NADIA AFIFI

THE SENTIENT

This is a FLAME TREE PRESS book

FLAME TREE PRESS
6 Melbray Mews, London, SW6 3NS, UK
flametreepress.com

US sales, distribution and warehouse:
Simon & Schuster
simonandschuster.biz

UK distribution and warehouse:
Marston Book Services Ltd
marston.co.uk

Thanks to the Flame Tree Press team, including:
Taylor Bentley, Frances Bodiam, Federica Ciaravella, Don D'Auria, Chris Herbert, Josie Karani, Molly Rosevear, Will Rough, Mike Spender, Cat Taylor, Maria Tissot, Nick Wells, Gillian Whitaker.

The cover is created by Flame Tree Studio with
thanks to Nik Keevil and Shutterstock.com.
The font families used are Avenir and Bembo.

Flame Tree Press is an imprint of Flame Tree Publishing Ltd
flametreepublishing.com

A copy of the CIP data for this book is available from the British Library and the Library of Congress.

HB ISBN: 978-1-78758-434-1
US PB ISBN: 978-1-78758-432-7
UK PB ISBN: 978-1-78758-433-4
ebook ISBN: 978-1-78758-435-8

Printed and bound in Great Britain by Clays Ltd, Elcograf S.p.A.

NADIA AFIFI

THE SENTIENT

FLAME TREE PRESS
London & New York

To my grandmother, Joan.

CHAPTER ONE

Wilderness

The Green line to Bedlam was the oldest train route through Westport, a clogged, aging artery through the city's industrial zone. Inside one of its trembling cars, Amira Valdez pressed her face against the cool window, exhaling with forced steadiness. She had not felt this anxious on a train since her escape from the Children of the New Covenant Compound ten years ago. The train shuddered as it passed over a battered section of the tracks. Amira clenched her fists, digging her nails into her whip-scarred palms, another remnant of the compound.

Amira's morning commute to the Academy was normally a pleasant one, but today was Placement Day, and far from ordinary.

She pulled away from the window, where the tracks ascended above ground and the dense, grimy brick buildings of the Riverfront district came into view. Academy students filled the train car, all prepared in their own way for the most important day of the year. A gangly young man with a green mohawk leaned against one of the central poles, muttering a string of equations. Another student grimly performed lunges near the door, inciting glares every time new passengers boarded. No one made eye contact. Talented students abounded at the Academy and assignments were limited. Assignments in space would be even rarer.

Space. Her mentor, Dr. Mercer, called it the world above the world. For Amira, the research stations orbiting overhead represented everything the compound was not – unburdened by the past, a place that welcomed the unknown and challenged the idea of the unknowable. She belonged there. But if she failed to place well in the Aldwych district, the epicenter of the city of Westport's Lower Earth Orbit industry, today's exams would mercilessly destroy her dreams of working spaceside. Those countless hours she'd spent as a lonely child, hiding on the roof and searching the night sky for space-bound shuttles, would mean nothing. She *had* to succeed. Amira chewed her lower lip, forcing down her doubts.

The outlines of Aldwych's imposing skyscrapers rose in the distance as the Green line turned east. A faint trail of smoke from the Galileo building signaled a recent shuttle launch. Amira ran her finger along the condensed window glass, tracing the shuttle's skyward path toward the stations. Waves of adrenaline pulsed through her small frame, growing stronger as she neared the Academy's stop.

You've waited a long time for this day, her inner voice encouraged. *You know you're ready. This is what you were meant to do. This is who you're meant to be.*

The train announced its arrival at the Academy with a dull, screeching wail. The student reciting equations switched to a torrent of expletives. As she stepped outside, Amira's heart quickened at the sight of the Academy's elegant, angular walls, the sleek architecture of its buildings amplified by the comparatively grim, industrial neighborhood that surrounded it. Despite Oregon's mild climate, the Academy adopted a distinctly tropical aesthetic. The school's founder conducted her research in the Brazilian rainforest and brought the jungle back with her. Synthetic palm trees lined the walkways and vines crawled over the self-consciously modernist buildings, their concrete walls made to look like timber. Amira touched the founder's statue every time she passed it, as though she could absorb the late scientist's essence through the marble.

The Academy's main building hosted the Placement Day trials. Its corridors were remarkably silent save for Amira's echoing footsteps and the occasional somber-faced student shuffling by. A dull-eyed teaching assistant ordered Amira to Room Four. *So her fate would be decided there.* Amira took a steadying breath and followed the instruction, striding with as much confidence as she could muster beyond the lecture hall.

A small, pale figure emerged from the lecture hall's towering doors. Amira's best friend, D'Arcy Pham, grinned excitedly, raising her fist in triumph. Though the knot in her stomach tightened further,

Amira returned the smile and they clasped hands briefly. D'Arcy mouthed the word 'Pandora' before turning around the corridor.

Amira blinked with surprise. The Pandora project, spearheaded by a team of elite Aldwych scientists, was really a collection of projects with one common theme – a desire to push the boundaries of science as far as law, budget and human understanding would allow. It was no surprise that D'Arcy, a top quantum programmer at the Academy who custom-made her own Third Eye, had placed well – but Pandora? The project was both unusually prestigious and clandestine, even by the standards of insular Aldwych.

And there it was – Room Four. Amira found no external indicators of what awaited her beyond the door, but she had a reasonable guess. She managed to evade one test in her ten years of study, but she would not face the panel without completing it. Just as police officers had to be shocked before they could inflict the pain of a nano-pulse Taser, Amira would have to lay her own mind bare before she could become an Academy-approved therapist and holomentic reader.

She exhaled, memories of glimmering space stations and night skies dancing in her mind's eye, and walked through the door.

★ ★ ★

Amira sat still, arms folded in her lap with sensory pads attached to her forehead and temples. She breathed deeply and closed her eyes when the first needle entered her wrist. The standard dose of Nirvatrene, cooling as it found her vein.

"Are you ready?" A lanky young man with horn-rimmed glasses pulled up a seat next to her, monitor hovering over his knees. "Nervous? I can change our background to a beach or park, or whatever you prefer."

"I'm fine." The walls were white, windowless and sterile.

"All right then. We'll submerge in a few minutes."

In the seconds before her thoughts would no longer be hers alone, Amira allowed herself a final moment of calculation. Her skills as a holomentic reader, the latest breakthrough in thought-visualizing neuroscience, did not interest the Placement Panel. This exercise was ultimately a psychological evaluation, intended to deliver a verdict on her emotional stability for a position that gave her access to patients' innermost thoughts. A verdict on the soundness of her mind, not what she could do with it.

The sensory pads warmed against Amira's face, joined by an odd, pulling sensation in the back of her head, as though an invisible hand tried to reel her in like a fish on a hook. She struggled to concentrate on the door, but it grew harder and harder to focus. The hologram table to her right projected images from her brain as she experienced them, in flashes of shapes and color that formed three-dimensional scenes. Initially dim and blurry, they took form while the man, her assigned reader, adjusted dials and dragged his fingers across a large monitor.

Amira clenched her fists. She fought to keep her expression neutral, but the glimpses of memory continued to appear, gaining clarity and strength under the reader's skilled navigation.

This was only the first step. The reader probed the first level of her consciousness and would move in deeper as he navigated the complex neural map in front of him. Any Academy student could learn to read the map of the human mind – the real skill, one Amira possessed in abundance, was knowing where to look.

Amira shivered. If this reader could find points of weakness the way she could, the next hour would test her like nothing else.

"Ok, Amira, let's start," he said. "In the interest of treating this like a proper therapy session, let's focus on a moment from your past and dissect what it means together. In your profile, it says you were originally born in one of the religious compounds in the southwest. Correct?"

Amira suppressed a sigh. As she had dreaded, she would have to relive the compound, the epicenter of all her traumas, to pass her final test.

"Yes," she said. No sooner had the words escaped her lips, the tugging sensation returned.

"What do you think of when you remember life on Children of the New Covenant?" he asked. An open-ended and vague question, a common tactic to start off a holomentic therapy session. Amira closed her eyes and centered her thoughts on the word 'compound'. Other words darted into her thoughts as well, along with images and sounds – of violence, of terror – that would never leave her, but she resisted, struggling to focus on the word alone and not the memories it evoked.

And there it was, clear and vivid on the nearby hologram – the compound, at night. It gave off an otherworldly light from a distance, its pale, round buildings glowing like craterless moons rising out of the Sonoran valley. It was the only source of light for hundreds of miles on those typical nights marred by ashy clouds or smog from the western cities. Its inhabitants left those cities generations ago to escape the modern world's liberties and license, but civilization still found ways to reach them.

With the luxury of distance and time between her and her place of birth, Amira let herself see the unsettling beauty of the place, the hushed calm that descended over the desert when the sunlight dissolved over the mountains. The solar power that fueled the compound left the pathways and low buildings glowing with an eerie, bluish light at night. But Amira knew the secret lives that existed within each of those orb-like houses, the hidden violence and despair contained within every wall. The way people disappeared, never to be spoken of again except in quiet whispers. The way women and girls barely ranked above livestock, a means to an end.

Her face grew clammy at the sight of the barbed wires around the compound walls and she pushed the image aside with effort, closing her eyes. Her heart quickened as sound replaced sight, screams and cries from old punishments. The burning of Chimyra, warm and thick in her throat, at the start of the Passage Ceremony. Another tug in her head.

The scene in the hologram shifted to a young girl with long black hair. No older than thirteen, the girl shivered on her knees in a small shed. She lifted her shaking hands to gaze at her palms, which were raw and bleeding in thin trails onto the floor.

"Amira? Are you ok?"

The man's voice, though distant, cut through her thundering heartbeat. Amira swallowed and nodded. Biting her lip in frustration, she redirected her thoughts back to her first image of the compound at night, but she could feel the man probing deeper into her thought patterns, the sensors warming slightly against her temples.

"Ok, let's focus on that memory for a minute. I see a lot of fear activated around the prelimbic cortex, very conditioned fear, of course. Why are you in that small space and what brought you there?"

Amira's mouth went dry. That was the first night she tried to escape, and the punishment was predictably severe. She had spent months building her resolve to leave, knowing the consequences of failure...and then she *had* failed. Residual pain flashed across her palms, and she balled her fists.

Opening her eyes, Amira could see the images in the hologram shifting again, from the shed to a large crowd in a clearing. Most were children or teenagers, rapt and bright-eyed, flanked by stony-faced adults in long black coats. No trees or clouds shielded them from a fierce sun, though shadows from nearby hills stretched in their direction. *The Gathering.*

Amira grimaced, trying to redirect her thoughts to the shed, to the smell of blood and fear, but it was too late.

"The Gathering?" the man asked with interest, dragging his fingers along the words that appeared on his monitor. "What does that mean? Is that what I'm looking at right now?"

He's good, Amira thought. He knew when to prod further and follow an idea, and when to hold back on what he suspected to be true. They were moving closer together toward a defining moment, one that ultimately brought her to this very room. A moment she never wanted the Academy, or anyone, to expose. She dug her fingernails into her palms.

"Let's focus," the reader said, not mentioning whether he registered Amira's mixed feelings of respect and resentment. "Tell me about the Gathering, and how it led to your first escape attempt."

"The Elders brought all of the children from the three biggest compounds together," Amira said carefully. "My compound participated in the Gathering, along with the Trinity and the Remnant Faithful compounds. Everyone here thinks they're all the same, but the compounds don't trust each other. They hate secular life, but they still have different doctrines, different cultures and methods from each other, which is why they fought separately by the end of the Drought Wars. The Gathering was meant to unify the compounds, make them stronger against outside influences trying to change them. To mobilize fractured communities against a common enemy."

In the hologram, a line of young girls walked along a rocky trail, Amira among them. She fidgeted with her silver lace veil, a flimsy shield over her hair and eyes that let splinters of sunlight through, and an older woman appeared at her side, swiping, cat-like, at Amira's hand. Further ahead, a similar team of boys marched in single file, singing one of the Trinity Compound's spiritual hymns. The Elder at the forefront sang louder than all the boys combined in a surprisingly rich baritone. He bore the same traits as most compound spiritual leaders – older, charismatic and zealous, or able to appear as such. He had multiple wives of various ages, who hovered silently around him like shadows.

"I notice the hike is gender segregated," the reader said, pulling Amira back into the room.

"It was for the Remnant Faithfuls," Amira said. "Although I'm sure the other Elders didn't object. My compound – Children of the New Covenant – was only strict when we became teenagers, but on the Remnant Faithful Compound, they separate boys and girls at the age of five, even within the family home. When they first arrived at the Gathering, the kids watched us like it was Sodom and Gomorrah in action."

The reader laughed lightly before raising his hand to extract a still image from the hologram, showing a blonde girl lunging at Amira. On the still-moving hologram, the girl shoved Amira to the ground, wiping her hands theatrically on her billowing dress. She kicked sand in Amira's face for good measure. The old woman leading the hike remained at the front, defiantly oblivious.

"What happened there?" he asked. Amira sighed.

"That girl came from the Trinity Compound," she said. "They saw those of us with darker skin as 'polluted' and unclean."

"White supremacy, from what I've read, is a core tenet of Trinity's values," the reader said bluntly.

"Less so than before, but it's still there," she said. "They believe that only light-skinned people can access the Nearhaven, the parallel dimension that's untainted by modern evils, when we die. It's part of what's kept the compounds from uniting, despite how small they are alone. Some of the Trinity Elders probably fought against the Gathering in the first place."

The hologram cut to the last day of the Gathering. Young Amira stood in the heart of the crowd, flanked by rocky hills and sparse patches of juniper trees.

In the absence of other outlets in the compounds, ceremony became a competitive sport. Children learned the rules of the game quickly, waving their arms in a trance the way they watched their parents pray at Passage and Unveiling ceremonies. Though most were too young to consume Chimyra, they knew enough to mimic its effects, swaying and shrieking at imagined sights from hidden worlds. The Elders had other tricks to convince their followers that they were glimpsing into the Otherworlds – tricks Amira only learned after escaping. Holograms, sensory machines and bubble screens embedded in the temples, parlor trickery enhanced by the hallucinogenic powers of Chimyra. But on Gathering day, they deployed no illusions on their youngest congregants. The ceremony relied on faith alone.

Three banners loomed behind the podium, one for each compound. The Trinity leaders stood on the platform, all Elders save for a teenage boy in the corner. The boy scowled into the distance, past the crowd in an impressive display of apathy.

Another young man, handsome and smiling, led the crowd in a hymn. The hymn they collectively swayed to originated from Amira's compound, no doubt a political concession on the part of the Trinity, the unmistakable leader of the event. Elder Avery Cartwright, hero of the Drought Wars and discoverer of Chimyra, was Trinity, after all.

The singer delivered the simple harmony with such conviction that Amira had hummed along, though by that stage, she no longer believed in the words. The simple melody struck a chord with her, reaching those deep corners of her heart that she kept hidden and buried, even from herself. Music, a binding agent in her loneliest moments.

The men at the podium surveyed the crowd with cold appraisement. Amira barely noticed the small group at the time, but with hindsight, they became sharp and clear in her mind's eye. Time gave memories power and form – with each revisiting, it illuminated new angles to the same moment. The singer raised his right arm and the children's voices swelled.

Through the Cataclysm's embers, I walk without fear
Through faith and submission, Nearhaven is near

A strange buzzing sound cut through the chorus and faces turned upward toward a pentagon-shaped drone, hovering ominously over the crowd. It darted from side to side briefly before it ascended and turned south. The children stopped singing and began chattering excitedly about the machine from the cities. Amira glanced at a widening gap in the crowd. Two compound men ran downhill toward the ceremony, arms aggressively waving. Scouts, alerting the presence of intruders.

Seconds later, loud bangs cut through the hum of voices, followed by colorful plumes of smoke. Panicked screams erupted, and the crowd scattered in every direction.

At the top of the surrounding hills, a pack of imposing armored hovercrafts, bearing the North American Alliance's insignia, materialized from nowhere. Armed men spilled from the sides of each vehicle, weapons pointed. They moved in formation around the frenzied throng's perimeter.

Amira's pulse rose in a sharp crescendo on the nearby monitor. She turned away from the hologram, gripping the sides of her chair to steady herself.

In the hologram, the younger Amira ran up a steep hill, panting as her thick floral dress billowed oppressively around her. She stepped over its hem and stumbled forward into the dirt, her nails digging into the hot sand. The sounds of the raid, cries and bursts of smoke canisters, grew distant as she zigzagged through the rising terrain.

A patch of color caught the corner of her eye and before she could turn, something shoved her forward and she fell on her knees. A boy, the same teenager who stood in silence on the podium, ran past her toward the top of the hill. Spitting out sand, Amira followed.

Running along the ridge behind the boy, Amira realized that she no longer recognized her surroundings. The cacophony of the raid vanished, leaving only wilderness, a harsh landscape of dead junipers and dust whipped by angry winds.

"Stop!" she called out to the boy. "Stop, we need to go back!"

The boy stopped but did not turn. Amira caught up with him, following his gaze.

Across the valley sat a house unlike any she had seen before. Perched atop a cliff, its sharp angles and sloping sides glinted in the sunlight, but its most striking feature was a beam of light rising directly from its center, clear through the high noon's haze.

The boy suddenly fell to his knees, clutching the sides of his head and rocking back and forth.

"What's wrong with you?" Amira cried. "What's happening?"

Amira's ears rang, faintly at first but louder with each passing second, her head pulsating as the ringing rose in pitch. She sank to her knees near the boy, who thrashed on the ground. The sound drowned out the wind, her own moans and her senses, as she buried her forehead against the hot earth. She twisted in an agony she'd never known, the sound cutting through to every nerve, down to her bones.

Then it stopped.

She lifted her head, leaving a damp patch of sweat on the sand where her forehead had lain. Something shifted within her. Her arms jerked and twitched of their own accord. She held her hand before her eyes and did not recognize it as her own. She willed her fist to close and it did, but the movement felt foreign and unnatural.

"This is the end," a thick voice said, and Amira realized she was speaking back in the Academy's reading room, where the man stared, transfixed, at the hologram. She tried to stand but her legs rebelled, sinking further into the ground. "We can stop now, it—"

"You're doing great, Amira, we just need to submerge a little further."

The sensors heated up again and Amira returned to the desert. Her heart fluttered in rising panic.

Don't let him see, Amira thought desperately. *Fight back.* For a moment, the hologram flickered, but she couldn't push aside the girl in the desert.

The boy went limp next to her.

The young Amira screamed and without warning, the ground beneath her disappeared. She floated high over the ridge, like a marionette bound to invisible strings, swaying in the air. She hovered over the body, her own, now motionless under a voluminous dress. Her long black hair whipped in every direction under gusts of wind and she instinctively tried to brush it aside, but her hands remained with the rest of her below. Mind and body, detached. A wave of peace washed over her, dissolving her initial sense of panic. The taste of rust filled her mouth, though she had no mouth or tongue to speak of in her detached state. It didn't bother her. For the first time that day, since the start of the Gathering, nothing aggravated or frightened her.

Someone, or something, watched her from her high perch. Eyes trained on her, felt more than seen. Neither predatory nor friendly, merely an observer to her own detachment.

Something else invaded her solitude. Something to her left. Tearing away from the surreal sight of her own body below her, she expanded her range of vision.

The boy floated beside her, hovering over his own body. He was not a solid object, like the shape on the ground, but she recognized him as the scowling, distant child who ran with her up the hill. A presence who sensed her, as she sensed him.

Her conscious mind remained in suspense, surveying the landscape and the small figures below her with detached curiosity, a spectator on a theater balcony watching someone else's story unfold.

In the distance, the strange beam of light from the house flickered, then vanished.

New figures came into view, men in black robes running along the ridge, and in an instant, Amira dropped to the ground, retching, her body her own again. The calmness of the moment vanished, but the taste of rust lingered in her mouth.

The Elders approached, running to the boy first. His face turned the color of curdled milk as they lifted him, but his eyes found Amira's before the men carried him away. The boy's head jerked to one side in a subtle gesture that Amira returned with a silent nod.

Say nothing.

Hands gripped the sides of her head and Amira gasped. The

interviewer removed the sensors. She pressed her head into the back of her chair, light-headed, a common sensation in the immediate aftermath of a reading. The room, with its white walls and monochromatic machinery, felt vivid and real compared to the foggy world of her memories, all sharp lines and edges.

"What happened there?" the man asked, unable to suppress the curiosity from his voice.

Something happened beyond her control years ago. At the time, she feared she had accessed the Conscious Plane, a level of transcendence forbidden without an Elder's guidance, but her years in the Academy had provided another explanation. Dissociation, the separation of mind and body. A known phenomenon, but rarely as extreme or pronounced as Amira's experience at the Gathering. The panel would declare her unfit to be a reader in response. Someone with a tenable grip on reality, they would pronounce with an appropriate mixture of firmness and empathy, could not delve into the minds of others. Despite her undeniable skill and years of hard work, a single memory would unravel everything. All those years, wasted.

Amira hesitated. She couldn't lie, at least not completely. Holomentic machines, though built to heal, also functioned as effective interrogation devices. The map of her neural activity would pick up an outright lie when the brain center for imagination, not memory, highlighted on the nearby monitor. The heat and fear of the Gathering fresh in her mind, she gripped the armrest to hide shaking hands. She could not go back to the compound, or end up on the street, as other compound escapees often did. She would not fail.

"I don't know exactly," she said slowly, a truth in the broadest sense. "But looking back, I think it may have been a panic attack where I disconnected somehow—"

"I'm sorry, I meant after you were found? After you and the boy got what looks like heatstroke. Were you punished for getting so far away?"

Amira gaped at him. Did he not see her separate from her own body? She recovered, arranging her face to show the shape of polite introspection.

"They didn't question me too much," she said. "The Feds arrested most of the Elders and their marshals for unlawful assembly. A power play. They have so little influence over the compounds that they couldn't pass up an opportunity to charge so many Elders at once. Everyone was frightened. The remaining adults took us back that night. The Elders were released by the Feds – by the Alliance forces the next day – on some technicality. The punishment came months later, when I tried to escape. I'm sorry, did you mean to continue the reading?"

"I did, but the machine's acting up," he said with a dismissive nod toward the holographic table. "It went black when you fell down next to that other kid who was freaking out. Not sure what happened, but it came back on when the men found you on the hill. I'll have to get it looked at, but I certainly have what I need for today."

He shook her hand and gestured her toward the door with a slight smile.

Amira exhaled audibly, breathing freely for the first time in the room, but her hands trembled as she walked down the hallway. Psychotic breaks, multiple personality cases, even the final brain signals of the dying – all could be captured in some form by the machine. But the holomentic device failed to display the moment on the mountaintop. Only death was undetectable by the machine. So either the examiner misinterpreted Amira's dissociation as a mechanical malfunction, or the moment itself was…what, exactly? Why had it failed to read that moment on the ridge?

The house in the middle of nowhere, anchored by the mysterious beam of light, hovered in her racing mind as she approached the panel room.

★ ★ ★

"Valdez? Amira Valdez? Excellent. Have a seat."

The room looked the same as every other in the Academy – spacious, polished, but lacking in charm. Amira liked it regardless, with its geometric furniture and high, echoing ceilings. Here, they would declare her fate.

The yawning window to her right overlooked the Academy's pool, an extravagant, costly structure flanked by synthetic palm trees and plastic lounge chairs. She had spent countless hours doing laps there and even more floating on her back, staring out through the clear ceiling as shuttles and helicopters passed silently overhead.

Amira did her best to ignore the crystalline water and focus on the panel before her. A severe woman and a short, round man sat behind a metallic desk. Both wore the requisite violet lab coats of senior professors. A flat screen on the desk's surface displayed a string of text alongside Amira's profile picture. It was taken several years ago, but she looked the same – light brown skin and angular face offset by her eyes, almost as black as her hair. She wore the same expression in her profile that she wore now – thoughtful and stern, except for her mouth, which turned up at the corners in a subtle, almost cryptic smile. The slight frame of her shoulders slouched in the image. She straightened her back and crossed her ankles, compensating for her poor posture. The man on the panel smiled brightly in her direction, but the woman scrutinized her in an unabashed manner.

"You know this already, but you passed your physical."

"Yes," Amira said. "Fifteen miles."

"You've also scored consistently high on your academic reviews," the woman said, running her long fingers across the screen. "Let's see...aeronautics, physics, some neo-quantum physics, genetic engineering, bioengineering. Excellent across the board."

Amira nodded, keeping her gaze on the stern woman's face. The professor's eyes were the color of dried olive pits, her hair cut in that fashionable, unevenly chopped style. Little warmth emanated from her person, or even a trace of personality, but then again, this was a meeting that required formality. A District of Aldwych Jury insignia was fastened to her breast pocket, indicating a position on one of the district's most powerful governing bodies, second only to the elite Aldwych Council. The man, on the other hand, was small and genial, with tufts of dark hair springing from his face and round features that reminded Amira of an affable koala. Her mouth twitched as the comparison set in, followed by a pang of guilt. Unlike the woman, he seemed kind, eager to tell her what she wanted to hear.

"And outstanding recommendations," the man added, nodding encouragingly at her. "Including one from Dr. Mercer himself."

"But your strong suit," the woman continued, "seems to be neuroscience, including holomentic interpretation, dream analysis and old-fashioned therapy. Your coursework suggests this is also where your true interests lie, multi-talented as you are. Very interesting, especially for a young woman with your...unusual background."

As she feared, the compound reared its ubiquitous head again. The woman paused, waiting for a response, but Amira was well versed in deflecting the topic. After months of planning for this moment, an offhand remark would not unseat her.

"It's an exciting line of study, and a rewarding one," Amira said. "We know the body so well, but the mind is something we're still just beginning to scratch the surface of."

"The community you came from is known for its interest in manipulating the minds of its followers," the woman said with shrewd eyes, scanning through a file on the desk's monitor. "Hallucinogenic drugs, forced mental conditioning, ideas of unified thought and action. Has that factored into your decision to specialize in holomentic reading?"

"Only in showing me the difference between science and manipulation," Amira said quickly. "The place I came from uses lesser technology to control others. I want to help people suffering from past trauma and study consciousness without bias. I want to help people control their own minds, especially where past trauma has made that challenging."

"Hmm. And where would you ultimately like to take those skills?"

Amira pulled herself upright in her seat. "One of the space stations," she said. "The Carthage or Volta, perhaps, or maybe even the Osiris station someday."

The woman snorted audibly. The man raised his eyebrows.

"The Osiris station?" he said. "Ambitious!"

"Quite," the woman said drily. "Very ambitious, especially for a young woman of twenty-five with only seven years of higher education. You are talented, of course. You've been through a lot and have a very compelling history, which never hurts in this atypical climate we find ourselves in. But to do research on one of the stations, especially the Osiris, is reserved for the seasoned and the true elite. Only the best in the world go into space, no matter how they score at Placement."

Amira nodded. The words stung, but she suspected the woman was not being purposefully harsh – the Academy had never assigned someone so young to the stations. The Volta station's chief scientist, Victor Zhang, was producing some of his best research at one hundred and forty-six years, and his advanced age was not an anomaly. And it was foolish to mention the Osiris – its notorious secrecy had inflated its myth in the public consciousness, inspiring wild theories about the station's purpose. An interest in the Osiris may have suggested a speculative mind, not a serious, inquiring one. Regret gnawed at the corners of her thoughts.

The man, reading her expression, chimed in. "But an excellent long-term goal. With the right inclinations and a willingness to work, you can do anything, and I truly believe that. If you—"

"After careful review by the board," the woman continued, "we have found an assignment for you that we believe will truly benefit all. You will remain here in Westport, so you can continue your classes part time, and avoid the usual break that throws so many of your promising colleagues back."

Amira stared at her, making eye contact for the first time in the room. "Here in Greater Westport?"

"Yes," the woman said with a wry smile. "You'll like this as well – it's with a little project underway at the Mendel-Soma building in the Aldwych district. You want to join the elite and push boundaries. The Pandora initiative has a special effort underway to do just that. A small team of geneticists experimenting with embryonic replication technology. No doubt you've heard of it?"

Amira's heart sank. She held the woman's gaze, silent as her heart pounded at the base of her throat. Of course she had heard of it. Everyone had. It was all over the news, debated in coffee shops, the focus of the media from every possible volatile angle. The last thing Amira wanted.

The woman waited for an answer, brows slightly arched. Amira smothered her disappointment and lifted her chin, plastering cool acceptance over a practiced smile. "Pandora. The Cloning Division."

★ ★ ★

"You must be very excited," the man with the koala hair said, trailing after Amira on short, waddling legs. "I'm Perkins, by the way."

She managed a smile. "I am."

They crossed the winding stairs that led from the Dunning Academy of New Science's main complex to the courtyard, a spacious quadrangle overtaken by lounging students and exotic plants. Amira moved as though the wind were carrying her, dragging her where it pleased. Under the deceptively bright Westport sky, the Osiris space station felt further from her grasp than ever. Before reaching the world above the world, she would have to survive the political minefield of Aldwych. Her lie during her Placement exam would not be her last. She forced herself to keep smiling.

"Ah, what a wonderful coincidence!" Perkins waved excitedly at a tall man in a white lab coat. "Dr. Barlow, yes? Do you have a minute? This is M. Amira Valdez, one of our best and brightest, and the newest member of your group. Amira, this is Tony Barlow, one of the doctors on the Pandora project."

"Nice to meet you." Barlow nodded distractedly in her direction.

"A very talented student," Perkins continued. "Brilliant at holomentic reading. She will be providing some much-needed psychiatric support that I believe Dr. Singh herself had requested."

"I may have heard something to that effect," Barlow said.

He paused, and Amira realized that he was staring directly at her right hand. She closed her scarred palm reflexively and returned his gaze. His expression was difficult to read, but she was clearly being viewed with new interest.

"Which Holy Community did you come to us from?" Barlow asked.

"Ah, yes," Perkins said before she could answer. "What a story! To escape from that awful place in the desert and end up here. Barely a possession to her name when she arrived, Dr. Mercer told me."

"Children of the New Covenant," Amira replied, careful to keep her voice neutral.

"I watched a Stream documentary on them," Perkins said.

"Fascinating. The New Covenants are a more diverse lot than the Trinity and Remnant Faithfuls, are they not?"

Amira glared with eyes like dark razors and Perkins snapped into silence. She turned away guiltily from the genial man's crestfallen face.

"Interesting." Barlow nodded again. "If you will both excuse me, I have a rather urgent meeting to get to. I look forward to working with you, M. Valdez." He shook both of their hands, giving Amira a final appraising look before he turned toward the main building.

"A strange man," Perkins whispered rather loudly as they watched Barlow walk away. He appeared to have forgotten Amira's glare. "But a very talented and brilliant one, they say. They're all like that, these men and women who devote themselves to the riddles of science. Aldwych demands the dedicated. I imagine you will feel quite at home among them, my dear."

CHAPTER TWO

Westport

When Amira arrived in Greater Westport ten years ago, armed with a tattered shoulder bag carrying clothes she would never wear again, the noise and chaos of the metro stations overwhelmed her. Now the trains incited a strange, kinetic excitement. The stop near the Academy was one of the city's main intersections, an imposing, towering strata of tracks, platforms and rusted stairs that rattled above and beneath the streets. The highest train level was also the fastest – the Gradient line, which traveled between cities on the continent, and the Bullet, which could reach anywhere Earthside in a matter of hours. The slowest routes remained underground and dated back over a hundred years, carrying rattling electric cars through Westport's scattered stations.

Amira knew them well. The Orange line took her to and from the Academy, but she could also get there through the Green and Gray lines. The Red line ran in a semi-circular path along the oceanfront through Northampton, Sullivan's Wharf and the Westport Harbor, turning toward bustling Midtown and the cloud-slicing towers of Aldwych.

Aldwych. A city within a city. Technically, a district within the city of Westport, but Amira knew better than to consider Aldwych part of any world but its own. Within its boundaries, elite scientists defined the laws. Justice existed for those who contributed to the district's power and knowledge, provided they knew their place within Aldwych's complex, delicate ecosystem, where even the color of a person's lab coat marked their caste in the scientific order.

Amira gazed numbly out the window where the station signs flashed by in a river of concrete. Her small frame swayed rhythmically in the train car, bathed in absinthe-green light. A battered, hologrammed TV screen delivered the news in static fits.

"...no official word yet on why ISP security forces were denied access to the Carthage station, but Mendel-Soma sources suggest that experiments with radioactive components made travel to and from the station too perilous at present, rendering inspections impossible.... In other news, the Volta station's chief, Victor Zhang, has been conspicuously absent from Aldwych press conferences in the last month."

An old woman in a brown coat coughed violently. Amira glanced at her briefly before training her eyes back on the TV.

"In the meantime, President Hume is considering a formal hearing on the genetic research giant's highly controversial 'Pandora' project, following the deaths of its two volunteer subjects this past summer. Much of the criticism has centered on the use of subjects that are perceived to be among the most vulnerable...."

Amira stood up. Why hadn't she brought music with her? Trying to drown out the news report, she could only think of New Covenant hymns, ones she hadn't thought of in years that came bubbling up from the dark undertows of memory. Songs of sin and salvation, of realities spread across space and time like beads on a necklace, some sparkling and beautiful, others marred and broken. A dull throb settled in her temples where the holomentic machine's sensors had sucked the past out of her.

Shrieking brakes signaled the train's approach to the Riverfront, and Amira departed, ascending from the grimy station to the familiar scent of foaming canal water and moss. Candy-colored graffiti lined the walls along the station's exit, bearing the usual slogans. *Remember the Cataclysm. Human Workers First. We All Bleed the Same (Except Robots, But Fuck Them).* She joined the frenetic rush of bodies that always greeted her as she stepped out into the sunlight.

It was an unusually warm late afternoon for September and the Riverfront's denizens gathered in force along the waterfront's main promenade. Young students crowded the walkway, spilling out of the neighborhood's many bars and cafés into a swelling tributary of heavily tattooed street performers, transients and artists with makeshift displays. The sun dipped behind the red brick buildings, illuminating the waterway and the crowd in a muted, peachy glow.

Amira loved to walk this street on cool summer evenings or warm autumn days, but today an invisible, suffocating fog weighed down on her, slowing her progress through the jostling crowd. *Pandora.* The word clung to her thoughts like a clawed jungle animal onto a tree. Lyrical and taunting. She pushed against her fellow pedestrians, twisting past a pair of musicians lazily strumming their guitars in harmony.

Placement Day had ended with a placement, one she would have never imagined. Her bewilderment swelled with each step, accompanied by a growing sense of injustice. Had the panel intended to sabotage her career before it even began? Had she been a fool to mention the Osiris station? Why else would she have walked away with Pandora's cloning project, the most hated endeavor in Westport, on her resume?

Her apartment was several blocks from the main waterway, close enough to hear drunken shouts in the later hours but far enough away to sleep through them. Affectionately named the Canary House due to the many birds that had overtaken its pipes and roof, it was one of several Academy-owned student residences in the area. The weathered brick exterior, coated in creeping vines, gave the Canary House a quiet charm.

Amira entered the common area, finding complete silence in the wake of Placement Day. A young male student with a mop of dark hair slept on a forest green couch, buried under a blanket of chemistry books, but the first floor was otherwise abandoned.

Amira arrived at her bedroom, one of eight on the third floor. A note taped to her door, written in a tight, distinctive scrawl, read 'Music & BBQ on the roof'.

Amira threw her bag unceremoniously on the edge of her wire-framed bed. Though cluttered with books and bio-paper, her room had little in the way of decoration; the only personalized features were a pair of cactuses along the windowsill and a large three-dimensional map of the human brain on her desk. Her only prized possession in the New Covenant, a hand-held telescope unexpectedly gifted by her father, had not made the journey to Westport. Not that she would be able to star-gaze through Westport's smog.

She forced the window open and stepped out onto the fire escape that led to the roof. The hum of music and animated chatter swelled near the top of the building. The scent of charred synthetic kebab hung in the air, sending a wave of nausea through Amira's body. Of all her stories about life in the compound, few details shocked her fellow students more than the fact that its residents ate real meat, slaughtered from living animals, in defiance of the Synthetic Meat Act. Most of the students were born well after bio-tech advances rendered synth meat cost-effective, leading to a ban on factory farming. Butchery was an alien and frightening concept to them, but one Amira knew well.

Amira stepped onto the roof and a pair of skinny arms slipped around her shoulders. D'Arcy's wide grin faltered slightly as her eyes met Amira's.

"What happened?" she asked. "You got placed, didn't you? There's no way—"

"It's Pandora," Amira said.

"You too?" D'Arcy said with an excited shriek. "I'm going to be in the quantum division, programming the Stream to work in space, to get ready for the Titan colony. We'll be working together. Do you know which team you'll be on?"

"Not a team so much as a den of wolves," Amira said, unable to suppress the note of bitterness. "It's the cloning project."

D'Arcy opened her mouth to speak and then closed it again. In the crowd at the center of the roof, several students shot brief glances in Amira's direction, their expressions a mixture of pity and suspicion. Word traveled quickly.

"But why?" D'Arcy managed to say, shaking her head. "You're not a geneticist. Why put a therapist on a cloning project?"

"I've got an idea." The voice belonged to Julian, Amira's friend and D'Arcy's long-term partner. He reached for the old-fashioned radio the Canary House students kept on the rooftop and raised the volume.

"The increased scrutiny of the Pandora cloning project," the radio announcer said, "comes as inside reports suggest that the third and last surviving subject of the project, an unnamed young woman, is in precarious health and displaying increasingly erratic behavior. The nature of her complications has not been revealed, but similar reports preceded the deaths of the previous two subjects, both of whom died while carrying their unborn clones in the third trimester. Pandora, a rare collaborative effort between high-ranking Aldwych scientists, encompasses a number of controversial and challenging projects. With the latest setback to Pandora's cloning effort, Dr. Valerie Singh faces renewed pressure to shut down a lifelong dream."

"So the last one's dying," D'Arcy said with disgust. "They're getting desperate. It's not just the compound crazies, everyone in Westport will turn on Pandora."

"Notice what they said, though," Julian replied. "*Erratic behavior.* It's not just a medical problem, or something to do with the cloning process. They need a neuroscientist because there's a psychological component at play."

"But what about the last two?" D'Arcy asked impatiently. "Did they both have nervous breakdowns and commit suicide? It seems unlikely."

"Maybe not so unlikely. They're using former compound girls, because they're the only ones desperate enough to volunteer. They—"

Amira turned away from her friends, leaving them to continue their argument as though she wasn't there. The ground swayed slightly before she remembered to breathe. She steadied her hands on the rooftop rails. Julian and D'Arcy's sparring voices faded into the background as the cityscape stretched out before her. The distant towers of Aldwych, normally a source of awe, even hope, never looked more ominous than they did now.

Amira replayed the interview with the Placement Panel in her mind, finding new hints in the woman's questions about her compound upbringing. Although cautious, she had greeted the assignment as an endorsement of her talent, to join the most high-profile experiment in North America. Now, her placement seemed too coincidental. Did the panel believe that, as a former compound girl, she could empathize with the dying subject in ways that others could not? Or was she being used as a political prop, a compound girl done well, to deflect from the young, pregnant woman dying in the Soma building? Amira's resume did offer a perfect counterbalance to the rumors shouted across the Stream that Pandora was exploiting some of Westport's most vulnerable citizens – a compound escapee, overcoming adversity to survive, thrive and help other compound escapees. Amira winced at the potential headlines, not that she was likely to warrant her own feature story. *Compound survivor, overcoming her past to help others. In Pandora, a chance to make a difference. Amid turbulent cloning effort, a story of triumph.*

Aldwych loomed over the city, its heart in more ways than one. All roadways, train tracks, air shuttle pathways gravitated to it, like a whirlpool dragging ships into an unstoppable current.

And the next morning, Amira would become part of that current; a new world in which she would either navigate or drown beneath its glassy surface.

★ ★ ★

That afternoon, the Blue line departed Westport under a gloomy, gray sky for the mountains northeast of the city. Amira gazed through the window with wonder, as beyond the Pines district the dense topography of brick and concrete slowly gave way to nature. Rows of vertical farms were Westport's final compromise with its surroundings. Located on the edge of the city zone, the towering structures were stacked with layer upon layer of lush farmland, its vines and branches hanging over the buildings' sides. The vines curled around the windows like fingers and Amira smiled to herself, imagining green hands emerging to wave at the passing train. The lower levels contained the final remnants of legal livestock, milk cows lazily chewing cud under artificial lights, while the upper levels carried everything from basic vegetables to exotic tropical fruits, each floor climate controlled to suit the produce's natural environment. Massive panels of vertical grassland sat on rolling green hills in the distance, their inclined surfaces rotating in the direction of the sun. Amira squinted, unable to find workers tending the farms. Had they been replaced by machines, spared from toiling under the cruel elements that she had been forced to endure in the compound? Or were they laboring somewhere in the structures' shadows, invisible to those who didn't want to see them?

The mountains drew near. Amira never tired of their familiar outlines, the quiet power of their permanence. The temperature always dropped slightly when the train crossed into the shade of the snow-capped peaks. The quiet unsettled her – living in Westport for so long, she sometimes forgot how silent and still it could be in the world's final stretches of wilderness. She shook off another residual memory of compound life, its bitter aura lingering after her holomentic exam.

Dr. Paul Mercer lived above Clementine, a mining town on a remote pathway into the mountains. Once Amira exited the station at the town's entrance, it required a bus ride followed by a brief hike to reach his property gate. He greeted her at the front door with outstretched arms and a warm smile.

"My favorite student!" he said. "How long has it been?"

They sat on the main deck, absorbing the sun's waning warmth and enjoying a breathtaking view of the mountains. Dr. Mercer's humanoid robot, named Henry, brought them glasses of iced tea.

"What's its purpose exactly, other than housework?" Amira asked Dr. Mercer in a soft voice when Henry returned to the kitchen, wondering if robots possessed a hearing range.

"Henry's a 'buddy' robot," the former professor replied. "You've encountered them, my dear, and know it's insensitive to use the term 'it'. Henry helps around the house, but I acquired him for company. Not in that way, of course, although other robots exist to serve all types of human urges. Henry is simply a friend, a source of conversation in my voluntary exile."

"I should have come to see you earlier," Amira began uncomfortably.

"Nonsense! I know how busy they keep you at the Academy. And especially you – I heard from Perkins about your assignment to Pandora."

Though Dr. Mercer had raised the very topic she made this trip for, Amira felt a compassionate curiosity about her former mentor, a man she hadn't spoken to in over a year. He took his time showing her around the house and discussing his remodeled deck, displaying the enthusiasm of the committed suburbanites he used to ridicule. Clearly, he appreciated Amira's company more than he would admit.

"Have you heard from others at the Academy, Dr. Mercer? Do you keep in touch with them much?"

"Not really," he said. "I rarely talk to anyone back in Westport these days. Perkins told me that he approved your assignment there, through old-fashioned email, of all things. I threw away my Third Eye, nightmarish devices if you ask me. Who decided that we need computerized contact lenses that actually block your vision? Anyway, your assignment – I have my issues with the Academy getting into bed with Aldwych, but I will say that they could not have gained a more deserving pupil. Frankly, you have more talent than most of those lab-coated clowns over there."

"Paul always speaks highly of you, Amira Valdez," Henry said. He was short, about Amira's height, with features typical of companionate robots – large, almost childlike eyes, a soothing voice and a soft exterior comprised of smooth, silvery fabric.

Amira smiled stiffly at Henry. Robots did not exist in the compound, but she had grown comfortable in her limited interactions with functional models in Westport, such as the police units that issued loitering tickets to curfew-defying bar patrons. Friendship robots, however, were another story.

"Dr. Mercer, you should come down to Westport more," she said, turning back to the professor. "It must get a little lonely up here. Everyone at the Academy would love to see you again."

Dr. Mercer waved his hand in a dismissive gesture.

"Westport has nothing else to offer me. Henry and I are perfectly happy up here. We go down to the little town once a week for lunch at the café and take a walk on the trails afterward. These new buddy bots are incredible, you know. My brother passed away a few years ago and it was hard. We were close, even as adults. When I purchased Henry, I set up a voice for him that sounded just like my brother's – his inflections, his speech patterns. Quite remarkable! You can program past recollections, so Henry can bring them up in conversation. We used to surf on this beach in San Diego, and Henry reminds me of our adventures by the water. Did I mention to you that my final retirement home will be in Baja? I have some beachfront property there, a parting gift from the Academy if you'll believe that, but the construction isn't done yet. Anyway, the old stories…it's impressive, almost like hearing voices from beyond the grave. A new era indeed."

Amira nodded, but the notion of reviving the dead's voices left a hollow sensation in her chest. Did Dr. Mercer really feel that this shivering set of silver limbs could replicate his memories of his brother? Amira hoped that her mentor's lonely life in Clementine had not dulled his judgment. She needed his advice.

When it started to rain, they retreated into his study, a warmly lit room flanked with bookshelves and various gadgets. A traditional holomentic machine stood in the corner, not remotely as sophisticated as the models available at the Academy. She wandered around the room, examining the motion-based photographs hanging from the walls – the professor waving with colleagues at the Academy, collecting awards at various ceremonies, passing plates at Thanksgiving dinners.

"So, my dear," he said. "The Pandora project...the creation of the first human clone! Quite a starting assignment. And quite a name, by the way. *Pandora.* Valerie Singh almost begs for the negative press."

He smiled encouragingly but Amira's eyes were distant, her thin brows fixed in somber lines across her forehead.

"Do you think they're just bringing me on as a prop?" she asked, finally articulating the question that plagued her all afternoon. "Using me to deter accusations that they're exploiting girls from the compounds?"

Dr. Mercer considered the question, leaning back in thoughtful repose in his oversized rocking chair. Amira always admired that about him, that he never treated any question of hers as insignificant.

"No, I don't think so," he responded. "That would be a foolish move, and the Pandora team are not fools. They've made mistakes, no doubt about it, but doing something that transparent would be laughed off by the people of Westport and they know it. No, Amira, I'm sure you have been given this assignment because you possess skills and talents they need. Don't doubt yourself."

"Should I be nervous at all then about this assignment?"

"Ah." Dr. Mercer smiled. "A lot to unravel with that question. I would say 'extremely cautious' would be a more appropriate response. This is a high-profile project full of high-profile characters, with considerable stakes. And the cloning effort is the most ambitious project that the Pandora group is attempting – that I know of, anyway. If it succeeds, it will be a watershed moment for humanity, one that will change how we have families and more deeply, how we perceive ourselves as navigators of our own evolutionary story. If it fails, however, as I'm sure your former home desperately hopes it will, the ramifications will be felt in Aldwych for years to come, and likely become a black eye on your resume."

"And I would take a good share of the blame if the subject dies," Amira said.

Dr. Mercer nodded thoughtfully. "You need to have your own interests at heart, my dear. No one else will protect you on Pandora, you can be certain of that. It just baffles me that the Academy is so eager to put young people in such a precarious position."

"Is that why you left?"

Dr. Mercer sighed and gestured toward one of the photographs, in which he stood smiling in front of the Avicenna building.

"I never approved of the Academy's pact with Aldwych," he said. "The district is too powerful and its reach extends into space, where the laws become murky and enforcement nearly impossible. Look at the Carthage, exploiting prisoners for test subjects. To offer our students to them was dangerous; I said it then and I see how true it is now. But the alliance with Aldwych had deeper problems."

"Science for profit."

"Well, that's nothing new," Dr. Mercer said dismissively.

Amira picked up a photograph on the end table. A small group of scientists posed in front of a statue in Aldwych Square. Amira identified several famous faces from Stream newscasts but didn't recognize others, despite the impressive array of badges on their lab coats. The caption below read, 'Associates and Friends of Sentient Cosmology'.

"You're not in this one, Dr. Mercer."

For the first time during her visit, Dr. Mercer's genial air faltered and he fidgeted in his chair. He eyed the photograph in Amira's hand.

"No, I'm not, thankfully," he said at last. "I avoided that rabbit hole, although there are many in that picture who I respect greatly. I keep it as a reminder of what happens when scientific inquiry becomes polluted by wishful thinking."

"Some famous faces there," Amira said. "Dr. Alvarez from Galileo, Felicity Knox from McKenna-Okoye's space division. Competitors, right? Why are they all posing together? Is this some kind of cross-Aldwych organization?"

"Yes, and you know them," he said. "They started recruiting at the Academy right before I left, despite many objections from faculty. They call themselves the Cosmics."

Amira knew of the Cosmics. They had become a regular sight on the campus's quadrangle in recent months, sweating in sleek, tailored pantsuits as they distributed pamphlets, paperbacks and free Eye downloads to passing students. A quick skim of their literature revealed it to be a New Age religion of some kind.

"Yes, the Cosmics," Dr. Mercer said under his breath. "It started off well enough, you know, as many things do. An astrotheorist developed a theory to tie together what we know about the universe – the Quantum world, dark energy, dark matter, predictive consciousness – with a spiritual understanding of our existence. Many of the founders were ex-compound, if you didn't know."

"No!" Amira said, horrified.

"There are some core tenets they share," Dr. Mercer said, pouring Amira another cup of iced tea. "The Conscious Plane, the level of existence where all things are bound together and the individual soul is subsumed into the whole. They also subscribe to multiverses, which science has all but conclusively proven exist in some form. But unlike your former community, they don't project morality to these different realities. There is no heaven or hell concept. What was it they taught you? If you eat your peas and have many children under holy matrimony, you go to the Nearhaven, whereas if you disobey the Elders, you go to—"

"The Neverhaven," Amira finished for him. "The shadeless and waveless world, in which the Cataclysm never ended, and the ground burns beneath your feet." She flushed. Even years later, she could recite the Elders' sermons to the word.

"Exactly. So the Cosmics are more benign than your Elders in that sense. But it's dangerous to try to fill in the gaps of our knowledge with anything other than scientific proof. That is what religion has tried to do for centuries, and these Cosmics are no different, even if they use scientific jargon to make it more palatable. They're everywhere in Aldwych now, and I fear they will try to remake the District in their image."

"Are they involved in Pandora's cloning effort at all, do you think?"

Dr. Mercer laughed.

"Henry will pitch me off a high cliff before Valerie Singh has anything to do with the Cosmics," he chuckled. "But that doesn't mean they're not involved in some way on Pandora, and it certainly doesn't mean they're not interested. Watch yourself, Amira. Watch yourself, and remember what drives you and what made you one of my best, most dedicated students."

The knot in Amira's stomach tightened at Dr. Mercer's warning, so starkly delivered. Her senses heightened, just slightly, as they had always done in the compound before an impending punishment – the birds chirped louder, the sun grew a little brighter through the window. The flickers of doubt that followed her from the Academy grew stronger. She was a neuroscientist, not a politician. Was she out of her depth in the political jungles of Aldwych?

They walked together along the gravel path leading to the main road down the mountain, Henry shuffling behind them. Amira stopped abruptly, facing Dr. Mercer.

"I'll come visit again soon," she began. "I should have come a long time ago, before all of this, but I've been so busy—"

Dr. Mercer raised his hand.

"Don't worry about me here. Life is for the young. Go forth and live! And if Pandora lives up to its reputation, I suspect I'll be hearing from you again before too long."

On that ominous note, he turned back, leaving Amira to continue down the path to the trains, alone.

★ ★ ★

"Are you sure you don't want to go out tonight? There are some great bars down by Sullivan's Wharf."

Amira studied D'Arcy's face, attempting to discern how badly her friend wanted to spend the night drinking before their first day in Aldwych. An enormous plate of Ethiopian *wat* lay between them, nearly stripped of injera bread and surprisingly flavorful synthetic lamb, along with a half-empty bottle of hybrid wine. The rich food left Amira sedated, dulling the anxiety of her conversation with Dr.

Mercer, and the coming day ahead. She hesitated.

"Don't you girls have an early morning tomorrow?" D'Arcy's father called from the living room. "You don't want to walk into those shiny buildings with hangovers."

"I'd prefer to stay here," Amira admitted, silently thanking Mr. Pham.

"Of course," D'Arcy said kindly, reaching for the wine bottle, as if to formally seal the decision to stay in. Although she shared a room with Julian in the Canary House, D'Arcy visited her father for dinner at least once a week. Amira accompanied her more often than Julian did, relishing the opportunity to cook and escape the Riverfront's exhaustive pace.

"Mind if we finish off the wine, Dad?" D'Arcy called out, refilling Amira's glass with a wink.

"I suppose you girls have earned it." A soft note of pride crept into Mr. Pham's gruff voice. "Although I'll never understand exactly what it is you do, no matter how many times D'Arcy explains it to me."

A stevedore, D'Arcy's father worked in Sullivan's Wharf, loading cargo destined for the space stations. On occasion, he accompanied the cargo to the Pacific Parallel itself, the offshore platform where one of Earth's two space elevators hurtled supplies and souls into space. Though the Stream provided countless images of the Parallel's loading docks, anchored in choppy Pacific waters, it fascinated Amira to imagine Mr. Pham nonchalantly pushing crates, syntharette in mouth, under one of the greatest structures ever built.

"Saving the world," D'Arcy said, her smile faltering as she turned back to Amira. She gestured upstairs.

D'Arcy's childhood bedroom was a living exhibit to her twenty-five years on Earth, a vortex in which no object, once it entered the room, seemed to escape. There were stuffed animals and long-deactivated play robots from her childhood, posters of Vietnamese pop idols on her walls, books on physics and programming that spanned her school years. Every time Amira entered, she discovered some new facet of D'Arcy, a relic of an old hobby or fascination. Patterns drawn on the walls that would eventually become glowing, intricate tattoos. D'Arcy sat on the bed, the bedspread covered with anime characters, and Amira could picture her friend as a girl of seven, building her first computer from the wharf junkyard's scraps.

The room rattled as a train passed overhead, sending the entire building into seismic fits and drowning out the distant, drunken shouts of stevedores returning from night shifts.

"I still can't believe you grew up here," Amira said, holding her glass of wine high as she joined D'Arcy on the bed. "It's like a completely different city by the water."

"It's as much a part of Westport as the Riverfront or Aldwych," D'Arcy said. "One of the few parts of the city that didn't get bombed out during the Cataclysm, so it was never rebuilt. It'll always be home. It made me realize what mattered to me. I saw the conditions that Mom and Dad worked in at the Parallel and knew I wanted a different life."

Outside the barred window, the moonlight caught the ripples in the Pacific waters. The indigo glow reminded Amira of the compound at night. Though she dreamed about the desert from time to time, she never looked back on it as home.

"Amira, you've had this dark look all night," D'Arcy said. Impatience tinged her normally warm voice. "Try to see the bright side. Pandora is pretty elite for a couple of students like you and me. You're on the most problematic part of Pandora, it's true, but you get to work with Valerie Singh and Alistair Parrish. It's not the space stations, but Pandora's still a big deal. It's where all of the great minds across Aldwych get together, break through their corporate barriers, and push the limits of science."

"Easy for you to say," Amira said. "You get to write code to make sure cat articles on the Stream work in deep space. Everyone loves the Stream. I'm stuck treating a dying girl on a project everyone hates, when I could be doing experiments on one of the stations."

"Why are you so bent on getting into space anyway?" D'Arcy asked. "I've never understood that."

Like an involuntary reflex, Amira's eyes turned back up at the night sky.

"Space is where the boundaries are really pushed," she said. "You know the psychology of space travel is a major area of study, especially with the Titan voyage. Learning how to keep people sane on long space missions, surrounded by nothing and hundreds of millions of miles away from home – I could make my mark there."

A textbook answer, but a truthful one. As much as D'Arcy may have wanted to, she would never understand the way Amira's heart swelled, as a child hiding on her rooftop, when something man-made passed across the night sky. She couldn't understand the hope the stations contained within their insulated, carbon walls, the potential for a better world than the restrictive life in Children of the New Covenant.

Nor could she understand that for Amira, the more physical distance she put between herself and the place of her childhood, the safer she felt. She wrapped her arms around her middle.

Realizing that her gloom was beginning to affect D'Arcy on a night of celebration, Amira changed the subject. An hour later, both sat cross-legged on the floor, laughing hysterically as D'Arcy's holo-camera displayed footage from last year's Climate Day celebrations at the Academy. The festival had devolved into pandemonium after an enterprising student botanist chose the day to unveil a new, fast-growing liana vine that responded to artificial light. Within hours, it had taken over the main auditorium and the neighboring swimming pool, emitting the smell of rotten eggs as it reached the chlorinated water. Students fled in a panic, as though the vines were a deadly nerve agent.

Amira drained her glass and stretched across the floor, wiping tears of laughter from her eyes. D'Arcy turned off the holo-cam, her eyelids drooping.

"It's kind of funny," Amira said.

"What is?"

"That man I met from the project, Barlow? He knew I was from a compound when he saw my hand. He asked me which 'community' I came from. I've never heard anyone from the city call them communities before. Only people from the compounds say that."

D'Arcy frowned slightly. "Well, he's part of the project and they've been recruiting girls from the compounds, right? Maybe he picked up the language from them."

"That's possible." Amira drummed her fingers lightly, Barlow's strange, appraising expression fresh in her mind.

D'Arcy pulled herself onto the bed. Her breathing grew heavy with sleep after several minutes. Amira joined her on the bed and succumbed to exhaustion shortly after, her sleep punctuated by dreams of the desert, the choking vines along the Canary House, and the relentless scream of oncoming trains.

CHAPTER THREE

Subject #42

It was still dark when Amira woke. She fumbled in the pitch black for her overnight bag, stepping on a small robotic toy that squeaked in protest. Cursing softly, she settled on black pants and a purple hoodie that she fastened tightly around her head – it had turned frigid overnight in the heatless room. Over her clothes, she threw on the lab coat issued by the Academy the day before – dark blue, the color denoting an apprentice researcher within the hierarchy-conscious Aldwych. She nudged D'Arcy awake, who grumbled in protest but pulled herself out of bed.

It was snowing steadily outside, blanketing the ground in grimy powder that crunched softly as they took long, hurried strides across the street. The block was silent, save for a few barking dogs in the distance. Through the fog and over the rusted buildings of the Wharf, Amira could make out the distant towers of Aldwych, always dotted with lights and visible throughout the city.

The Red line was relatively quiet when they boarded, but gained new passengers exponentially as the train neared downtown Westport. Initially, they were mostly commuters. Stony-faced businessmen in expensive suits, teenagers with neon hair sheltered under their oversized headphones, and grim technicians in white lab coats; all jostled for space and avoided eye contact as best they could in the confines of the narrow tin shuttle. Tourists joined the throng from the downtown stops, their left pupils flashing brightly with each snap of their Eye cameras. Affectionately called the Third Eye, the models no longer required voice commands, and operated entirely on the thoughts of their users. A device that fit onto the eye like a contact lens, many now came with custom colors and patterns, leaving most people Amira encountered with mismatched eyes, one pupil shining with the Eye's distinctive glow.

A man next to Amira blinked twice and a small globe materialized in front of his eyeball, a hologram that flashed temperatures in different cities as it spun. Though impressed, Amira shuddered when the small globe retreated back into his eye, dissolving like water when it touched his pupil. Likely nursing a headache, D'Arcy still couldn't resist laughing from her corner seat. Amira's fear and distrust of Third Eyes had become a running joke between them. Beyond her squeamishness, Amira couldn't fathom how people crossed streets and carried on conversations with a screen perpetually covering half of their vision.

Turning away, Amira stared ahead as the train moved above ground and over the streets, where the glass skyscrapers of downtown Westport reached dizzying heights, higher even than the mountains that framed the city.

She nervously gripped the safety rail inside the train car. Her Academy briefing papers offered few clues as to what she would encounter today. Beyond the media's rampant, varied speculation on Pandora, the state of the project and its players remained a mystery. The two famous scientists behind the cloning effort, Valerie Singh and Alistair Parrish, the greatest living geneticists by most accounts, wielded unmatched fame and influence in North America. Though never officially married, they had a child together. Most interestingly for Amira, Parrish owned the Carthage station, where he divided his time between experiments in the Soma building.

The lights in the train car flashed. A group of tourists let out a stream of curses.

"All Third Eye devices have been deactivated as we enter the Aldwych District," a mechanical voice chirped through the speakers over outraged cries of protest. "In accordance with the Station Alliance Ratification, all camera and video functionality is prohibited. Have a nice day."

One by one, the lights in the passengers' eyes flickered out, leaving their pupils dull and unseeing.

The snow had turned to sleet by the time they reached the Aldwych station. The train car hummed with anticipation, tourists jostling for a view of Aldwych's main square. On the other side of the car's windows, commuters in lab coats of various shades streamed silently toward the main complex.

Upon exiting the station, Amira paused despite the strengthening sleet at Aldwych Square. A hand touched her shoulder and D'Arcy waved goodbye before walking toward the Soma building. Amira lingered, as D'Arcy must have sensed she would, to take in the imposing semi-circle of skyscrapers that marked the heart of Aldwych. Amira allowed herself a moment of reflection amid the throng of tourists. She once milked cows and received beatings when hair escaped from her veil. Had she not managed to board that train years ago, she would be another compound congregant, writhing under the effects of Chimyra in hopes of becoming no one, a cog in a machine of oppression. In less than an hour, she would officially become a scientist of Aldwych.

The Mendel-Soma Complex, which housed the Pandora project, could be seen all over Westport as part of the Aldwych skyline, but nothing did justice to the scale of the building up close. While most of the surrounding skyscrapers shone despite the overcast skies, encased in effervescent light blue or glassy white, the Soma had grown dull under the abrasion of time, the murky color of black onyx. The Soma's two separate buildings coiled around one another like strands of DNA, twisting until they eventually broke apart and splayed upward into the sky. As they separated, the two towers remained connected by a series of cylindrical walkways. The diverging towers supported the Soma's highest level, a rotating, disc-shaped structure topped by an antenna that disappeared into the clouds. The spinning disc reminded Amira of a holomentic machine.

Angry shouts cut through the wind and rain, through which a crowd of protesters lined both sides of the complex's entrance. They waved signs with the usual anti-cloning slogans, some accompanied by gruesome drawings of mangled infants, a vivid imagining of botched clones, along with lurid caricatures of a woman who could only be Valerie Singh. The protesters leaned fiercely over the fences meant to contain them, waving fists and shouting at the hunched figures who rushed into the building. Locals, Westport natives who had rejected Aldwych's official line on the pioneering benefits of human cloning. The compounds, as Julian had noted many times on his radio show, had been noticeably silent about the cloning attempt, despite the use and deaths of their former congregants. No formal statement of condemnation or the usual Stream propaganda. Their silence on the matter left a dark shadow in Amira's thoughts.

"A warm welcome on your first day," a soft voice said to her right. Stunned, she turned to face Tony Barlow.

"Dr. Barlow!" she gasped. "I didn't see you—"

"A bad habit of mine, I'm afraid, Miss Valdez, making myself known at the wrong moment," he said. He raised an oversized umbrella above them.

Amira flinched slightly at the gendered title but accepted the shelter from the downpour.

"Apologies, I meant to say M. Valdez," he added with a knowing look, exaggerating the 'em' sound before her surname. "Bad habit from another time. I personally don't see the need for this gender-neutral language, but it's a good habit to have in a research environment, I suppose. Shall we go in?"

The last person to refer to Amira as 'Miss' was a compound Elder, right before administering a beating. Amira cringed when the crack of the cane across her back resonated in her memory, but she followed Barlow toward the Soma building.

They advanced toward the entrance under a hail of slogans and waving placards. Most of the demonstrators who lined the walkway screamed nonsensically at tourist and scientist alike, but a single figure to her right caught Amira's eye: a tall, dark-haired man whose eyes sank into his gaunt face. He locked his gaze on her as she passed through the gauntlet. A cold knot formed in the pit of her stomach, accompanied by a strange ringing in her ears. She did not recognize the man, but had experienced the same cold, devouring glare many times over in the compound, the look men cast upon the young, the female, the minds and bodies they could control but never own in entirety.

"Is it always like this?" she asked Barlow over the roar of the crowd.

"It's become worse in the last month," he said casually, staring ahead. "After the deaths of the previous subjects, it has obviously dominated the news. But it's neither here nor there. It's a free country, and these people have the right to their convictions and fears, unfounded as they are. I have some business in the mezzanine to attend to, but I'm sure you can find your way up. It's floor 235 – top floor. It's good you're early, you'll have to go through quite a bit of security for your first day. No one is allowed in who isn't meant to be there."

★ ★ ★

Under the guidance of Naomi, the project's animated, pink-haired secretary, Amira stood behind a wide glass window of the 235th floor's main laboratory, where Subject #42 lay in deep sleep. A collection of monitors near her bed indicated steady vitals. Above a circular platform in the center of the room, a hologram displayed the swirling colors and occasional flashing images of the conscious mind at rest.

The subject looked very young, barely into adulthood, with straight, deep-red hair that framed a delicate, heart-shaped face. One of only three subjects who successfully conceived during the cloning initiative, and the only one still alive. Though she was beautiful by any standard, her beauty was more interesting than striking, her face a patchwork of sharp angles and softness. Her brows were furrowed slightly, and her small mouth turned downward in stern contemplation. The round heaviness of her abdomen overwhelmed her tiny frame.

Naomi handed Amira a portable screen. A moving picture of the subject's face sat at the top of the screen alongside the name: 'Hull, Rozene. Mendel-Soma Complex Subject No. 42'. The text below her image read:

Demographics

Age: 19

Sex: Female, XX

Gender: Woman-conforming

Birthplace: New Mexico, USA (Trinity Compound)

Alternate names: Unknown

Consents given: Signed. All necessary medical treatment authorized.

Medical History

Allergies: Penicillin, Cats

Prior pregnancies: None

Pre-birth DNA modifications: None

Possibility of cancer, Alzheimer's, heart disease in later years due to lack of preventative care at subject's place of birth.

Background and Mental Evaluation

Subject admitted to occasional alcohol use after moving to Westport but denies experimentation with illicit drugs. Precise sexual history is unknown, but interview responses suggest that Subject is around 75–80 per cent heterosexual. Subject was raised in an isolated religious compound, known as the Trinity Compound, where physical and emotional abuse is known to occur, although subject has refused to provide details on either account. Despite apparent trauma at references to her upbringing, subject occasionally expresses religious views and ideations, including fears of an afterlife in a series of parallel dimensions known as the 'Otherworlds' (a prevalent belief in compound life). The affect ranges from blunt to volatile emotional fluctuations, including anger and depression. Possible bipolar personality, category 6, with self-aggrandizing tendencies. Class 3 suicide watch: Constant monitoring and periodic restraints are recommended.

Amira grabbed a pair of goggles hanging near the door.

"Are you going in already? She's asleep," Naomi said.

"I'd like to start by observing her dream patterns," Amira said. "If there's no issue with that."

A panel of machinery and monitors flanked the sleeping subject from both sides. The holomentic device stood apart from the other equipment. The machine's appearance was deceptively simple, a box-like device with a wide, spinning, disc-shaped platform at its top where holographic images were displayed from a subject's subconscious. Two interactive screens protruded from its sides, like a pair of outstretched hands waiting to be touched. Its reach, however, extended beyond its unassuming exterior. With the newer holomentic models, Amira could change its settings at her mental command, make the holographic disc follow her movements or even use the new submergence command to enlarge the holographic display, filling every corner of a room with the sights, sounds and sensations of a person's deepest, darkest memories. Amira pictured the shed of her Placement Day exam filling this room with its dusty, lightless oppression, and resisted a shudder.

Amira ran her fingers lightly across the reader's many buttons and dials, letting their familiarity bring her a semblance of calm – the first calm she'd felt in days. This was what she knew; within the sterile confines of the ward's glass walls, she was in control. Exhaling deeply, she pulled up a chair beside the subject.

She pulled the goggles over her eyes, took another deep breath and extended her hand. *Sensor to me*, she thought, enunciating each word in her head, and a robotic arm glided across the table and into her open palm. She attached the arm to the reader; red wires ran from the center of the machine to a series of sensory pads placed around the subject's head. She flipped a switch on the monitor and thought, *Read.*

The kaleidoscope of color began to move and rotate at a faster pace above the holographic platform, twisting into a series of blurred, indecipherable shapes. *Limbic pre-conscious*, Amira thought, and the sensor responded to her command, humming softly as the sensory pads on the subject's head glowed. A haphazard reel of images materialized on the hologram platform in rapid succession – the moon glowing over a desert landscape, a blurred figure with a stethoscope, a large ship in the dark. There were sounds as well, though they were faint; high-pitched laughter, footsteps, the growl of an all-terrain engine.

Amira's throat tightened at the familiar sound and she ran her thumbs across the palms of her hands. The holographic images had taken a reddish tint – the color of fear.

"Let's submerge," she muttered softly. "Limbic pre-conscious, REM dream state." The sensor obliged, and the hologram spread beyond its platform across the room, covering the floor until Amira stood in the center of a small classroom with paneled walls and uneven floorboards. A dirt-caked window revealed a dry, baked landscape of red sand and a cloudless sky. Though it was an optical illusion, Amira blinked several times to orient herself to the shift in her surroundings.

A small girl with dark red hair stood at the head of the class before rows of young children, none older than ten. Two adults, a man and a woman, flanked this young version of Rozene Hull. The man swung a strange, glowing baton at his side. The older woman, short with burly arms, spoke in a faint, distant voice, as though she were trapped underwater.

Raise auditory sensors, Amira thought, and the woman's voice rang clear.

"Recite it again, Rozene, without swaying your arms this time," the older woman said. "Keep them still."

"It's the only way I can remember," the young girl replied in a small voice.

"These are Elder Cartwright's words!" the teacher bellowed.

"How they are said matters. They must be spoken with reverence, and you will say them that way, from memory, if we must stay here all day. Again!"

The girl exhaled and raised her chin. "And from the ashes of the Cataclysm, the Elder of Elders found peace within the Conscious Plane, becoming one with all things good and evil. Through this tr-transcendence, the Plane gifted him with Chimyra, so that others may see Creation's glory, and a new c-covenant was born in the desert...." Her arms began to sway back and forth as she searched for the next phrase.

"Arms, again!" the woman shouted, and in a swift motion, the baton struck Rozene on her shoulder with a hideous cracking sound. The girl shrieked at the electric jolt and dropped to her knees, clutching her arm as, to Amira's horror, a deep crimson stain spread across her shoulder. Rozene gave a terrified wail as the man pulled her back to her feet and pressed her arms tightly to her sides. Amira's shoulders twitched involuntarily, as though shaking off the sting herself. That weapon was new to her, although similar punishments existed in the New Covenant Compound.

"Now continue," the woman said in a cool, threatening voice.

The young Rozene hiccupped and sobbed, looking around desperately for help that didn't exist, not within the Trinity Compound or the empty miles around it.

"And through Chimyra, the people opened doors that only the f-faithful could pass through, and saw the g-glory of the Nearhaven, w-where the virtuous may find life after life."

Amira approached the center of the classroom, passing directly through the children in their desks. They sat in frozen silence, adopting the stillness of animals sensing a predator's gaze. Nearby, the sleeping subject twitched slightly, audibly muttering the words in time with the frightened, younger version of herself, and Amira realized that she too was joining in the prayer out loud, one she learned years ago in a similar classroom, the prayer that united the compounds in the height of the Drought Wars.

"And to those who turned away from the natural order of the universe, and our destiny among the stars, they w-will find a world, a Neverhaven, more terrible t-than imagining, shadeless under skies where the Cataclysm rages without end. Waveless, where the waters are filled with terrible poison. The ground shall crack b-beneath their feet and their souls torn asunder, a terrible – a-a terrible and righteous r-retribution of rock…and thunder."

The classroom scene faded under a haze of blue – the color of relief and tranquility – and the brightly lit laboratory returned to view. The holographic platform turned pitch black. The lab assistant, Naomi, approached from her silent corner of the room.

"She's now in the delta stage of sleep," Amira said softly. "A deeper level. We need to submerge further into her consciousness to see what she sees."

She turned the dial and the hologram began to punctuate with crackling flashes of red and blue light. Sounds echoed around the room, distant and indecipherable. Laughter or shouts, mixed with the faint pulse of chanting. Then once again, new sights materialized in the hologram, but unlike the classroom scene that unfolded moments ago, they were blurred around the edges and never spanned the breadth of the room.

"Record," Amira whispered, hoping that the scanners at the Soma were sophisticated enough to capture the rapidly shifting images. They flashed into focus and transformed into a whirling dervish of noise and color. Scenes appeared and disappeared in seconds – an old man digging beneath a full moon; a doctor's office; a disembodied pair of legs strapped into stirrups. Next, a large auditorium ribbed with sensory screens that reached to the high ceiling, packed with men, women and children in white robes, writhing and sobbing under the obvious effects of Chimyra, their fingers crooked and bent at odd, claw-like angles. A tall Elder stood at a podium, his mouth moving without words.

Amira tried to zoom in on the preaching figure, but the sobs turned to shrieks and the floor collapsed beneath the crowd, sending them tumbling and falling through darkness that gave way to a canvas of stars. The writhing figures floated silently in space.

"You see," the Elder's voice boomed through the void, "how we stand together in the space between our universe and the next one. Our worlds are like beads on a necklace, and through Chimyra, we stand on the thread that binds. Sin and selfishness infect this holy place! It rots us from the inside. Do you faithless wish to see the punishment that the Conscious Plane promises for sinners? Look!"

The stars swelled until they became bursts of fire. The blackness of space gave way to a landscape stripped of trees, fierce smoke seeping from cracks in the ground. The wreckage of an airplane loomed before the now-screaming crowd, burnt bodies crawling from its sides.

The sleeping woman jerked her head from side to side and Amira closed her eyes. When the Elders sought to frighten the compound faithful with glimpses of the Neverhaven, they invoked iconic images from the Cataclysm – thousands of planes falling from the sky, into oceans, farms and cities. Though Amira had not been born at the time of the Cataclysm or the years of war that followed, she felt as though she had lived it, many times over, as this sleeping subject had done during the Passage Ceremony.

The plane wreckage burst into flames, the scattered bodies hissing as they dissolved into the ground. Screams rose into the air.

Suddenly, pulsing flashes of red light and a loud buzzing filled the room.

"What's happening?" Naomi cried.

"She's waking up," Amira said. She pulled off her goggles and turned the machine off. "The red tones indicate a high state of fear, so she's pulling herself out before the dream escalates."

The images on the holomentic machine vanished.

The subject's eyes opened and she drew several sharp breaths as though emerging from icy water. She leaned upright, searching wildly around the room before recognition set in. Her dark blue eyes fixed coldly on Amira.

"Who are you?" she demanded. Her voice was high, almost girlish, but with a harsh, ringing quality.

"Rozene, calm down, no one's hurting you," Naomi said in hushed tones, grabbing Rozene's wrists with clearly practiced speed. At her touch, Rozene lunged forward, grasping furiously for the wires fixed to her temples.

Amira took a step back.

"Is she a Fed?" Rozene yelled. "Here to carve me to pieces when I die like the others? You don't know what's wrong with me. None of you know anything! You'll let me die! Me and my baby!"

Her wrists slid out of Naomi's grip and she shifted her fury toward the source; the holomentic machine. For a heavily pregnant woman, she grappled at the equipment with surprising strength while Naomi pulled at her elbows, fighting to regain control. Naomi panted with the effort of restraining Rozene while Amira stood in stunned silence, rooted to the ground. "She's here to help, she's a—"

"You think I'm crazy!" Rozene continued to claw at the wires, albeit with less conviction. "I'm not crazy. I wasn't crazy before I came here, it's the drugs you give me that are making me crazy. All I do is sleep, and these dreams...."

"Sedate her now," a light, calm voice said, and Amira gasped.

Valerie Singh stood at the ward's entrance. The scientist leaned against the door frame, observing the scene with a nonchalant detachment that suggested they were discussing the weather at a picnic.

Rozene collapsed back into the bed and burst into tears. The outburst, the rise followed by the crash, reminded Amira of her first course with Dr. Mercer, when he brought the class to the last operating Westport asylum. The elderly patients shifted between despair and sudden bursts of rage in the blink of an eye, the supposed product of chemical attacks during the Drought Wars. She pitied and feared those haunted survivors in equal measure. The small woman in front of her, shoulders slumped with exhaustion, inspired only pity.

Naomi pulled a syringe from her coat in a swift, furtive motion and in seconds, Rozene's head tilted to one side, the small features on her tear-streaked face relaxing as she slipped back into unconsciousness.

Amira recognized Dr. Singh immediately, from her countless appearances on television and the Stream, but she was taken aback by how diminutive the famed geneticist appeared in person. Dark-skinned with black hair tied into a tight, elegant bun, Dr. Singh had an aura of effortless composure that was offset by calculating green eyes. She wore the signature black coat reserved for Aldwych's highest-ranking researchers, its lapel decorated with a variety of medals and pins, compact trophies from a long, eventful career.

"You must be Amira Valdez," she said. "Our new assistant from the Academy."

Amira cleared her throat, glancing back at the now catatonic Rozene. She struggled for words.

"Yes."

"I'm not up to date on how modern therapy is taught these days, but I would think the goal would be to help the patient, not instigate a nervous breakdown."

Amira flushed. "Before I can do anything to help, I need to understand what's happening to her and why. I can't tell from her profile summary how the previous psychiatrist was treating her."

Dr. Singh smiled with cold appreciation at the subtle retort – both women knew there had not been a dedicated psychiatrist on the project before today.

"Is it safe to sedate her in her condition?" Amira continued, emboldened.

"Safer than the alternative," Singh said.

She turned to the monitor displaying Rozene's vitals and ran her hands pensively over the screen. "I understand the science of cloning and of genetics, and there is nothing medically wrong with M. Hull. She should be healthy and on her way to the history books, as should I be, delivering the first true human clone to the world. She should not be in danger, but for some reason, she is."

She paced across the room and Naomi jumped out of her path.

"The previous subjects both died with no clear and conclusive medical explanation," Singh said. "With the physical options ruled out, it's obvious to me now that the problem we are facing must be a psychological one. Stress can attack and corrode the body more fiercely than any cancer. And we know that young women from the cesspools known as the compounds" – she nodded at Amira – "are especially vulnerable to both."

Singh paused, staring at the monitor again with an indecipherable expression. Amira bit her lower lip, absorbing the sting of the insult in silence.

"This vulnerability has its advantages, though, at least for us," Singh continued. "Babies are born in the compounds without genetic manipulation, not even to prevent cancer or Alzheimer's, which is standard practice in any city. While primitive, it does make the process of cloning and manipulating the embryonic DNA much easier. Fewer complications than those we encountered with regular subjects – until these final stages of pregnancy."

Singh resumed her pacing. Though she was in constant motion, her movements were never hurried or suggestive of uncertainty.

"I will not waste your time or mine with false niceties," she said. "I did not request a holomentic reader, and certainly not a student, but the decision has been made. You are here because people with more power than me" a note of clear contempt crept into her smooth voice – "decided to make it so. But since you *are* here, your role should be extremely clear. Fix my subject. And failing that, get her to the point where she's sane enough to keep herself and this fetus, special as it is, alive for the next few months. The world is watching us."

CHAPTER FOUR

Submergence

The bitter cold front that gripped Westport for the last month finally gave way as the sun fought through the dense Pacific clouds, turning the pavements slick with melted snow. Westport's residents had been long accustomed to periodic snow throughout the year and knew to embrace the warmth whenever it reemerged.

"A rough first week?"

Amira nodded, tearing into a slice of pizza with grim ferocity. Julian and D'Arcy sat across a narrow table, shoulders touching.

They sat outside, taking advantage of a warm Westport night. After passing through several Riverfront bars, they found an all-night diner that overlooked the murky canal, the perfect place to begin the grim transition to sobriety.

Julian leaned back into his seat in drowsy contentment. Rail-thin with dark brown skin and a large mop of curly black hair, he fidgeted with the animated air of a happy drunk unwilling to concede the night's end. D'Arcy sat calmly, twirling the saltshaker with her thin, pale fingers. She shot Amira a sly smile. They had run into each other several times in Aldwych that week. Amira always did a double-take at the sight of D'Arcy in conservative, professional attire. D'Arcy had earned a reputation as a wild bohemian at the Academy, due to her ever-changing appearance. On this particular night, her strapless dress revealed a string of tattoos and tribal scarring down her left arm along with a new henna pattern around her neck, made to look like twisting branches. Her dark, razor-straight hair was contrastingly simple, hovering above her pale shoulders. In Aldwych, however, D'Arcy played the game.

"I feel like you've been hiding from me," D'Arcy said, waving the pizza in a mock-threatening gesture. "I came up to the Soma yesterday to drop off some code and that adorable assistant said you were logging a session in the back rooms, 'not to be disturbed under any circumstances'."

Amira laughed, imagining pink-haired, bubbly Naomi parroting her warning at D'Arcy.

"Sorry about that," Amira said. "Like you said, it wasn't an easy week."

"So that poor girl isn't getting any better?"

"No," Amira sighed, her thoughts returning to Rozene. "She doesn't trust me, so I haven't even tried a waking reading yet. I've just been monitoring her dreams for now. She's sedated for at least half of the day – special sedatives that are supposed to be safe for pregnancy, but it doesn't seem right."

Following the outburst on the first day, Amira and Rozene's rapport had not improved. Remembering the learned bigotry of the Trinity Compound, Amira wondered if Rozene's hostility derived from Amira's skin color, but the young woman treated others on the project, including Valerie Singh, with comparative respect. To allay concerns that Amira was a 'Fed', Naomi had revealed that Amira had escaped from a compound as well. Amira had been downloading recordings from the holomentic machine at the time and Rozene laughed aloud from the bed, a shrill, mocking sound of disbelief. When Amira admitted that it was true, she had come from the Children of the New Covenant, she felt an odd sense of flattery that Rozene had considered it impossible, followed by guilt at her own desire to be as far removed from this broken woman as possible.

Once she accepted the fact of Amira's compound past, Rozene's distrust of her only grew. Amira would catch Rozene staring at her as she arranged the lab equipment, watching with a hungry, searching expression. Amira did not need to read her thoughts to know what question plagued Rozene – how had this compound girl ended up here?

Amira smiled grimly. "Valerie Singh thinks I'm an idiot. She has this way of looking right through you, like you're a piece of decoration on the wall. Some cheap painting of a fruit bowl." Accustomed to endless praise at the Academy, Amira was stung by

Singh's dismissiveness to an unexpected degree. Though Amira tried to return the indifference, she desperately wanted to prove herself to the geneticist, a woman who validated her loftiest ambitions. Dr. Singh came from a notoriously volatile region in India after the Drought Wars, where girls attended school under the cover of armed guards, before thriving in cosmopolitan Kolkata. Amira had hoped that Dr. Singh's background would provide a source of common ground, an illusion quickly dispelled in the last few days.

"Well, we're all idiots compared to the famous Dr. Singh," Julian said. "Even this one here." He nudged D'Arcy affectionately. Amira had only known them as a couple, having met them both on her first day in the Canary House. Both studied in technical fields, although Julian's true loves were his radio show and artwork. Julian had claimed the empty attic of the Canary House for his art, covering its walls with rich colors of paint and chalk. Amira visited the makeshift studio frequently to escape the heat of her own room, as well as to take in the dystopian, surreal landscapes that stretched around the ceiling.

"I need to make some progress," Amira continued. "Dr. Singh thinks the subject – Rozene's – health problems at her age are mostly psychological at this point, so the onus is on me to figure out how to mitigate them."

"Mitigate?" D'Arcy asked, her thin brows arching slightly. "Isn't it obvious why she would be under stress? She's a guinea pig who watched the previous batch of subjects die under 'mysterious circumstances'. I don't blame her in the slightest for being in a panic. And I also find it strange that two – *two* – healthy young women just dropped dead and miscarried, don't you think?"

Amira bristled at the contempt in D'Arcy's voice.

"These are the best geneticists in the world," she said with a hint of defensiveness. Though it had only been a few days, she was now part of the Pandora team. "And this is Westport, not compound territory. There's no conspiracy and no malice. That's what the anti-cloning religionists want you to think."

"The world isn't divided cleanly between the forces of scientific truth and the compounds," Julian said with uncharacteristic gentleness, a by-product of the alcohol pulsing through his system.

"Westport isn't as perfect and pure as you make it out to be, Amira. We're all human, after all. There are bound to be prejudices, mistakes made. And at the end of the day, it's money, not knowledge, that fuels Aldwych."

Amira wrinkled her nose before hiding her frustration in another slice of pizza. Julian never failed to mention the world's nuances and complexities, but spent little time experiencing life outside of the cities. For Amira, Westport was more than an adopted home – it saved her from the misery, the pseudo-life she would have lived out in the compound. Even on her worst days, she remembered that fact.

She sighed, gazing down the promenade. The chains of light from the nearby bridge reflected in the canal, its black water swaying rhythmically with restless, breaking waves.

"What's going on down there?" Julian called, pointing at the lower walking path that lined the waterway. Near the bridge, a small crowd gathered around something on the ground. A skinny teenager with a red mohawk prodded a stick toward a small, dark object before backing away nervously.

"Some junkie hyped on Elysium," D'Arcy said under her breath.

The kid looked around, confused, and saw Julian waving above him. "It's a bat or something," he shouted back. "We're trying to get it to move, but it looks hurt."

Amira leaned over the rail. It certainly looked like a bat, a more familiar sight to her than to Westport natives, who treated any non-domesticated animal as an exotic creature to be coveted and feared in equal measure.

"Let's check it out," Julian said eagerly, and he ran down the walkway steps. D'Arcy smiled down at the scene with a bemused, forcibly detached air, but followed closely behind to watch the excitement. Amira remained seated.

"Look, it's trying to move!"

"It might be a baby or something, maybe it can't fly yet...."

"How can you tell?"

"Something going on down there?" A male voice, closer than the crowd by the canal.

A man had taken the seat opposite Amira, nodding in the direction of the expanding crowd along the river.

Amira blinked with surprise at the man's sudden appearance. Where had he come from? "Just a crew of drunks who've apparently never seen a bat before," she said.

The man was unshaven with a wry smile that enhanced his sharp, not unhandsome features. It was difficult to discern his age – by Westport standards, he could be as old as forty or as young as his early thirties in a compound, where time turned at a faster, harsher pace. His worn jacket looked several sizes too large for him, drawing attention to his slight frame. A web of tattoos peered out behind his long sleeves, extending to his wrists. The man's eyes were red, bloodshot, and there was an odd glow around his pupils that did not come from a Third Eye. Not used to the Westport pollution, perhaps. He stretched casually back into the booth.

"Not impressed with the flying rodent, love?" he asked. His accent was difficult to place, a hybrid of Standard North American and one of the United Kingdom's countless regional inflections.

"I dissected a few, before that became illegal," she said. In truth, she had never dissected a bat. The creatures were ubiquitous in the desert, hovering in dark swarms outside of her bedroom at night, but Amira decided to avoid any hints of the compound.

"So, another science kid." He leaned in closer toward her with a confiding, playful grin. "This city is full of them. Is anyone here not an Academy student or a struggling artist?"

"We get the occasional visitor," she replied. Though she was beginning to tire of the uninvited tablemate, a sense of politeness drove her deeper into the conversation. "Are you from Westport?"

"Nah, I'm an outsider myself," he said, before taking a drink from D'Arcy's abandoned water glass. "Name's Hadrian Wolfe. I came down from the North American Space Harbor a few days ago."

The North American Space Harbor, commonly referred to as NASH, was the largest human-formed structure in space, an enormous gateway station for research hubs that cruised through Earth's lower orbit. The space elevator connected the Pacific Parallel to NASH, which rotated in line with the Earth in geostationary orbit, enabling the elevator to transfer cargo and workers into space. In addition to the business of scientific research, NASH also played host to the thriving space tourism industry.

Amira smiled, reaching out to shake his extended hand. "Well met."

He leaned back again, watching her flick crumbs of pizza crust from her fingers. Aside from Julian, Amira always felt uncomfortable eating in front of men. On the rare occasions when she woke up in a room that was not her own, she snuck out in the early hours to avoid the threat of breakfast.

Julian and D'Arcy lingered at the base of the canal walkway. The bat fluttered its wings in a feeble, erratic attempt at flight, pushing off the ground and careening sideways until it landed again to a cacophony of groans from the expanding crowd.

Hadrian Wolfe chuckled before turning back to Amira. "You don't seem happy for someone on a night out, at least not like your friends over there."

Amira shrugged. "It's been a long week."

"Long week? Trouble with classes, or something tied to the work you do?"

The pointedness of the comment disarmed her. *The work you do.* Though his demeanor remained open and casual, Amira, whose job centered on extracting information from people, recognized the early stages of an interrogation.

"So, you work at NASH?" she asked, gesturing upward to the sky.

"Most of the time. Sometimes, my work takes me to the other stations or back to HQ here in the 'Port. And sometimes, to Aldwych."

The breeze from the river passed through her, bringing a cold, sober realization with it. He continued to smile but his light blue eyes were now probing, alight with unveiled purpose. This was no chance encounter.

"You're ISP," she said, her pulse kicking up a notch. International Station Police. An investigator for NASH.

"How'd you guess?"

"You have that undercover space cop look."

"I wanted to chat with you in a more relaxed setting, Amira Valdez," Agent Wolfe replied. "And explain how you could help us both."

Now sober in every sense of the word, Amira grew tense and rigid in her seat. When she remained silent, formulating her response, he continued.

"I work at the Space Harbor," he said, nodding upward to the cloudless sky, where, on the clearest of nights, Westport denizens could see a bright light over the ocean that marked the enormous station. "And keep an eye on the goings on at the research stations spinning around above us – stations run by the companies in Aldwych, including your new employers at the Mendel-Soma building, where Pandora resides. You've no doubt heard the news that something is going on at the Carthage station – Alistair Parrish's station."

"I haven't," she lied, trying to inject innocent curiosity into her wavering voice. Wolfe nodded with a smile.

"It's gone dark. No one allowed in or out. NASH tried to board and someone high up got my superiors to back off. To cut a long story short, I think – I *know* – that it has something to do with the Pandora cloning project, and I need information."

Amira didn't respond. She drummed her fingers along the chipped plastic table to conceal her shaking hands. The world around her continued its predictable dance – drunken crowds laughing and clutching bottles as they migrated along the canal, oblivious to the battle of wills underway, of two parties calculating their next step.

The agent broke the silence.

"You don't trust me. I get that. But you're a smart girl, Amira Valdez. You must realize that you're not surrounded by trustworthy folk at the Soma. You've got no reason to protect a team of labcoats running a reckless, failing experiment, and throwing you in as a political prop before the ship sinks. You're a pawn in a game you don't understand yet, love. A compound refugee done well, brought in to save the day – that's a convenient trick to pull when they're killing compound girls. You know as well as I do that laws are being broken, it's just a question of—"

"Aldwych has its own laws," Amira interjected, her voice shaking despite her best efforts to remain calm and clinical. "And at the end of the day, you're a glorified space cop. You have no power within the district itself. That's why you're talking to me. And you have *no* proof that anyone's been *killed*."

The agent's wry smile remained fixed on his face, although a distinct hardness settled in his eyes.

"Not yet," he agreed. "But Aldwych isn't an island, or the walled-up Vatican City it pretends to be. It's in the middle of Westport, and if the city's laws are being broken, the hammer will come down, along with everyone who tries to cover up what's happening in that shiny building."

"First you try to flatter me, then you insult me, then you threaten me," Amira said, her voice rising. "If you're investigating Pandora, why haven't I seen you at the Soma or heard anything on the Stream—?"

A burst of loud cheers interrupted her speech. The small bat, wings flapping in a desperate frenzy, rose above the crowd to wild applause. It hovered off the ground for a moment, as though basking in its moment of triumph. At last, it ascended, becoming a dark smudge over the picturesque waterway. The crowd dissipated, resuming the drunken trek along the canal in search of new diversions.

"You *know* why," Wolfe said as they turned back to face each other, and for the first time, his smooth demeanor cracked. He lowered his voice to a tense whisper. "Listen, love, you don't know half of what you're dealing with. Valerie Singh and Alistair Parrish, the stories on the Stream...they don't even scratch the surface. What's going on right now—"

"I'll take care of myself." Amira rose to her feet. Indignation at this man, for interrupting her one night of respite with threats and riddles, overrode her fear. Julian and D'Arcy, back from the canal, stood hesitantly out of earshot. "I suggest you do the same."

Before the agent could respond, she was gone, dissolving into the throng of revelers along the sidewalks of the Riverfront, into the heat and noise that ran like a tireless current through the streets.

★ ★ ★

All was quiet on the 235th floor except the sharp click of Amira's heels pacing the length of Rozene's ward. Amira paused in front of the expansive glass windows on the room's northern side, gazing out at acres and acres of Westport, a dense topography of buildings, trainways and lights that stretched without pause from eastern mountains to sea. From her dizzying perch in the Soma, no building stood above her. The city lit up each night, revealing the dark, snaking trail of the river that cut into the dense lights of the Riverfront. The Canary House stood too far away to identify, but she could tell the neighborhoods by their lights and traffic – the neon glow to the east marked the infamous Satyr Road, a trail of sex shows, clubs and assorted vices cutting diagonally through the center of the city. To the west were the coastline and the harbor, where the winking lights of incoming ships and freighters marked the day's final shift from the Pacific Parallel.

Behind her, the macabre theater of Rozene's subconscious unfurled in the center of the room. The subject herself lay in deep sleep nearby. While the pregnant woman appeared calm in her bed, the hologram revealed a younger version of Rozene, crouched and trembling from head to bare, dirty toe.

Amira fidgeted with her coat sleeves and resumed her pacing, casting a glance at the monitor that covered the nearest wall.

Subject's anxieties, while many, settle on a particular recurring nightmare that appears at multiple stages of sleep, she thought as strongly and clearly as she could, and the words transcribed themselves onto the screen. *The dream always begins the same way – the subject sits in darkness, confined in some type of shed or other enclosure.*

Rozene's silhouette was illuminated by a narrow beam of light that peered through the wooden entrance. Head bowed, her eyes darted frequently to the door, as though she were expecting someone, or something, to come through.

The door to the enclosure then opens – Rozene recoiled under the invading light – *and two figures appear and pull her out. The dream then cuts, as dreams often do, to a new place.*

The scene shifted from the shed to a well-lit auditorium. Rozene sat on a flimsy chair atop an elevated stage platform, facing an excited, chattering crowd. Shoulders slumped forward, her clay-red hair hung like two curtains on either side of her face, a wispy shield against her audience. Rozene's features in the dream were harsher, a cruel parody of her real face, but this was typical in holomentic readings of a person's dream state. Dreamers often presented themselves as less attractive, women especially. Rozene's self-perception was unforgiving, likely a defense mechanism in the Trinity Compound, where pride was one of woman's many sins.

The subject sits before a large crowd during an Unveiling ceremony at the compound she used to reside in. Amira recorded her thoughts. *To clarify, an Unveiling ceremony is – oh, shit!*

Amira stood on her toes to delete the word 'Hadrian' from the transcribed text. While the cognition-capturing technology in the Soma building was more advanced than the software available to the general public, the background thoughts of distracted users still snuck in from time to time.

"Turn off Thought Reader, switch to Voice Only," Amira barked at the monitor. Her thoughts now invisible to the computer, she silently cursed the inefficacy of modern technology.

A week had passed since her meeting with ISP Agent Hadrian Wolfe, but she frequently replayed moments of their encounter on that night along the river. *Valerie Singh and Alistair Parrish, the stories on the Stream...they don't even scratch the surface.* What had he meant? It was well known that Parrish had been in a tumultuous relationship with Singh for years, the subject of endless gossip among Westport's elite. They remained colleagues after their separation, but while Valerie Singh spearheaded the groundbreaking cancer gene discovery, Parrish always retained a higher-ranking position as the head of the Carthage space station. Amira began to wonder if he was the ranking official who requested her on the Pandora project, given Dr. Singh's clear lack of enthusiasm at her presence.

Amira exhaled and resumed her monologue, circling the hologram.

"The subject sits on the podium during the Unveiling, her wrists bound with zip ties to the arms of a chair. She does not appear to be in any immediate physical danger, but brain wave readings during the dream indicate a high level of fear and apprehension. To clarify, an Unveiling ceremony is a religious ritual that takes place on most compounds, regardless of denomination. They serve many purposes, but are usually collective events that use drugs to elicit confessions from a perceived sinner, show the punishments they will face in a hellish parallel world known as the Neverhaven and encourage public shaming.

"Another woman walks up to the stage, approaches the subject and begins a sermon. She mostly addresses the crowd, but occasionally points back to the subject, or walks behind her and grabs her roughly by the hair. Most of what she says is unclear, no doubt because the subject cannot remember the exact phrases, but it is clear that the subject is being publicly shamed before the compound for some transgression. Some phrases do stick out in the subject's memory enough to hear them – see previous report on dream dated March 20, 2227."

Amira could recite the words herself after days of sitting at the sleeping woman's bedside, watching the same dream unfold every time she turned on the holomentic machine.

As Amira circled the scene, the preaching woman's voice rose into clarity:

"Do you truly think, brothers and sisters, that it is enough to transcend through the power of blessed Chimyra, ask for forgiveness and have your sins washed away? No! For the soul is not a slate that can be wiped clean at regular intervals, when it is convenient for us. No, the soul is a sieve, through which the tribulations and temptations of life gather and pass through us. The weaker our defenses, the more fragile our spiritual foundation in this dimension, the more we are corroded through sin, and that damage is irreparable!"

"An atrocious metaphor," Valerie Singh had scoffed while listening to Amira's report. "Do those compound housewives need religion explained to them in terms of kitchen utensils to get the message across?" Tony Barlow, on the other hand, had listened raptly during the briefing but said nothing.

The woman in the dream continued, turning with a dramatic flourish toward Rozene. "This Child in Faith comes to you a sinner."

Amira paused to massage the back of her neck.

"The woman's voice fades in and out as the dream progresses," Amira continued in a tired voice. "The subject looks around at the crowd, down at her feet, and— wait. Wait! Stop recording!"

The hologram obediently froze in place.

She approached the center of the hologram. Rozene sat

motionless in the chair, while the frozen woman was twisted in place, pointing back theatrically at her. Rozene, however, stared directly to her right, in the direction she continuously looked at throughout the dream. No matter what was happening or being said, Rozene only focused on one point in the room.

Amira knelt in front of Rozene, whose face showed unmistakable fear and also, to Amira's surprise, revulsion. Amira followed Rozene's wide eyes across the room, to a single row of spectators seated separately from the sea of congregants.

"Zoom in – and stop," she said, and the hologram focused further on three figures in the front row. From their build, they appeared to be male but Amira could not be sure, as their faces were blurred beyond recognition. The other congregants all had faces, clear and defined, but something clouded the three men's faces, like drops of water on a finished painting.

"What is that?" a soft voice spoke behind her and Amira jolted. Rozene sat awake, shifting lethargically and staring at the frozen scene in front of her.

"Rozene! When did you wake up?"

"I feel like all I do is sleep," Rozene said. She leaned back in her bed with her arms delicately crossed, watching Amira warily.

Heart still pounding, Amira distanced herself from the blurred figures.

"This is a holographic image taken from your brain patterns while you were dreaming," Amira said with the warmest tone she could manage. "Does it look familiar to you at all? We also had Unveiling meetings back at— where I grew up."

Rozene's eyes narrowed.

"This is from my head?"

The tone in her voice hinted at another impending outburst.

Appear calm, Amira thought. *Make it seem natural that her innermost secrets are on display in the middle of the room.*

"From your brain patterns, yes."

Rozene ran a small hand over her belly self-consciously, as though the sight of her younger self brought her pregnancy into painful focus.

"I— I remember this one," she said slowly. "I was shamed at

other Unveilings for other things, but this was the last one before I left." She closed her eyes and shuddered, as though trying to shake off the memory.

"Rozene...."

"I'm not talking about it!" she said, color rising in her cheeks. "You can see it all for yourself anyway."

Amira's initial compassion for the young, damaged compound girl had quickly given way to frustration. Rozene's memories, while layered with trauma, did not differ greatly from Amira's own experiences on the compound. But while Amira thrived in Westport, Rozene seemed to be a woman in a state of suspense, neither moving forward nor retreating in the face of adversity. And now, perpetually sedated and, for all intents and purposes, a science experiment, she continued to refuse Amira's help.

"Please, I only want to know one thing," Amira said. "That group of men you were looking at, during the Unveiling – do you know who they were?"

Rozene looked at Amira as though she had grown a second head. In explanation, Amira pointed back to the still-frozen scene, at the three blurred men.

"You seemed to know who they were," Amira continued. "And you were clearly afraid."

"Of course I know who they were, I—" Rozene said before pausing, shaking her head in confusion. She breathed in sharply, eyes darting from the blurred men back to Amira.

"No, I don't understand...but they were, they were..." she stammered as the monitor began beeping, displaying her heart rate in an alarming crescendo. Tears of frustration welled in the corners of her eyes.

"I don't know anymore, I'm too tired!" she spat.

"I'm sorry," Amira said quickly.

An idea struck her. In a subtle motion, she slid her hand to the touch screen obscured behind the monitoring equipment and switched the Thought Reader back on. As she hoped, Rozene's thoughts began transcribing on the smaller screen. Her confusion was evident in the phrases that appeared: *Names won't come. No one to remember...after me. Thunder. Trapped in the fog.*

"Don't worry about it now," Amira continued as Rozene wiped her eyes delicately with her fingertips. "Do you want a sedative to help you sleep?"

"No more drugs," Rozene protested, but with less defiance. Outside the window, night had taken over Westport and the landscape pulsed with the energy of millions of lights and bodies in motion.

Amira glanced at the screen transcribing Rozene's thoughts. *Ship. Hadrian Jones...best friend...will help me.*

Hadrian. The hologram came back to life on the other side of Rozene – first, flashes of a docked ship strewn with lights, followed by a face, a smirking man with piercing eyes. The same face she first encountered at the Riverfront only days before.

Amira leaned against the wall to steady herself while Rozene watched her in confusion. The NASH investigator, if he was even a real investigator, knew the subject of the Pandora project. Rozene even considered him to be a friend. She called him Jones, although he introduced himself to Amira as Wolfe, but there was no mistaking the man. How did they know each other, and what was Hadrian's motive for approaching Amira that night?

"When did it become easy for you?" Rozene asked Amira abruptly. "To live this life away from...from home?"

"I don't know if it ever gets easy," Amira said. She opened her mouth to continue speaking, but the words caught in her throat and for a moment, an understanding passed between them; two young women far from a home that was never home, navigating an alien world that would never know them as they knew one another.

"Listen, I know you don't trust me," Amira said in a gentler tone. "But I am here to help you. I know I can fix whatever's happening to you. We're both survivors because we had to be. We survived...the places we left, and you will survive this."

Rozene turned away, eyes shining with tears. For a moment, she seemed ready to speak further, but instead leaned back into her pillow and closed her eyes.

Amira grabbed her transcriber, hands trembling slightly, and left the ward. The last hour yielded more progress than the entire week, but before she could begin her waking therapy sessions with

Rozene, Amira had a more immediate challenge to face. She knew it the moment Rozene could not identify the three mysterious men in her dream.

Someone, somehow, had tampered with the girl's memory.

CHAPTER FIVE

The Soul is a Sieve

The docks north of Sullivan's Wharf were a graveyard for ships that had served their purpose, either through obsolescence or the natural, corrosive decay of industry. Freighters and ferries that once carried cargo and passengers to the Pacific Parallel and beyond reclined in rows across the docks, swaying faintly in the current or parked ashore with rotting hulls and broken windows. The remains of a large cargo ship sat aground, a series of metallic beams in the shape of a battered ribcage, blanketed in moss. Somewhere in this maze, Amira hoped, a man in a ship held clues to the mystery of Rozene's memory.

Removed from the traffic of the city, the dockyards were dark, silent and isolated. A high barbed fence lined its perimeter, the occasional security camera acting as sentry near the main gates. Amira darted past the first camera. She pulled her gray hoodie tightly over her forehead and pushed the fence in search of its inevitable weak point. Running her thin hands along the metal wire, she found a torn opening and entered the shipyard.

It was D'Arcy who led her to this place. When Amira mentioned, omitting the essentials, that Rozene's memories included an illuminated, abandoned ship, D'Arcy knew the ship in question. The stevedores all knew of the one ship in the old dockyards that was inhabited, and they all kept their distance.

"Something strange going on there, according to Dad," D'Arcy had said. Amira had promised not to go wandering around looking for it. As the lights from the street disappeared deeper into the shipyard, Amira hoped she wouldn't regret her lie.

Moving swiftly and silently around the rusted skeleton of a narrow passenger boat, she reached the main pier, where she found the docked remains of a sizable cruise ship, the same one displayed in the hologram in Rozene's ward. Streams of lights hung from the top and sides of the ship, the only source of illumination in the shipyard. Lights also glowed from the ship's interior. The crisp smell of salt water mingled with the odor of stale trash.

Amira stood before the pier and noted another camera at the base of the gangway. Though she felt a rising sense of dread at the ship's quiet entrance, she needed answers.

"Who's there?" a muffled voice barked, causing Amira to jolt and nearly slide off the pier. She spun around to find no one.

"What do you want?" the voice called out again, and Amira saw a metallic bullhorn fixed unsteadily on the rail of the walkway.

She caught her breath.

"I'm here to see Hadrian," she said clearly. "I…need some information. For a mutual friend."

"Who is this?"

"My name is Amelia Sandoval. I work in Aldwych, in the Soma complex, with someone who lived here once."

There was a pause, and a deeper, calmer voice replied.

"Come on in."

The entrance hall of the cruise ship was a shadow of what it must have been in its prime when it traversed ports across the Pacific. The carpeting and wallpaper had been stripped, making every footstep echo and ricochet off the high ceilings. Wires ran along the flayed concrete walls. The lights on the central chandelier had been replaced with green bulbs that gave the expansive room a sickly hue.

A cluster of teenagers, some of whom appeared as young as thirteen, gathered at the far end of the room while others peered down from the mezzanine. More children flooded the upper levels, running and shouting raucously along the walkways above them. A pair of boys on the lower level spun around in circles with flailing arms under the unmistakable influence of Elysium, their distant expressions ecstatic. Elysium was a popular drug in the cities, so Amira was not surprised to discover its popularity among compound escapees, who found it a gentler substitute for Chimyra.

Amira pulled her hoodie down and approached the other end of the room, where the small group hovered around an archaic computer. Several faces turned to her in curiosity.

"I'm looking for Hadrian Jones," she said.

A man emerged from the crowd, the only visible adult on the ship besides Amira. He flashed a ghoulish smile at Amira and dipped in a mocking bow. Lean and of medium height, his muscled arms were lined with three-dimensional tattoos and tribal scars. His eyeballs were tattooed as well with yellow irises, the black pupils unnaturally large and glowing with the predatory luminescence of an animal at hunt. In retrospect, Amira realized that his red eyes during their first encounter were caused by heavy contact lenses designed to conceal his eye markings.

Amira felt a wave of pity for Rozene. Could she truly consider this man to be her closest friend?

"That would be me," Hadrian Jones replied with a thicker version of the accent he greeted her with in the Riverfront. "Welcome to my humble little boat, *Amelia*."

More teenagers gathered to watch the scene unfold, some leaning over the rails on the mezzanine's upper level. Though his demeanor was jovial, Amira sensed that he had not expected her to trace him to this ship, an unlikely home for a NASH agent.

With that advantage in mind, Amira decided to be direct.

"I'm here to talk about Rozene Hull," she said, her voice low but controlled. "I need to learn about her time on the Trinity Compound."

Hadrian rolled his head back melodramatically, throwing his hands up in the air as though inquiring of the heavens.

"She gave you lot her real name – her real name! Something isn't rigged right in that brain of hers."

"What is this place?" Amira asked, unable to contain the question any longer. "Do you live here?"

"Guilty as charged," Hadrian said cheerily. "When I'm not causing trouble in NASH or pestering drunk Academy brats, I'm here with my many, many children. My home is their refuge, as long as they want it."

"Is Hadrian Jones your real name?"

"Does it sound like a real fucking name? Do I look like a fucking Jones?"

Laughter echoed through the room. A young girl in her underwear sat on a large crate against the wall, her bare feet dangling back and forth like a child's on a swing. She tilted her head and giggled loudly, triggering a second wave of taunts from the observers.

Hadrian moved closer to Amira. His wolf-like eyes narrowed as he peered into her face. Unwilling to give ground, Amira stepped sideways and Hadrian mirrored her, the two circling one another slowly.

"You don't look like you were one of mine," he said in a low, thoughtful voice.

"So, these are compound children who escaped," Amira said as a way of deflection. "Why are they all here? There are charities and state resources in Westport for refugees."

More scattered laughter.

"Some go there for sure," Hadrian replied. "They learn better before long how the *system* works, and find their way here on my little yacht, where they get real help."

"It worked for me," Amira said, realizing at once that it was a half-truth. Dr. Mercer, not the state, had discovered her and seen her potential.

"Nice for you," Hadrian sneered.

"But you're ISP! This must be illegal."

"And I'm shaking in my little boots," Hadrian replied merrily. "Let's just say I've been in law enforcement long enough, love. I've watched them fuck up time after time and found a better way. So I got me this little ship, rigged it up with the best security apparatus an ISP badge can buy – or borrow, steal, whatever – and the kids started coming. They pass the word on to new kids from the compounds, and they all jump at the chance to be here."

"Why is that?"

"Why, love? They get protection from the old life and a perfect little gateway into the new world. They're with their own people to start, so they live with folk who understand them. They can acclimate to city life here."

One of the kids on Elysium had started pulling off his clothes, tripping over his pants in the process and falling to the ground, his expression still rapt.

Amira raised her voice. "There have to be better places for them. Places where they aren't half-naked and high."

"I'm an altruist, simply performing a necessary service to help Westport's most vulnerable residents," he retorted with a smile. "But you didn't answer the question, love – why didn't you end up on my ship?"

"Why would I?"

He let out a low, delighted cackle.

"Do you think old Hadrian was born yesterday, love?" he asked. "Do you think I can't spot a compound girl when I see one? You can try to hide it all you want, and you may fool some of them out there, but not Hadrian Jones. You know, I didn't even know you were a compounder when I met you by the river? There was no file that told me, but I saw it the minute I looked at your pretty little face. You all have that same look – the same fucking haunted look, no matter what you're doing, like you're waiting at any moment for something to come out of the shadows."

In a sudden motion, Hadrian lunged forward.

Amira jerked back, nearly losing her balance.

He laughed again, the throaty rasps echoing across the walls. Many others laughed as well, but the mood of the room was shifting from bemused curiosity into something more assertive, even hostile, and Amira could sense the crowd's growing impatience with their intruder.

"I didn't come here to talk about myself," Amira said. "Rozene is in trouble."

A sullen-faced boy came forward, listening intently over Hadrian's shoulder.

"What's wrong with Rozene?" he asked in a quiet voice.

Amira opened her mouth to speak but fell silent under the boy's sad, stern eyes, unsure of how to articulate the cloning subject's precarious situation.

Her mind is unraveling. She's dying.

"I warned her," Hadrian said. "She didn't listen – the labcoats must have made a deal with our Rozene, just like they did with Nina and Jessica, rest their souls. Something she couldn't say no to. Always getting crazy ideas in her head, too; she wants to be part of something big. But she's in deep now. A bit like you, eh? You must think you're better than our poor Rozene."

"I think someone's trying to hurt her on purpose," Amira said carefully, avoiding mention of Rozene's tampered memory. "I don't know who yet, but my job on the project is to search her mind, and I'm getting clues that something suspicious is going on. And if that's the case, then the other two deaths may not have been accidents."

The room went completely silent.

Hadrian paced, his rough features frozen in a mask of contemplation. Behind those unnatural eyes, Amira could see him processing this new revelation, rethinking his next approach. She gestured him outside, away from the small army of curious children, and he followed.

Cool air hit her the moment she left the ship, bringing with it the sharp stench of seawater and rust. Outside on the gangway, they faced each other.

"So, what is it you're hoping to get from me, love?"

"You know things about the Trinity Compound. And about Rozene's time there."

"Of course."

"And you want to know more about Pandora, for your own ISP reasons."

"She remembered!" He pointed at her, tone mocking.

She ignored his reproach and said, "You might be able to help me piece things together. I have recordings from Rozene's dreams where I need some gaps filled in. Tell me what you know about the Trinity Compound, so I can help revive her memory."

"Our little compound girl here is a smuggler as well as a sneak," Hadrian said with a subtle smile. "Got permission to carry that footage out of Aldwych, did you?"

"I have stills," Amira continued, ignoring the legal implications, her pulse pounding at her neck. "Stills of an Unveiling ceremony at the Trinity Compound. I'll need you to identify three men for me and tell me what's important about them."

"And what's in it for me?" Hadrian asked.

"New information about Pandora."

"You already gave me that," he replied with a knowing gleam in his eye. "You've confirmed some of Hadrian's long-standing suspicions, love. What else?"

"It could save Rozene."

"Do I look like little Rozene to you?" Hadrian asked, his voice suddenly adopting a softer, more menacing quality. "I asked what was in it for me?"

"I – it would—"

"Nothing!"

"What do you want then?"

"Love, if I'm going to help you out, I'll need something in return. Payment in kind."

It was Amira's turn to laugh.

"I'm an Academy student on subsidy," she said. "I have no money."

"It's not money I need," Hadrian said, his smile widening. "Here's what you'll do for me before I help with whatever this memory is and look at your little home movie. There's a new drug somewhere in the Soma building. I mean brand new, still being tested, not even on the black market. Called Tiresia. You're going to find it and get it for me. All of it. And then I'll tell you what I know."

"That's impossible," Amira stated flatly. "They would know if one test tube was missing, and I can't just walk through any part of the Soma. There's no way for me to get it out."

"That's my price," Hadrian replied indifferently. "You're a resourceful girl, or you wouldn't be where you are now. You'll figure it out."

Amira shook her head in a quick motion, as though trying to shake herself out of a dream.

"What is Tiresia?" she asked. "What does it do?"

"Never you mind about that, love. I want it, is all you need to know. It won't be labeled as Tiresia, mind, but you'll know it because it'll be the only thing in the Soma stores that's *unlabeled*. Packed in a small box. Won't look like much, but it's plenty, I've been told."

"Even if I manage to get it, how do I know that I can trust you to keep your end of the deal? There are no guarantees that you'll know who the three are, or that you won't simply lie about it."

In a sudden motion, Hadrian grabbed Amira by the wrist and brought his face close to hers, his breath warm with the scent of burnt tobacco.

"You can't trust me, love, but you also know you can't trust your labcoat friends in Aldwych," he hissed. "You haven't told anyone there about this memory business, have you? Not the good Dr. Singh, not even your friends, right?"

When she didn't respond, he chuckled softly and shook his head.

"You're stepping into the wolves' den, *Amira Valdez*," he said in a voice barely above a whisper. "You don't even know how deep you are yet. Even I don't tangle with the Trinity Compound, or anyone at Aldwych who's keeping their secrets."

Her eyes widened. With one comment, her growing suspicion and worst fear was given voice. Could there be a Trinity spy on the Pandora project?

"I see we're thinking the same thing," he said. "Now *go*."

Her head was spinning. Though Hadrian was noncommittal about his ability to identify the three mysterious figures from the Trinity ceremony, it was clear to Amira that he knew who the three men were, or at least had a highly educated guess. He had also suspected, as she had begun to, that someone on the Pandora project was connected to the Trinity Compound, protecting them. This, however, begged another question. Who on Pandora would do such a thing, and why?

Amira tightened her hoodie around her face as she gingerly slipped through the opening in the shipyard fence. She walked several blocks in the direction of Sullivan's Wharf. Suddenly, a hand gripped her arm from behind, seemingly materializing from the darkness. She screamed in shock and whipped around to come face to face with Hadrian again.

"What are you doing?" she shouted.

"We need to talk further," he said, maintaining a firm hold on her wrist. "Somewhere far away from the kiddos."

As the adrenaline gradually subsided, her terror gave way to anger.

"You scared the shit out of me," she spat.

"Get used to it," he said, finally loosening his grip.

Amira massaged her wrist, glaring at him with pointed defiance, but she made no move to fight or run.

"I could scrap our deal and report you straight to ISP," she said. "Tell them about your little hideaway, if you're going to attack me in the dark."

Hadrian lunged forward and threw an arm around Amira's

midsection, reaching furiously into the pockets of her sweatshirt. After a silent minute of breathless struggle, they broke apart, Hadrian triumphantly holding the thin glass disc that stored Rozene's neural image readings. *Property of the Mendel-Soma Complex* ran, almost mockingly, across the disc cover. He patted his jacket pocket lightly where the disc now lay, revealing the faint outline of an electromagnetic gun in the process.

"And now we're even," he continued. "We've both got something on each other. So, let's talk."

⋆ ⋆ ⋆

The Three Sirens Tavern was typical of the many bars around the dockyards – dank and noisy. Its patrons were sailors, stevedores and other workers who profited, however narrowly, from the many ships that passed through greater Westport. It was approaching midnight; a sizable crowd remained, night shifters in need of a drink before the dark walk home. A man with a guitar sang at the end of the bar, his voice drowned out by the louder chorus of drunken chatter that echoed off the musty walls.

Amira and Hadrian sat facing one another in a small cul-de-sac in the far corner of the pub, quiet enough to converse comfortably but loud enough not to be overheard. Away from the audience of the ship, Hadrian lost much of his theatrical showmanship, but he still drew curious looks for his flamboyant appearance. He took a swig from his bottle. Amira had not touched hers. Exhausted and nauseous, she needed her faculties for the impending confrontation, one she could not afford to lose.

"You don't want your drink?" Hadrian asked, eyebrows raised mockingly.

"I'm not in a drinking mood, seeing how I'm being blackmailed," Amira replied, her voice tart. Despite her reluctance, she reached for the bottle, but kept her lips closed as she mimicked a long drink.

"That's the best time to be in a drinking state," he said gleefully, before his tone became serious. "It's in your best interest to cooperate with me, love. You don't realize it yet, Amira Valdez, but I'm the best ally you could have right now."

In a swift motion, her hands darted toward his jacket pocket and emerged with his copper-toned badge. She traced the text with her fingers – *Hadrian Wolfe, NASH Investigator.* It sounded like the name of one of the Saturday morning cartoons she watched at the compound and she laughed aloud.

"So what do I call you?" she asked abruptly. "Are you Hadrian Jones, like I heard in Rozene's thoughts? Or Wolfe, like your badge says?"

"Hell, maybe I'm neither and my real name's Captain Crunch. You can call me whatever you like, but on the ship, just call me Hadrian. The kids, they know what I do but I don't tell them more than they need to know, you know?"

The scars on her palms shone in the dull tavern light. She curled her hands into her sweatshirt and sank back into her seat. The warmth of the crowd did not overcome the cold, which permeated the brick walls. Over Hadrian's shoulder, the man strummed his guitar with closed eyes, oblivious to the indifferent crowd.

"Am I boring you, love?" Hadrian's voice cut through the din.

"If you're an ally, you should know that I don't respond well to threats," she said.

"Which is why you're here and not sitting with a silver veil and fifty kids in the desert," Hadrian said. "You know what, love? We need what my bosses at NASH call a team-building exercise. We are mates, whether you know it or not yet. So as a gesture of goodwill, ask me some questions and I'll answer them."

After a minute of sullen silence, during which Hadrian finished his beer, she relented. Her first question, though not the most important, nagged her above all others.

"Where are you from? I can't place your accent, but some of the things you say, the way you say them, remind me of compound speak."

He laughed and gestured toward the bar for another beer.

"You've made sure to load that question plenty," he said with a conspiratorial grin. "The short answer is, I'm from Birmingham. Born there, anyway. I've done my share of travel, so I'm a Brummie by way of many places."

"Did you live on a compound?"

"Not me, no."

The phrasing of his answer intrigued Amira but she decided not to pursue it, shifting to the most important question.

"Did Rozene tell you why she left the Trinity Compound?"

"Everyone leaves the compounds for some variation of the same reason," Hadrian replied with unexpected gravity. "Except for the boys who get thrown out, of course, so the older men can have all the young girls to themselves. I've got some of those in my ship. They take their time to adjust. Anyway, the problem for little Rozene was also one of those older menfolk. An Elder wanted to marry her and she didn't want to marry him – and so here she is."

They sat in silence. Amira's breaking point in the compound was not that different from Rozene's. Arranged marriages were standard at the Children of the New Covenant, with polygamy reserved for Elders. Children were the imperative. Part of being able to ascend into the next world was to add new souls to this one. Though Amira attempted to escape before, the night she succeeded was the day before she turned sixteen, the day of her Inspection. Though her mother never gave her details of what the Inspection entailed, she put the pieces together. She would be examined by the compound's doctor for overall health, fertility and most importantly, purity. There was no good outcome. Passing Inspection meant that she would be declared ready for a husband, while failing on the grounds of infertility or suspected impropriety meant 'disappearing' from compound life, never to be spoken of again. Amira knew she had to leave that night, whatever the consequences.

Hadrian drained his beer.

"What do you know about the Trinity Compound?" he asked.

Amira paused.

"I know about it," she said slowly. "Elder Cartwright founded it, after inventing Chimyra. I met people from the Trinity a long time ago, when the compounds tried to unify. I know it's big, much bigger than where I lived, at least. Our parents used to threaten us – me and the other girls. They'd say if we didn't shape up, they'd send us to the Trinity, where they knew how to deal with girls like us. 'Learn your prayers, or you'll get your lessons at the Trinity. You think you have it bad here, you could be at the Trinity.' There were stories, but it's hard to say what's true and what isn't."

"They're not just stories, love," Hadrian said. "It's not a good place to be a woman or a girl. Anyone, really. But that's not what NASH cares about. They're on the radar for something else."

"NASH?" Amira asked, surprised. "Investigating the Trinity? Is that why you met me that night, wanting to know about Pandora?"

Hadrian nodded.

"So when you said that even you don't tangle with the Trinity—" Amira said.

"A white lie for the kids' sake," Hadrian said. "As captain of their ship, I take kids from all compounds and keep my head low. But as a NASH man…."

Hadrian leaned forward, the deep etches under his eyes dark in the bar room light.

"I'm going to show you something," he said. "If you're going down the rabbit hole, you need to see what could bite you at the end of the tunnel."

★ ★ ★

At nearly one o'clock in the morning, Hadrian ushered Amira inside the deserted police station. His makeshift cubicle was cluttered with paper folders and books, resembling the ransacked remnants of a widower's attic more than a working station. It was a longstanding custom for Westport police to cooperate fully with their counterparts in space, due to the limited jurisdiction they both possessed over Aldwych. They habitually shared resources, intelligence and even office space with one another, something Hadrian had taken full advantage of.

Amira's head throbbed under the harsh fluorescent lighting, her irritation amplified by the dying ring of the single bulb above Hadrian's cubicle. She grabbed a cup of coffee from the nearby vending machine, which also offered gray-tinged curry bowls and some decidedly questionable sushi, the synthetic salmon turning mossy green, while Hadrian rummaged furiously through his desk.

"Here!" he called out, waving a glass disc.

As Amira settled in his chair, his face turned grim.

"What I'm about to show you – well, play for you – is classified," he said. "This hasn't gone out on the Stream yet, so the public knows fuck all except that Victor Zhang hasn't been seen—"

"Victor Zhang?" she asked, bewildered. "The head of the Volta station?" Amira recalled the news report on the train back from Placement Day, how Victor Zhang hadn't been seen in weeks.

He slid the disc into the side of the computer screen. It was a holographic computer, albeit a very antiquated one, but the disc did not have any image to display. Hadrian's own voice came in first, his tone perfunctory.

Recording delivered to NASH Investigative Headquarters at 17:00 hours, March 14, 2227.

The slightest of pauses was followed by another speaker, also a man, but with an unnaturally low voice that had clearly been distorted to prevent identification. He spoke in the slow, heavily enunciated speech of the compounds.

We have the criminal scientist Zhang in our custody to answer for the crimes he has committed against the cosmic order in the name of his vanity. He has nothing to say to you now, but we will allow him to repent once his trial is over.

Amira shrunk back into her seat as her heart pounded violently, not in response to the words being spoken by that disembodied voice, but to the horrible screaming that was audible in the background. Terrible shrieks that rose in volume until they devolved into a howl of unmistakable agony.

We call on the other colleagues of Zhang to end their pursuit of the abomination of human cloning, which is the most grievous affront to the laws of the universe, bound by the Conscious Plane. Valerie Singh and Alistair Parrish, if you continue in your plans to mock the natural order, you will answer for it not only in the eternal embers of the Neverhaven, but in this one.

The screaming faded into silence and after a pause, a third voice, thin and tired, began to speak. From the monotonous clip of his tone and the occasional break in his speech, he seemed to be reading aloud from a written statement.

My name is Victor Zhang, the Chief Researcher of the Volta station and a member of the Aldwych Council. I am speaking to renounce my participation in the Pandora cloning project and implore Doctors Singh and

Parrish to follow my example, before it is too late for them, as it now is for me. I understand that I am beyond repentance. The soul is a sieve, and my sins have gathered and followed me to my ultimate corruption, which led me to believe that I could play God. I hope for atonement with my death and with my renunciation of my role in the terrible crimes of Aldwych.

Another pause followed. Amira felt a dizzying wave of adrenaline as her vision narrowed into a single tunnel, until her surroundings became something terrible and distant. Then it came – the unmistakable sound of a single gunshot. The recording ended.

They sat in silence, but Hadrian watched her with interest. She had audibly gasped when Victor Zhang had uttered that familiar, bizarre phrase.

"The soul is a sieve," Amira said at last. "I heard that same thing while reading Rozene's dreams, one about the Trinity Compound. It's a strange phrase. I heard nothing like that in the New Covenant."

Hadrian looked tired. He sighed and observed her carefully.

"Well then, love, that goes along with our suspicions that the Trinity was behind this," he said. "They're the biggest of the compounds, and the only one we reckon has real reach beyond the southwest. They managed to capture Victor Zhang here in Westport, we suspect. It was all kept quiet, of course, but now that NASH has this tape, it won't stay quiet forever. I knew him. He was a good man." His voice tightened at that last sentence, and he cleared his throat.

"They're all shook up at NASH," he said. "But the higher ups think this is a one-off thing, a group of fringe fanatics who got lucky. I don't think so. They've got weapons, from what my kids tell me, and they have the will – plenty of it. You heard it – a clear threat to your doctor friends at Pandora.

"So now you know what I'm after, Amira Valdez. I don't have any backing from NASH on this, and Valerie Singh and Alistair Parrish haven't been cooperating with me either."

"They know about Victor Zhang?" Amira asked, horrified.

"Of course, we had to tell them that their colleague is dead and they were both threatened by his killers. They weren't happy, mind, but it didn't change anything fundamental. The show must go on.

And neither thinks they're at risk. Like the people above me, they don't think a group of nutters from a compound can reach them."

"But they reached Victor Zhang!" Amira said.

"They did. But you have to understand something about these people, love. They're powerful folk, living legends, and they've been hearing that about themselves for a long time. They've started to believe in their invincibility, that a simple group of religious fundies can't touch them. And here's my second point: they underestimate the compounds and the folk that live there, see them as nothing more than backward simpletons beneath scrutiny. Everyone always has. I'm sure you've even experienced that, to a point."

Hadrian smiled slightly at her and yawned deeply before grabbing a vial from his drawer. He swallowed a pill and closed his eyes.

"I don't know what to think anymore," Amira said. The events of the last few hours were finally catching up with her, and she wanted nothing more than to retreat to the Canary House and fall into dreamless sleep. "Everyone seems to think that because of where I came from, I'm different, and that I have some kind of special insight. But I don't. I'm just a student trying to live my life. I don't want to get pulled into this."

"You don't have a choice," Hadrian said bluntly. "The Trinity wants to stop the Pandora folk from cloning our Rozene, and you're part of Pandora now, whether you like it or not. If someone on the inside is working with them, they know who you are and you're not safe anymore."

A knot formed in Amira's stomach. D'Arcy had been assigned to the Pandora initiative. Though she wasn't involved in its cloning project, did the Trinity care? Was she, too, compromised?

"But even if you could walk away, you won't," Hadrian continued. "You're like me, love – you need to find the truth in things. It's what separates us from the compounds, where they want every mystery in the universe answered for them, because they fear not knowing the *what* or the *why*. Whatever is happening, we need to stop it together, Amira."

★ ★ ★

That night, she dreamed of the compound, and the time she fell from the roof of her family home. She had snuck out through her bedroom window, where she had been confined as punishment for listening to music on the Stream ("City filth, straight from the Devil's mouth," her mother had screamed before slamming the door). Earlier that day, she had asked her teachers for proof that only child-bearers entered the Nearhaven, pointing out that Elder Cartwright's second wife never had children, which earned her an immediate lashing and subsequent suspension.

Crawling along the ledge of her home's second floor, she grabbed the rusted stepladder that led to the roof. In her dream state, she glided more than climbed, her body floating effortlessly as her hands flew from rail to rail. The white rooftop glowed under the moonlight, the color of bone, its smooth surface cool against her feet.

In the desert, the night sky was more vivid and expansive than any painting. Though she understood very little then about the universe and its countless galaxies, staring into the night sky made her feel alive and small at the same time. Every night she made it to the roof, she cupped her hands in imitation of a telescope and peered through its fleshy lens into the cosmos. Though her parents told her that the stars showed the gates to parallel worlds, she only cared about what she could see. Potential new homes and new life in this reality. New places to discover, new riddles to solve.

She paced the length of the roof, the moon hovering close to the distant mountains, when she stumbled too close to the ledge and her foot found air. Amira fell slowly in her dream, the stars and trees spinning past her on the way to the ground. Sneaking out of the house at night was a dangerous precedent in the compound, especially for a young girl. As a result, when Amira's mother ran out to the sound of her cries and found her curled in a ball in the grass, she marched Amira straight into the house, forcing her to limp through a broken ankle, pulled her into the kitchen, and pressed her hands directly on the still-hot stove where they had cooked tamales for dinner.

Amira jolted awake, clutching her hands where they hissed against the metal grooves years ago. The dream felt real, as real as the sweat running down her forehead. The compound, try as she may to wipe it from her mind, continued to exist hundreds of miles away, where some other young girl might be screaming in her kitchen at this very moment.

Perhaps there *is* no escape from the compound – only levels of separation.

But I have *separated*, Amira thought. *I'm not Rozene, or those children running around Hadrian's ship. I know my home, and it's here.*

With that reassuring thought, she drifted back into sleep, gently tracing the palms of her hands.

CHAPTER SIX

Contraband and Cosmics

When Amira arrived on the 235th floor the next morning, the elevator doors parted to reveal a ward in crisis.

The doors to the ward flew open, followed by a flurry of movement. Staff in white scrubs swept a large bed down the hallway, ornamented with swinging tubes and drips, shouting instructions to each other. Stunned, Amira barely stepped aside in time as they advanced on the elevator. The bed passed by, revealing Rozene's small, colorless face in the middle of the chaos, her eyes rolled back, her veiny neck arched like a rigid cat.

Naomi greeted Amira in a flood of tears. Through fits of sobbing, she explained that Rozene awoke with chest pains and heart palpitations in the early hours of the morning. The emergency team arrived as she fainted. Amira sat in a daze, numbly feeding Naomi a steady stream of tissues. Through Amira's shock, the first sensations of failure set in, leaving her cold and hollow.

"It's terrible," Naomi sobbed. "This is what happened the last time to the other two, before, you know.... I don't know if I can go through this again!"

"Can I see her?" Amira asked. Rozene's pale face, the eggshell-whites of her rolled eyes, filled Amira's mind. Was that the last time she would see the young woman, barely out of the compound, alive?

"Not at the moment, M. Valdez," Tony Barlow interjected, causing both women to jump at his sudden presence. Barlow possessed an uncanny ability to materialize from thin air. "Dr. Singh is in the emergency room with her now, and she is the best equipped of all of us to handle things in their current state."

"What a day." Naomi sighed. "And Dr. Parrish had to come in today, of all days."

Barlow nodded grimly but said nothing. Still reeling from the revelations of the last twenty-four hours, it took Amira a moment to recall that Alistair Parrish had arrived Earthside from the Carthage station this morning, ostensibly for a routine visit to the Soma. The endless publicity meant that Pandora, and the cloning project in particular, was likely to dominate, if not monopolize, his time.

They waited in silence. Naomi anxiously fidgeted behind the protective shell of her receptionist's desk. Tony Barlow wordlessly scrolled through data on the wall's three-dimensional screen. Amira sat on the edge of Rozene's now-empty bed, hands in her lap. The days since she discovered Rozene's altered memory had passed by in a blur, but time was now at a standstill. Had she been too late? Did the person who tampered with Rozene's memory decide to take a more extreme course of action?

The ward's doors flew open and Valerie Singh walked briskly into the room. Her brow was knitted into a frown. She motioned them with a quick gesture to follow her into her office.

Dr. Singh closed the door behind them.

"She's out of immediate danger," she said, and Naomi sighed audibly in relief. "M. Hull was approaching the point of premature delivery, but we were able to reverse the early labor process and stabilize her. No harm to the fetus that we could see. We ran the usual tests, with the usual results." She turned to Barlow with a slightly arched brow and he nodded silently in response.

"But she's ok?" Naomi asked.

"For now, M. Nakamura," Dr. Singh said. "Our subject will remain with us for the near future, at any rate."

"Do we know what happened?" Amira asked.

Singh pivoted in place to face her with an icy stare. "*We* know as much as we've known since yesterday, M. Valdez," she responded smoothly. "*We* see symptoms of heart palpitations and syncope with no underlying medical condition, so *we* can only infer that the cause is extreme stress or ongoing psychological trauma."

Barlow and Naomi took this as their cue to exit the room.

"Dr. Singh," Amira said in a low voice. "I think I've finally figured out an effective way to treat Rozene, but I need more time."

"She is two weeks away from her third trimester," Singh said. "Time is a luxury we may not have."

"More time," Amira continued. "I've made some breakthroughs in the last week. The root cause *is* psychological. It's not just post-traumatic stress from her childhood, although there is plenty of that. It's her memory that's behind this, damaged memories in her parahippocampal processing."

Dr. Singh frowned, her mouth tightening into a thin line. Whatever she had expected to hear, she was clearly taken aback. She opened her mouth to respond when the door swung open. To Amira's surprise, D'Arcy entered.

"Dr. Parrish is here," D'Arcy said. "He wants cloning, interstellar Streaming and de-radiation all briefed together this afternoon."

Dr. Singh sighed irritably. D'Arcy stole a wink at Amira.

"Our fearless leader arrives," Singh said drily. "We'll continue this discussion later, M. Valdez." The statement carried a hint of an ominous note. Amira's throat tightened, and she felt a brief nostalgia for those first few days on Pandora, when she had been dismissed as a mild irritant.

As Amira left Dr. Singh's office, she sensed an opportunity amid the morning's crisis.

"Naomi," she whispered. Naomi was feverishly scrolling through emails. "We need to get a resupply of Nirvatrene. Dr. Singh wants a full case ready for Rozene when she returns."

"Oh, Amira, I'm swamped at the moment," Naomi said as she stretched her hand across the three-dimensional monitor, zooming in on a message with Dr. Parrish's face next to it. "I need to rearrange Dr. Singh's calendar for tomorrow, and there's that upcoming interview on the Stream—"

"Want me to take care of it?"

"Could you?" Naomi asked eagerly. "Can you get into the medical stores?"

"I'd be happy to, but have I been given the clearance to go to 202?"

"Here, take my ID in case you need it."

Surprised, Amira accepted the card.

Though she had access to Floor 202, the next steps to finding

Tiresia, Hadrian's price for cooperation, would be the real challenge. Amira would need to search the Soma's medical stores, an endeavor that could take weeks of research and scouting. The scare this morning, however, demonstrated that Rozene may not have weeks. *Time to improvise.*

Amira caught D'Arcy at the ward's main door.

"This is going to sound crazy," she began, ignoring D'Arcy's mock-terrified smile. "But I wouldn't ask for this favor unless a life literally depended on it. I need you to Cloud me."

"Are you crazy?" D'Arcy whispered, dragging Amira by the arm in the hallway. She pivoted her head around like a wild owl, scanning the walls and ceilings for monitoring devices. "Amira, what are you planning?"

"Rozene went to the emergency ward this morning," Amira said. "She's getting worse and I don't know how much time she has. In order to get the – the help I need, I need to get something from the medical stores that I'm not supposed to know about. If I'm caught, or someone reads my mind later, I need the next thirty minutes of my life Clouded, so they can't see it."

"You're going to steal something and want me to help cover your tracks," D'Arcy said succinctly. As a programmer, she had a knack for reducing a complicated scenario into zeroes and ones. "You know I believe you and I want to help, Amira, but this is my career on the line as well."

"Please, D'Arcy," Amira said. Shame burned down her neck as she met D'Arcy's eyes. "If I'm caught, I'll deny your name to the grave. All you have to do is switch the Clouding on and off again when I get out."

They descended the stairwell toward Floor 202 to avoid elevator cameras. After Amira had attached the sensory patch underneath her long hair, where skull met neck, she leaned over the stair railing and raised her thumb. Several floors up the stairwell, D'Arcy lifted her hand in response and activated the Cloud code from her personal computer. A cold sensation spread from the pad through Amira's head and down her spine. She gripped the railing, adjusting to the light-headed, buzzing sensation of the memory-blocker. Though she would remember the essentials, as the name hinted, the Cloud would dull her senses as it placed her short-term memories into a jumbled archive that would render them meaningless in a holomentic reading. At least, that was the hope. She slid an encrypted Two-Way communicator into her left ear.

"Are you ok?" D'Arcy whispered, her voice reverberating in Amira's ear. "Can you hear me clearly?"

"I'm adjusting," Amira said, with more confidence than she felt. She exited the stairwell.

Tentatively stepping onto the 202nd floor, Amira was greeted by a short, humanoid robot who introduced himself as Sparkes. As Naomi previously explained to Amira, he was more computer than standard robot, his processor synchronized with the Soma's archives and medical stores, serving as a friendly interface for the complex's daunting inventory. Despite this, he had smooth palms for retrieving files and medicine, and the retractable blades below his elbows revealed another purpose – to protect the Soma's archives if needed.

Amira held Naomi's badge in front of Sparkes's swiveling, orb-like eyes, hoping his skills did not include facial recognition.

"Identifying," he said in a soft, pleasant tone. His voice sounded fuzzy and distant under the effects of the Cloud, as though her ears were filled with water. "Welcome, Naomi Nakamura. How may I assist you today?"

Amira hesitated. Requesting the Tiresia directly was foolish, lest she create a red flag and incriminate herself and Naomi in the process.

"I'm not sure of the name, unfortunately, but it's a new trial medication," she said, peering over Sparkes's shoulder. Rows upon rows of shelved inventory stretched across the length of the room, orderly and brightly sterile. "Is there a section for new medications that I could browse?"

She cringed internally at the clumsiness of the lie, though Sparkes and his ilk could only understand words, not infer the intent behind them. Not yet, anyway.

"You are not authorized to search directly," Sparkes replied neutrally. "You must request an order that I will retrieve."

"I see," she said, fumbling for a response. "Well, I can go back and get my, um, supervisor to confirm the name. In the meantime, can you pick up an order for...for Oniria. And the usual supply for Subject 42: a ten-pack of Nirvatrene, thirty milligrams."

As Sparkes turned to the far-left corner of the room, Amira darted in the opposite direction. Though the Cloud left her with a strange tingling sensation, her reflexes remained sharp. She had picked a woefully outdated medication for Sparkes to find, which she hoped would translate into a long search, but could only count on ten minutes at the most.

She charged through several rows of shelved inventory, pulsing with adrenaline. Her eye caught a glass reflection down one aisle. As she reached it, the shiny surface turned out to be a monitor, framed by a series of glass cabinets stacked with vials. Someone had marked each vial with handwritten labels. Trial medications.

She didn't dare try to run a search for Tiresia using the monitor, if it would even be searchable. Though all drugs were supposed to be logged into the system, she suspected that something Hadrian Wolfe was so eager to get his hands on would not be found in official records. *A box without labeling*, he had warned her.

Amira opened the glass case with trembling fingers. Sparkes could return at any minute.

With rising frustration, she pushed aside boxes and vials, all marked with the usual clinical nomenclature. She paused. Her fingers lingered on the lowest wooden shelf, which had become transparent where her hands had touched the surface.

A glass cover.

Her heart danced. Shifting to her knees, Amira moved cases aside and felt for a hinge. She lifted the lower shelf, revealing a hidden layer of storage underneath the glass cover. In the narrow dark space, a small black box rested alone. She blinked several times, focusing her vision through the effects of the Cloud. A number ran across the container's front – 08012216.

Tiresia. It had to be.

Wheels turned softly on the other side of the room. The box resisted her desperate attempts to unlock it or pry it from the shelf.

"D'Arcy?" Amira whispered into the Two-Way.

"I'm here," D'Arcy said. She sounded as tense as Amira felt.

"First, I need you to create a distraction to keep Sparkes busy," Amira said. "Quickly."

Silence on the other end. Fighting back panic, Amira placed a finger in her ear but before she could adjust the Two-Way, a crash erupted in the bowels of the inventory aisles. A thud, followed by the rippling of shattered glass.

"I hacked into the inventory server with my shadow account, made an assistant robot knock some things over," D'Arcy said, voice tinged with remorse. "I won't be able to look Sparkes in the eye again. Amira, what's going on?"

"I found what I need, but can't get it out of the container," Amira said. "Since you're in the system, can you unlock it?"

D'Arcy cursed softly. Amira gave her the number. "Found it," she said. "Oh, Amira, this is quantum encryption. The code is basically a series of probabilities. This is going to—"

"Please, can you try?" Amira whispered, standing up to peer around the aisle. Still no sign of Sparkes. "I need to get out of here now, with or without it."

"Hang on," D'Arcy said. "If I synch my laptop with the encoder from my Eye, I can run a script...yes, I've got it! No guarantees this will work, this is Aldwych-level security. Give me two minutes."

Amira pressed her forehead against the wooden shelving, fighting back the foggy sensation in her head. Whether it was the Cloud, the Two-Way device or raw fear, Amira didn't know. If she succeeded today without losing her job, Amira vowed to spend an evening free of technology. A drink on the Canary House's rooftop, under the stars.

The numbers on the box spun, the combination changing to zeroes. A sharp click, and the top opened.

Shaking, Amira clutched at the thin vials inside. She stuffed them into her lab coat pockets. All contained a clear liquid, surprisingly cold despite the lack of refrigeration. She closed the hidden shelf door.

She had done it. All that remained was beating Sparkes back to the front.

Amira sprinted toward the entrance. When she reached the main hallway, she slowed her gait. Sparkes rolled around the corner.

"Your order is complete," Sparkes said, leaning forward on a pivoted waist to present a tray, which Amira accepted, still panting from the run.

"Everything ok?" Amira gasped. "Sounded like a commotion back there."

"Inconsequential cleanup exercise," Sparkes said with a crispness that could have been interpreted as annoyance. "Anything else I may assist with?"

Just as she prepared to say no, another idea struck Amira.

"Actually, Sparkes," she said, "can you provide me with a list of medications administered to the previous two Pandora subjects? The names were Jessica Alvarado and Nina Leakey." Amira had never heard the two names spoken aloud within the Soma complex, but profiles of Jessica and Nina dominated the Stream after the news of their deaths broke last summer. Julian repeated both names on his radio station, loudly and often.

The robot's eyes blinked at her, depthless but unreadable swirls of black. There was no reason, of course, for robots to blink, or for an archival machine such as Sparkes to even appear human, but that was how they were made.

Seconds later, she held the dead women's records in hand, both marked in red as 'highly classified'.

She returned to the stairwell, tapped on the door twice and entered. Almost immediately, the effects of the Cloud dissipated, sensation returning to her fingers. She sighed with relief, her hearing sharp and clear again. As she pulled the pad from her neck and the Two-Way from her ear, she looked up to see D'Arcy give her a final wave before she exited the stairwell.

Taking the stairs back up to the ward, Amira flipped through the files. She received profiles of the previous two subjects on her first day at the Soma, but the details were suspiciously scanty, abbreviated footnotes on two lives cut short. Assuming they had not been edited, the records in her hand might fill that gap.

Both of the files contained a list of medications, including known treatments before and during their terms as Pandora subjects. Neither young woman had received the now common embryonic pre-treatments for cancer and other genetics-based diseases. In addition, neither was given the generous dosages of health supplements that most city-based residents grew up with. They, like Amira and all compound residents, were genetically unaltered from birth, a biological relic of a more primitive time.

They became Pandora subjects around the same time frame and died within days of each other, just shy of their third trimesters. A final photograph in Nina's file revealed a wide face drained of color, unambiguously dead. Amira slid the photograph to the end of the file with shaky fingers. A note in scrawling handwriting recommended that the project avoid recruiting a replacement subject. *One less potential death all over the Stream*, Amira thought as she flipped through the pages.

Amira scanned the last page on Jessica Alvarado's file, frowning slightly as she reached the end of the list. She read it again, then turned to the end of Nina Leakey's record. The same drug appeared in both women's files, administered during their time as subjects.

"Txxxxxa. Approved experimental therapy – confidential."

It had to be Tiresia.

★ ★ ★

She returned to the ward as quietly as she had left it. Rozene remained in the emergency room. The thin vials chimed softly together in Amira's coat pocket, nestled between the folded medical files. Keeping them was dangerous, but she was not ready to part with the information they contained.

Amira pulled out the Oniria, cradling the fragile vial between her fingers. She smiled at her own quick thinking – she'd requested the archaic medication to keep Sparkes busy, but it also offered a potential treatment for Rozene. Amira witnessed it being administered to volunteers in her early days at the Academy. Oniria was once used to treat patients with extreme stress or trauma by inducing vivid, waking dreams that a therapist and patient could witness and discuss together – ideal for exploring suppressed memories, provided that Rozene would cooperate.

The Tiresia was her more intriguing possession. Why had an unofficial trial drug been administered to two cloning subjects in precarious health, and why did that very same drug interest Hadrian? Was it some pioneering medication meant to aid the cloning process or something more sinister? If its purpose was sinister, why did someone include it on the file? Amira could not ask these questions of Valerie Singh without revealing how she discovered the information. Instead, she would hold on to the Tiresia as collateral until she made headway with Rozene's memory.

After dropping the approved medications at Naomi's desk, Amira stopped in front of Singh's office. The sounds of a heated argument drifted beyond the barrier of the door.

"From what I can see, there is no progress to speak of," Alistair Parrish said. "I'm only here for an hour before I hear about a new medical crisis this morning, the same pattern as we had before—"

"There *is* no crisis," Singh interjected. "We had her stabilized within an hour. I am not worried."

"Well, you might want to start worrying!" Dr. Parrish snapped. "If this got out to the Stream, after everything that's already happened...don't forget, the interview with Harrison Harvey is two weeks away."

"Yes, of course," Dr. Singh responded. "Press briefings are naturally at the top of my agenda."

"Don't be flippant, Valerie!"

"I am far from flippant."

"If I may interject—" a third voice intoned.

"And what's he doing here?" Parrish asked, his voice rising in outrage.

"Dr. Barlow is here at my request, as a consultant," Singh replied with a hint of impatience. "This is, after all, still my project."

"For now."

"On to more important things," Barlow said. "What is most urgent is monitoring the cell growth rate as we move into the third trimester. So far, fetal development is occurring as we'd expect, but we have to monitor the impact that M. Hull's stress may have on the child."

"How's your student working out?" Parrish asked abruptly. "Should we cut her loose? Or keep her until the press dies down?"

"She stays for now," Singh said firmly. "As I have said countless times, the problem with our subject is psychological, an area that none of us, perhaps forgiving Barlow somewhat, are qualified to speak about. We will wait and see if our addition from the Academy can tell us something new."

Amira sighed in relief, surprised and moved to hear Singh defend her after their earlier exchange.

The door flung open and Amira found herself face to face with Alistair Parrish. He was tall with copper-toned hair. A neatly trimmed beard framed his open, animated face. Access to the best anti-aging treatments in Westport kept his appearance youthful for a man in his fifties, his true age betrayed only by his eyes, which carried that sunken, haunted quality earned through life's trials. Like Valerie Singh, he wore the black lab coat of a senior researcher, and a red badge with the Atomic symbol across the lapel, signifying his membership of the powerful Aldwych Council. His stern expression quickly morphed into a broad, warm smile.

"Ah! You must be M. Valdez."

"Just letting Dr. Singh know that I ordered the Nirvatrene," Amira said swiftly. Singh nodded indifferently and then closed the door behind her.

"So, M. Valdez," Parrish continued. "I hear that our patient is out of immediate danger." He gestured toward Rozene's room.

Amira found herself walking in step with the legendary genetics pioneer.

"Yes, she sh-should be," Amira stammered. "She's resting now, but I'll be evaluating her later today."

"Excellent." His tone carried no lingering traces of his outburst moments ago.

Through the window into the main ward, Rozene was in deep sleep, her brow tightly furrowed as it often did when she dreamed. Her face was paler than usual and her arms bruised in several places from IVs, but she otherwise appeared the same as she had the day before. One arm lay draped across her ever-increasing belly as her chest rose and fell.

"Very young," Parrish said sadly. "She looks like a child. Reminds me of Maya, in a way."

Everyone in Westport knew the story of Alistair Parrish

and Valerie Singh's only child. When she was twenty-two, a car struck Maya Parrish off her bicycle in the Rails, the thoroughfare where Aldwych's elite lived. The story shocked Westport, a city unaccustomed to many accidents after the adoption of the Auto-Navigated Vehicle Promotion Act. When it emerged that a motorist had disabled the self-driving mechanism in his car, it prompted a citywide ban of all human-operated vehicles.

Maya remained in a coma, living through her twenties as a lifeless vegetable. While undoubtedly a tragedy for both geneticists, Alistair Parrish disappeared from public life for three years before resuming his career as the Carthage station's head researcher. "*I am happiest in the tranquil dark of space,*" he famously said at his returning press conference. "*Westport carries too many painful memories for me.*"

"That was going to be the original name for this project," Parrish continued. "The Maya project. I wanted to name it after her. Had you heard that?"

"No," she said carefully.

"But Valerie opposed it, and she had a point. Too sentimental and loaded for an already controversial effort. In addition, Maya in Hindu mythology means illusion, mirrors of deceit. It would play into the public's anxieties, that we are creating an illusionary human, something artificial. Ridiculous, but there you have it.

"Instead, it became the Pandora project, a nod to the fact that we want to open boxes of knowledge that could never be closed again. A name especially fitting for the cloning effort. A human woman created by the gods out of clay. A clone. Although in hindsight, Amira, was it really the better choice? Do we think ourselves to be gods? We all know how Pandora's story ended. Ills unleashed on the world, with only a sliver of hope remaining."

They stood in silence, watching Rozene through the ward's window. Amira saw a kindness in Parrish that was noticeably lacking in Singh and for a moment, considered opening her own box of secrets – the tampered memories, the mysterious men with blurred faces, the unexplained and ubiquitous presence of Tony Barlow. In the end, Dr. Mercer's warnings restrained her. *Watch yourself.*

★ ★ ★

Infinity Park was one of the few open spaces in Westport that remained defiantly urban, without the sound-canceling perimeters and dense ceilings of vegetation within the newly designated 'Green Zones'. Amira would jog through the Green Zones when she wanted to escape the cacophony of the city, but those occasions were rare. Infinity Park, on the other hand, was an open mixture of grass and concrete from which one could watch trains scream overhead against a backdrop of towering buildings that caught the waning sunlight.

It was the start of April, meaning that spring should have arrived, but seasons became less predictable each year. Random blizzards struck into late July and after heat waves during spring, when the park would become overrun by excited residents drawn like shivering plants to the sunlight. Soon enough, many predicted, there would be no seasons at all, only days subject to nature's whims.

Such warnings meant little, however, when the sun warmed the sidewalk and the scent of newly planted grass permeated the air. Amira sat cross-legged on the mossy turf opposite D'Arcy and Julian, digging her toes into the cool grass. They drank cheap wine out of plastic cups. Like most of the sunbathers in the park, D'Arcy was topless, displaying a new three-dimensional tattoo of dancing flames (temporary, she assured the group) along her left side. Though Amira had moved well beyond the laced veils and long dresses of the compound, she refused to join the casual public nudity that was commonplace on warm days in Westport. Her compromise was a sheer white top draped loosely over her shoulders. Julian's left eye flashed when his Third Eye took pictures of the cloudless sky.

Julian and D'Arcy were heatedly discussing rumors of a Westport resident who had designed an Eye that could be used not only in Aldwych, where the devices were disabled, but in the space stations as well.

"It's impossible," D'Arcy said flatly.

"But the guys on the second floor swear it's true!" Julian said. "It's supposed to be quantum-level encryption, which is how it can bypass all of the security the labcoats made."

"The technology isn't there yet," D'Arcy said. "Believe me, this is my area. There are true quantum computers in places like Aldwych and the stations. The Stream is obviously quantum as well, but to design an Eye at the quantum level...no way."

Amira sat upright, struggling with images spinning past her line of vision.

"How's that Eye working for you, Amira?" D'Arcy called playfully.

"It's…." Amira's voice trailed away as she struggled for the right obscenity. In her left eye, she could see her friends sitting on the grass, while the right eye was a dizzying tornado of images and words – calendars, articles, search results – changing faster than she could process them.

"You have to focus your thoughts into one, single command," D'Arcy said kindly, with subtle amusement in her voice. "Think the words 'send message', for example. Think those words and nothing else."

Amira followed D'Arcy's advice, her heart leaping with excitement as the screen simplified into a list of contacts, all familiar names of Academy students. As she tried to scroll down the list, however, the screen changed to display a series of Stream articles about Iceland.

"Why is it showing me pictures of glaciers, D'Arcy?" Amira asked in a low voice as Julian burst out laughing.

"Oh, it must have been your background thoughts again. The trick is not to make them *forefront* thoughts and—"

"And I'm done." Amira pulled the lens from her eye with a little more force than necessary and handed it back to D'Arcy, who smiled sheepishly as Julian continued to howl. "I'll stick to regular computers where I can switch off the mind-reading, thanks."

"I still think you could master it if you try."

Julian stood up.

"As much as I'd love to stay, I need to get ready for the radio show," he said, leaning down to give Amira a hug and kiss D'Arcy. "And I thought you were both going to get some classwork done."

Amira cast a dark glance at the textbook nestled in the folds of the blanket, beside the hummus plate – *Crossing the Void: A Theory of the Psychosocial Effects of Interstellar Space Travel.*

"Isn't that what the Carthage does?" Julian asked. "Study the effects of space on the human body and mind?"

D'Arcy raised a hand, counting off with her fingers.

"The Carthage is Parrish's station, and that's what they do using 'voluntary' prisoners," she said, unreadable under her wide sunglasses.

"The Volta is Victor Zhang's, although who knows who's running it after he disappeared – they research radiation in deep space and energy sources for long-term space travel. The Hypatia – dark matter and energy. The Nineveh – tied to that super-telescope, looking for habitable planets. And Amira, tell him about the Osiris."

"What's there to tell? No one knows."

"Exactly," D'Arcy said with a gleeful clap. "Well, whoever runs it knows, but we don't even know who they are. It's like the Area 51 of space. They might be partying with aliens for all we know."

Julian laughed. "I get it. And no room for the arts up there – unless that's the deviant stuff the Osiris is studying. I'll leave you both to it."

D'Arcy rounded on Amira the second Julian was out of earshot. "What the hell is going on, Amira? We're in Aldwych less than a month and I'm *Clouding* you. Do I even want to know?"

Amira cradled the textbook in her lap, the answer stuck in her throat. Her ears buzzed, as they had in the Soma when she stole the Tiresia. As a fellow Pandora team member, Amira could tell D'Arcy certain things. But explaining that she stole a mystery drug for a rogue space cop who ran an abandoned ship of compound refugees? Even D'Arcy had her limits.

"What I'm about to tell you has to stay between you and me," Amira said. "No one else on Pandora can know, because I can't trust anyone except you. That also includes Julian, your data, even that diary you keep in your Eye."

"As long as you don't have to Cloud me every time we talk," D'Arcy said, raising her wine-filled cup with sufficient gravitas.

Amira relaxed. They inched closer together on the picnic blanket.

"I think – I know – that Rozene's memory has been tampered with," Amira began. "Probably to hide something she knows. A secret. I don't know what or why, but let's just say that I learned of a drug called Tiresia that might be connected to it somehow. That's what I took from the Soma medical stores. And sure enough, it was on the classified records of the two previous subjects, the ones who died over the summer."

D'Arcy gasped. "Could it be some kind of miscarriage drug? Something to make them lose the clones?"

"I don't think so," Amira said. "Plenty of those exist already. But if you're trying to stop a clone from being born, that's an obvious, incriminating way to do it. It's something else. And Nina and Jessica – the two former subjects – didn't have any of those medications in their records. Their death records show sudden, unexplained heart failure and cessation of neural activity, which is incredibly strange for two women in their early twenties. When the cause of death can't be explained through charts and readings, it looks more likely that their conditions were psychologically induced."

"Or by this Tiresia," D'Arcy said.

"I don't think so," Amira said. "I don't know, but it must be more than a poison. It's something classified – it was marked on the women's medical charts, but isn't on Rozene's record. It's doing something, but maybe indirectly. Causing stress, and that's what's actually killing the Pandora subjects."

"It doesn't seem right," D'Arcy said. "Lots of people suffer in all kinds of ways, and they don't just drop dead. That can't really happen, can it?"

"Have you heard of the Nocebo effect?" Amira asked.

"*Nocebo*," D'Arcy said slowly. "Is that like the placebo effect? Where you think the meds are curing you, when it's just a dose of sugar or something?"

Amira nodded. "*I will harm.* One of my first classes with Dr. Mercer, he told us this story. Back in eighteenth century Vienna, these medical students decided to play this prank on a teacher's assistant they hated. They ambushed him after class, held him down and told him he was going to be decapitated. They pushed his head on a block and blindfolded him. One of them then wrung a wet cloth so that a drop of water fell on his neck. He felt it, thinking it was the cold of a blade, and died. Right there, on the spot."

D'Arcy raised her eyebrows behind her thick sunglasses. "He believed it enough that it happened."

"Exactly. The mind-body connection – doctors have known about it to some degree for centuries, and we're only now really understanding how powerful it can be. There are other examples, too – that Dancing Plague in the sixteenth century, when people in this village literally danced themselves to death for no reason. Even when I grew up in the compound, I remember this one summer, the Elders held a sermon where they accused the entire congregation of violating the natural order – you know, immodest dress, sinful thoughts, the usual. At least ten women had to be carried out of the auditorium for seizures. And it wasn't for show – these were real seizures. Now that I've been at the Academy, I know the difference. The Elders said it was possessed spirits from other dimensions leaving their bodies."

"Guess I learned something new," D'Arcy said with a sigh. "Our thoughts can kill us."

"Not just anyone," Amira said. "It's not common, and we have a better idea now of why that is. Certain types of people are more susceptible to the Nocebo effect. The first are those who have strong belief-based cognitive wiring – religious people, in other words, or those who were raised and conditioned to operate heavily on belief over rational judgment. The second type involves people with suppressed or damaged memories. In addition, there is usually an injury or inherent imbalance to the hypothalamus that's needed to trigger an aggravated stress response – meaning, stress that doesn't just wear you down over time like it does for most people, but literally attacks your body in the here and now."

"Compound girls would be the poster candidates," D'Arcy said. She leaned forward, tearing some blades of grass and rolling them between her fingers. Lines stretched across her forehead as she sat still, lost in thought. "So," she said in a low voice. "You're thinking someone used this Tiresia to tamper with the women's memories to hide something, and maybe kill them with the stress caused by the distorted memory. But why tamper with a memory? Why not just take it out completely, if you want to keep someone quiet?"

Amira drew a deep breath. "It's very difficult to erase an entire memory," she said. "Especially a vivid one like Rozene's. You would have to not only extract the memory itself from a complex neural maze, but also remove anything that could *trigger* the memory. Think of it like pulling out a tree, along with all the roots deep in the ground. It's almost always more effective to change the memory or remove certain details."

"So someone took the easier way—" D'Arcy began, but Amira shook her head.

"Not just anyone can do it," she said. "You need to really understand neuroscience and holomentics to do it properly. And even then.... It can cause serious trauma for the person whose memory has been removed. Serious emotional trauma, especially if it's a strong memory or a significant one in their development."

D'Arcy nodded sadly. "So that could be the problem with this poor girl?"

"It could," Amira said. "There could also be problems in the cloning process, I don't know. But this fits with what I've seen of Rozene. She became really confused when I pushed her to recall these three men. When your memory is altered the way hers was, you don't know what's real and what isn't, but you know something isn't right – with your thoughts, your past, your sense of, well, your own being. And that kind of stress corrodes the mind, and then the body."

"Why would someone go to all of this trouble?" D'Arcy asked. "Especially if they're a scientist. If they're caught, that's attempted murder. Why throw it all away?"

Amira had been considering the same question.

"If Julian were here, I'd know what he'd say," D'Arcy said with a faint smile. "Money. Maybe a Soma rival in Aldwych who's not part of Pandora – the Galileo, for example – wants to learn the technology but get credit for the first successful cloning. Maybe they're hoping to kill Pandora with bad publicity. Or maybe this man – or woman – is just opposed to human cloning and is willing to pay any price to keep it from succeeding."

The sun was beginning to set when they packed to leave, and the world around them embraced the haziness of dusk, the lemon glow of sunlight giving way to long shadows and the rising chorus of invisible crickets. Slightly drowsy from the wine and heat, Amira and D'Arcy walked together along the pathway to the train station, arms linked. D'Arcy had thrown on a shirt for the return home.

Something caught Amira's eye and she pulled D'Arcy to their left, toward the center of Infinity Park. An outdoor theater had been built at the hill's base for plays in the summer. On its main stage, a woman in an elegant dress, too formal for a hot day, addressed a large crowd. Although it was too distant for Amira to hear, the crowd appeared to be hanging on to the woman's every word.

"Have you learned about the teachings of the Cosmics?" An older man materialized next to them, dressed in a poorly made suit but wearing an eager, open smile. He handed Amira a pamphlet and walked away.

"What is this shit?" D'Arcy murmured, as Amira flipped through the pamphlet.

"*Sentient Cosmology*," Amira read aloud. "*A science-based approach to understanding the universe and our purpose in it. Our understanding of the quantum world and dark matter has confirmed what humans have known for centuries. The world is more than the sum of what we know and see, and our consciousness plays a vital role, the driving role, in the fabric of the cosmos.*"

"I've heard of them," D'Arcy said thoughtfully. "I've seen them recruiting at the Academy, putting up posters and such."

Amira nodded.

"Dr. Mercer told me about them," she said. "The Cosmics. Ex-compound people and those who want a lighter version of compound teachings."

Amira observed elements of the compound in the lecture – though the spectators were sharply dressed, some even in Aldwych lab coats, they bore the blank, hungry stares of the congregants at the Passage ceremonies. Unlike at the compound, posters behind the speaker displayed quantum equations and satellite images of deep space, as well as detailed diagrams showing the fabric of matter and antimatter between the stars.

Amira gripped D'Arcy's arm and pointed to the front row. Alistair Parrish sat near the center of the crowd, his face wet with tears.

"That's Alistair Parrish!" D'Arcy whispered excitedly.

"It is." Amira had never heard of Parrish's involvement with any religion, New Age or otherwise. The geneticist, though one of the most famed scientists in all of Aldwych, and esteemed almost to the point of worship by his colleagues, was not a religious figure.

"You'd think he'd be smarter than this," D'Arcy whispered, smirking slightly.

"Even the smartest people will look for answers anywhere they can find them," Amira said. She felt defensive on Parrish's behalf, but couldn't say exactly why. "Anyway, it's none of our business what he chooses to believe."

The crowd burst into applause, Parrish included. The spectators rose at the speech's conclusion and exited the park. Parrish wiped his eyes and made his way up the steps, disappearing into the crowd.

"Time to go?" D'Arcy asked, nodding in the direction of the sun, which was dipping lower toward the crystalline horizon of the ocean.

Amira cast a final glance at the crowd and gasped. Alistair Parrish had appeared again at the top of the theater steps, now joined by Tony Barlow. Though distant, their body language and gestures suggested that their exchange was not an amicable one.

"Barlow," Amira said. "He's on the Pandora cloning project as well. He's the one who knew I was from the compound."

"They don't look friendly," D'Arcy noted. "What does any of this mean?"

Amira shook her head. Something, perhaps. Or nothing. Every new discovery unraveled a new thread of questions.

All of this ties back to Rozene, she thought. *Rozene's mind is where the answers lie, deep in the shapeless fog of memory.*

CHAPTER SEVEN

Shadows and Silhouettes

They began the same way each time – a young girl with deep-red hair in an enclosed, dark shed, her back pressed against the wall as she peered through shafts of light. Amira forced back her own memories of the shed in her past, and asked the requisite question.

"Where are we, Rozene?"

"Nowhere," Rozene moaned loudly, and the shed on the holomentic platform vanished, replaced with static, like an old television searching for a signal. After a moment, the static became Rozene sitting in a Westport café, smiling nervously at the strangers around her. The occasional morning commuter smiled back but no one spoke to her. The ill-fitting clothes, the lack of an Eye, the learned hesitation – all revealed her to be a compound girl. A barista brought her a mug of coffee, topped with leaf-shaped foam, which Rozene tried not to disturb as she added sugar. The room was bright, the colors vivid as all of Rozene's concentration was focused on this mundane image, a brief happy moment after her escape. The hologram changed to reveal a younger version of Rozene as a child sitting in a kitchen, jumping excitedly as a woman placed a bowl of fried cactus on the table. Despite her frustration, Amira once again felt a painful wave of sympathy for Rozene – in her desperate search for a positive memory, these were the best she could muster.

Amira sighed and stood up, placing her sensor to one side, and checked Rozene's vitals on the nearby monitor. The dosage was correct. Rozene's brain patterns showed the near-conscious, waking dream state that Oniria was supposed to induce. Rozene sat in a nearby chair, head slumped to one side as her arms dangled listlessly over the armrests.

"Try to relax, Rozene," Amira said, fighting back frustration. "It's painful, I know, but it will help you get to where your mind doesn't want to go. Whatever happened in that shed, you need to face it. Believe me, I've been through similar things in the New Covenant. I know what you're facing."

Rozene's head twitched and jerked at the sound of Amira's voice, and she made a low sound in the back of her throat.

"What's that, Rozene?" Amira leaned closer, and Rozene turned to face her.

Rozene sat up, her eyes opening widely. "Enough. I can't go through this again."

"Rozene—"

"You say you know what's it's like, but you'll never know! I don't want you in my head, bitch, so get out!"

Stunned, Amira turned off the holomentic machine, the image of young Rozene frozen in mid-jump, a child not caring where she landed. Rozene sobbed bitterly while Amira removed the pads from her temples, dismantling her intricate apparatus with shaking fingers after another failed day.

The long elevator descent from the 235th floor gave Amira ample time to trade her shock for frustration, even anger. How could Rozene assume she had not overcome similar demons, that her time in the compound was different? Though her early years in Westport were difficult, Amira always knew friend from foe. She never lashed out at those who helped her.

But was she truly Rozene's friend? Perhaps Rozene saw an opportunist, rather than a fellow survivor, in Amira. From her vantage point, it was not an unreasonable conclusion. Amira wore the same lab coat as those who administered the sedatives. At the end of each day she left, to a home and friends. The life that Rozene failed to find in Westport.

As Amira passed Aldwych's main square and its statue of a man and a woman pointing to the heavens, she glanced back at the Soma building. The lights on the highest floor were still on. Somewhere on a lower level, D'Arcy worked a night shift, testing the Stream connection on a satellite in the Asteroid Belt. Amira entered the train station, feeling more distant from Rozene than ever before. Instead of relief, it left her hollow like the base of a dead tree, its roots rotting beneath the surface.

★ ★ ★

Rozene greeted Amira with an open grimace the next day, but her glare shifted to a look of surprise as Amira settled into the ward.

"What's that smell?" Rozene asked.

"Something new I thought we'd try today," Amira said, and she opened a container from her bag to unleash the scent of fried cactus into the air. She endured a late night to make it. After tracking down the unusual ingredient in the Riverfront's all-night groceries, she created a successful batch following several disasters in the Canary House's scarcely utilized kitchen.

"I haven't had cactus in ages," Rozene said with unmistakable longing. Amira began setting up the holomentic machine.

With the familiar smell in the room, Rozene drifted into the waking dream state with the first injection of Oniria. Amira asked her the usual carefully phrased questions about the compound and the shed once again came into focus on the hologram. Rozene's pulse quickened but Amira continued in a calm voice.

"Stay with me, Rozene. This shed, is it in the Trinity Compound? Close to home?"

Rozene breathed in deeply, taking in the smells of the cooking, and nodded. The hologram remained unchanged, the young girl's back still pressed against the wall of the shed. Amira's heart skipped. *It's working.*

"Why are you here, Rozene?"

"I don't know." Her wide eyes were glassy and her head lolled slightly to one side, but her voice thickened with tension.

"You seem frightened," Amira continued, toggling the settings on the machine in search of a new angle to the scene. "You never take your eyes off the door, where the light is coming from."

"Follow the light always, for that is where you will find the higher Plane," Rozene recited mechanically. A line of scripture from the local prayers of the Trinity, Amira assumed.

"Rozene, what's on the other side of the door?"

Rozene suddenly shrieked, twitching violently in her chair. The younger, holographic version of Rozene in front of her was also shrieking, as water began to pour in through cracks in the shed door.

Cloudy water bubbled and rose in the enclosure, reaching up to her knees in seconds. Rozene, young and translucent, and Rozene, adult and tangible, both shivered.

"It's only water, Rozene," Amira said gently. "Hold your breath and let it come."

★ ★ ★

"How was that time better, M. Vald— Amira? I nearly drowned." Rozene eyed Amira warily but accepted the second serving of fried cactus.

"First of all, you weren't going to drown," Amira said, eating from her own bowl next to Rozene's bed. "It felt real, I'm sure, but you weren't in any danger. But that was a big breakthrough, Rozene. You stayed in the shed and didn't fight it like the other times. You were great."

Rozene continued to eat, but her face relaxed into something nearing pleasure – at the food, perhaps, or the rare compliment. For most compound girls, praise was a jewel rarely gifted, and usually earned at a high price.

"But why the water?" Rozene asked after a lull. "I don't remember ever being flooded before. Not enough water where we came from."

Where we came from. Amira formed her own satisfied smile at this new, subtle camaraderie. Perhaps involving Rozene directly in interpreting the memories wasn't a bad idea. She seemed to relax more every time her voice was heard, her opinions respected.

"I think the shed is real but the water isn't," Amira said. "The water is a metaphor of some kind, which we usually see in dreams instead of memories, but this is no ordinary memory. The water represents something dangerous outside, something that scares you. Something happened to you after you came out of that shed, back at the Trinity. To find out, we'll have to get you to leave the shed and confront it, whatever it is."

"Sounds like fun," Rozene said drily, resting her plate on her belly. "By the way, can you make the cactus with adobo sauce next time? My grandma made the best adobo cactus salad every holy day."

From that point on, Amira continued bringing cooked food that reminded Rozene of peaceful times at home. Though dark memories dominated most holomentic reading sessions, happy memories could possess their own quiet power. In the moments before death, Dr. Mercer had taught Amira, the brain will search for moments of joy, as those moments reflect who people truly were, what they aspired to be.

Amira learned more than she ever imagined about Rozene Hull since the start of their sessions, but there were still gaps in both women's knowledge. To Amira's surprise, Rozene could not recall the details surrounding her escape from the Trinity Compound nor what prompted her to leave, other than the broad explanation of being terribly unhappy. Amira suspected that at least one of the three mysterious men at the ceremony played a key role in Rozene's departure, and whoever had tampered with her memory had been forced to remove the man from other crucial moments in her young life, leaving fragments and shards of the past that Amira would now have to sift through.

Rozene's family was, in many ways, typical of most families in the compounds. The middle of ten children, a commendable number for an observant compound family, Rozene followed her older sisters around the compound's orchards, playing barefoot under the shade of the hybrid-citrus trees. The family prayed, fought, endured silent meals. The husband ruled over the wife, the wife ruled over her children and the older children terrorized the young, a hierarchy of retaliation from which no one emerged unscathed. Her older brothers served as marshals for the Trinity's leadership, responsible for keeping outsiders away and, most importantly, keeping the faithful in.

Nightmares of the Neverhaven plagued Rozene as a child, the product of classroom indoctrination. The dreams worsened once she became old enough to take Chimyra, administered each night after dinner. Under the Chimyra, dream and waking blurred in the young girl's mind, always unsure whether she was hallucinating, sleepwalking or dreaming in those late hours, when Elders warned that the barriers between worlds weakened.

The holomentic display showed Rozene's childhood dreams, vivid and fraught, as she escaped her room and crossed the Trinity at night, avoiding the glowing pathways that weaved around dome-like houses. The temple loomed over her with each step she took, its spiral steeple coiled like a disfigured hand waiting to grab her. The nearer she drew to the compound's front gate, to freedom, the heavier her legs became. She stepped into the main road, shining through the dark like a streak of captured moonlight, and her feet would melt into the pavement, followed by her legs, until she dissolved, screaming and melting, into the ground. In her final moments, she glimpsed the Neverhaven, a terrible world welcoming her for the sin of imagined escape. Rozene always woke up sobbing, her sheets wet with sweat and urine. Her father reacted to the nightmares by striking her across the face with his leather shoes, her mother silently working in the kitchen through the sounds of her cries.

Despite her silence, Rozene's mother provided comparative comfort and benevolence during her childhood years. Recollections of her mother, always in the kitchen slicing vegetables or bent over in the garden, were tinged with a warm blue, the color of tranquility. This changed abruptly when Rozene turned eleven and her eldest sister married.

"What are we watching now, Rozene?" Amira asked. She removed her protective goggles to witness the hologram directly, showing the Hull family gathered around the dining table. Rozene's mother wailed with her arms stretched across the oak table, cutting through the usual silence.

"We just got the news," Rozene said numbly. "My older sister, Evelie, died that afternoon. Her husband found her in the backyard, by the pond. Her head was under the water."

"What happened?" Amira asked, though she guessed at the answer.

"He said she killed herself," Rozene said. "He found out she strayed with the aid workers who brought in food and supplies from the cities. At least five men, he said. He gave her the chance to repent at the Unveiling ceremony, but she drowned herself to avoid the shame and...and atone for the dishonor she brought on him. He found her there when he came back home."

"Did your family believe that?"

Rozene's hooded eyes hardened, but her lip trembled slightly as she spoke. "I don't know. It didn't matter. The shame was terrible, the whole compound knew the story, and Mama was terrified that we'd never recover because of what happened with Evelie."

Rozene's memories of her mother took on a different tone from that point, their interactions wrought with fear and distrust. Her mother would watch Rozene closely, eyes narrowing each time she entered a room, as though searching for some hidden signs of debauchery. She buttoned Rozene's shirts tightly about the collar each morning and insisted on her wearing a thick scarf whenever she left the house instead of the more revealing head veil, calling her long red hair a temptation for any man who crossed her path. She lectured the young girl about virtue and chastity, saying that a girl was like a newly blossomed flower, and every transgression, every mistake was like tearing off a petal, one by one, until only the wilted stalk remained. It escalated until she would strike at her without warning, raving incoherently that she was a future whore and temptress in the making, destined to ruin them all. Though Rozene may not have recognized it, Amira saw a semblance of love – as compound mothers interpreted love, anyway – behind the cruelty, a mother's desire to protect Rozene from her sister's fate. Amira wondered whether her own mother whipped her with a similar motivation, or if she just relished having power over someone, anyone, in a place where she held the lowest position possible – a barren woman, unable to carry a child after Amira.

Rozene also changed. The girl who played barefoot in the sun was gone, and the young woman who replaced her learned to walk in the shelter of her own shadow.

* * *

Hadrian remained seated as Amira crossed the ship's entrance hall. Still wearing her lab coat from her shift at Aldwych, she met his yellow eyes with grim determination.

"She says she doesn't have that thing you want, Hadrian," one of the children called behind her. Scrawny and no older than thirteen, the boy had insisted on frisking her at the ship's entrance like a nightclub bouncer.

"I'm still working on it," Amira said by way of reply. She had, of course, procured the mysterious Tiresia with unexpected ease, but Hadrian didn't need to know that. She needed collateral.

Amira wondered if Hadrian sensed this, following her advance across the room with a knowing smile. If he did, he didn't pursue the matter.

"The lady comes without bearing gifts," Hadrian said loudly, his voice echoing throughout the high room. "Which means she wants something else from her new buddy Hadrian."

"Tony Barlow," she said smoothly. "What do you know about him?"

Hadrian's eyes lit up with interest, even a flicker of surprise. There was a pause while he seemed to consider her question.

"I know him," he said. "Man's got access to the stations, so I run into him up at NASH from time to time. Why the interest, love?"

"I don't trust him," Amira said. "He knows about the compounds and there's something going on with him and Alistair Parrish. He's everywhere on Pandora but I don't know what he does."

"So you think he's your man to watch." Hadrian finished the thought for her.

"Look into Tony Barlow and tell me what you know," Amira said firmly.

"I can do that," he said softly, advancing across the room. "But don't forget that anything I do depends on our deal. I'm not a charity, love."

With a subtle shift of his arm, his NASH badge glinted behind his jacket. Amira hesitated, but watching Rozene cower under beatings and threats from men all day renewed her defiance. She cowered under similar threats once, but never here. Never in Westport.

"We both need each other," she said, grabbing his jacket lapel and pulling it over the badge. Hadrian stepped back, surprised. "I can cause as much trouble for you as you can for me. But I like us better as friends. Let's keep it that way. I want to know about Tony Barlow. Help me out and I'll do the same."

Hadrian gave her a mock salute as she exited the ship. She continued without acknowledging the gesture, face flushed in triumph. A small victory, for herself and Rozene, in which she refused to break or bend under another's terms.

★ ★ ★

Energized by the success of the reading sessions, Amira continued the Oniria treatment. After several days of exploring childhood memories, the time had come to revisit the shed.

Soon, they were back within its cracked wooden walls, only this time it was the heat of the sun, not water, that fought to break through.

"Let me out," Rozene howled, banging her small fists against the door. "Please, I'll burn alive in here!"

"Rozene," Amira said, addressing the actual, comparatively sedate Rozene beside her, shoulders slumped to one side like a broken lever. The subject's eyes squeezed shut and a single bead of sweat ran down her forehead. "Breathe deeply and don't panic. Look around the shed. There's a shovel to your right."

"Yes, there is," she said lightly, as the dream version of herself stopped pounding on the door and began moving her hands wildly over the ground.

"It's propped against the wall," Amira said calmly. "Maybe you can use it to break the door open."

Rozene grabbed the handle of the shovel and Amira heard the agonizingly familiar hiss of skin burning. Shrieking, the holographic Rozene dropped the shovel while the catatonic, real version rubbed her hands together in agitation.

"There's no way out," the two Rozenes cried in unison.

"There is. There's always a way out."

Amira switched off the holomentic machine, the disc slowing its spin while Amira disentangled Rozene from the apparatus. Rozene smiled and closed her eyes, a gesture of relief, but she shook out her fingers as though cooling them from a burn.

Rozene recovered after a lunch of cactus salad, even snorting with laughter when Amira joked that every compound must have the exact same shed, designed by Elder Cartwright himself, to support his war against teenage girls. After trading stories of milder transgressions that sent them to the shed, they resumed the reading.

"Do you know why you're here, girl?" a man asked Rozene.

Rozene sat in a small office surrounded by men in matching black robes. Her parents stood anxiously to one side. Trinity posters and slogans adorned nearly every inch of the sand-colored walls. The same words and phrases, arranged in different ways. A faint but fiery voice came from a radio on the windowsill, delivering a sermon in crackling fits.

Rozene gave no indication that she heard the question. A large horsefly buzzed overhead and she followed its path toward the window, watching it rap against the glass.

"Rozene, speak when the Elder addresses you," her mother snapped.

"The last time you found yourself here," the Elder continued, "your mother caught you at Elder Ron Ballard's guest house, with his daughter Marlee and other delinquents, watching pornographic filth from the cities."

"It was just a movie," Rozene said quietly. "It was a comedy about a fashion designer we found on the Stream."

On the hologram, additional memories interrupted the scene in the office – a group of girls gathered their skirts across a dried-up creek; the same group circled around a television, engrossed in snapshots of the world outside the Trinity, where women wore bright colors and long, free hair that snapped with the wind. A halo of light framed a single girl in each memory, the same girl. Marlee, the daughter of an Elder's second wife, smiled shyly at Rozene, her round face framed by thick, curly charcoal hair that bounced with each step she took.

"Don't try to make excuses," the Elder said, his voice rising with a snarl. "Anything from the cities is filth and poison. Their music, their movies, their so-called 'free press' – all of it created to promote selfishness. It is through the collective, not the individual, that we bring new souls into this world and learn the mysteries of the Conscious Plane. The cities, and every last sinful soul inside them, are destined for the Neverhaven, and you are evidently ready to burn with them."

Muted sobs arose from a neighboring room. Rozene turned away from the window and stared in the direction of the cries.

"I've tried everything, Elder," Rozene's mother said, thumping her chest with theatrical fervor. "You see how she is. We take Chimyra every day and never miss Unveilings, and yet we're afflicted with these daughters. They know what awaits them but don't seem to care! After her sister's disgrace, I'm doing all I can to keep her away from boys and men alike. I follow her to school. We keep her bedroom door open at all times and her window locked with three bolts. We drill the fear of the shadeless world into her bones. And what do we get in return? Crimes against nature under my own roof!"

"Your husband's roof," the Elder said coldly. "Do not forget your place, Mrs. Hull. You have indeed failed with yet another daughter. Barely out of girlhood and already steeped in perversion."

The hologram shifted to another scene, of Marlee sitting on the edge of Rozene's bed, the book of Elder Cartwright's sayings in her lap. Her fingers danced over the pages, as though she were playing an invisible instrument, while Rozene read a passage from her own copy in a monotone. Their knees touched on the bed, each stealing glances while the other read. Both girls sat upright and rigid as footsteps rose from the creaking stairs just outside the open door. Rozene's eldest brother passed, casting a leering glance at Marlee before heading downstairs, magnetic-rifle in hand. Summoned to pursue another escape attempt, the third this month.

At the sound of the front door closing, the book slid from Marlee's fingers to the floor. The girls fumbled together on the far corner of the bed, tugging at buttons and sliding hands underneath thick blouses and skirts. Their lips met, carefully at first, but with growing hunger as Rozene lay back against the headboard, pulling Marlee closer. Marlee snatched her veil off, sending thick ringlets of hair springing in every direction.

A shriek came from the far end of the room. The girls separated in a split second, untangling and darting to opposite sides of the bed. Rozene raised her head, struggling with her loose veil, to find her mother at the room's open door, horror and rage etched into her thin face.

In the office, the Elder held a folded whip at his side, considering Rozene carefully. A large bottle of Chimyra bulged from the pocket of his robes, no doubt to enhance the effect of whatever punishment awaited. Another cry, louder and pleading, came through the wall.

"This is a crime for which an Unveiling alone cannot atone," the Elder said. "But before we begin, you may beg for forgiveness."

Rozene suddenly looked directly at the main Elder with the whip, her eyes alight with fury.

"You think you know the universe's plan for me," she said. "Well, I only answer to the Plane that binds the worlds, not some angry, dirty old middleman. Half of the community is sick because the Feds cut the medicine rations and all you care about are what teenage girls get up to."

Her mother gasped, in time with Amira. Rozene sat back in her chair, her chest rising and falling underneath her heavy dress. Her eyes danced with rage and excitement, relishing the reaction she inspired. Two men advanced, each one grabbing an arm. The main Elder stared incredulously back at her, the thin wisps of his beard trembling with fury.

Amira also stared at the hologram in surprise. She had been on the receiving end of Rozene's flashes of defiance, but did not expect to see Rozene lash out at a Trinity Elder. If Amira had delivered a similar speech to the New Covenant Elders, she shuddered to think of the punishment she would receive – and she had accepted many in her time there.

"Do not concern yourself with men's affairs," the Elder growled. "We will deal with the sick. Your concern is to learn obedience, to be a wife and mother, to bring children into this world in place of those that ascend to the Nearhaven. Three days in the shed should help you think about your priorities. No, don't take her yet! The lesson isn't over."

The men holding Rozene's arms bent her over the desk. Her father turned away, but her mother nodded approvingly at the main Elder. As the first blow fell across her back, Rozene gritted her teeth but didn't scream. The blows continued and the scene in the office faded into the background, replaced by the comfort of Marlee's smiling face, lips slightly parted. The Elder pried Rozene's mouth open, spilling Chimyra down her throat. Marlee's face began to blur and distort, changing into a man's. Rozene howled in rage.

"Stop!" Rozene cried angrily as Amira removed her goggles. "That's private." Her face reddened to match her hair before she turned away with damp eyes.

"I'm sorry," Amira said gently. "We can stop for today. I'm afraid nothing is really private anymore, Rozene. Not in here, anyway. We'll try not to linger on those memories unless we need to. And try not to be ashamed."

Rozene scowled and turned away, looking out the window.

"Look, I understand," Amira said. "I lived on a compound too, and went through the same thing you did. We all did."

And it was true. She did not have an equivalent of Marlee, but she remembered those late afternoons in her bedroom, when she would twist her bedroom pillow and place it between her legs, rocking back and forth against it with her eyes trained on the lock on her door. Her parents caught her more than once and doused her with cold water as punishment while she crouched naked behind the shed. When her nipples tightened and swelled from the cold, she was doused again and beaten until her back was numb.

Rozene avoided eye contact with Amira for several days after the reading, speaking as little as possible. Amira avoided the topic of Marlee, until she could no longer ignore the aftermath of the Elder's discovery.

"How did your parents respond after the day in the Elders' offices?" Amira asked.

Rozene sighed, but leaned back in her chair, surrendering to the Oniria's effect.

"They kept us far away from each other, but you know that already," Rozene said. "They also decided to find me a husband. An important one."

At these last words, Rozene flinched, jerking her head to one side. *The memory.* Amira turned the reader's dials, following the reaction. The hologram obeyed, unveiling a wide panorama of the Trinity. Amira directed the holographic platform to the open floor in the ward's center, expanding it to fill most of the room.

The Hulls' home stood at the far end of the Trinity Compound, under the shade of the foothills that ran along its eastern border. Rozene walked each day across the compound to collect water at the wells, an exhausting task in the hot summer months. She dragged a metal case of water in each hand, sweating through her shapeless floral dress. Hover-carriers existed to carry water, but Elders encouraged manual labor in place of Unveilings when appropriate. Her skin was beginning to brown under the blistering sun and her river of smooth long hair clung to her back in rivulets of deep red – Rozene always removed her scarf the minute she evaded her mother's watchful eye.

The ground rumbled at the approach of an all-terrain vehicle, its engine growling in protest as it hovered inches above the parched earth. The marshals frequently patrolled the eastern edge of the compound, the only side protected by mountains rather than walls and barbed wire.

Rozene kept her brisk pace as the hovercraft approached, her eyes carefully trained on the ground in front of her. The engine softened to a low, deep vibrato as it slowed to a halt, the vehicle still suspended in the air. She looked up, squinting through the sun's glare, at a group of men towering above her atop the hovercraft. At the center was a very tall man in a long, tan coat. She tried to shield her eyes from the sun to get a better look at him, but his face was obscured by the shadow of his wide hat. As Rozene tried to look even closer, her pulse rose dramatically on the monitor and everything in the hologram, sky and earth alike, turned a dusty red.

"Rozene," Amira said sharply. "Who is that man?" Amira walked to the center of the hologram and moved her hands apart to expand the image of the patrol. As she suspected, his face was not merely shaded but blurred beyond recognition. Another tampered memory.

Rozene shook her head in agitation. She twitched in her chair, arching her back to accommodate her heavily pregnant frame.

"I can't see," she said. "I…I don't know."

"Open your eyes."

Rozene's heavy lids opened groggily, blinking as though she were waking from a long, deep sleep. Her eyes widened as she noticed the scene in the ward's center. A surreal experience, Amira knew, to have your mind's eye presented to you in such clear detail, like a still reel from a movie seen too many times.

"Let's keep going," Amira said. "You were carrying water when the patrol stopped next to you. What happened next?"

Rozene frowned and exhaled slowly. "I remember they were interested in me, but I didn't know why at the time."

She closed her eyes.

The frozen figures came back to life. The man, his face still obscured, turned to another man next to him and nodded. This second man, shorter with a long beard, asked Rozene for her name. She replied cautiously, and the vehicle sped away.

"That was it?" Amira asked. "There was nothing more?"

"I...don't think so."

"There's something significant about this memory, Rozene. Try to think about it. Who is that man in the all-terrain? There's something about him that's important, that maybe even ties in to why you left the Trinity."

Rozene ran her hands through her hair as she contemplated the scene, her fingers brushing against the sensory pads attached to her head.

"Our Elders wore coats like that," she said. "So he is – or was – important in the compound. The Elders are mostly older men, although sometimes a younger one will move up quickly. The rest are marshals like my brothers. They aren't important."

"Let's keep going. Count backward from ten to one...."

Suddenly, the scene dissolved, replaced by a fleeting image of a man with a shovel, standing under a bright moon. Then, the hologram turned pitch black and silent, punctuated by the soft sounds of a woman breathing. Amira sat tensely beside Rozene as the darkness spread to the corners of the ward, dimming the lights around them. The breathing stopped abruptly, as though someone was holding their breath, followed by the faint trace of footsteps, growing louder.

"Rozene," Amira said, her voice tight with fear. "What's happening?"

But Rozene was lost in the memory, her eyes closed tightly. A small sound escaped from her throat. Something shifted in the dark, and the faint outline of a figure appeared in the hologram, growing taller and taller as it neared the center of the room. Amira realized at that moment that the hologram displayed the memory from Rozene's viewpoint directly, rather than the usual wide lens perspective of the holomentic display. Only the most vivid and recent memories were displayed from the subject's direct viewpoint, too raw to be experienced with the luxury of distance.

The figure stood over Rozene's bed. Rozene's breath quickened, but she remained still. Silently, the figure leaned forward, revealing a face covered by a surgical mask and a white cap. It moved as a ghost would, without voice or footsteps. Rozene squeezed her eyes shut and willed herself to wake up. She opened her eyes. The figure was still there, hovering in the same place over her bed. Her eyes burned with sweat trickling from her forehead, causing the figure's face to blur. It held a finger up to its lips in a conspiratorial gesture of silence.

Then, to Amira's horror, the other hand came into view, holding a syringe full of clear liquid.

Rozene screamed.

The figure vanished.

The ward brightened again as the two women sat there, breathing rapidly. The holographic platform stood empty, the disc continuing to rotate.

"Someone came into this room late at night," Rozene finally said, turning to Amira with wide eyes. "Here in this room. I thought it was a nightmare, but I remember now. It was when I first came here, more than once, after they...implanted the...the cell and I became pregnant. What does that mean?"

For a moment, Amira leaned against the wall, speechless. Though it had been her longstanding theory that the modification to Rozene's memory had been deliberate and malicious, it was still shocking to see the evidence materialize literally before her eyes. Had Jessica Alvarado and Nina Leakey endured the same treatment?

She finally managed to clear her throat. "I'm going to find out. I have to report this, and we'll figure out what happened. I'd do it now, but we're the last ones here. I can find some security in the meantime. Maybe I can get Sparkes to stay outside your room—"

"No!" Rozene cried. "You can't report it! What if it's *her* who's behind this? It could be all of them!"

Amira frowned. For all her faults, she had come to doubt that Valerie Singh herself would directly sabotage her own project. Rozene, conditioned to distrust, would not be so easily convinced.

"Rozene, I'm just afraid it isn't safe."

"Of course it's not safe! I know that. But maybe if we keep going, I can get my memory back and find out who it was. You can't let anyone know."

Amira squeezed Rozene's shoulder, a brief gesture of comfort that surprised them both. After all she had seen Rozene survive, it pained Amira to place her in more danger. But Rozene was right. They had made significant progress that night. The discovery of another memory within Rozene's subconscious, the mysterious man on the all-terrain vehicle, meant that they were closer to his identity, assuming he was one of the three men in the ceremony.

Rozene buried her face in her hands. "How did I end up here? Why did I let this happen? Maybe this is my punishment for everything I've done."

"I think I may have pushed you too far today," Amira said, leaning forward and gently removing the pads from Rozene's head. "Get some rest. We'll continue tomorrow. Let me know if you remember any unusual dreams when you wake up."

Rozene removed her hands from her face, her cheeks shining with tears, and nodded. She patted her belly mindlessly and pulled herself back into the bed.

"I noticed your hands," Rozene called out as Amira walked toward the exit. "The scars on them. Are they from…from back home?"

Amira raised her hands, exposing thin white lines that snaked across her palms. The scars that lasted long past the pain, anger and thick, suffocating fear that accompanied them. Scabs of an old life that Amira had not yet buried entirely. Could it ever be buried? Amira didn't know.

"I was caught the first time I tried to escape," she said. "They brought me to the Elders' offices in the Temple, not unlike what happened to you. They gave me two choices: be chained outside the front of the temple for the rest of the night with an entire vial of Chimyra or take twenty lashes with their cable." She remembered it well; it was a thin whip comprised of hundreds of even thinner wires, the texture of a silver lock of hair, each strand charged with electricity.

"I was so cold by the time they brought me in," Amira continued, "that I would have taken anything other than going back outside again. And nothing makes shapes in the dark move like Chimyra. So, I held out my hand and took the twenty lashes."

"All twenty?"

"It ended up being about ten. The Elder insisted that he carry it out himself, punish his own flock and all of that, but he had terrible arthritis. His wrists gave out halfway through, and he sent me back home."

"The stronger sex in action," Rozene said with an arched brow.

And for the first time, they shared a genuine, open smile.

CHAPTER EIGHT

Thirst

The road carving through the narrow valley was the same reddish brown as the surrounding rocks, the sand, even the sky. The cool moisture of early morning hung in the air as Amira breathed in deeply, lungs free from Greater Westport's smog. She did not know where she was, but the desert reminded her of the New Covenant. Her unease entwined with an odd sense of relief, the feeling of coming home after a long journey.

She walked down the dirt road, her boots sliding on the wet ground. Vultures called to one another in the distance but otherwise, she was alone.

The road curved and Amira took the path down the side of a steep hill to find a large house on her right. The structure, comprised of wood and clay, blended into the hill behind it, as though it had grown out of the rock. The open front door revealed nothing but deep, inviting blackness inside.

Terror seized Amira. Though she did not understand it, she knew danger surrounded the house and that she had to get as far from it as possible. She tried to back away, her eyes trained on the entrance, but her legs grew heavy and sluggish. Her arms numbed, her strength deserting her as fear coursed through her body.

In an instant, the house silently burst into flames before her. The fire melted the clay walls at alarming speed and licked furiously against the wooden beams until they collapsed into the flames. Heat surrounded her, despite the distance from the burning structure, and she coughed and struggled for air.

She woke up, chest heaving and slick with sweat. The same dream visited her every night, only with different houses and settings. Sometimes, it would be a cottage in the mountains, other times a glass house by the ocean, but it was always accompanied by that same fear, followed by the fire.

Her bedroom was still dark except for the array of devices charging along her walls, forming angry red eyes staring at her. The window, slick with humidity, brought warm blue light into the room's center.

Amira crawled out of bed, naked with her long dark hair tied back, and pushed the window open. She could feel the breeze from the Riverfront as the streets near the Canary House came to life in the early morning. Students headed to the first wave of exams at the Academy, joined by joggers along the canals and commuters trekking to the trains.

What did the nightmares mean? Amira did not know which outcome she feared more – that she was going mad, breaking under Pandora's weight, or that she wasn't mad at all and the dreams meant something she did not yet understand. The rush of heat felt as real as the plants on her windowsill. She had no memory of a burning house, or anything in her past that might inspire such a dream. Was it symbolic, similar to dreams of flying or losing teeth? Or a warning? Amira knew only that she wanted them to end, to regain the few hours of peace left to her.

She drummed her fingers against the cracked windowsill. In the distance, the lights of Aldwych glowed through the morning fog. The district never went dark, no matter the hour. Rozene probably slept, or perhaps began to stir, on the Soma's highest floor, awaiting another grueling day of needles, tests and cruel invasions into her thoughts and fears. The first, muted light of dawn appeared as the brick walls of the Riverfront came into focus under the emerging sunlight. In the distance, the first shuttle to NASH departed from the Galileo building, leaving a trail of smoke through the pink sky.

Aldwych. She loved and feared the district in equal measure. The city held the keys to the space stations, the world above the world, and held the power to keep her from it. For the first time since her assignment, however, there was hope.

★ ★ ★

"There are several types of dreams," Amira said, hands twitching in her coat pockets. She faced her small but imposing audience – Alistair Parrish, politely engaged, Tony Barlow, unnaturally still and focused, and Valerie Singh, distracted and impatient. Amira detested formal briefings, and explaining her work to two of the world's most famous scientists did little to help matters. By the door, D'Arcy gave her an encouraging thumbs-up, having just delivered her own briefing on the successful Stream signal near Mars.

Amira cleared her throat. "Three main types in total. The first type of dream is what we refer to as 'processing' dreams. These are the most common type of dreams we have – they help us organize our brain and process new experiences, take in the information that we receive each day. For example, if you watch a documentary about, let's say, the rainforest, you may dream that you're in the jungle that night, as your brain takes in the new visuals and sounds you were exposed to.

"The second type is a memory-based dream. They're similar to the first type but far more significant, because they concern longer-term memories that have had a lasting impact on the person's psyche. These memories may be traumatic, or simply be related to significant events in a person's life. It is this type of dream that I'm triggering in Rozene with the Oniria treatment."

"Only older, lasting memories," Barlow said thoughtfully. "And why exactly are you focusing on this, M. Valdez?"

Amira paused, choosing her words carefully. "From the holomentic readings, I believe that *part* of the problems that Rozene— that the subject is experiencing is due to traumatic memories from her past that have been distorted, which can cause severe psychological distress. And that, you know, can translate into physical symptoms."

While the two men nodded silently, Singh immediately came to attention.

"Distorted?" she asked sharply, raising her dark brows. "Distorted how? As in suppressed memories?"

Amira clenched her fists in her pockets, struggling to keep her face impassive. Nothing escaped Dr. Singh. Remembering her promise to Rozene, Amira channeled her inner politician, searching for the vaguest response.

"Maybe," she said. "It's not yet clear to me what the cause *is* exactly. But if I can bring these memories to the surface, however painful they are, they can be dealt with more effectively. All memories distort with time and they evolve into something rosier or something worse. What I'm seeing is what Rozene remembers, not a true account of the past. But there are severities in the distortions, pieces that are missing that suggest something extremely painful is behind it."

"I keep hearing words like 'stress', 'trauma' and 'pain'," Singh said, her shrewd, narrowed eyes betraying the light, casual tone of her voice. "And I question whether this is the best therapeutic approach for a pregnant woman in her third trimester who has experienced multiple trips to the emergency room."

"Valerie," Parrish said with exasperation. "We haven't had another incident since this treatment of M. Valdez's has started, have we? And what other alternatives have we not exhausted already? You have stated to me *many times* that you suspect our subjects' problems are psychological in nature, which is, frankly, not your area of expertise."

"No, it isn't," she agreed icily. "But it is in Barlow's realm, somewhat. Dr. Barlow, what are your thoughts on this?"

Tony Barlow smiled placidly, as though he and Singh had just shared a private joke.

Amira recalled his seemingly heated conversation with Parrish at Infinity Park and felt a renewed sense of unease.

"Consciousness is an incredible field," he said. "That is my area of expertise, if you did not know, M. Valdez, one I am leveraging for several Pandora sub-projects. Why don't you tell our friends here about the last type of dream one may experience?"

Amira stood dumbfounded. Barlow's responses, while always delivered with the same tranquil monotone, were never predictable.

"Well," she said. "The last type of dream is what we call a 'preconjective' dream. We still don't fully understand how or why, but studies have shown that some dreams appear to provide insight into events that have…not yet transpired, a warning of things to come."

"Seeing the future?" Parrish asked with interest.

"Not exactly," Amira said. "Not quite like that anyway. You've probably had one or two. Where you're in a place or see something familiar...déjà vu is often the byproduct of a preconjective dream. You dream something before it happens, only it may not happen exactly how you dreamed it. Sometimes it's hard to tell what came first, the dream or the waking experience."

"The beautiful fog of memory," Barlow said with a smile. "Some theoretical physicists and cosmologists have latched on to the idea of preconjective dreams, seeing them as evidence that time itself is not real in the true sense, but a way in which we are forced to make sense of reality. We need a sequence to our lives, or else there would be chaos. And the alternative consciousness of the dream world may be where we get to cheat a little, to be sentient beyond our narrow window into life." His lips curled in a subtle, secretive smile that left Amira squirming slightly under his gaze.

"This is obviously fascinating," Singh interjected drily. "But I fail to see what this has to do with the unorthodox mental experiment that my subject is now enduring. What about it, Barlow?"

Amira could not help but admire the skill with which Singh could inject contempt into the most benign of phrases.

"I would like to see where Amira's approach leads," Barlow said. "The mind is an ever-fascinating thing, and since she's started this unusual treatment, it makes sense to let it unravel and see the end results."

So he wasn't opposing her work, at least not outwardly. Amira had heard nothing from Hadrian about Barlow, but she had researched him further on her own. As Singh had said, Barlow's specialty area was consciousness. He was 'detailed' to Pandora, meaning his work and research findings were not owned by the project – an enviable position for an Aldwych scientist, as most were contracted with specific corporations, sometimes for decades. Aside from those searchable facts, his profile lacked personal details, such as age and family. Either he had no past to speak of, which was strange, or he had a past to conceal, which Amira found more likely. Everything about Tony Barlow was open to interpretation, from his cryptic smiles to his conversations, which were insightful but revealed nothing. The more she crossed paths with Tony Barlow, the more she confirmed her suspicion that he was a man with his own agenda, and likely a dangerous one.

Singh sighed. "That will do for now, M. Valdez. I have some tests to run, and then she is yours for the remainder of the day."

* * *

Singh kept her word. The battery of tests left Rozene tired and melancholy, so Amira began the reading session without the Oniria.

"Tell me what happened after you encountered the man in the all-terrain vehicle," Amira began. "The one you can't identify."

"I remember I was pulled from school after," Rozene said, and the hologram displayed the young girl lying on her bed, her tear-stained face fixed on the ceiling. In the next moment, she peered downstairs, where an Elder sat in the kitchen with her parents, deep in conversation. She then walked along the street outside, a beam with two buckets of water balanced precariously on her bony shoulders. Sensing Rozene glance at the hologram, Amira pointed to the corner and the holographic disc floated out of Rozene's line of vision.

"Did you see your friends much after that?" Amira said, thinking of the earlier memories of Marlee.

Rozene glared at Amira, as though sensing her train of thought. She shook her head.

"My life was nothing but chores and prayer. I barely had time to myself but when I did, I prayed for a better life, one that was mine. After a while, I stopped doing that, because I knew it would make me crazy. I almost looked forward to getting married, just so I'd have other things to do with my time."

The hologram in the corner began to display one of Rozene's fantasies. Young, thin and glamorously dressed in modern clothing, she held a baby with one arm and a toddler on her hip. She smiled at someone Amira could not see.

"Is that why you agreed to join the Pandora project as a subject?" Amira asked, watching the laughing Rozene in the hologram.

"I always knew I wanted to be a mother," Rozene said. "Even if it means having a baby…this way. Do you think it's true what the

Elders said? In the Trinity, they told us that clones are evil because the Conscious Plane won't recognize them as souls. That they'll never be able to ascend to the Nearhaven when they die, just stay here and create imbalance in the dimensions."

"I think they're more afraid of babies born outside of traditional compound marriages and reproduction," Amira said, ignoring the theological component of Rozene's question.

"That's what I believe too," Rozene said, relieved. "But anyway, life here didn't work out the way I expected. It was hard when I first came to the city. All my life, everything was controlled. When I ate, who I spoke to, what I said. The freedom here was more than I could take, I guess. When I signed the contract with Dr. Parrish, I had food and people to watch over me, and part of me wanted that again."

This self-awareness surprised Amira. Rozene wanted to be loved above all else, to find purpose in others. A goal she chased at a high price.

"But you still don't remember when you left, or why?" Amira asked.

"No. I know I wasn't happy, but that's nothing new."

"Ok. Let's try another round of the Oniria. Just relax your arm...."

In the hologram, Rozene cowered in the shed again, only this time, sand poured in through the cracks in the walls. Panicked, she pounded frantically on the door with small fists. The sand hissed down the wooden planks and formed pools around her bare feet.

"Help!" Rozene cried frantically. "Help, I can't breathe!"

"Rozene, we've been here before," Amira said in her calmest voice. Next to her, Rozene jerked her head rhythmically, but otherwise remained still in her chair. "You can find a way out. There's only a wooden door in the way."

In the hologram, Rozene pressed her forehead against the door, catching her breath as the sand continued to pour in. Suddenly, her hand plunged into the ground and emerged holding a shovel. She swung the shovel at the door with all her strength, throwing the full weight of her body as she struck the lock over and over. With a final, violent swing, the door gave in and swung open.

When she stepped outside into the quiet desert, there was no longer a flood of sand pouring through the cracks. The sharp sliver of the moon, waning in a narrow crescent, hung low in the night sky. Its bright, blue light caused the sand to shimmer and glow, illuminating her surroundings.

Rozene stepped tentatively away from the shed, following the sound of nearby voices. Though it was dark, she could see movement from shadowy figures in front of her. She touched her face, surprised by a trail of blood streaming from her nose.

This is it. Amira's hands trembled on the machine's dial as she sharpened the scene. *Submerge.* The desert scene spread from the platform to engulf the room. Dread accompanied her excitement – the sudden appearance of blood suggested imminent violence.

Rozene's memory came into sharp focus in the hologram, new details materializing with each step she took. Bruises appeared on her arms and her dress was now torn and stained with dirt and blood.

"What's happening?" Rozene cried in the hologram, bewildered at the changes to her appearance.

A man appeared behind her and shoved her roughly to her knees. Three other young girls waited on their knees nearby; her school friends from other memories, though Marlee was absent. Two sobbed and trembled in open terror, the third stared mutely ahead in sullen resignation. They were guarded by a group of armed men, all wearing black ski masks.

"Four this time, Sarka?"

The silky voice belonged to a tall figure who Amira instantly knew as the same man who watched Rozene carry water on that hot, dusty path. He had the same narrow frame and long tan coat. His face was no longer blurred. He looked to be in his fifties, with graying hair and pale blue eyes that surveyed the scene with chilling calculation. Amira approached the hologram as she realized that the bulges on the man's temples were not protruding veins, but wires underneath his skin. City-level technology on a compound holy man. But why?

"Caught them before they reached the highway," the man named Sarka said, his voice high and reed-thin. He was stocky, with a full beard that failed to conceal a weak chin and a round, blunt face. His entire body trembled with nervous, aggressive energy, as though he were an incredibly dangerous wind-up toy turned to the last gear. "Look who we found here, Elder."

The gray-haired man leaned down to face Rozene.

"Rozene Hull," the man said softly. "I'm disappointed."

She remained silent, staring into the distance.

"The girl's brother got them past the gates," Sarka said. He gestured toward a young man flanked by a pair of marshals. Rozene's brother's face was heavily bruised, blood leaking from the side of his swollen lower lip. He stole a terrified glance at Rozene, but she stared wordlessly ahead.

"You know I choose my brides very carefully," the Elder said, turning indifferently away from Rozene's brother. "Virtue and obedience are qualities I value above all. It seems I may have misjudged you."

As though coming out of a trance, Rozene turned sharply to face him for the first time.

"You're a disgusting old man, and I'll never marry you," she said with fierce conviction. Her eyes danced with that same defiant anger she had unleashed in the Elder's office.

Another flash of a different Rozene, one without fear. Amira knew immediately that Rozene would pay for that.

"No, you won't," the Elder said, and his cool, velvety voice carried more danger than all his armed henchmen combined. "You're no use to me now. But you can watch the others first."

He nodded to the group of men standing behind the girls. Wordlessly, they grabbed them and began tying them to wooden planks that had been lying nearby. Another man dug a series of shallow holes in the sand. When one of the girls realized what was happening, she tore away from her captor's grip and took a few steps before collapsing to the ground, falling to her hands and knees and wailing uncontrollably.

"Stop your squealing," Sarka said before grabbing Rozene by the hair and shoving her toward the remaining plank. She knelt in apparent shock, but as Amira drew closer to her, she could see that every joint and muscle in her body was trembling.

The first of the girls had been bound to a plank and was pushed backward into the first shallow hole, so that she remained on her back with her head in the crevasse and her feet lifted several inches off the ground. She lay in silence at that precarious angle, her arms limp underneath the bindings. The other two girls were placed in the same position with only their heads below ground, the one girl continuing to sob in shuddering gasps. Sarka grabbed each girl by the hair, one by one, and tipped a substance into their mouths. To Amira's surprise, it was not Chimyra, or any strain she had seen. Instead of the usual cloudy, blood-orange color, the liquid was clear, administered sparingly. As the men began to shovel sand over their faces, the real Rozene shuddered and twisted in her chair, a frightened gasp escaping from her throat.

"Talk me through what you're seeing, Rozene," Amira said, noting Rozene's heart rate spiking to alarming peaks on the monitor. "What happens next?"

As though on cue, Sarka finished tying Rozene up and pushed her with a kick of his foot into the last hole. The other three girls choked and gasped as the men shoveled silently and the sand crept across their faces. Sarka grabbed Rozene's face and she received her own dose of the strange substance.

"I can't!" Rozene cried.

Amira caught Rozene underneath her arms before she slid out of her chair.

Rozene coughed and spat imaginary sand away, her shoulders jerking in time to the scene in the hologram, to her own burial. The sand began to vibrate, the grains pulsing to a silent, terrible rhythm.

"I need air!"

"Rozene, keep breathing!"

Scarabs, red and black, emerged from the sand, crawling over Rozene. The girls beside her screamed.

"I can't breathe!"

"This will end soon. You have to let it happen."

"I need water!"

Amira ached to tell Rozene that it was all over, that they were in Westport and far from the Trinity's reach, but she knew that the memory had to be experienced, fully realized, to undo the damage done to Rozene's fractured subconscious. The strangled cries of the young women were unbearable, but Amira forced herself to keep looking. The men shoveled the last of the sand over Rozene's face.

Darkness blanketed the scene as the women's heads were fully submerged underground. Muffled sounds broke through the silence. The thud of desperate legs thrashing against wooden planks. Male voices, cold and amused, coming from somewhere far away. Nearer, muffled cries and coughs.

Amira's heart hammered. The entire room had turned pitch black, mirroring Rozene's time under the sand. It became more unbearable by the second. Rozene had to come up soon, to escape. She had survived, after all.

Finally, light streaked across the room as one of the men dragged Rozene by her feet out of the earth. The other girls had also been yanked from their makeshift graves. They retched and gasped for air, spitting out sand as they were wordlessly unbound. Too weak to stand, they rolled on the ground, shuddering and struggling to restore air to their lungs and wiping sand out of their eyes.

Out of the darkness, the scene resumed on the holomentic display. The men stood around them, mutely surveying their gruesome work. The Elder turned back to Sarka, his waxen features and clear blue eyes coming alive with a smile that froze Amira to her bones.

The wires on the Elder's temples illuminated, sending a blue, glowing current across his forehead and around his ears. He raised his arms in a slow, open arc, his thin fingers curling in time with his smile.

The four women rose from the ground to their feet in tandem, raised with a macabre flourish like vampires from a sandy coffin. Dazed, they turned to each other, when Rozene's arm swung like a deadweight and struck the girl beside her. The second girl turned to the third, ripping the front of her dress open, while the third responded with another lumbering strike.

The men howled with laughter as the women continued their jerking, marionette assault. Sarka clapped his hands like a child excited by a new toy, glancing at the Elder, whose temples shone like blue embers as he stared with deep concentration at his captives.

The fourth girl had lunged at Rozene and kicked her to the ground. The proximity to the sand that had nearly suffocated her sent Rozene into renewed terror, sputtering and shrieking as she writhed near the wooden plank.

The hologram, now encompassing the entire room, spun and tilted. The ground was falling, or they were rising, until the hologram shifted to a bird's eye view of the scene. Below, the compound men continued laughing as the four female bodies jerked and swung under the Elder's apparent command.

Amira stood up and marched into the center of the room. She stretched out her hands, tingling with adrenaline, and moved them together. The hologram disobeyed her and did not move the scene closer, remaining in the hovering position in the sky. Behind Amira, Rozene twisted in her seat.

"My mouth," Rozene muttered. "I taste metal."

Cold shock seized Amira. The taste of rust, the high vantage point. Amira knew this sensation. Heart pounding, she spun in space, scanning wildly around the room. Another familiar sensation seized her, and undoubtedly Rozene as well. Eyes upon her, watching, from somewhere unseen.

At that first sense of being watched, the hologram vanished. The ward became the ward again. Machines and counters rose from the floor like a dollhouse room, surreal in its mundane familiarity. Amira returned to the holomentic machine but before she could act further, the holographic image reappeared over the platform.

The view had shifted back to the ground, where the Elder now lowered his arms. The four women all collapsed in perfect unison. One of the men clapped Sarka on the shoulder.

"It worked," he said. "Just like they said."

"Silence," the Elder barked.

"Water," Rozene whispered. In the hologram, she pulled herself up on all fours before collapsing again, eyes dull with shock.

"Let this be a lesson you never forget," the Elder said. "You all sought to abandon your families and your faith for a life of sin. But that life is not what you imagine it to be. You may enjoy your freedom for a day, maybe even a year, but soon, you would drown in filth and descend to the Neverhaven, as you nearly did tonight."

He paused, smiling appreciatively at his closing metaphor, and walked back to the compound.

"Water," Rozene gasped again.

Amira brought a glass of water to Rozene's lips and held her head back carefully. The effect of the Oniria had not worn off yet, and she had to be brought out of her waking dream state slowly. The hologram had shrunk back to the platform and they were no longer in the desert. A series of images appeared and dissolved in rapid succession on the disc – the Elder leering at Rozene while she carried her water and blinked back the sun, the same man conversing quietly with her mother in the Hulls' kitchen, and then the Unveiling ceremony, three men's faces now clearly visible in the crowd. The hologram faded with a final sight – a young girl with long red hair running down a desolate highway in the direction of the setting sun.

When Rozene awoke, she immediately clutched the glass in Amira's hand, gulping water as though her throat were on fire.

While Rozene drank a second glass of water, Amira sat down, gripping her knees as she processed all that she had seen. The hidden memory, revealed at last. Torture, followed by a strange detachment that mirrored Amira's own experience at the Gathering. The holomentic display, failing as it had done during Amira's own Placement test. The Elder, fueled by a strange, glowing halo, commanding others as Elders could only dream of, although the impossible feats were likely an exaggeration from Rozene's active imagination. And a strange liquid, administered to Rozene and those other, wretched women, before the terror began. A thin, clear liquid, delivered in shivering drops.

Amira shuddered and closed her eyes. Was it possible? Was it the same liquid, Tiresia, that she had stolen for Hadrian?

"Amira?"

Rozene peered into Amira's face. Concern revealed itself behind her hooded eyes. Collecting herself, Amira drew her notepad toward them, leaving the cat-sized screen hovering between them while she conducted the post-session interview.

Rozene spoke clearly when Amira asked about her escape.

"At first, I was too afraid to try anything again," she said as Amira helped her back into her bed. "But a few weeks after…what happened, Elder Young – that was his name – decided he still wanted to marry me. He already had seven wives. I was locked in my room after they caught me, but my parents had to let me out after a while, to help with the chores. I crossed the mountains by our house the first morning."

"During the day?" Amira asked in surprise. Rozene nodded.

"It was risky because there was no cover, I know. But no one would notice if I was gone a few hours during the daytime, right? I had to fetch water and work in the gardens. After I made it over the mountain, I kept walking until I found the highway. They probably didn't notice I was gone until dinner."

"And you followed the highway north?"

"All night. It was terrible, I was so thirsty. I cried and tried to drink my own tears. I came to a bus station as the sun was coming up. I had no money, but I told the driver where I came from and he let me sleep on the bus. When I woke up, I was here in Westport."

"How do you feel now?"

Rozene ran her hands up and down her pregnant belly, pondering the question.

"My head feels clear at last," she said. "Like a weight inside me is gone and I can see properly again. Does that make sense? I'm so tired, though."

Something caught the corner of Amira's eye. Singh stood on the other side of the glass door, her arms folded. How much she had seen was unclear, but when their eyes met, she gave Amira an appraising nod and walked away.

Amira sat with Rozene for the remainder of the afternoon until Rozene finally drifted into a deep sleep. Amira replayed the Oniria session on the holographic platform, which continued to shift to the bird's eye view before the lapse in display, and paused at the final moments when Rozene returned to the Unveiling Ceremony, the three men revealed at last.

Amira downloaded the entire session onto a disc. She was now ready to visit Hadrian again, with his mysterious Tiresia. If the strange liquid in Rozene's memory and Tiresia were one and the same, Amira needed answers and had no desire to keep it in her possession. She also needed to unearth the remaining men's identities. Besides Elder Young, Rozene had recognized one of the other men but didn't know his name, only that he was 'powerful'. The third man was a stranger to her, though he looked familiar to Amira. She wasn't surprised to learn that Sarka wasn't one of the three figures in the front row; though he played a key role in Rozene's punishment, he was clearly a useful thug, not a compound power-player.

Amira stood still, hairs raising on the back of her neck. She sensed a strange shift in her surroundings, as though something had moved out of place, and turned back to the hologram in the room's center. The three men in their seats were no longer observing the podium on which Rozene stood.

Instead, their eyes locked directly on Amira. Not in her general direction, but on her, as though she were a figure in the auditorium.

Amira shrieked, leaping up from her chair. The men continued to stare at her, suspended in time. She froze as well, rooted to the ground as her heart immobilized in her chest, until she jerked forward to sprint toward the door. When she looked back after several steps, however, the moment had passed. The men resumed their original positions, eyes turned back to the spot where Rozene sat in penitence in the Trinity's auditorium.

Wordlessly, she removed the disc from the computer and left the room. What had happened? Had her mind, overburdened with stress after a long day, played a cruel trick on her? Holomentic readings did not interact with the reader beyond obeying commands to move, shrink or expand, but that gave Amira little comfort – either the impossible had occurred, or her hold on reality was starting to weaken, just as Rozene's had reversed course.

Valerie Singh met her in the hallway.

"I have some tests to run on M. Hull now that she's asleep," Singh said. "But the monitors in my office show stronger vitals, more in line with those of a normal pregnant woman at this stage. It looks as though it has been quite a day for you both."

"Her memories have been restored, from what I can see. Hopefully, she's out of the woods."

Singh smiled.

"Whether we are out of the woods or not, you've done a good day's work, M. Valdez. I suggest you leave on time today, for once." Still smiling, she passed a speechless Amira and entered into the ward.

★ ★ ★

"Do you have my payment?"

Amira held the vial of Tiresia triumphantly up to Hadrian's face and, in a swift motion, he swiped it out of her hand. He stared at the label, shaking the glass slightly.

"Ta, my dear," he said, handing the glass over to a solemn-looking boy of about seventeen. Hadrian addressed him as Lee, the same boy who had asked about Rozene on Amira's first visit to the ship. "Ok, that's your payment met – let's look at your little movie collection."

"Let's talk about the Tiresia and what it does."

"Unimportant and not your business."

"It is neither of those things," Amira snapped, again channeling Singh in her sharp voice. "I risked a lot to get it, and you're going to tell me what it is."

"All in good time, love, but not in front of the kiddos here. First, let's find out who your new friends are."

Hadrian possessed a surprisingly sophisticated computer system in the cruise ship's old gymnasium. In addition to the security apparatus monitoring the surrounding shipyard for intruders, the ship was equipped with a full three-dimensional holographic platform, although a more archaic version than the models in the Soma. A group of older teenagers set up the hologram. Hadrian shooed them all out of the room, except for Lee.

"Consider him mini-Hadrian," he said to Amira. "What I know, Lee knows. Near enough, anyway."

The hologram unfolded in the center of the room, car-sized, displaying the final image of the Oniria session. Rozene, head slumped at the center of a stage, the three men seated apart from their congregants. Lee grimaced and stood by Rozene, as though to protect her.

Hadrian circled the platform, scrutinizing the three men in the ceremony. The children chattered outside and Lee rapped the door in sharp warning.

Hadrian pointed to the man in the center.

"That's Elder William Young," Hadrian said definitively. "Most powerful man in the Trinity Compound. Got all the usual qualities of a good compound holy man – a little charm, some political know-how. Likes to keep company with scary men and little girls."

He leaned forward, the blue monitor light reflecting his face, and pointed at the dark-haired man on Elder Young's left, his gaunt face fixed on Rozene with hollow eyes. His frame was tall and wiry, but he gave off the impression of considerable strength, as though his every movement had purpose and calculation behind it.

"This charming chap here is Andrew Reznik. He's the good Elder's second in command. Dangerous motherfucker. The Trinity kids here have told me some stories that would make your hair stand up. I don't know what you're planning to do with all of this, love, but I hope your plans keep you far the fuck away from Andrew Reznik."

Amira leaned in closer to the hologram. While Young's posture was relaxed and authoritative, Reznik sat upright in his chair, as though poised for attack. What really struck Amira, however, was the lack of emotion on Reznik's face. His eyes were cold and unreachable, observing Rozene's humiliation with detached indifference. The longer Amira looked at Reznik, the more unsettlingly familiar he seemed. A sense of déjà vu.

The protest line outside of Aldwych. The skin on her arms tightened, shrinking as chilling realization struck her. She had seen him in the crowd, his cold eyes staring back at her with the same detachment he directed at Rozene. A Trinity man, Elder Young's deputy, lurking outside of the Soma.

Hadrian snapped his fingers and Amira turned back to the hologram.

The third figure, a middle-aged Asian man in a black suit, sat to Elder Young's right. Though his posture was alert, his face looked puffy. Hadrian studied the suited figure with narrow eyes, tilting his head as though hoping to gain some new insight from the man's polite, engaged expression.

"Now this is a riddle," he murmured softly, scratching his chin.

Amira nodded. She had noticed something odd about the man the minute his face was revealed.

"He's not compound," she said.

"No, he's not," Hadrian agreed, continuing to peer into the man's face. "That fancy suit, that smile of his.... He's a city boy, that's clear. Probably not used to the dry climate and the pollen, with that swollen nose of his. Not a convert either, I reckon. He's watching this shit show to be polite. See that look on his face? He's got no clue. He's out of his element here. No, I reckon he's some kind of guest of the good Elder there."

"But who is he, and what's he doing at the Trinity?" Amira asked. Lee shrugged.

"Your guess is as good as mine, love," Hadrian said. "But now you've got me interested. I'll see if any of my kids know anything, or if we can get an ID on him. If you've got any contacts who can put a name on the suit here, I'd start talking to them."

⋆ ⋆ ⋆

Amira's mind raced late into the night, long after the last students had stumbled into their rooms from the Riverfront bars. She gazed out the window, where the stars glimmered faintly through the cracks in the clouds. The earlier joy and relief at breaching the wall of Rozene's memories had proven short lived. Someone had gone to great lengths to keep the identities of those men secret, and now that she'd witnessed the horror of the Trinity Compound, Amira knew they had good reason.

That night, she dreamed of her own escape from the compound.

The memory was vivid, of moonlight reflecting off the New Covenant's glowing white buildings on a cloudless night, the Temple's spire reaching up to the heavens. Everyone had convened at the temple for the Ascension ceremony that night, to remember and attempt to see those who had ascended to the Nearhaven. Their chanting could be heard from the western walls, the first obstacle Amira climbed after escaping through her bedroom window. Since she was already under lock and key, no one would have expected her in the auditorium that night. The ceremony would keep her parents occupied – something big had happened in the cities, her mother warned, a sign of the end times that required fierce prayer – but Amira only had a narrow window of time in which to act.

Surrounded by dead grass and thirsty sagebrush, Amira crouched in the desert beyond the compound walls, skinny arms locked tight around her knees. Her airy blue dress provided little shelter from the night chill and her feet were bare, her white shoes suspended in barbed wire somewhere along the compound's walls. She dug her toes into the cool sand and waited.

She shivered and ran her fingers absent-mindedly over the thin scars across her palms, a reminder of that first escape attempt. Whatever the outcome, this one would be her last.

Amira traced the grim outline of the northern mountains as her eyes slowly adjusted to the dark. Without warning, her surroundings were illuminated when a piercing beam of light traveled across the ground in front of her. The searchlight passed over her head, inches away.

She crouched, motionless, against the prickly brush. She didn't dare breathe. Something caught the corner of her eye. Her muscles went rigid with fear.

A rattlesnake coiled within biting distance, stirring under the invading glow. It let out a low hiss.

Her heartbeat pounded in her ears.

The snake regarded the intruder with caution.

A silent prayer played on her lips. *Let it go on. Let me leave this place.*

After a moment of hesitation, the reptile recoiled back into the rocks.

She exhaled softly, returning her gaze to the beam's circular path.

Amira learned to welcome silence in her years of being locked away, in her room and sometimes the compound stables. Those long hours of confinement had prepared her for that moment, when opportunity struck.

The beam traveled around the other side of the compound's wall. The darkness returned and she ran.

She tore across the sand at breakneck speed. Without a flashlight to guide her, the desert flora turned against her and whipped mercilessly at her face and legs. She kept running, darting left and right, occasionally collapsing into the sand, only to pull herself up and continue the charge to the northwest range. The tattered backpack she carried over her shoulder, holding the barest of her possessions, began to weigh her down. Her chest burned and her sides ached as she ascended the mountain rim in long, steady strides. Each step was agony; the soles of her feet grew bloody under the relentless assault of rock and thorns. The salty grains of sand stuck to the open cuts and sent shooting pain through her ankles. Despite the pain, she did not slow down. This escape was different – she knew where to run and what she had to do.

When would they notice she was gone? No sirens sounded, only the fierce pounding of blood in her ears. Someone would surely check on her and trigger the alarms. Even her mother would alert the authorities without hesitation. The barbed wires and searchlights were secondary to the New Covenant's true strength: the watchful eyes of family and neighbors.

At the top of the ridge, Amira collapsed on her knees and sobbed, weak with exhaustion, her throat raw and ragged when she sucked in the cold air.

As she knelt in the sand, a distant, deep rumbling drew her eyes upward. The clouds above her had parted in a wide gash through which she could see the starry canvas of space and an enormous shuttle moving across the sky. In all her years of stargazing, she had never seen a shuttle this close. Though over a hundred miles above her, its red and blue lights flashed and translucent smoke streamed behind its roaring engines. Her arm stretched out almost involuntarily and for a fleeting second, her thin fingers reached up toward the glowing, propulsive object so far above her. In that solitary moment, she could see it all; its engines spinning while men and women in lab coats teemed behind egg-shaped windows. She stood rooted to the ground beneath her, weighed down by a sudden, powerful purpose. Her heart pounded at the base of her throat until the shuttle disappeared once again behind the clouds.

One day, she would go to space. Whatever purpose the universe had for her, she would find it there.

A nearer, more familiar engine growled, reverberating across the ground. She leapt to her feet like a deer at the sound of a gunshot. The lights of an all-terrain hovercraft traveled away from the compound's gates at a steady, unyielding pace across the desert like a hungry gull over water. A wild fear gripped her and she ran.

There was no alarm this time. No need to alert the entire compound if they did not intend for her to return. A single bullet would suffice, straight into a shallow, unblessed grave.

Amira charged forward with a speed she never knew possible. Her legs burned as she weaved through the jagged pines and boulders across the ridge. She was no longer running uphill. Her energy returned, fueled by adrenaline. She crossed the flat peak and stared down into a narrow gully in the mountains.

And there was the train, exactly where it was supposed to be. A secret from an unexpected ally – an aid worker who refused to let her hide in their convoy but revealed another opportunity for escape. He had told her the truth. Relief shot through her limbs. She could make it. She *had* to.

She raced toward the base of the rocky gorge along the dark, winding path. The train's engine bellowed, and she pushed herself faster down the steep gorge. But she teetered too far forward on the sloping land. She stumbled and crashed to the ground, sliding down the rock face as the momentum carried her downhill. She held her breath as her body flailed and crashed against rock. Somehow, she had to remain silent. A bitter taste flooded her mouth, something wet leaking from her lips. Blood, from biting her cheek. She scrambled to her feet, fighting back pain and rising panic. She couldn't stop now. Not this close.

A branch lashed the left side of her face and she careened diagonally down the valley on a bed of loose dirt and pine needles. When the ground flattened at the valley's base, she fell forward on her knees.

"I see her, she's there!" cried a man's voice behind her, triumphant.

The train was no more than one hundred feet away. The smell of diesel burned in her nostrils.

Freedom within her reach.

Amira jumped to her feet and raced for the nearest freight car. *Run*, she chanted in her head. *Run!*

A pair of spinning light beams flashed in front of her. She cast a fleeting glance over her shoulder.

The patrol had found her. The vehicle worked its way down the gorge, a pair of searchlights darting at its helm.

She locked her sights on the train and pushed harder, her lungs screaming for air.

Move, she mouthed desperately. *Please move.*

The train came to life with a jolt. Its wheels creaked and spun fitfully before lurching forward.

"Stop!" cried that same male voice, booming through a megaphone. "Stop the train!"

An adrenal, animalistic rush crashed over her, propelling her alongside the boxcar. Her hands reached out and gripped the ladder. Her feet flew off the ground. With the last of her strength, she swung her body toward the rail and pulled herself upward. A series of loud cracks rang against metal. Bullets. The patrol fired at her. She clung to the back of the freight car, arms and feet locked around the ladder rungs.

The train gained speed.

More gunfire sprayed the side of the train. Ricocheted near her, over her head, within inches of her body. The patrol vehicle glided alongside the train but lost ground quickly.

Straining her neck, Amira finally turned her head to face her pursuers. The lights of the hovercraft grew smaller and dimmer in the dark of the desert. As the train turned a sharp north over the mountains, she allowed herself to believe, at last, that she was free. She tugged at the veil around her hair, releasing it into the fluttering wind. Elation flooded her chest. Tears broke free and streamed down her cheeks. She had made it. The compound, its Elders, Chimyra, and disciples, held no power where she was going. She clung to the ladder with weakening arms, letting a long-suppressed sob erupt from her chest. For the first time, she breathed in free air.

CHAPTER NINE

Entropy

Jessica Alvarado and Nina Leakey died on June 14, 2226 and June 27, 2226, respectively, days shy of their third trimesters. As a result, when Rozene entered the third trimester and her pregnancy was officially pronounced 'stable', the reaction in Pandora was triumphant. Naomi whistled at her desk, Amira received warm nods of recognition in the Soma's hallways, and even Singh carried a certain bounce to her step. D'Arcy and the quantum programming team congratulated the cloning team as only they could, posting a Stream message from the Nineveh satellite in the Asteroid belt, complete with a montage of viral baby videos. Eventually, the team boldly announced its lack of failure, the headline reading, 'Birth of First Human Clone Approaches as Healthy Subject Enters Final Trimester'. The story ran across the Soma's exterior screen, where it was greeted with jeers and shouts of derision by protesters outside. The remainder of Aldwych welcomed the news – the entire district had felt the effects of the controversy surrounding Pandora and welcomed a positive headline.

Parrish returned to the Carthage station after thanking the team. The blockade of the station was lifted with no explanation of why it had been instated in the first place. The Stream reported that all appeared normal at the Carthage, as much as a prison research facility could be considered normal.

The upbeat mood on floor 235 even infected Rozene, already improved in mind and body after the last, fateful Oniria session. The weight of her fractured past removed, Rozene's troubles shifted to the more typical complaints of a young woman in her final weeks of pregnancy – aching limbs, the oppressive weight, fear of the moment of birth and the chaotic months that would follow.

"Feeling better today?" Amira asked upon entering the ward.

Rozene did not reply, engrossed in the screen resting on her formidable belly, round and firm as a hard-boiled egg. Amira leaned over her shoulder to find a series of Stream articles on baby names running across the monitor.

"Names from ancient mythology," Amira said softly. "Scientific pioneers who changed the world. Notable characters in fiction to give your baby a unique name."

Rozene looked up with a mischievous smile.

"I can't believe Dr. Singh's letting me name the baby."

"Well, it is yours," Amira said, laughing. Rozene beamed, her face brighter than Amira had ever seen.

"I know," Rozene said. "But it's a big deal. Her name will be in history books, every textbook on biology and genetics to come."

Amira gave Rozene's shoulder an affectionate squeeze, hearing Singh's voice behind Rozene's words.

"Have you decided on a name?" Amira asked.

"I think I have," Rozene said, grinning.

"You're not going to tell me, are you?"

"I'll keep this one to myself," Rozene said.

Of course Rozene craved privacy, so cruelly denied during her long pregnancy. Her innermost secrets laid bare under Amira's holomentic talents. As Amira's own dreams continued to plague her, she tried to record them on the archaic holomentic machine she took on loan from the Academy. D'Arcy had walked into her room to find Amira sitting cross-legged on the floor, a burning house on display on her computer monitor. Amira told D'Arcy she was watching Stream viral videos, another lie that rolled off her tongue but left a bitter aftertaste.

Sparkes rolled into the ward, carrying a tray of pills.

"At least I'm off the sedatives," Rozene said, swallowing back the pastel cocktail of medication. Sparkes remained by the door, pacing back and forth.

"I asked if Sparkes could keep an extra eye on you," Amira said by way of explanation. Rozene caught Amira's dark look of warning and nodded with grim understanding. Neither had forgotten the masked figure with the syringe. The intruder, whoever it was, clearly meant Rozene or her clone harm.

The aura of celebration in the Soma enveloped Amira, but she resisted its pull, unable to completely sink into its comfort. Though free from the effects of the tampered memory, Rozene was not out of the woods, as the memory itself had revealed. The person who had tried to harm Rozene remained out there, perhaps within the walls of the Soma itself, perhaps plotting their next move.

★ ★ ★

It was well after sunset when she returned to the Riverfront. The residents of the Canary House had converged on the common area for Singh's highly anticipated interview on the Stream. Students pressed themselves mercilessly together on worn couches and spilled over onto the floor, exchanging drinks, Academy-approved macrobiotic snacks and predictions for the hour-long exclusive with the Pandora project's figurehead. After weeks of feigning ignorance and resisting questions from her fellow students, Amira was more excited than anyone for the status of Pandora to go public.

Julian and D'Arcy greeted Amira excitedly when she entered the common area. Amira found a spot on the thinly carpeted floor, which reeked of stale beer. Several students shared meaningful glances as Amira took her seat.

"Do you know what she'll be saying, Amira?" D'Arcy squeezed in tightly with Julian and two others in a large armchair.

"Not really," Amira replied, accepting a beer from a classmate. "I know she's not looking forward to it, though."

"Well, it's not her job," Julian said. "Doing the rounds, talking to reporters who want to take her down. Everyone's tuning in for a bloodbath."

"This is Westport, not the compounds or the dark ages," Amira retorted. "They might ask her tough questions, but it won't be like that. She's one of the greatest living scientists."

Julian sighed and D'Arcy shot him a warning look.

"I just think you see this place with a rosy tint is all, Amira," Julian said warily. "Westport isn't a fucking utopia where everything is fair and civilized, and because of where you came from, you forget that. You want to see the best of this place, but women still have it bad, working people like D'Arcy's dad still suffer. It's the same shit in a shinier package."

"There is no comparison!" Amira said with vehemence, thinking back to Rozene's memory in the desert, the sand covering the young girls' pale, frightened faces. No matter how many stories she shared of the compounds, Julian would never truly understand what it meant to live through it, to survive girlhood within their walls. For all their self-professed enlightenment, the people of Westport clung to their preconceptions like torches, waving them in the air but ignoring the puddles of darkness they couldn't reach, the corners of human experience they couldn't understand.

Someone made a bowl of popcorn and D'Arcy passed it along to Amira with an apologetic smile. Amira shrugged. She liked Julian, but he reminded her of a child in a kitchen, trying to touch things even though they had burned him once. He never knew when to leave something unsaid, or didn't care enough to hold back. But this night was about Pandora, her and D'Arcy's moment. She accepted a handful of popcorn, a peace offering.

The noise of the crowd died down. Someone retrieved the live Stream feed from their Eye and projected it onto the screen. In moments, a three-dimensional Valerie Singh materialized in front of them, sitting cross-legged with folded arms in what Amira immediately recognized as the inner courtyard of the Soma building. The camera had been angled so that protesters remained hidden from view.

The interviewer for the exclusive was Harrison Harvey, a former biologist turned media personality known more for his flamboyant outfits and headline-grabbing statements than for his research contributions. He sat opposite Singh in a lilac suit that immediately sent D'Arcy into fits of laughter. Amira was impressed by Singh's ability to keep an impassive expression on her face as he slicked back his paper-white hair, cleared his throat loudly and began.

"Good evening, Westport, and hello, world! I come to you tonight from the imposing Mendel-Soma complex in Aldwych, the beating heart of Westport.

"I am joined here by the pioneering geneticist whose breakthrough work removed cancer from our genetic code. Her research has lengthened our lives, and now she seeks to fundamentally change how we create new life under the always fascinating, always boundary-pushing Pandora project, in which she is attempting to produce the first fully formed human clone."

He turned to Singh and continued in a melodramatic, somber tone.

"But the Pandora project has not been without struggle and tragedy. Last summer, Westport was rocked by the deaths of two young women who bravely volunteered for the project. Many began to question both the feasibility of the Pandora project's cloning method and the regard for the safety of its subjects. However, the news from the Soma tonight is only positive, with reports that the anonymous subject now has a clean bill of health as she enters the third trimester. Is that correct, Dr. Singh?"

Valerie Singh cleared her throat.

"It is. Both the mother and fetus are doing well. We are monitoring her closely, but I am highly confident that there will be no further issues in the final trimester. The first human clone will arrive into the world safely."

The room broke into excited chatter, as many looked back at Amira for confirmation. Julian leaned forward and gave Amira a congratulatory pat on the shoulder, but she continued to watch Singh.

"What exciting news!" Harvey said.

"We owe our success to an excellent team that includes—"

"Hold, please, just one moment, Dr. Singh," Harvey interjected airily. "Before we take a break for our sponsor for the night, Namaste Superjuice – Empower and cleanse your life! Now, we're bringing our viewers an exclusive look inside the famous Soma building with the project's brainchild, Alistair Parrish."

The screen then cut to a recording of Harrison Harvey and Alistair Parrish conversing as they sauntered through the Soma's main walkway.

"I'm sorry, Amira," D'Arcy whispered. "Do you think Dr. Singh was going to mention you by name?"

"No idea," Amira said before she downed the remainder of her pilsner and reached toward the coffee table for a second drink. She never cared for the heavy craft beers popular in the Canary House, but the cool drink countered the rising heat in her face. She could only imagine Singh's reaction to the glowing attention given to Parrish, who had spent most of the project's duration thousands of miles above them.

"Dr. Singh," Harvey continued. "Given all of the controversy and tragedy surrounding the Pandora project, I must ask this question – do we even need human cloning? Is it worth the hurdles to attempt such an endeavor? Cloning is still banned in most countries and is a universally unpopular idea."

Singh carried a hint of a smile as he spoke, polite but masking subtle irritation at the question. Without missing a beat, she nodded her head.

"There are many benefits to human cloning that go beyond the obvious," she said. "It opens the floodgates for a further understanding of our genetic makeup, which can lead to cures for diseases and even slow down the aging process. However, the most important implication of cloning, for me at least, is its ability to combat infertility and liberate women from the biological shackle of motherhood to which they are now constrained. We live much longer lives than our ancestors did, we study and work longer than ever, but women still have a narrow time window in which to reproduce. With cloning, according to the model that Pandora is pursuing, that will change to the benefit of all women."

Someone behind Amira let out a low whistle. "Lady had that one rehearsed."

"Interesting that you should bring that up," Harvey said. "Because many of your critics – and there are many – argue that your agenda is to change the very fabric of our society with your project, by allowing women to reproduce *completely* without the, ah, assistance of men. To remove the need for men, you could say. Females creating copies of themselves. What if that becomes the new order of things, and we have women outnumbering men by overwhelming numbers? Couldn't men become extinct?"

"Is this real?" D'Arcy asked in disgust over the jeers of other students.

As she watched some of the male students stare intently at the screen, Amira realized that the question was a valid one for many viewers beyond the Canary House, a question that spoke to their own anxieties about a world with cloning.

"The current cloning method uses female embryo replication, it's true," Singh said. "For the first replication attempt, we intend to use the simplest and safest approach, which is a subject hosting a clone of their own DNA. Of course, once the technology is proven successful, we envision being able to modify the early genetic code as we do now with standard pregnancies, where we can determine a host of different factors – eye color, skin tone and, of course, biological sex. In other words, male clones will become a reality someday."

"Someday. What do we do until then?"

"I doubt this will replace the conventional method of reproduction anytime soon," Singh responded drily. "But what it does do is provide women with alternatives that allow them to have children on their own time and on their own terms."

"But some may not see it that way, Dr. Singh."

"Are we supposed to slow down human progress to protect a few male egos?"

An uncomfortable silence followed. Harvey sputtered as he attempted to formulate a counterattack. Singh sat patiently, her eyebrows slightly raised in a parody of polite interest.

"Well, she's not going to make any new friends tonight," Julian said under his breath.

"I don't know about that," D'Arcy said. "I'm liking her a lot more now."

Amira's beer was empty again. As she returned from the kitchen with a cranberry vodka, Harvey continued to press his argument from a different angle.

"Dr. Singh, you say your motives for this controversial project are about strengthening options for women, not weakening men?"

"Of course. Presumably, one can happen without the other."

"Was that always your view?"

"Excuse me?"

"I have here—" Harvey raised a thick paper document with a theatrical flourish, "—an article you produced back when you were a student in Mexico City. In it, you address—"

"How exactly is this relevant?" Though she appeared calm, there was no mistaking the irritation in her voice.

"All I'm doing is quoting your own words. Let me continue then, doctor. In your paper, which is titled 'On Reproduction and the Modern Woman', you include the following text – and viewers, I am quoting Valerie Singh verbatim, you can find old copies of her article all over the Stream – in which you state:

Though it may run contrary to emotion and remain unpopular to say so, women have been shackled by the burden of motherhood throughout history and they remain shackled to this day. For millennia, religion and social structures have defined women first and foremost as vessels of reproduction. In present times, as women navigate their way through education, the professional world, and an increasingly revolving door of relationships and pseudo-relationships, the ever-present question hovers over them, the albatross of femininity – should I, will I, have a child? Am I complete, loved, self-actualized without this step of life, though it is one that will constrain me physically, emotionally, intellectually?

The brave new age of modern genetics promises to eliminate the burden of continuing the human race from women's shoulders. Asexual reproduction is the first step, allowing us to reproduce without the aid of men completely, the final and ultimate goal being the divorcing of childbirth from the female body.

Harvey looked up from his papers gravely, his animated demeanor replaced with a stern solemnity.

"How do you respond, Dr. Singh, to these revelations?"

"This is no revelation," Singh snapped. "As you just said, it is all over the Stream. I had many views as a young student that I no longer have now. I'm sure the same could be said of many people."

"You must have changed somewhat, because only five years after this article was published, you gave birth to your first and only child, Maya. The same Maya Parrish who our viewers know was victim to a terrible tragedy years ago."

An unpleasant knot tightened in Amira's stomach and she took a drink, finding only bitter ice in her glass. She twisted back to the coffee table to pour another cranberry vodka, minus the cranberry.

When Singh offered no response, Harvey continued.

"Did you ever consider her, at the time, to be a shackle?"

D'Arcy gasped. Julian shook his head. The entire common area was silent, waiting breathlessly for Singh's response.

The camera zeroed in on Singh's face, which remained composed and firm.

"I will not take part in this distasteful circus," she said coldly. "Since you clearly have no interest in the topic at hand, this interview is over."

She smoothly removed the microphone from her collar and walked away.

"Holy shit," Julian breathed as sporadic applause broke out in the common room.

"Of course they had to try to bring her down a peg," D'Arcy fumed as she extracted herself from the tangle of bodies on the armchair. "And did Alistair Parrish get any of those questions? No, and he owns the project!"

The room was spinning, the floor swaying from side to side like a ship's deck in turbulent waters. Amira's glass was empty again – she needed to slow down. The noise of the chattering crowd, excitedly discussing what had just transpired, rang in her ears as she stood up. She reached sideways to the wall for balance, veering toward the entrance.

The remainder of the evening was a disconnected puzzle of lost hours, snapshots of time interspersed with periods of darkness. In one moment, she and D'Arcy argued heatedly behind the mossy walls of the Canary House.

"I can't believe you're defending what Julian said," Amira remonstrated, loud and slurring.

"That's not what I meant," D'Arcy said. "All I said was that the way Valerie Singh was treated just now is what Julian was talking about. A powerful woman getting taken down a notch, it happens even in Westport."

"You have no idea how good you've had it," Amira said. She stumbled slightly, lifting her glass to keep it steady. "This city saved my life, but people here don't understand...." She paused, fumbling for the right words.

"We're your friends, Amira. Julian and I. We want you to be happy, we just think you tend to see things in black and white, and it's going to hurt you."

"Julian thinks he knows the compounds better than I do," Amira said, raising her voice. "And you treat me like a child because you see me as one. Forever stunted by where I came from."

"That's not true, Amira!" D'Arcy said in a tearful voice.

"It is," Amira said. "You take his side because you agree with him! You see me as a child. I'll always just be that backwater compound girl, no matter what I do."

She tore herself free from D'Arcy's grip and marched down an alleyway. She drained the remaining contents of her glass, warm liquid spilling down the sides of her mouth. Distant shouts followed her along the canals on the way to Infinity Park. Instead of entering the park, she changed direction and stalked to the nearest subway station. A sharp smell of garbage greeted her at the entrance and she staggered to a trash can. She leaned over and vomited forcefully inside it. She followed the crowds to the Red line and stumbled onto the westbound train, ignoring the jeers and catcalls around her, before everything went dark again.

When Amira regained her senses, she felt eyes on her, though she could not make out faces through her blurry, unfocused vision. Someone was holding on to her arm and steering her forward, and she cooperated as best she could.

"Hadrian!" A young male voice called out. "We need your help."

Someone placed her in a chair with a bottle of water in her hands, which she immediately, gratefully depleted. It had a distinct tangy flavor Amira recognized from other regrettable nights as Bottled Rehab, a popular brand of enhanced water designed to speed up sobriety and prevent hangovers. A second bottle found its way into her hands and as she continued to drink, the room came into focus. She was on Hadrian's ship, in the main mezzanine near the entrance. Lee, the quiet teenager who ran Hadrian's computers, hovered close by, watching her with solemn, paternal concern. Behind Lee, young teenagers of both sexes ran around the mezzanine, stumbling in fits of wild laughter across the hallways. Bottled Rehab was undoubtedly in perpetual demand on Hadrian's ship.

"Our fearless visitor returns," a familiar voice said, and Hadrian's face suddenly loomed into her line of vision. He was wearing his contact lenses, his eyes red in the corners, and a security badge gleamed on his blue jacket, suggesting a recent return from NASH.

"How – how did I get here?" Amira asked, the words sticking in her throat.

"My boy Lee found you skulking around outside," Hadrian cackled. "Letting your hair down tonight, love? Didn't think you'd be the type to let the drink overpower you, but you look like a girl fresh out of the compound. Can't hold your liquor after all this time in Westport?"

Amira opened her mouth to retort, but closed it as her stomach lurched and the room spun again.

"I'll take her to one of the safe rooms," Lee said, lifting Amira gently by her arms.

"It's where we take the girls and the occasional bloke who've had too much, to keep them from making decisions they'll regret more than a little," Hadrian said with a smile, as Amira stepped forward carefully. "You need to sleep this one off."

Through her inebriated haze, Amira smiled back.

"You're not that bad, are you?" she asked dreamily, slumping against Lee.

"Don't tell the others," Hadrian said with a wink.

Amira, with significant support from Lee, passed a narrow entryway into the ship's sleeping quarters. At the end of the hall, two older teenage girls stood side by side, one armed with what appeared to be a high-grade stun weapon, likely a gift from Hadrian's NASH inventory. The girls nodded at Lee and stepped aside.

Through a cracked door, a young girl of about thirteen, still wearing her compound head-cover, sat on the edge of her bed and sobbed loudly. In the next room down the corridor, an older girl in a bright, sequined tube top lurched forward to slam the door but not before revealing pinpoint-sized pupils behind cloudy eyes – the unmistakable effects of Elysium.

"All stages of life on display," Amira murmured. She winced at her incoherence, but Lee seemed to understand her and nodded.

"Everyone's excited when they first come here," he said. "Then they try to be free for the first time, and it's too much when you've never had it before, and the freedom scares them. Some go back and forth, between the old ways and the new."

"And then you learn that the new world isn't what you thought it was," Amira said with bitterness. They had found an empty room and she collapsed onto the bed. "The perfect world that kept you going every night, that gave you the courage to escape, doesn't exist and all you get are new battles to fight."

The room was no longer spinning, but faces emerged and vanished in her mind's eye – D'Arcy, Harrison Harvey, the twisted faces of angry demonstrators outside the Soma – and she swatted angrily at the air.

Lee sat on the end of the bed, eyes fixed downward.

"Rozene talked like that before she left," he said. "She used to come here a lot, to the safe rooms. It was too wild for her out there. She left the Trinity because she wanted peace."

"You care about her a lot, don't you?" Amira asked softly, her voice teasing. "Were you in love with her?"

Lee's ears turned pink. He fixed his gaze on the floor, the carpet patterned in colors reminiscent of vomit, of which the floors had undoubtedly seen plenty.

"I just want her to be happy," he said. "She was my friend when she was here – she was kind even though she was unhappy. She deserves to be happy. Is she going to be ok?"

Lee finally faced Amira, his expression anxious and searching, and Amira immediately regretted teasing him moments ago. She patted his shoulder awkwardly.

"She will be," she murmured. "We'll see to that, together."

Her promise delivered, she closed her eyes and surrendered to exhaustion.

★ ★ ★

Amira left in the early hours of the morning, before the ship began to stir. She couldn't stomach Hadrian's inevitable mockery over her behavior the previous night. She could barely stomach the bottle of water in her hand, each sip churning a tempest of nausea that overwhelmed her senses. Better to retreat and nurse the tattered shreds of her dignity alone.

The window in Amira's room at the Canary House was slick with the steady rainfall that blanketed Westport on spring afternoons. The low purr of the water against the glass was soothing, almost hypnotic, but did nothing to abate the cruel pounding in Amira's head. Bottled Rehab, despite its assurances, failed to reverse the consequences of the previous night. The headache was minor compared to the sickening sensation of guilt over her fight with D'Arcy. D'Arcy's room was empty when Amira returned in the early hours of the morning, so she had likely spent the night in Julian's dorm on the third floor. Wherever she was, Amira would have an apology ready once she materialized.

Amira sat cross-legged on her bed, against all the protests of her aching body. In front of her, a small hologram rose through her computer monitor, bearing Dr. Mercer's face.

"I doubt the great Valerie Singh is losing sleep over whatever comes out of that clown Harvey's vacuous mouth," Mercer said. "I wouldn't overinflate last night's debacle in your mind."

"I took it pretty hard," Amira said drily, massaging her temples.

"I'll spare you the lecture," Mercer said. "Let's talk about more important things."

"Pandora."

"I'm thrilled that the crisis was averted on Pandora, no doubt in part due to your talents," Mercer said. His voice rang out in static fits through the hologram, so Amira had to lean forward attentively to follow him. "But give me the real story, without the Aldwych spin – will this girl really give birth to the first human clone? Did you discover why the earlier attempts failed?"

"Dr. Mercer, please promise me you won't share this with anyone."

"I'll take it to the grave. Henry, too." Henry had made several brief appearances in the outer edges of the hologram, but to Amira's relief did not participate in the conversation.

Amira revealed the discovery of Rozene's tampered memories.

"Tampered? As in deliberately, maliciously tampered?"

"Definitely tampered. I used waking Oniria therapy to resurface them."

"Ah, clever! Not a conventional approach."

"I got the idea from you. Advanced Holomentic Interpretation, in my fifth year."

"And when you uncovered these memories, did you reveal who the culprit may be?"

Amira hesitated. To tell Dr. Mercer everything – the horrors of the Trinity Compound, the mysterious visitor at the Revival ceremony and the shadowy figure who hovered over Rozene in the night – would jeopardize his safety.

"I don't know who did it exactly," she said. "But someone on Pandora must be helping, someone with access to the Soma. I don't know who to trust."

"It's Aldwych, my dear. Trust no one."

"I wonder if the Cosmics are connected to all of this somehow," Amira said, recalling the heated exchange between Dr. Parrish and Tony Barlow at Infinity Park.

"Interesting, although make sure you're not mistaking their ubiquitous presence in Aldwych for complicity or involvement. But tell me, why do you think so?"

"Alistair Parrish is one," Amira said thoughtfully. "But he's in charge of Pandora, so why would he sabotage his own project? Tony Barlow might be one as well. I'm not sure."

"Tony Barlow?" Dr. Mercer asked, surprised. "Barlow is on Pandora?"

"He is, but I don't know his role. Dr. Singh called him a consultant. Do you know him?"

"From long ago."

When Mercer did not elaborate, Amira continued.

"I've wondered about him. He said something that suggested a connection to the compounds."

In the hologram, Mercer leaned back in his chair, his face wary and grim through the static blur.

"Tony Barlow's area of interest is consciousness, and in that area, he is exceptional. His interest in the compounds began years before when he studied the effects of human prayer on the mind. No doubt he has an agenda on Pandora, whatever it may be. But I would be shocked if he were involved in the unpleasantness you have uncovered."

"But who then?" Amira sat upright, reaching for a cold cup of coffee perched on the windowsill. "The compounds hate the idea of cloning more than anything else in the cities. I remember when there was first talk about legalizing human cloning. They thought the end times were coming. Women reproducing without men, and who knew if those cloned babies would be admitted to the Nearhaven? So whoever is doing all of this must be connected to the compounds, right? These girls all escaped the compounds and could have spoken publicly about life there. They were also part of a project that the Elders would do anything to stop. What if someone decided to kill them to take care of both problems together?"

"A good theory."

"But what am I missing?"

"Maybe nothing. But remember that it is not only the compounds that take issue with human cloning. You and I live in something of a bubble, Amira, and outside of it, there are many people from all walks of life who have anxieties about this project and what it means. And frankly, with these mysterious deaths and Valerie Singh's *myopic* mishandling of public opinion, this project hasn't done much to calm their nerves."

Amira nodded, thinking back to the fervid demonstrators she passed each morning, angry men and women with no connection to the compounds. No obvious connection, at any rate. But many Cosmics had come from the compounds, forging another way of living from its teachings, adapting them for the cities. They evolved into a new community. Just as D'Arcy had evolved from collecting scrap metal in Sullivan's Wharf. Only she, Amira, remained an oddity within this chameleon-like city, unable to blend in or plant her drifting feet on solid ground.

Amira shook herself back to the holo conversation.

"Things have relaxed a lot at the Soma since Rozene's health scare ended, but the protests haven't stopped. They're actually worse. A few people were even arrested yesterday."

"Yes, Henry and I have seen footage on the Stream when I bother to connect into it," Mercer said. "In a way, the project is even more of a threat to its many critics now that it is actually succeeding. The concern for the girls was genuine for some and a bit of a red herring for others, an opportunity to show that cloning is a doomed endeavor. I hope there are still those wise enough in the Soma to see that Pandora is not out of the woods yet. Far from it."

As Amira readied to sign off, something pressed into her thoughts. Something she couldn't ignore, that haunted her sleep and gnawed at her waking hours. Mercer, more than anyone else, might be able to help her.

"Dr. Mercer, I've been having these strange dreams. The same dream over and over again. A house on fire. The house and the place always change, but it always ends the same way."

"What is your reaction when the house catches on fire?"

"Fear," she said. "Terrible fear, the sensation of heat, and then I wake up."

"Before your brain is forced to simulate pain, which almost never occurs in a dream – almost never."

"Am I going crazy?" she asked. "None of it makes sense."

"I know you," Mercer said with a smile. "I know how your mind works. You're wondering if these are preconjective dreams you're experiencing."

"Is that possible?"

"I don't see why not," he said. "But don't let these questions and doubts consume you, Amira. Push the dreams aside and focus on the facts. I sense you're keeping me at arm's length, for whatever reason, but I urge you not to. You say you uncovered memories from this woman's past – law prohibits you from sharing this outside of Pandora, of course, but if you can send me anything to investigate, I will. Henry and I will look into the Cosmics further, in case there is a connection. In the meantime, take care of yourself, my dear. You are never alone."

CHAPTER TEN

Rock and Thunder

The Soma building's courtyard transformed into a place of celebration as Aldwych's most prominent luminaries prepared for the clone's arrival. The attendees included politicians, scientists, journalists and academics, sipping cocktails and exchanging pleasantries on a warm afternoon. Members of the Aldwych Council were all present, with the noticeable absence of Alistair Parrish, who had not been seen in public in recent weeks, and the head of the Volta station, Victor Zhang, whose disappearance was discussed less with each passing day. Life in Westport moved quickly, and with a lack of new developments on Zhang's whereabouts, the story soon moved from a main headline into the bowels of the Stream, where conspiracists shared theories around kidnapping, staged kidnapping and other forms of Aldwych-based intrigue.

The subject of the party herself, naturally, remained on the 235th floor, far removed from the festivities. After less than an hour of polite small talk with vaguely familiar faces, Amira grew restless. Before long, she found herself back in the ward, sitting awkwardly on the foot of Rozene's bed while her black cocktail dress crawled up her thighs. D'Arcy and Naomi joined them as well, and the four women shared slices of cake and stories while Sparkes dreamily paced the length of the ward's entrance.

"Are you allowed?" Rozene asked as Amira handed her a slice of cake. "Wait, of course you are." She flushed.

"No more rationing for me," Amira said with a smile. She turned to D'Arcy and Naomi, smiling at their perplexed faces. "Non-pregnant women on the compounds are usually subject to a strict diet once you turn thirteen. We use Nutrient-Sensors, like they have here in the cities, to track calories, macronutrients and expended joules. Keeps girls thin for the Elders, but also gives an incentive for married women to be pregnant as much as possible."

Naomi shuddered, zealously attacking her own slice of cake. D'Arcy glanced at Amira and raised her glass of wine with a tight, apologetic smile. No, D'Arcy and Julian had no idea what compound life was like. Maybe D'Arcy was beginning to understand. With that concession, Amira tilted her own glass in a silent toast, burying their argument.

Rozene cast nervous smiles at her new guests but appeared grateful for the company. D'Arcy had not yet met Rozene, being confined to unrelated programming work on the first floor, and Amira watched with quiet pleasure as they developed an easy rapport. Rozene spoke little, however, listening with growing amusement while Naomi animatedly recounted the story of a demonstrator outside of the Soma who caused a scene by breaching the security perimeter. Like Amira, Naomi had already worked her way through several glasses of wine, punctuating her story with high-pitched giggles and pauses for recollection.

"So once he breaks through the barrier, he runs in right through the door – big guy, six-foot-four and scary looking. He's holding this picture of a little baby with two heads and something like hooves for feet, the works! They've gotten more creative with their posters the last few months. Anyway, everyone in the lobby freaks out, of course, and he sees Dr. Singh in line for coffee and goes right for her. I'm standing by the elevator, thinking she's in trouble and wondering where security is and if we even have real security. He's charging at her, his face all red and angry, and she turns around and gives him this look."

Naomi straightened up and did her best impression of Valerie Singh's most contemptuous expression, sending Amira and Rozene into fits of laughter. D'Arcy, less familiar with Dr. Singh, stifled a giggle. Amira finished her glass. Memories of her last tangle with alcohol fresh in her mind and stomach, Amira had started the evening with Bottled Tolerance, the less popular cousin of Bottled Rehab, to dull the effects of the wine.

"And he just freezes. Here's this giant man, holding this awful picture in his hands, and she says 'Yes?' and he slouches over like he's a kid being scolded for stealing cookies! They stand there like that for a minute and the entire lobby is just silent. It's never that quiet – even when we leave here at midnight! After a while, he says something to the effect, 'You're doing the Devil's work', throws the picture at her, and runs back outside."

"And what did Dr. Singh do then?" Amira asked, still chortling.

"Oh, she just grabbed her coffee, kind of raised one eyebrow like she does, and walked on by like nothing had happened."

"She's officially become my hero," D'Arcy said. "That interview with Harrison Harvey was a start, but this seals the deal."

"What would it take to get a reaction out of that woman?" Amira mused, relieved to be back on comfortable terms with D'Arcy.

Rozene looked at them with a conspiratorial smile. "I wouldn't want to find out," she said.

As Naomi and D'Arcy left to get more cake downstairs, Rozene's mood turned introspective.

"I'm afraid I'm not ready for all of this," she said, running her hand along her belly.

"Oh, Rozene, don't worry," Amira said. "This is one of the best places in the world to give birth, despite everything. Now that you're better, the labor will be fine."

"No, it's not the labor that bothers me. I've seen plenty of them in the Trinity. I know what's coming. It's what happens afterward – what if there's something wrong with it? What if it isn't normal?"

"The baby? Of course it will be!"

"You don't know that," Rozene said quietly. "I saw stories on the Stream when I was looking up names.... No one knows what she'll be like because this has never happened before. And what if... what if my problems have hurt her somehow?"

Amira took a pausing breath, formulating her words carefully.

"You're right," Amira said, noting how Rozene described her impending child as 'her' for the first time. "We don't know for sure. But I have faith in Dr. Singh on this. And if she isn't normal, would you love her any less?"

Rozene shook her head. "I know I signed up for it," she said. "And I knew she wouldn't live a normal life. But I'm worried about all the tests she'll go through, now that I've been through them. I want her to be happy. Jessica and Nina – the other two girls – talked about that a lot. Did you know them?"

Amira shook her head.

"They were from the Trinity as well," Rozene said. "But I didn't know them back on the compound. They had escaped before me, so of course I only heard terrible things about them. Harlots, spies, the usual. We became friends on Hadrian's ship, but they both joined Pandora a week after I met them. I signed up later, when things got too hard. As bad as it was, I'm glad I got to spend time with them again, before...summer happened. I think they'd be happy to see me better. They would have liked you."

They sat in silence, air shuttles traversing Westport through the expansive window. Amira would have liked them, too, if they were anything like Rozene. Smoke and fog choked the sky that day, countless lights from the panorama of buildings blinking through the haze. No matter what the elements threw at Westport, the city embraced it, made it a character in the landscape.

Before Amira took the elevator to the ground floor, leaving Rozene with Sparkes for company, she noticed that neither D'Arcy nor Naomi had returned yet. Perhaps Dr. Singh had forced them to remain at the party.

Amira considered whether it was worth the risk to refill her wine glass. But given all that she had overcome with Rozene in the last few weeks, small talk with a few Aldwych dignitaries seemed like a benign challenge. Especially in exchange for another drink. She called the elevator.

Halfway to the ground level, an alarm sounded.

The elevator came to an abrupt halt. Amira jolted violently. Her raised hands hit the wall. The main lights went out and a small emergency light flickered on above the elevator buttons. She pulled the circuit box back, hoping desperately for a manual override. She fumbled for several seconds, and then found a narrow lever that opened the doors. She pried them apart. The elevator had stopped halfway between floors, so she slid out to exit, cursing her tight dress and heels.

The alarms stopped.

She stood on the mezzanine just above the main ground floor.

The vast, echoing room was completely silent. The hairs on Amira's arms and neck stood to attention and a dizzying wave of apprehension washed over her. Only minutes ago, they had laughed over a security breach. But something was seriously wrong.

Rozene. Amira had left her alone with Sparkes upstairs. She needed to get back to her. She crept toward the railing that overlooked the ground floor, stepping as quietly as possible.

The silence was broken by a low, strangled sob, followed by a chorus of frightened voices all speaking at once.

"Everyone calm down!"

"Stand back!"

"Let her go!"

"Whatever you want, we have nothing to do with it, so *please* lower your weapons."

Amira inched closer and peered over the railing. The party guests were now inside and crowded at one end of the wide floor. On the other side, a group of men fanned out across the room, their faces covered by ski masks. Several held electromagnetic guns and large knives. One of them clutched D'Arcy, his knife glinting as he pressed its tip against her pale throat.

Time froze, leaving an agonizing space between seconds. Amira's knees buckled. Her hands caught the railing before she fell, her gaze locked on the sharp point of the blade pressed to the fragile skin of her best friend's throat.

A short, muscular figure stepped forward beside D'Arcy and her captor, waving his gun in front of him as he spoke.

"Whoever switched the elevators off needs to turn them back on," he yelled.

Amira recognized the high, thin voice immediately from Rozene's worst memory. Sarka. A violent chill spread through her limbs.

"Do it now, or we'll start with this one!" He gestured at D'Arcy, who stood rigid under her captor's grip. Her body shook, visible even to Amira, but her pale face was set with grim defiance.

Amira scanned the crowd, her heart pounding hard against her rib cage. Singh was nowhere to be seen, nor was Barlow. Naomi stood in the front of the crowd, hands covering her mouth and her eyes wide with unmasked terror.

After a pause, an elderly man stepped forward and walked toward the receptionist's desk to reactivate the building's systems.

"Faster!" Sarka yelled. One of the generators stirred as power returned to the elevators. Bile soured Amira's mouth. She needed to act. Quickly.

The elderly man reappeared behind the desk, frail but rigid.

In a swift moment, a *crack* echoed across the room.

The old man collapsed onto the floor to the sound of terrified wails.

The masked intruder holding D'Arcy made a jerking motion.

A knife flashed. D'Arcy fell to the ground as blood splattered grotesquely across the marble floor.

Amira clapped her hand to her mouth, muffling her cry. *No, D'Arcy!*

The crowd scattered in earnest, screaming and running frantically in all directions. Several of the men fired their guns up in the air, one waving the flag of the Trinity Compound – an eagle grabbing a flaming, bloody heart, flanked by four crosses.

D'Arcy scrambled away on all fours, leaving a trail of blood in her wake. Naomi crawled toward her, sliding in a swelling puddle of blood, and hauled D'Arcy under a table. At the epicenter of the frenzy, one of the men saw Amira, terror-stricken, on the mezzanine and raised his gun.

Amira whipped around and sprinted toward the elevators.

"Rozeeene," Sarka cried tauntingly, stretching out the last syllable like a child playing hide-and-seek. "We're coming for you. It's time to go home!"

The elevator doors closed on the frantic scene.

Amira trembled in the narrow space, her arms folded tightly as she shifted from foot to foot, anxiety coursing like ice through her veins. Realizing her heels were still on, she kicked them both off, preparing to run. The ascent to the highest floor was agonizingly long and she could do nothing but stand there and watch the floor numbers climb, adrenaline coursing through her veins. The men would have begun their ascent shortly after her. She had minutes, maybe seconds, to get to Rozene first.

Once again, the elevator stopped abruptly and Amira lost her balance, lurching forward. Someone had deactivated the elevators for a second time. Curses and banging sounded below. The men were also trapped in their own elevator. She squeezed through the doors onto the 211th floor and sprinted toward the stairs.

Amira ran and pivoted around the winding steps. Her legs burned and she gasped for air, but she climbed without pause.

Echoing footsteps rose from the stairwell. The men had also escaped their elevator shaft and were following closely behind.

Amira sprinted into the ward's entrance area. Sparkes stood at attention. The robot would not be aware something was wrong until the security lockdown on the elevators was reinstated. "Lock the doors!" Amira screamed as she ran past Sparkes into Rozene's room.

"What's going on?" Rozene asked, bewildered, as a sheer layer of a clear material descended from the ceiling, fortifying the existing wall of glass between the ward and the offices, creating an additional protective barrier in Rozene's room. The door locked behind them, bolts loudly snapping into place.

Amira hunched over, her breathing heavy and ragged. As their eyes met, Rozene's widened in fearful understanding.

"They're here," Rozene whispered. Amira nodded, turning to look along the walls, the cabinets and drawers for something, anything, that would help them.

Rozene screamed, a raw, terrified cry that cut Amira's ears like a serrated blade.

Amira whipped around. Three men in long black coats stood on the other side of the glass wall, watching them. They removed their masks. Sarka glared with wild, hateful eyes, Elder William Young gazed into the ward with calm interest, and Andrew Reznik stood apart from the other two, his cold blue eyes locked on Amira. Sarka cradled a large electromagnetic gun, shifting his feet like a boxer before the first bell.

Amira and Rozene froze. They stared at the intruders, hardly daring to move. While she faced the Trinity Elder and his lieutenants for the first time, Amira's head flooded with questions. How had they made their way in past security? Why had help not yet arrived? How long could they hold them off in that room? Was there a traitor within Pandora who led them here? A thin trail of smoke rose behind the men. Sparkes lay scattered across the floor as a collection of charred gears and limbs.

D'Arcy. Amira shuddered, the trail of blood from her friend's neck still vivid in her mind's eye. Had Naomi stopped the bleeding in time? Would help arrive too late? A cry formed in the back of Amira's throat, threatening her composure, but she forced her terror back.

In a sudden movement, Sarka aimed his gun at the glass wall and fired. The wall shuddered under the impact, sending ripples out in all directions along the surface, but remained intact.

Failing to breach the barrier, Sarka paced along the wall like a caged predator, scanning for a weak spot along its defenses. He paused, then swung his weapon with full force against the wall. The violence of the impact caused the wall to bend, but not break.

Rozene shrieked and retreated behind her bed. The two women exchanged frightened glances. Sarka paced the length of the room and struck the wall again, first with deliberation and then with uninhibited rage, swinging with wild abandon. He fired another shot in desperation before returning to blows with the end of the gun. Reznik also paced, panther-like, with control and deliberation, never taking his eyes off his prey.

The glass door shivered with each blow of Sarka's weapon. Amira walked as calmly as possible toward the panel that controlled the room's settings. Her face inches away from Elder Young's, she avoided his eye while activating the distress indicator and keying in a message with shaking fingers: *Under attack. Send armed support.*

Elder Young watched her with a leering smile as she backed away from the glass. Nearby, Sarka continued to strike the wall mindlessly, while Reznik kept an eye on Rozene. He glanced momentarily at Amira. Her ears rang faintly, dulling her senses, and she closed her eyes to push it back in her mind.

"This one thinks she's brave," Elder Young said softly. "I know who you are, Amira Valdez."

She ignored him and withdrew, joining Rozene on the other side of the bed. As Sarka continued to swing viciously at the glass wall, the thinnest of lines spread from the center of the barrier outward like a crack in ice, widening until it would inevitably shatter.

Rozene turned to Amira, her eyes round with panic.

"They're going to get in!"

She was right. There was no time to wait for help. The glass would shatter in a matter of minutes, maybe seconds. New masked figures joined the three men on the other side of the glass – reinforcements.

Amira scanned the room desperately, looking for something useful. There were various things that could be used as weapons to defend themselves, but they were outnumbered and nothing could outmatch the electromagnetic gun.

There were no exits either. The only ways out were through the glass entrance or the windows.

"The windows," Amira whispered under her breath.

She ran to the cabinets behind Rozene's bed and flung the doors open. When she emerged, she threw an oxygen mask at Rozene.

"Put this on," she said quietly. "Get ready."

"A-Amira," Rozene stammered. "What are you doing?"

Amira ran past the windows, looking out of the Soma. They spanned most of the walls around the building. She scanned the room for something heavy.

Elder Young's glassy eyes widened in anger when he realized what she was about to do.

"Faster," he said sternly, as Reznik and the other men joined Sarka in striking the glass. "Faster, bring it down!"

After a final, defiant glare at the Trinity men, Amira grabbed two syringes from a nearby table, lifted a chair and threw it with a forceful swing into the opposite window. It bounced away with a loud thud. Cursing, Amira grabbed the chair again, striking repeatedly at the window with all her strength. A crack formed down the center. With a a final battle cry, Amira threw the chair a second time. The glass shattered into pieces and scattered like fractured marbles across the floor as wind tore into the room, sending sheets and papers flying. She fastened her oxygen mask, grabbed Rozene by the elbow, and pulled her out through the window onto a narrow ledge.

Both women shrieked as cold winds greeted them outside. They stood on a concrete surface that encircled the building and shielded them from the dizzying, teeming city far below. It was wide enough for two people to walk side by side, but the wind was shockingly powerful, whipping their hair and clothes in every direction while they pressed their bodies against the smooth wall and inched their way sideways along the building. All instincts screamed at Amira to run back inside, where the wind could not hurtle them over the edge, but the sound of shattering glass pushed them onward. They took slow, faltering steps toward the building's corner, Amira struggling to look anywhere but down. She fought the urge to cry, to scream, to imagine falling to her death. Instead, she moved sideways, one step at a time.

Pink skies signaled the early stages of dusk. They were on the eastern tower of the Soma. Toward the center of the building was a walkway that connected the two main towers together, one level below them. If they could reach it, they could reenter the building and attempt an escape through the West Tower.

Rozene moved in front, inching sideways along the narrow ledge while she clutched her midsection for balance. Though the mask concealed most of her face, her eyes widened with shock and she faltered at each burst of unrelenting wind. A faint yell sounded behind them. Heart pounding, Amira twisted her neck to look back.

One of the masked henchmen stood on the ledge, the barrel of a magnetic gun visible in his raised arm. He advanced, teetering with each clumsy step.

A gust of wind spun around the building. The man's foot slipped off and the rest of his body followed. He disappeared over the edge, faster than he could scream.

Rozene stopped, sinking down against the wall until she sat precariously along the ledge. She pulled the mask from her face, gasping with eyes squeezed shut.

I can't, I can't, she mouthed.

Amira pulled out one of the two syringes from her pocket. A stimulant balancer, designed to help a person function through shock. Safe enough during pregnancy. Inching forward carefully, she gripped Rozene's arm and pressed the needle into her skin. Rozene shivered but did not resist. After a moment, her eyes snapped back open and her posture transformed from limp to rigid. She looked fearfully at Amira.

"We have to keep going," Amira yelled, though the wind drowned out her words. "We can make it to the other tower. We're almost there!"

She grabbed Rozene's arm again and Rozene pushed herself up, steadying her swelling frame before they resumed their trek along the building's exterior. Amira stole a final glance at the open window before rounding the corner of the building, but no one else followed.

The walkway stretched directly below them. Both women slid down carefully, so that they were standing on its shiny glass roof. A gust of wind blasted Amira. She slid onto her knees.

Rozene screamed. Amira pulled off her own oxygen mask and brought it down with all her strength on the walkway's ceiling, hoping for the same weak glass as in the windows in Rozene's ward. After a few strikes, it gave, and they lowered themselves through the sharp, broken glass onto the walkway, Amira helping Rozene down.

Back inside, safe from the elements, Amira sank onto all fours, pressed her head against the floor and let out a strangled sob. She didn't dare scream – not yet.

There was no sign of Elder Young and his men – Amira assumed they were not suicidal enough to chase them around the outside of the building, but they would not give up their pursuit so easily.

Silently, they made their way across the still walkway into the western building, Rozene clutching Amira's hand. The cityscape flanked both sides of the open walkway and Amira wished desperately to be on the ground, to disappear into the dense web of roads and alleyways below. Upon reaching the western building's interior, Amira flung the stairway entrance open, nearly colliding with Valerie Singh. Rozene shrieked.

"Dr. Singh!" Amira gasped. "They're…they're looking for Rozene."

Singh nodded wordlessly, motioning them into the stairwell.

"Quick," she said. "There are men above us, on the landing roof. We need to go down."

Rozene moaned in pain as they descended the stairwell.

"I gave her a stimulant," Amira said in a low voice. "A safe one from our stocks."

"She needs more than that," Singh replied, her voice breathless.

"The trauma...she could deliver early."

Shouts echoed along the stairwell and the three women froze. There were men on the stairwell several floors down, the tops of their heads pivoting as they ran up in single file.

"We have to go back up," Amira said.

"No. Through the door!" Singh ushered them through the exit. They were on the 224th floor, at one end of a long hallway.

Rozene stumbled and Singh linked arms with her while Amira supported her on the other side, the three women running together toward towering double doors on the other end of the corridor. Singh swiped her badge and they entered the Soma's morgue.

Rozene crumpled when she realized where they were. Tears streaked down her face and she retreated to the exit, but Singh gripped her arm firmly and pointed ahead.

"We need to go in there," she said gently, pointing to a smaller room shielded with a glass wall, not unlike the one on the 235th floor.

"They got through the wall in Rozene's room," Amira said softly as Singh swiped them in. "They fired a few times and when that didn't work, they just bashed their way in."

"This has special protection," Singh said. "They'll have a harder time on these walls. And even if they get through, they won't find either of you."

Before Amira could answer, they entered a narrow, sterile room flanked on both sides by a high wall of freezer units. The room's center hosted several tables for autopsies, thankfully empty at present. At the far end of the room, glass cases containing human heads suspended in blue liquid lined the wall. The heads were the color of chalk with metallic tags fastened at their temples, from which a bright current pulsated, sending translucent streams of light through their brains. Each case had a placard underneath it. Though not close enough to read them, Amira knew they contained the names of important figures: scientists, leaders, anyone wealthy or connected enough to place their dreams of immortality in the Soma's hands.

Amira stood, transfixed, before the array of floating tombs until a frightened sob broke her concentration. Singh ushered Rozene toward the freezer doors, where Nina Leakey and Jessica Alvarado had undoubtedly ended their short tenures in the Soma.

Singh pulled one of the freezer doors open.

"Inside, quickly," she said. "And you, Amira, get in one on the other side."

Rozene shook her head, wringing her hands.

"I can't, please, no...."

"You must," Singh said with uncharacteristic softness. "There's an emergency latch inside, in case someone is locked in by mistake, so just pull on it once the coast is clear. You can do this. Everything will be fine."

Singh handed a vial from her coat pocket to Rozene.

"Take this once you're inside," she said. "It will stop labor if it begins. I'll disable the freezer so that it doesn't show the unit as occupied from the outside. Don't be afraid. I won't let harm come to you or the life you carry."

With that, Singh persuaded Rozene to lie on the slab and quickly closed the door.

"What about you?" Amira asked, pulling herself into a unit on the opposite wall.

"There isn't time," Singh said, rushing over to disable Amira's freezer. "I can redirect them somewhere else. What *is* important is keeping her safe."

"But—"

"You must promise me, no matter what happens, that you do not leave until it's safe." Singh's face hardened, her insistence radiating from every feature. "No matter what you hear, you must do this. Promise me, if something happens to me, that you will finish what I've started and see this through to the end."

"But I don't know enough to—"

"You do. Promise me."

Before Amira could answer, Singh slammed the door shut, encasing Amira in darkness.

It was unbearably still. Amira could run, even fight back if needed, but to be motionless was the cruelest state. She tried her best to breathe quietly over the deafening sound of her heart pounding.

Singh's footsteps trailed further away when they were interrupted by a loud banging sound, followed by more footsteps. Their pursuers had arrived before she could make her exit.

"It's the cloning heathen!" Sarka said, his voice now unmistakable to Amira. He followed his introduction with several shots of his gun. Another gun fired as well, and after a pause, a series of thuds and curses. From the sounds being made, the men seemed to be striking at the glass, as they had done in Rozene's ward.

Sarka let out a howl of rage.

"It's childproof," Singh said in response.

"Woman." The voice of Elder Young, though soft, cut through the chorus of his men's furious retorts. "We're not here for you, though you are a grievous sinner against the natural order. But if you stand in our way, you'll meet the sentence you deserve. *A terrible retribution of rock and thunder.*"

Singh laughed. Amira had never heard her laugh before. Light and airy, Singh's high-pitched laughter could not have felt more out of place in this room, at this moment.

"Let us in, woman."

"Where is my subject?" Singh asked. "What have you done with Rozene?" Amira felt a flutter of relief, impressed with the quickness of the lie and the convincing tone of outrage in which Singh delivered it.

"You tell us, woman," Elder Young said smoothly. "She was running down this tower with another young female. Why don't you come out and we can find them together?"

Amira held her breath, her clenched fists sweaty. To her relief, Rozene also managed to keep silent across the room.

"We both know I'll do no such thing," Singh said. "You have no hope of getting in here with your little toy guns. Why don't you sit around and wait for the police to come and pick you up? They should be on their way shortly."

"We don't fear your police."

"And I don't fear you."

A pause followed. Amira thought back to Rozene's memory in the desert and the way the girls struggled for air as the sand covered their faces inch by inch. She held her hands in front of her face, feeling the distance between her body and the cold metallic ceiling above her. *This is only temporary. This is a moment that will dissolve into memory with each passing day. A story to tell, of the time I nearly died.*

A new series of footsteps, loud and fast, echoed outside, joined by new voices.

"We found it on Floor 202, just like he said. We looked under the trial drug shelving and found the box, but it was empty. Everything gone."

"Gone? Cosmos curse you all!"

The Tiresia, Amira thought. They wanted it as well, whatever it was, and found the hidden box in the medical stores empty. If she made it out alive, she vowed silently, she would have some questions for Hadrian Wolfe, or Jones. Whoever he truly was.

"There's no time now," another voice interjected, one that was unpleasantly familiar. "We'll have to get Barlow, he knows the formula."

"*You!*" Valerie Singh shouted, and Amira's heart sank at the fear and rage in her voice. "How could you, Alistair?"

"I'm sorry, Valerie," Alistair Parrish replied, each word heavy with sadness.

"How long?"

"Does it matter now?"

"Did you give them Victor?"

No response. Amira clenched every muscle in her body to stop herself from shaking. She had not felt this kind of fear since she left the compound on that cool summer night, charging down the rocky hill as the sirens blared. The fear of the impending, the sense of things beginning to unravel.

It happened quickly; the familiar chime of a card swiping, the slide of the glass door opening.

"Tell us where they are, woman," Young said softly.

"No!"

"I'm sorry, Valerie," Parrish said. "It's for the best."

"No!"

The distinctive, ringing shot of the electromagnetic gun sounded, followed by a soft thud. Amira clamped her hands to her mouth, squeezing her eyes shut. She listened to the slow, methodical footsteps of the men entering the inner morgue.

"Look!" Sarka cried. "On the wall."

"Cowards," Young said, and Amira realized they were referring to the frozen heads. "Desperate to live again because they doubt the justice of the Conscious Plane. Now they reside in the Neverhaven, which will get a new arrival shortly."

"The bitch is still breathing!"

Young spoke again.

"Where is the Tiresia, woman?" he asked, louder than before. "Tell us, and we'll end your pain."

Amira could not hear Singh's response, but what she said made Sarka shout a string of obscenities before firing his gun again.

"We could have dragged that out," a new voice said. There was no emotion in the words, merely a statement of fact. Amira wondered if this was Reznik speaking at last; the cold, low timbre of the voice matched his gaunt face.

"There's no time," Parrish said, his voice etched with agitation. "We need to find Barlow! Something happened to the Tiresia stores. He must have made some preparations to hide it, but he would never destroy it entirely. Those are the last supplies in existence, and you know all too well what it takes to make more of it."

"Our deal was two-fold," Elder Young snarled. "The drug and the girl. I can't mobilize the compounds without both. I know your cursed wife will have made efforts to protect her abomination. They must be close."

Mobilize the compounds? Amira resisted a gasp of shock. He couldn't mean it.

"We cannot lose the Tiresia," Parrish said.

"The girl matters more to my congregants," Elder Young said. "They want to see a sinner pay for their crimes, and I'm going to deliver that retribution. Help me, or our deal ends in this room."

Parrish cursed.

"Let's start in here," he said.

Metal clanged as the men tried to open the freezer doors on the far end of the room, without apparent success. Valerie Singh must have locked the entire row of freezers before the men arrived. Sarka unleashed another string of curses, obscene but not blasphemous. Her own parents used to curse in a similar fashion. She was clammy and light-headed with fear, but did her best to keep her body rigid so that the men would not hear her tremble against the freezer's walls.

"Parrish, open them!"

"Valerie would have put in a code."

"Don't test me!" Young snarled. "We're running out of time."

"There are more efficient ways to find out if they're here," Parrish said, not masking his contempt when addressing the Elder. "Give me that gun. No, I don't need the whole damn thing, just pull out the electric coil at the base."

And Amira realized what he planned to do. In a single motion, Parrish intended to smoke them out of their hiding places in the worst way possible.

As quietly as she could manage, she reached into her pocket and found the second syringe she had seized before escaping the ward, still unused. Though the stimulant had worked effectively on Rozene as they made their way around the building, it also had the side effect of dulling senses and pain. Hopefully, it would be enough. She could not reach her arm in the tight confines of the freezer without making a noise, so she pushed the needle into the side of her leg. A rush of warmth pulsed through her body. She placed the cylinder between her teeth and bit down as hard as she could.

Footsteps again, drawing closer to her side of the room. Parrish would reach her first. The space between each second was agonizing, almost unbearable.

Parrish struck the freezer doors with the coil. The electric current ran down the wall of metal freezers. She knew it was coming, but the jolt of pain still made her heart stop. Her back arched and twisted, but she did not scream.

"What are you doing? We need her alive!"

"This won't kill her," Parrish responded as his footsteps trailed away to the other side of the room. "But it will hurt, and we'll hear them."

Amira, still reeling from the shock of electricity, listened apprehensively. Rozene's stimulant was still in effect, but her condition was undeniably more fragile. *Stay silent*, she thought desperately.

Before Parrish swung, a stifled sob echoed from the freezer wall.

"In there, she's on the other side!" Sarka cried out excitedly.

"No!" Rozene cried out, and it sounded as though she were flinging the freezer door open and attempting to climb outside. "It'll hurt the baby, please don't."

"This is no baby, Rozene!" Young said over the noise of a scuffle, and Rozene began shrieking. "It's an abomination against God, and I'll carve it out of you myself if I have to! Parrish, help them! Restrain her and let's go."

"Dr. Parrish, no, they'll kill me!"

A loud crash sounded, followed by the noise of glass breaking and water flowing. Rozene's screams trailed away, until the room was silent again.

Amira waited, trying to control her shaking. Singh needed help, but the danger had not passed. She pressed her hands, numb with shock, against her lips, silently counting the passing seconds. *Ten. Twenty. Thirty.*

More silence. No voices, no screams or footsteps. After several agonizing minutes, Amira reached for the emergency latch. She struggled to find it, almost giving in to panic, when her fingers found the cold metal and the door sprang open.

Blue liquid covered the floor at the far end of the room, along with a grotesque medley of detached heads, explaining the earlier crashing sound. Sarka had smashed the glass casing carrying the dead, the Trinity's final assault on the Soma.

Singh lay on the floor near the autopsy table in a pool of thick blood. Amira knelt beside her. Her fingers found three shots in Singh's chest and stomach, and one near her temple that spurted blood with each jerk of her head. Her elegant bun was still in place, though streaked in dark red, her features relaxed. Her olive-green eyes had turned glassy and depthless.

Amira examined the head wound with shaking fingers, overcome with panic.

"Help," she said in a low moan, desperately pressing her hands against the bubbling blood. "Somebody help, please!"

Then, as she crouched in a pool of the dying woman's blood and sobbed helplessly, something shifted in the air around her. Rust-tinged saliva flooded her mouth, accompanied by a dull ringing in her ears. The hairs on her arms rose like blades of grass at the instinctual sense of being watched, formless eyes boring into the back of her head. Amira left the floor and hovered high above the bloody scene. Below, she could see Valerie Singh and herself, still frantically shouting and trying to stop the bleeding. She floated in the air as though she were submerged in water, tranquil and distant. Images appeared, sights and memories that were not her own, but seen through another's eyes; the top of a hill where children played with rainbow-colored kites, overlooking the unmistakable skyline of Kolkata, followed by a podium where an old man handed her a diploma, then a young woman, with reddish-brown hair and almond-shaped eyes sitting on a bicycle, smiling over her shoulder. A sense of peace settled within her, as though she were coming home from a long, exhausting trip, and she sank backward into something she could not see, but she did not resist its warm, inviting pull.

Amira returned to the ground, her bare knees sticky with blood. Figures in black armor surrounded her, the laser lights of their weapons pointed directly at her head. Still dazed, she drew her bloody hands away from Singh's head wound and looked up at the nearest figure standing over her.

"Everything will be all right," she said softly.

Someone shouted something she couldn't understand. Her ears rang again. She reached her hand out and stood up.

Out of nowhere, something large and solid struck at the side of her head, and she fell into black again.

CHAPTER ELEVEN

Allies

Amira regained consciousness to the smell of blood and stale coffee. She touched her throbbing forehead, feeling a damp bandage in place. The blood was her own. Her hands strained against tight cuffs as she massaged her temple.

The room slowly came into focus. The coffee smell traced to the two policemen in the corner. The small, well-lit room contained a table and the chair she occupied.

She slumped to one side, dizzy. The officers chatted with one another quietly, ignoring her. Both appeared human, which struck her as odd, since robots handled most routine police work. Still in her black dress, Amira had somehow acquired a white lab coat while unconscious. From a blue coat to white, an unprecedented promotion. Perhaps it had been thrown on her as a courtesy in the cold, barren room.

Noticing her stir, one of the men pressed the door open and called out into the hallway, "She's up, detective!"

A man with straw-colored hair entered, a large folder tucked under his arm. His lazy gait revealed a confidence that belied his youth, as he looked no more than a few years older than Amira. His well-polished badge hung loosely around his belt, which emphasized his tall, wiry frame.

"Amira Valdez," he said in a low drawl that injected skepticism into every syllable. "I'm Detective Dale Pierson with Westport PD. I apologize for how you got here – you were ordered to put your hands on the ground and you failed to do that. Now, the law in this city prevents me from keeping you handcuffed unless you prove to be a verifiable threat. Can I expect you to cooperate if I remove the bindings?"

"Where—" Her mouth was parched and fuzzy, as though her cheeks were stuffed with cotton. "Where am I?"

Ignoring her, he leaned forward and briskly unfastened her cuffs. "I am *also* legally required to offer you water, food, a bathroom break and a total of ten minutes of personal time, be it prayer, self-reflection or meditation, blah blah etcetera, before the formal process begins. As you are not formally charged yet, but a person of very high interest in a presumed terrorist attack, you do not have a right to an attorney under the 2204 Preservation of North America Act."

Amira rubbed her wrists where the cuffs imprinted red marks. Her head cleared and the events of the night came back into focus. D'Arcy, clutching at her opened throat. Dr. Singh, lying in a pool of blood. And Rozene....

A string of questions spilled from her mouth.

"What happened? Did you stop them? Is D'Arcy alive? Where's Rozene?"

"That's what you're here to help me with."

"I don't understand. Dr. Singh, did she – did she survive?"

Pierson's mouth twitched and his eyes, the color of faded brown brick, flickered briefly with amusement.

"She *is* alive, actually," he said. "It's pretty incredible. I was sure she was gone but those Aldwych doctors can pretty much bring you back from the dead these days. But the doc told me that the skull fractures from the gunshot did some serious damage to her – what was it again – temporal lobe and cerebellum. He said that signals to her something or other were shut off for so long, that—"

"She won't recover," Amira finished. "She'll be in a coma for the rest of her life."

"Figured you'd come to that understanding, being an educated lady and all that. Profile says you're a student at the famous Dunning Academy by the Riverfront. Not bad for a runaway cult member."

"Listen," she said, searching desperately in his eyes for some understanding. "They will hurt Rozene and the baby if we don't find them quickly. They must have something planned or they would have just killed her right away. They could be back in the Trinity Compound before long—"

"So you know which compound they operate in," Pierson said triumphantly. "And your old home is something different, according to your file. Here it is – Children of the New Covenant. So how did they reach out to you?"

"How did they…what are you talking about?"

"The Academy assigned you to the Pandora project over three months ago. Were you supporting your compound friends before then, or did they contact you after you got access to the Soma?"

Amira stared back in disbelief. In the space of a few hours, the worst possible outcome had transpired. Valerie Singh was comatose, likely lost forever. Rozene was missing, dead, or worse. And Amira, as a former compound resident, was Westport PD's natural suspect.

"You have to listen to me," Amira said in a low voice. "I had *nothing* to do with the Trinity's actions. Or any compound's actions, for that matter. But you're right: they didn't act alone. Alistair Parrish was there, he helped them escape. I heard him, when they came for Rozene. He let them shoot Valerie Singh! *His former wife, and mother of his child.*"

The two police officers by the door laughed but Pierson narrowed his eyes, irritated.

"Why would Alistair Parrish sabotage his own project?" he asked. "It makes no sense. Unless someone else can vouch for what you're saying—"

"The only other person who can is in a coma," Amira said heatedly. "But she can still talk to us. Give her a holomentic reading and get someone to tap into her recent memories. Trust me, it won't be easy but they can be extracted before she deteriorates further. You have to be quick and find Parrish now before he disappears!"

A man strode into the room and whispered in Pierson's ear. The detective made a gesture for Amira to pause and followed the man into the hall. Several seconds later, Pierson's voice exploded from the hallway.

"Why does everything have to be a fucking jurisdiction battle?" he shouted. "I'm sick of these turf wars. She's in our custody, this happened in Westport and we're dealing with it! The Aldwych Council can have her once we've filed our own charges and finished our own fucking police work. Tell them no!"

The Aldwych Council. Parrish sat on the Council, the governing body that determined most of Aldwych's internal affairs, to the irritation of many in Greater Westport. If the Council wanted her in their custody, Amira guessed that the reason was nothing advantageous for her.

"What do you mean fucking NASH wants her, too?" Pierson howled. "What does NASH have to do with anything?"

"This attack is connected to a crime we believe happened on one of the stations," a familiar voice stated glibly. "We just have a few questions for her, and then you can keep her. I have my warrant right here."

Hadrian.

Unleashing a torrent of obscenities, Pierson stormed back into the interrogation room. Hadrian followed closely behind. He wore a starched white shirt and NASH jacket that concealed his more colorful tattoos, but still looked out of place next to the officers around them with his bloodshot eyes and unshaven face. Hadrian glanced casually in Amira's direction but gave no outward signs of recognition. Taking her cue from him, Amira turned angrily to Pierson.

"Now what's going on?" she asked, slipping indignation into the words. "Who is this?"

"This is Inspector Hadrian Wolfe," the detective said with forced composure. "He has some questions for you related to your compound friends. So in the spirit of *interagency cooperation*, I'll hand it over to you, Inspector."

Pierson left the room and Hadrian took the opportunity to lean over Amira, shielding both of their faces from view from the remaining officers.

"You have to find a way out of here, love," he whispered. "Aldwych is coming for you."

"How can I—" Amira whispered back, then Hadrian winked with a subtle gesture at his coat pocket.

Sounds of a scuffle erupted in the hallway, followed by a loud bang. Shouts and curses devolved into violent coughing, followed by thick, white smoke streaming into the interrogation room.

"They're here," Hadrian said. "Let's go!"

He grabbed her arm and ran past the two police officers, both on their knees already retching and gasping for air.

Hadrian and Amira covered their mouths and crouched low into the hallway to find a small battle underway.

A team of police officers, including Pierson, took shelter behind a wall of boxes, firing stun guns at a line of intruders in bright red uniforms. The fighters wore gas masks and powerful armor, their fluid, irregular movements suggesting that they were not robot, but human.

"Who the fuck are they?" Pierson yelled over the gunfire. "You're all under arrest!"

Whoever they were, they did not fire with the intent to kill, using stunners instead of electromagnetic fire.

"There she is!" one of the masked intruders shouted.

Amira lunged toward Hadrian's coat pocket, where he gestured earlier, and retrieved a finger-thin metal rod with a small button. Though she was not law enforcement, she had seen enough crime videos on the Stream to guess its purpose.

"Fuck!" Pierson yelled as Amira crouched down and raised her arm in the air. She pressed her thumb down on the button. She was quick – the end of the rod erupted, sending a translucent wave through the air in every direction, rippling like a stone thrown in smooth water and sending bodies to the ground.

The pulse from the aerial stunner struck the top of Hadrian's head, rendering him limp and helpless. He fell against the wall with a violent thud.

Police officers and mercenaries lay unconscious on the floor with one exception; Pierson was also quick, having ducked down immediately at the sight of the stunner. He crouched on his hands and knees, momentarily dazed.

Their eyes met and Amira scrambled to her feet, sprinting in the opposite direction.

They charged down the hallway. A rush of air to her right side whipped at her hair, accompanied by a large cracking sound. Pierson's stun gun narrowly missed her. Before he could fire again, she rounded a sharp corner down another pathway, her feet skidding on the marble floor.

Two women emerged from a side room into the hallway, barely managing a double-take before Amira collided with them, knocking them to the ground.

"Stop her!" Pierson cried.

The women shrieked again as Pierson tripped over them and smashed into the floor with a harsh thud. Amira barreled through a door leading to a stairwell and descended. The stairs were cold and unforgiving, but though still barefoot, she kept up her furious pace. She would have no hope of exiting through the front door of a police station, and the others would regain consciousness soon. Her only hope was another way out.

Another door awaited at the lowest stair level. Without any alternatives, Amira slammed through shoulder-first. The room on the other side was pitch black. Without an Eye or a handheld device to light the way, she moved forward blindly until her shaking hands found a handle. She pushed through and stepped outside, the cool air of early morning blasting her cheeks and hair.

She was behind the police station. Rows and rows of solar train tracks stretched in front of her, spanning several hundred feet and flanked on both sides by streetlights. It was still dark outside and quiet, the city not yet stirring. The long line of tracks glowed with reserve solar energy and electromagnetic currents that ran below the glassy surface.

Footsteps echoed from the stairwell.

Amira took a deep breath and ran at breakneck speed across the tracks, leaving a fading trail of green, glowing footprints on the surface behind her, an effect of the dormant sunlight beneath the track's surface.

Pierson burst out of the door. "Stop!" he yelled. "You'll get hit, you crazy bitch, stop!"

Amira continued to run.

"Amira," Pierson said. "I've put my gun away! Turn back before you kill yourself!"

A meaningless gesture – electromagnetic weapons were notoriously unpredictable near maglev tracks, and he would not risk firing, just as he would not risk following her all the way across the railway.

When Amira continued to run, he resumed the chase. His footsteps, hesitant at first, gained speed behind her. She neared the other end of the tracks, her shadow dancing under the streetlight as her ghostly footprints faded behind her.

The ground rattled and Pierson shouted in panic, leaping to the center platform between two of the tracks. Seconds later, a high-pitched wail announced a train's arrival, followed by a long streak of green light shooting along the tracks between hunter and hunted. By the time it passed, the lonely roads were silent again, and Amira was gone.

★ ★ ★

It was too dangerous to return to the Canary House. The police or the armed goons at the station had probably placed the building under guard now, perhaps combing through her room at that very moment. Though she had never seen the uniforms of the attackers before, Amira guessed that they were mercenaries. Either Parrish hired them directly, or the Aldwych Council had on his behalf. Pierson's shock was justifiable – security at Aldwych was handled by Westport PD within the district, and by NASH at the corporate space stations. Hiring mercenary fighters was a serious violation of the city's laws, and the fact that someone was willing to send them to attack a police station to capture Amira meant that she had accrued dangerous and desperate enemies.

She stopped in a thrift store and used the last of her cash to pay for a pair of biodegradable slippers. Cameras blinked from the store's corners, but she kept her head low. Her feet had already begun to blister and bleed, and she had more walking to do.

The Academy was certainly off-limits, as was D'Arcy's family home in Sullivan's Wharf. There was only one logical place left to go. Moving swiftly across alleyways and underneath bridges, she cut through the city's heart to the dockyards as the sun peered over the skyline.

★ ★ ★

Hadrian's crew was expecting her. She passed the speaker phone on the gangplank without a single threat or sarcastic comment and found the shipmaster back on his perch with his castaways, gathered around a large screen in the entrance hall. Hadrian still wore his suit from the police station, although his tie was now wrapped artfully around his forehead. Though she left him unconscious in the middle of a firefight, Amira did not feel the faintest trace of surprise to find him back on the ship.

"The lady of the hour!" Hadrian boomed, looking over his shoulder when Amira walked in. "We're catching up on your Aldwych adventures, us and the whole damn world. As a side note, you could have given me just a little warning about the stunner. My head feels like it's been fucking split in half."

Hadrian spoke with an almost giddy lilt, but the young faces fixated on the screen were etched with deep anxiety, terror even, as they watched the display of the Trinity Compound's power in Westport.

The screen was divided into multiple panels from different facets of the Stream, all covering scenes from the previous night – helicopters circling the dark towers of the Soma, the Trinity flag hanging out of a broken window, men and women in formal dress carried out on stretchers and stock images of Valerie Singh, her arms folded and her expression stern. Rozene was noticeably absent from the news feeds, but Stream commenters referenced the 'missing clone girl' feverishly in the side panels that ran below the headlines.

The room spun a little.

"Get some food and rest, missy!" Hadrian said. "Find an empty cabin room, *mi casa es tu casa* and all. And when you wake up, we'll see if we have something better to share." He cast a meaningful glance at Lee, who nodded. The boy's face was the color of sour milk and more haggard than Hadrian's, but he navigated his computer with grim purpose.

Clutching a sandwich wrapped in tin foil, Amira sank back into a cabin bed near the mezzanine, resting her clammy forehead against the white-paneled wall. Every muscle in her body ached and her head throbbed. She started to eat and suddenly felt famished, biting into the stale bread like a wolf attacking a carcass.

As she stretched across the bed, Amira thought of the ship's residents, refugees of a failed dream in the desert who wandered the hallways seeking shelter from the world outside. She returned to that day she disembarked the train in Westport, frightened but hopeful.

Now, she was a runaway seeking shelter once again, adrift in a deep ocean current where the land was out of her reach, no matter which way she turned.

When she finally faded away, it was into a deep, dreamless sleep, her first in months.

⋆ ⋆ ⋆

If Hadrian was giddy before, he was beside himself with jubilation when she arrived in the ship's gym, the small, musty room where they previously viewed Rozene's memory.

"Sleeping Beauty is risen!" he greeted her, gesturing her forward. "And you have a visitor."

A blur with dark hair rushed forward and D'Arcy threw her arms around Amira. Stunned, Amira clutched her friend close until she winced with pain and pulled away. A heavy bandage covered D'Arcy's throat and right shoulder.

"You're ok," Amira said and immediately burst into tears. The full weight of the last twelve hours struck her at once – the loss, the fear and now relief.

"It wasn't that bad," D'Arcy said, wiping her eyes. "He missed the jugular, so the cut ended up more on the shoulder. The doctor told me that if I hadn't moved in that one second, I'd probably be dead."

Amira recalled the way the masked attacker had swung the knife and the way D'Arcy had been forced to crawl in her own blood. Raw, unfiltered hatred bubbled inside her. Elder Young, Sarka, Reznik and the faceless thugs who followed them – they would face justice, and not the interdimensional kind they preached in the compounds. Real justice, in this world.

"Do we know who they were?" D'Arcy asked.

"Yes," Amira said, her voice still choked with emotion. "It was the Trinity Compound, Rozene's compound, that came for her. I tried to get her out, but they were armed and we were trapped. They took her alive and shot Valerie Singh. But that's not all – Alistair Parrish was there, D'Arcy. He helped them."

D'Arcy clapped a colorless hand to her mouth.

"The Trinity is definitely planning something, but there's more to it than that," Amira said. "Dr. Parrish was helping them, for a start. And when they were looking for us, one of them said something about this drug they were searching for. They needed Barlow to get more of it."

"Barlow? You mean the drug you stole from the stores?"

"Thanking me yet, missy?" Hadrian called out, clapping D'Arcy affectionately on her good shoulder, but still making her wince. "Old Hadrian has a reason for every season. Got that little vial away from some very bad folk."

Amira's head swam, absorbing Hadrian's words. She had assumed that Tiresia had been a black-market drug that Hadrian wanted for the usual reasons – money, recreation, power. After the events of the previous night, it was clear that Tiresia was no ordinary drug.

Perhaps sensing Amira's line of thought, Hadrian gestured her and D'Arcy toward the computer screens.

"Come on then," Hadrian said. "I've got some top-rate footage here."

A slight girl of about sixteen was combing through a long string of data on a monitor, chewing the ends of her dreadlocks. Nearby, Hadrian, Lee and a group of teenagers gathered around a small screen.

"Hadrian," Amira said tensely. "I have to find Rozene, and quickly."

"That you do," Hadrian said. "But you're a wanted woman now. Lots of folk looking for you when they should be tracking our Rozene down. You need to lie low here for now. We've been on the search while you were catnapping. Look."

Amira leaned forward. A young woman with short, spiky black hair lay on a hospital bed and addressed someone off-camera.

"Wait," Amira said to D'Arcy. "That's you!"

D'Arcy smiled. "They didn't waste any time," she said. "Got wheeled out to the hospital and had cops in my room the second they finished bandaging me."

"I know you're not telling me everything." Amira immediately recognized Detective Dale Pierson's low drawl as he addressed D'Arcy on camera. "Do you really expect me to believe that Amira Valdez made *no* attempt to contact you or speak to you since yesterday? That she didn't come back to your residence?"

"I'm in the hospital," D'Arcy said. "Getting stitched up."

"All the more reason for her to look for you."

D'Arcy rolled her eyes.

"She's one of the top students at the Academy," D'Arcy retorted. "She's not stupid. Why are you after her? She had nothing to do with the attack on the Soma! You should be asking for her help, if anything."

"Did she ever talk to you about problems on the cloning project? You are a fellow Pandora colleague, after all."

"No."

"Did she ever mention any pressures she was under, from her superiors or somewhere else?"

"No."

"Then what the hell did you two talk about? You're her best friend, or so I've been told."

"Oh, you know...boys. Our periods. Girl stuff."

"How are we seeing this?" Amira asked Hadrian. "Do you have access as an ISP—"

"Nope," Hadrian said cheerfully. "They kicked me out of their shared system completely after that business at the station. I had my kids do a little foraging through the PD's archives and found a whole folder with your name all over it."

"You hacked into the Westport Police's server?" Amira asked incredulously.

"Well, Lee hacked into it," Hadrian said. "With a little help from Hadrian and his connections. Lee, you know how they say parents love all their children equally? It's fucking bullshit. You're my favorite, Lee, of all of my kids!"

The screen switched to Julian, who was in the middle of his own heated exchange with Pierson.

"Think about this logically—"

"Just answer the question!" Pierson snapped.

"I am answering your questions," Julian replied in a calm but insistent voice. "What I'm asking is why Amira would assist a group of religious fanatics at a compound she didn't grow up in, when she ran away from that life years ago? What incentive would she have?"

"Oh, you tell me," Pierson replied sarcastically. "Maybe she wanted to go back, and this was her ticket home. Maybe she never really left!"

"That's bullshit. Anyone who knows Amira knows that's the last thing she would do. She hated that life and she's moved as far away from it as possible. She's a star Academy student with a top assignment in Aldwych, why would she throw that away?"

"Are you going to start cooperating?"

"I'm done cooperating," Julian said. Next to Amira, D'Arcy beamed. "Unless you have some legal reason to keep asking me stupid shit, I have better things to do."

"Don't think we're done here," Pierson warned.

"I'll bring a lawyer next time. Idiot."

"Remind me to apologize to Julian," Amira said to D'Arcy, while Hadrian howled with laughter.

"My boyfriend," D'Arcy said to Hadrian in explanation.

"He's a keeper," Hadrian cackled. "This is my favorite one. I've already had Lee download it to my Eye. Oh, and there was one more."

The screen switched to a young woman seated behind a table, and Amira sighed with relief to see that Naomi appeared uninjured after the attack. Though visibly shaken, Naomi sat upright while Pierson interrogated her.

"But Amira was with me the whole time," she said.

"When the terrorists entered the Soma?"

"Well, no, not then, but right before. We were all up with Rozene – with the subject, and she stayed up there when I went down for more cake. Then a crowd of men burst through the door and shot their guns in the air and…." She buried her face in her hands and sobbed.

"Poor Rozene," she continued, wiping her eyes. "You need to find her. She's in so much danger this late in her term."

"She wasn't as interesting," Hadrian said impatiently. "He stuck to facts with her, asking the same question about fifty times, and didn't sound like he got anything. If it was me interrogating her, I'd have pushed a little harder."

"What else did you find from the police files?" Amira asked. Though the display of support from her friends was heartening, it revealed nothing about the Trinity or Rozene's whereabouts.

"We're still going through the data," Hadrian said as he leaned back in his chair. "But we did learn about your mystery man."

"The man in Rozene's memory of the ceremony?" Amira asked eagerly.

"The very same." Hadrian swiped his hand in front of Lee's monitor and a man's face leapt from the screen to the center of the room, expanding to the size of a bookshelf. The face of the third man in the Unveiling ceremony. Hadrian twisted his wrist and the man's features began to change, shifting subtly to form another, similar face.

D'Arcy gasped. Amira blinked several times, moving closer.

"That's Victor Zhang," Amira said.

"The one and only," Hadrian said, turning to the now-shifting face so that his own expression was unreadable. "Got an Alias treatment on the black market, or maybe even just a face-scrambler injection. Of course, he's – *was* – too famous to pay a visit to the Trinity Compound without some kind of disguise. Lee played around with it for half a day before figuring it out. Can't believe I didn't recognize him myself."

Victor Zhang, a Cosmic, had visited the Trinity in the past, even attending an Unveiling ceremony. The scientist's calm, polite expression as he observed Rozene's humiliation lingered in Amira's mind, followed by his own screams during his recorded execution. What had he promised or given Elder Young, before their relationship had soured?

"So Dr. Zhang, Andrew Reznik and Elder Young were the three men who were scratched from Rozene's memory," Amira said. *Before I came along*, she added in her own mind. "And Zhang is dead, meaning we have no more clues or leads."

"Oh, how you underestimate your friend Hadrian," Hadrian said with a dramatic, wounded gesture. "Do you think we just sit around here playing Scrabble and sharing cat holograms from the Stream, love? That there's a chance in Hades, or the Neverhaven itself, that old Hadrian wouldn't keep track of Elder Young's comings and goings?"

"Are you saying that you're spying on Elder Young?" Amira asked, turning to Lee for confirmation. The boy nodded, stony faced.

"As you have undoubtedly deduced by now," Hadrian continued, "the good Elder has some friends in high places in Westport, in the literal and figurative senses. He doesn't have much of a digital trail compared to a city-dweller, but he has an ID that he uses when he's in town. Even uses his own name, boring as it is."

"Near-full access in Aldwych," Lee said, counting names off on his fingers. "The Soma building, Galileo Enterprises, the McKenna-Okoye complex and the Avicenna. Sometimes lists an address in the Rails, the neighborhood where all the Aldwych scientists live. Even more crazy, he has NASH access."

Amira exchanged a stunned glance with D'Arcy. The Trinity's highest Elder, a man who had tortured and killed a leading scientist, given free rein to roam Aldwych's halls. And to space – the world above the world Amira had dreamed of reaching since she first thought to look up at the sky. Nausea bubbled within her.

"How did you find all of this out?" D'Arcy asked. Lee's face lit up with a rare, impish smile.

"We have an informant, you might say," Hadrian said.

"Who?" Amira asked.

"One of my former kids," Hadrian said, scribbling on a grease-stained napkin before handing it with a flourish to Amira. "He – sorry, *she* – works on the Satyr Road, and it just so happens that Elder Young is one of her regulars. He pays her a visit when he's in town and needs a break from his teenage brides. A former Trinity girl, but the old git doesn't recognize her, given that she looked plenty different when he kicked her out. Her talents go beyond her night job, though. She knows her tech and may have something that could help you if you're really going to start digging into the Cosmics to find our little Rozene."

"Hang on," D'Arcy said. "Why are we starting off at the Satyr Road when these people are probably miles away now? You don't think Rozene might still be in the city, do you?"

Hadrian sprang out of his seat and waved his finger at her, as though pleased with the question. He paced in front of them, the children pulling back to give him space. In that moment, Amira once again took in the entirety of his alarming appearance – the web of tattoos along his arms that seemed to protrude out of his flesh, the scars that shone white on his neck as he stood in the shadows of the ship, and the unsettling wolf-like eyes that always glowed with feverish animation yet revealed nothing of the man behind them.

"Let's talk this through," he said in the casual tone of a professor asking his class to consider a tough math problem. "They could take her to the Trinity, but that would be obvious and a long trip for a small army of men and a pregnant girl. After the scene at the Soma, the Feds might finally decide to pay the compounds a visit. But the Trinity is secure, in its way, and I'll bet Elder Young has some hideaways up his sleeve in the event that he wakes the sleeping tiger and gets raided."

Lee and several of the other children gaped in disbelief and Amira understood why. The idea of the government raiding the compounds, any compound, was inconceivable to them. The Gathering was the last time the compounds faced a direct challenge from the outside world. Amira's pulse quickened as she remembered what Elder Young had said. *Mobilize the compounds.*

"But they could also still be in Westport, or somewhere close by," Hadrian continued, turning to the gym's single oval-shaped window, through which a sliver of moon peered inside. "They have allies here now, who the fuck knows why, and I bet those Cosmics have a fancy pad somewhere with lots of security to keep her hidden. Still risky, though – Westport is a big city, but we're good at stepping on each other's toes."

"Why keep her alive, though?" Amira asked in frustration. "Elder Young said, 'We need her alive'. But why? He wanted to marry her once. Is that still his plan?"

The girl with the dreadlocks snorted loudly.

"She's damaged goods," Hadrian said by way of explanation. "I doubt the good Elder would even pawn her off to one of his men at this point. She's lived in Westport too long and had too many chances. No, my guess is that this is much bigger than little Rozene, bless her, and they're doing this to make a statement."

Amira exchanged a confused look with D'Arcy.

"Have you been away from the compound that long, love?" Hadrian asked. "Think about it. Remember when you broke a rule back home, got caught stealing cookies or diddling yourself in your room? What did they make you do as punishment? Besides getting a beating or two, what did you have to go through each time?"

"Unveiling and community penance," Amira said, and the horrific realization gripped her. "They're going to execute her in public!"

"Blast it on the Stream is my guess," Hadrian said. Lee turned pale.

"And they need to do more than that," D'Arcy added thoughtfully. "They'll want to show how wrong it was to clone her in the first place. They won't just let the baby live, will they?"

"No," Hadrian said, no longer smiling. "They could do a few different things, thinking off the top of my head, but my bet is they'll get mini-Rozene out of her, if she hasn't gone into labor already, and get it all mutilated, to show the world what happens when you upset the Conscious Plane, or whatnot."

Amira closed her eyes, suppressing a resurging wave of nausea. Lee walked out of the room, but not before Amira saw his ashen face twisted in horror. Hadrian was right; for something as spiritually threatening to the compounds as human cloning, the Trinity would make the most brutal statement possible. Even Harrison Harvey, a city figure, spoke of women reproducing without men completely. What could frighten Elder Young more than that?

"We don't know that for sure yet," D'Arcy said, glancing sidelong at Amira with a nod of reassurance. "They could want a ransom, even, or have a list of demands like people have been doing for centuries."

"Maybe," Hadrian said. "Mayhap the Cosmics also want our Rozene for something, and that's part of their deal – they let the Cosmics do what they want with her, which is why they didn't blow a hole through her head the minute they saw her, and then the Trinity can take over at the end."

Amira sank into a chair, overwhelmed by the sense of dread coursing through her body. Her focus surprised her. Perhaps she was at her limit, and her mind could no longer handle a protracted state of panic. Too much was out of her control – Rozene could be under torture or worse at that very moment, and though no one admitted it, not even Hadrian, they were grasping at straws to figure out her location.

The Stream cut back to the Soma and a wave of anger washed away her guilt and fear. This was not only an attack on the city she loved, imperfections and all, but on each young escapee gathered around the screen who, like herself, sought control over their lives. They no longer felt safe from the compounds' reach. There was also Amira's debt to Rozene – her patient, friend and fellow refugee. Valerie Singh's final words to her were to keep Rozene safe and see Pandora to its end, and Amira would have to find a way, for both their sakes.

As the children slowly retreated to their cabins, Amira turned to Hadrian to ask the final question that haunted her since the Soma attack.

"The Tiresia," she said in a low whisper, and his sharp yellow eyes met hers directly. "The Cosmics and the Trinity found the box of vials empty. The vials I gave you."

"Did they now?"

"They know it's all gone," Amira said.

"They're not fools, love."

"What is it, Hadrian?"

"What is what?"

"The *Tiresia*!" she said with venom. "What does it do?"

"No clue."

She opened her mouth to scream in frustration, then closed her eyes and exhaled. Hadrian waited patiently beside her, his head cocked in a mocking gesture of innocence. Calming down, she clasped her hands together and faced him again.

"If you don't know what it is or what it does, why did you have me steal it?" she asked.

"Because somebody far more important than the two of us asked me to," he said. "Get it out of the Soma, he said, whatever you do, get it out and keep it safe. And that's what I'm doing. I didn't ask anything beyond that."

Amira laughed, loudly enough that her bitter peals of mirth echoed across the room's battered walls. Yet another riddle.

"I guess I won't bother asking you who it was this time."

"Oh, you've guessed the answer already, love," Hadrian said with a wicked grin. "Tony Barlow. He and I go way back, guess I forgot to mention that, and I owe him some. Smart guy, that Dr. Barlow, so when he asks for a favor, it's for a good reason."

"You lied," Amira said. "When I asked you about Barlow and you promised to look into him."

"I did," Hadrian said matter-of-factly. "Barlow wanted his drug hidden and his last supplies away from men and ladyfolk with ill intent, and I didn't want you knowing more than you needed to. Keep you under the radar, as it were. Too late for that now. You've made yourself many enemies by fixing our Rozene. Want my advice? Don't make another one out of me. We're on the same side, love."

As Hadrian sauntered toward the door, he turned one last time.

"He asked about you quite a bit. Barlow. Seems *very interested* in you, Amira Valdez."

CHAPTER TWELVE

The Satyr Road

The Satyr Road cut diagonally across the heart of Westport, a bleeding artery of neon lights and glistening cars that snaked through the city's congested center. The bright sheen of new rainfall only enhanced the effect of a place that produced its own radiance, however artificial it may be. Brazenly painted signs and video screens spanned the length of tall buildings, advertising multi-story complexes of sex shops, performance clubs, virtual rooms and more private, intimate services. Women and men posed on display in artfully lit glass windows, advertising their wares, inspected and admired by passersby along crowded sidewalks.

Amira and Lee tried to feign ease with their surroundings, but the compounds' obsession with sexual purity was a hard lesson to unlearn, even with years and miles of distance. Beyond its general licentiousness, however, there was much about the Satyr Road that unsettled Amira – artificial, silicone bodies displayed like meat through glass panels, the mile-away stares behind every worker's eyes, making human and robot faces impossible to distinguish. Then there were the darker offshoots of the main road, the alleys behind alleys, where robots with children's bodies were furtively advertised. 'Keep Real Children Safe', the campaign slogan read. Amira turned away in disgust, resisting the urge to yank the signs from the window. Instead, she grabbed Lee's elbow and continued ahead. They could not afford to draw any attention to themselves.

After several blocks, Lee regressed to staring at the pavement, and Amira wondered whether bringing the quiet teenager as a backup was, at best, pointless, and possibly even dangerous. D'Arcy worked for Pandora, Hadrian drew too much attention and Julian was undoubtedly being watched. As a result, Lee became her accomplice for the night.

"This is the one," Amira said, pulling Lee down a narrow alleyway past a window of robotic women in provocative poses that a nearby sign promised were 'the authentic human experience, inside and out'. In the alleyway, they entered a narrow building with a faint 'Hotel' sign above it and into a musty room with fading, mold-colored carpeting. There was no reception desk or any evidence of service. Creaking stairs, also shabbily carpeted, led up several flights to the address Hadrian provided, the number '42' barely readable on the door.

Amira rapped the door sharply.

She fidgeted anxiously, pulling her sleeves over her wrists. Since her own room at the Canary House was no longer safe, she was forced to borrow clothes from the girls on Hadrian's ship, all considerably younger with less-developed frames. Her black sweater itched and crawled up her navel, and the eggplant-hued jeans she managed to squeeze into pressed at her mercilessly from all sides. Most of the girls on the ship discarded the signature lace veils and shapeless compound dresses within days of escape and opted for the tightest and least comfortable clothes available. One restriction traded for another.

The door flung open and a striking woman with long, layered bronze hair peered out, scanning her two visitors under heavy eyelids. She made a delicate gesture with her hand to beckon them inside.

"Hadrian let me know you were coming," Maxine St. Germaine said in a melodious voice that revealed neither warmth nor displeasure at their arrival. Maxine's dimly lit apartment could not have been further removed from the dour, stale hallway. The contrast was so evident that Amira paused to readjust her eyes to the wealth of rich colors and textures inside. Tapestries hung on the wall to their left, classic scenes of geisha walking over bridges beneath cherry blossom trees and pouring cups of tea. Ornate stone sculptures sat on end tables, male and female figures with limbs entwined in various contortions. A large screen on the opposing wall ran in the background, depicting scenes of a less subtle nature that turned Lee's ears red. The furniture was simple and utilitarian, glass tables and leather couches with clean lines, glowing warmly under the delicate streaming lights that stretched along the walls.

They followed Maxine behind a curtain that partitioned the front area, clearly designed with her clients in mind, from the remainder of her apartment.

Behind the curtain, the back room had the chaotic quality of an artist's studio, but instead of canvases and paint, wires, gears, microchips and a wide assortment of tools covered every surface. A high-powered microscope rested in the corner next to a compact molecular beam epitaxy. Amira recognized other tools and instruments associated with computing, although she suspected that D'Arcy would understand most, if not all, of the room's impressive array.

Lee let out a low whistle, reaching out to touch the microscope.

"Not a bad setup, eh?" Maxine said, pulling up a red velvet chair to sit. "Drink?"

She jerked her thumb at a bottle of vodka on the table in front of her, and when they both shook their heads, she poured herself a glass.

"I have a nice little side operation here, as you can see," Maxine continued, lighting a cigarette. "Mostly tech that you can't get through the normal channels. I can enhance Eyes, quantumize smaller computers, fix outdated systems. Some of my clients have things done on the side and some aren't clients at all. There's no shortage of folk here in Westport in need of some discreet upgrades."

She laughed airily.

Amira searched her heavily made up features for any trace of her former masculinity, but found none. Maxine's frame was narrow and delicate, strategically pneumatic in the appropriate areas, though her shoulders and collarbone jutted out prominently, the final remnants of awkward adolescence. Few Westport natives took advantage of the latest sex-transitioning procedures, due to early screenings for genetic variations and less rigid gender roles, but compound refugees were known to request transitions when they arrived in the cities.

According to Hadrian, Maxine's past was one of unwelcome births, assigned male when she was born in the Trinity Compound. At the age of fourteen, puberty greeted Maxine with more trauma than most, bringing facial hair but no deepening voice, and a body that remained soft and round.

Maxine's parents knew something was wrong, but did not confront the issue until the hot, turbulent summer when the changes could no longer be kept secret. Maxine wearing the starched, trademark white shirt at ceremonies, unable to conceal growing breasts. When the boys lined up to receive Chimyra, Maxine always stood out as the shortest. After an official inspection, surrounded by horrified relatives on a cold, late night, she was pronounced by the Trinity's healer as neither entirely man nor woman, unfit to submit to a husband or hold dominion over a household. When the Elders expelled her, she held her sobs in the back of her throat while passing through the front gate, because boys were not supposed to cry. In Westport, she became Maxine through a few strategic surgeries, though she chose to leave some 'ambiguities' – as Hadrian referred to them – for the parts of her body she was comfortable with, a uniqueness that made her marketable on the Satyr Road.

"Does it pay well?" Lee asked with interest, gesturing at the equipment.

"Well enough," Maxine replied, smiling slyly. Her movements were fluid, exaggeratedly feminine, whether for the clients or herself was unclear. "It's hard to make an honest, safe living through whoring these days, and I can't say I miss it. You know why that is? It's those damn robots. They've just gotten too good, and the punters have gotten worse in response."

"The intimacy robots?" Amira asked apprehensively.

"Of course. Robots that play for pay. It's terrible. You're competing with a literal fuck machine, so not only can they out screw you, there's none of the usual mess that comes with a real person. You know, dryness, smells. Do I need to get graphic? Anyway, to make it even worse, the men can do what they like when they dabble with the metal, any violent act they can think of, and the virtual simulations give them all kinds of ideas. The robots can be programmed to act like they love it, or to scream and cry, whatever the client wants. Disgusting. They don't want human pussy anymore, and when they do, the few remaining working girls don't want to deal with it."

When neither Amira nor Lee could manage a response, Maxine let the silence settle in the air before continuing.

"What I've finally learned is that you can't compete with the 'bots, at least not on their level. Most of my income is through my programming these days. My few remaining clients are more interested in the pillow talk than the sex, spilling out their sad little hearts or unloading their day on someone who'll listen at the hourly rate. They can't program a woman's mind yet in those 'bots, our subtleties, the secrets we carry in our smiles. We've still got tricks you can't mimic in a machine, believe me."

Lee had inched back at least a foot away during Maxine's speech, as though he were attempting to dissolve into the corner wall.

"So one of your clients is Elder William Young, correct?" Amira asked hurriedly. Lee's expression mirrored Amira's disgust, although Amira shared none of his confusion about Elder Young seeking company on the Satyr Road. Amira had experienced enough life to know the positive correlation between the zealous and the hypocritical.

Maxine's eyes, blazing in indignation seconds ago, hardened as they met Amira's. She cradled the burning cigarette between two fingers, scattering a trail of ashes onto the floor. "Yeah, he's one of mine," she said. "The holy man himself, sent me out crying into the desert. Called me an abomination against nature. But seems he likes a little abomination on the side, when his flock isn't looking. It's satisfying, in a way. He thinks he's using me, when I'm feeding everything he mutters in his sleep to Hadrian. How is dear Hadrian, by the way?"

"Same," Lee said neutrally.

"Right. He told me everything. Well, the important parts at least."

Amira nodded. "And?"

Maxine put out her cigarette and rested her chin on her hand, her eyes calm and distant.

"I've been thinking since I got word from Hadrian," she said. "Trying to recall something that might be useful. Most of his rambling is about how important he is back home, how I should read the teachings of Elder Cartwright and other shit you'd expect a raving compound hypocrite to say. But he did mention going up to the stations for the first time in a long time."

"Did he say which station?"

"No. Wait, yes. The Carthage."

Alistair Parrish's station. Amira's heart fluttered with excitement.

"Notice anything strange in the last few weeks?" Lee asked.

Maxine narrowed her thin brows.

"He did cancel last week," she said slowly. "And then he rescheduled his appointment last night to today. Nothing that weird about it on its own, until you put together what happened at Aldwych last night."

Amira nodded grimly. Had it really only been twenty-four hours since the attack? The time since Rozene disappeared felt both far too quick and agonizingly prolonged.

"So he's coming tonight?" Lee asked, glancing furtively at the long table of equipment behind Maxine.

"In about half an hour," Maxine replied. "I see that look on your face, Lee, but don't get too brave. He never comes alone. There'll be guards outside, armed with the best magnetic guns that Westport connections can buy. But I think there's a way I can help you."

She pulled herself off the chair with an effort, sighing softly, and knelt to open a small cabinet below her work bench.

"This has been a little project of mine," she said, rummaging through the cabinet. "It's not perfected yet, but you'd make an excellent guinea pig. And if it does work, this should help you quite a bit." She emerged holding a small case, which she presented to Amira.

"Take out your Eye," she said.

"I don't wear one." Amira winced, eyeing the case with new suspicion.

"You don't? Oh, you are a real compound girl! I didn't care for them myself when I first got here – too much mental clutter, right? Then I saw what you could do with them – put this on."

"What's so special about this Eye?" Lee asked as Amira cautiously balanced the lens on her fingertips.

"First, it can bypass the Ocular Registry – you know, which identifies who's wearing the Eye by scanning your eyeball – so you can override it with another person's ocular print."

"Meaning I could wear the Eye and pass off as someone else?" Amira asked.

"Exactly."

"That's nothing special," Lee interjected. "You can get fake ID Eyes from lots of places. It's a common black-market thing."

"True," Maxine said. "But that's not all. If it works, it'll also scramble the security override that keeps ordinary Eyes from operating in certain places where they're blocked to commoners like you and me."

"Meaning Aldwych," Amira said slowly. Entering Aldwych with every scanner greeting her as William Young meant unprecedented access.

"Not just Aldwych," Lee said. "NASH, the space stations, government zones. So she'd be able to hit the Stream in those places?"

"The Stream, and the local quantum servers that connect to it," Maxine said proudly. "It's those powerful servers in Aldwych and NASH that shut your Eye down in the first place. But my Eye can fake a quantum data stream, so the systems see what they think is a friendly device, part of their own architecture, and the disabler doesn't activate."

"If it works," Lee added softly, but he was already gazing with envy at the small lens on Amira's finger.

"Assuming it works. But if it does, think about it. These Cosmic freaks Hadrian told me about, the police, Aldwych...there'd be no secrets they could hide from you."

"But we still need to get her into those places," Lee said. "They have all kinds of security, including facial scanning. Amira's a fugitive now."

"Well, I can't fix *all* of your problems," Maxine said with a slight bite in her voice, raising her eyebrows at Lee. "I can't give you Elder Young's face, dear, and you wouldn't want it. But you won't be able to get to these places without it."

"What do you want for this?" Amira asked. For the first time, she handled the lens with excitement. The Eye meant limitless access in places where she needed it most.

"It's yours," Maxine said.

"I can't just accept it."

"You can," Maxine said firmly. "We need to take care of our own. I grew up on the Trinity, if you didn't know that, and I haven't forgotten what they did to me. Not just sending me out to die in the desert. It took me a long time to accept who I am, to love myself. And I knew Jessica and Nina as well, when I lived on Hadrian's ship. If I can help you do right by them, for all our girls, I will."

Amira nodded.

The plan was simple in theory. When Young arrived for his appointment, the Eye would activate its hacking script to upload his identity. They had to be close for the upload to work, but once it was complete Amira could travel anywhere on Earth or space under the identity of William Young, unaffiliated Aldwych associate.

Amira and Lee would hide behind the partition in the back of Maxine's apartment while the hack script ran. After, they could exit down the fire escape.

They barely finished finalizing the plan when a loud rapping on the door signaled Elder Young's arrival. Maxine disappeared behind the curtain and Amira slid in the Eye. She blinked a few times and shuddered at that unpleasant pulling sensation as the Eye activated, a flurry of text and graphics appearing in the right corner of her vision.

Amira reeled, trying to shift her focus to Lee, the room, reality, but the Eye was no less overwhelming than the last time she used one in the park. The screens alone were not the only navigational challenge – Amira could not understand how Westport natives could converse, work and cross busy streets, all while reading whatever their Eyes ran in the corner of their vision.

Elder Young burst through the door and Amira snapped back into focus. She pressed against the wall, fighting back a rush of rage. On her right, Lee peered through the curtain, scowling with unmasked venom. To her relief, a sidebar in the corner of the lens displayed the progress of the download. Maxine's hack was working.

"Right on time," Maxine said smoothly.

"Did someone ask you about me?" he asked furiously.

"What are you talking—"

"No games!" he shouted, his voice thick with panic. "Someone followed me here, so I'll ask you again. Has anyone come by and asked you about me? Said my name? Answer me, whore!"

Amira and Lee exchanged nervous glances.

"I don't know what you're talking about," Maxine replied

indignantly. "I haven't seen or heard anything strange. Is it safe for me now? Do I need to get extra security?"

"Never mind," Young snarled.

Amira peered through a gap in the curtain. Young threw his jacket on the couch and paced the length of the room, the tension visible in his rail-thin frame. He had predictably eschewed his usual compound attire for a very unsanctioned visit to the Satyr.

Maxine slid behind the bar, assembling a cocktail.

In the corner of Amira's eye, the bar read *thirty per cent.*

"Can you believe that attack on the Soma yesterday?" she asked casually over her shoulder.

"What?" he asked distractedly. "Oh, yes. A terrible tragedy."

Amira dug her nails into her palms.

Maxine did not press for further details. She handed him a drink, the color of old aquarium water, garnished with an olive. As Amira watched him down the drink and pour his second, a new burst of fury erupted within her, so strong that even her eyes burned. To see Rozene's abductor and Dr. Singh's attacker in person again, after barely escaping from the Soma, was surreal. She fought the urge to burst through the partition and confront him, to grab him by his throat and demand Rozene's location. Reason kept her in check – if Maxine was right about the armed guards outside, she would become just another stain on the hallway carpet.

The bar reached *fifty per cent.* Amira's pulse raced and she shifted her feet back and forth, willing the colored meter to move faster across her eye.

"You need a vacation," Maxine said wryly, stretching out across the sofa.

Elder Young downed his second drink. For the first time since bursting into the apartment, he scanned her delicate frame.

"Vacation embodies the sin of idleness and I am never idle," he said in a sermonic tone. "I have important matters to attend to back home. Some unexpected surprises to address."

Amira's stomach tightened. What were the 'unexpected surprises' Young had to address? Had something happened to Rozene?

The bar read *seventy per cent.*

Maxine said, "How do you know someone's following you? You

really scared me when you came in here, you know."

"You're filled with questions today," Young said, more with contempt than suspicion. "Not that it concerns you, but a business arrangement of mine was not meeting my needs, and I decided to change the terms. Something my business partners may not take too kindly to. A new fire to put out."

"Metaphorically speaking."

"If all goes well," Young said with renewed menace.

Ninety-five per cent.

"You could call the police if you think it's serious."

"I'm tired of talking," Young said with irritation.

"Right." Maxine turned on her music, loud enough to drown out all other sounds in the room.

The bar reached *one hundred per cent*, followed by a greeting across the Eye screen: 'Welcome, William A. Young'.

She signaled to Lee and they took slow, cautious steps out of the back window, already opened in preparation. The crisp night air filled Amira's lungs as she stepped carefully down the fire escape. Police sirens wailed in the distance but the surrounding area was quiet.

Above her, Lee grabbed Amira's arm.

"Do you hear that?" he whispered. The music continued to rattle the tattered curtain inside. Amira shook her head.

Then it happened. The *boom!* of a door being kicked down. Screams of shock and anger. A loud scuffle.

"What's going on?"

"Grab the Elder! Take him alive!"

"Stun them! We don't need corpses."

The alley's breeze whipped at the parting curtain, revealing a knot of bodies, armed with fists and weapons. Figures in red uniforms brandished magnetic guns that they resisted firing, and instead grabbed at other men in black robes. Maxine crouched behind the counter. She screamed as a chair crashed into a computer across the room.

The curtain closed, ending the snapshot of a kidnapping in progress. That was Amira's assessment, in the seconds allowed her. The Cosmics had sent the same crimson fighters who tried to seize her in the prison to capture Elder Young and apparently surprised his guards. The Elder's guards fought back, and Amira had no desire to stay to confront the winning side.

"Back out the window," Lee whispered. "Go!"

They scrambled down the fire escape, feet clanging against the metal steps, but there was no time for silence. Lee nudged her from behind and Amira quickened her pace, eager for the first time to return to the well-lit Satyr Road.

They reached the alleyway and ran toward the main drag of the Satyr Road. Amira's eyes caught sudden movement and she screamed.

Two new figures appeared in front of them, blocking off the main road. The streetlight framed their silhouettes and Amira recognized the taller figure, the sharp tips of hair and gaunt jaw. Reznik, looking as cold and cruel as he did her first day on Pandora. Lee grabbed Amira's arm and pulled her through a door to their right.

Panting, Amira and Lee stumbled up a flight of stairs, burst through the next door, and emerged in a department store comprised entirely of adult wares. They ran, careening past lurid mannequins, through racks of corsets and leather, pushing startled shoppers aside and knocking over shelves. A crash came behind them. Amira cast a quick glance over her shoulder. The two men raced toward them, Reznik's piercing eyes trained directly on her. He moved quickly and would easily catch them in an open space.

They crossed the length of the store and sprinted down a ramp into the busy street, weaving through the dense crowds toward the station. *Westport train schedule*, Amira thought as clearly as she could manage through her panic. A second later, the Eye displayed the train schedule for the nearest station, with the Red line due to arrive in three minutes. She nudged Lee and pointed at the station sign down the street. He nodded.

The entrance to the subway resembled the neck of an hourglass as crowds filtered inside. Amira and Lee were separated by the sea of bodies, all sweaty arms and cursing faces, and carried down the human current until they passed the bottleneck and broke free, sprinting toward the Red line.

"Welcome back, William," a voice greeted Amira as they crossed the ticket barrier. As they followed the signs down to the trains, a scuffle erupted behind them.

"Sir, you need a pass!"

"Let me through!"

The train welcomed them with open doors when they reached the tracks. They stood anxiously in the back of the farthest carriage, waiting for the men to burst through the ticket barrier. Across the walkway, the other train departed south.

Reznik and his accomplice charged down the steps. Lee and Amira shifted tensely behind the other standing carriage passengers in hopes of dissolving into the crowd.

Just then, through the sea of faces, Reznik's eyes found Amira's. Her ears buzzed again, ringing over the screeching of passing trains. He shouted at his companion.

The men charged at the carriage door. Amira waited helplessly, willing the doors to seal shut as the glass panes glided slowly, far too slowly, and the final call for boarding echoed across the platform.

The last instant, the doors closed.

Reznik's accomplice crashed against the sealed door, drawing alarmed stares from the other passengers as the train moved north. Its acceleration drowned out the man's final howl of rage. Reznik stood still, his eyes following Amira through the carriage's back window, until the train left the station and the ringing in her ears abated.

* * *

"You're sure you weren't followed?"

"Hadrian, I checked twice before we crossed the fence," Lee said. "And Amira's new Eye has a sensory tracker. There was nobody on the street."

"Your new Eye," Hadrian said in a cheerier tone. "Coming in handy, eh?"

It was already midnight. Drunken shouts echoed along the ship's hallways. When Amira and Lee returned, visibly shaken and hair damp with sweat, the children followed them to the makeshift headquarters of the gym, where Hadrian locked the door to their smaller group.

D'Arcy bit her lip tensely during Amira's retelling of the events on the Satyr Road.

"What I don't understand, though, is why those Cosmics went after Elder Young," Amira said. "The same ones who tried to take me from the police. I thought the Cosmics were working together with the compound. Unless something changed."

Hadrian smiled knowingly at Amira. "Got any fancy theories on why that is, love?"

Amira frowned, leaning back against the wall. She had the same question.

"There are several possibilities," she said. "Maybe Parrish went rogue and tried to take Elder Young against the instructions of the Cosmics. I doubt that, though, since someone pretty high up sent those mercenaries to the police station. More likely, the Cosmics are now going after the Trinity. Maybe something caused the Trinity and the Cosmics to fall out, and they're now fighting each other. I was surprised the compound would work with people who they see as heretics. I remember how much they hated and distrusted anyone from the cities."

"A falling out between compound and Cosmic might work in our favor," Hadrian said. "But it's time to dig into what happened, whether they got our friendly neighborhood Elder or not."

An hour passed. Lee resumed his research at his computer, joined by Hadrian. Amira gratefully accepted a cup of tea from D'Arcy. With the Soma closed after the attack and the ever-present risk of being followed, D'Arcy had remained on the ship. After finding the kitchen, she had brought some civilization to their debauched surroundings in the form of herbal tea and square-cut sandwiches.

Lee suddenly stood up and motioned for them to join him.

"These are the security cams from the South Satyr station," he said, pointing to the monitor. "Look, there we are."

The grainy figures of Amira and Lee barreled across the screen, running into the open train door.

A minute later, the two men followed. Amira felt a rush of satisfaction reliving the moment again, when they crashed head-first into the closing door.

"Here," Lee said. He zoomed in on Reznik and the second man, on his knees with his mouth open in a furious wail. "I got their faces. Reznik's not in the system, but the second one might be."

"See if he has any arrest records," Amira said. "Or if he's been on police tracking."

"You think my boy's an amateur?" Hadrian said. "While you were talking, Lee's hacked my own NASH account with the password I just changed, to keep him on his toes, and combed half of the files in Westport—"

"Not Westport," Lee said quietly. "NASH. Look at this."

The man appeared on the screen again, his scowl enhanced by a fresh black eye. Two men stood at either side of him, walking him through a security checkpoint.

"This happened minutes ago," Lee said. "That's him, entering the Carthage station. Only him, see? Looks like the Elder won the fight at Maxine's place, but this one got picked up later. Already in space hours after arrest – they must have shuttled him right from the Galileo building."

Hadrian let out a low whistle.

"Parrish's station," Amira whispered.

"The one where they use 'volunteer' convicts for the station's experiments in exchange for a reduced sentence?" D'Arcy asked.

"That's the short of it, love," Hadrian said. "A clever set up Parrish wangled there. Researching the effects of space on the human body is a hard sell for most, but worth the risk if you're a lifer in some corp-run prison. And a great place to take folk you want to question – or disappear."

"So the Cosmics found him," Amira finished the thought. "And brought him up to the Carthage as a prisoner. But he might know where Rozene is!"

Amira turned to Hadrian.

"I need to go up to the Carthage station," she said.

Silence followed. Hadrian threw his head back and laughed and, upon seeing Amira's serious, stony expression, laughed even harder.

"It's the only lead we have," Amira said. "If I can get this Trinity man and read him, it's our best chance of finding out where Rozene is. He was guarding Elder Young, so he must be important enough to know. And the Carthage is a place to disappear people – Rozene might even be there, under Parrish's control."

Lee began rattling off the reasons it would be impossible. Everyone got to NASH one of two ways: through shuttles privately owned owned by companies at Aldwych, or on tourist shuttles at the Parallel, both of which had layer upon layer of stringent security. The Parallel ran facial recognition scans in addition to retinal ones, so her Eye would only get her so far. The Carthage, a glorified prison colony masquerading as a research station, had even more security hurdles to clear.

Amira nodded as Lee spoke, but had made her decision. She would go into space. It was the only logical option at this stage, and it was what she would do.

"It's a place for prisoners," Amira said. "And you're an ISP agent."

"You're thinking that I take you there in cuffs," Hadrian said shrewdly. "Now that it's open to NASH again."

"That might work," Amira said, thinking aloud. "Until Westport PD figures out who I am and come for me. Parrish wants Elder Young, right? That's who I am, according to my Eye. Bring me to Parrish, and he'll gladly welcome you into the Carthage."

Hadrian exchanged a glance with Lee, who nodded with fierce approval. Rozene's face appeared on a nearby monitor, a generic, smiling stock photo from the Soma, which revealed none of her past sadness or the suffering to come.

"It's crazy enough, it just might work," Hadrian noted. "Hell, even *I* think it's crazy."

The decision made and the plan set, Amira left for the ship's sleeping quarters. D'Arcy retreated to her own room, afraid to leave the ship in case she lured the Cosmics to their hiding place.

Settled in her cabin, Amira used her new Eye to contact Dr. Mercer. She was seeking out reassurance and sound advice, but instead she found her mentor packing for a swift evacuation of his mountain home.

"I received a tip off that the Aldwych Council is coming for me," he said hurriedly while Henry zoomed in and out of the frame of Amira's lens, carrying piles of clothes. "Well, not the Council directly, but they'll send some hired goons to ask about our conversations. I've already talked to that damn detective, rude little weasel that he is, and I suspect he'll be back with more questions as well. We need to be quick, my dear. They're probably tracing my calls. Who is William Young, anyway? I almost didn't accept the call."

"Never mind," Amira said. "It's a long story and I don't want to waste your time. Dr. Mercer, do you know what the Cosmics actually believe and why they would help the Trinity?"

"No, Henry, leave everything in the kitchen. We just need clothes and anything computerized!" Dr. Mercer barked over his shoulder before turning back to Amira. "The Cosmics...well, I got in touch with some old contacts since our last conversation, people who have been members in the past. Have you done any research on them yet?"

"A little on the Stream," Amira replied. "They believe that consciousness drives reality and not the other way around. And that there is a collective consciousness, like the Conscious Plane."

"Yes, they are in agreement with the compounds on that front. They call it the Conscious Plane as well. If every living, conscious entity on this planet were to expire tomorrow, would there still be rocks, land, sea, the moon orbiting around us? The Cosmics would say no, that the material world and our conscious interpretation of that world are interdependent. And there is compelling evidence to support that, starting with the Double Slit experiment and early quantum theory. They believe that this interdependency can be observed in the Conscious Plane."

"So they believe it's proven and observable?" After years of dismissing compound teachings as fantasy, Amira paused at this revelation. Perhaps instead of pure fiction, the compounds had woven their own threads into something truthful and useful.

"Yes. Dark energy may be an output or measurable component of this binding level of reality. Our consciousness is, of course, driven by the complex neural mapping of our brains, but the age-old question is whether consciousness exists without the brain or extends beyond a living entity. There is evidence that there is a wider consciousness beyond our own perceptions, a shared sentience. There has been some success in detecting it – monks who have spent a lifetime in deep meditation, near-death experiences, certain hallucinogens and drugs. Your former home with its Chimyra – basically an enhanced hallucinogen, developed in a lab by an enterprising Elder. More than just an 'out-of-body experience', it is a connection to a wider entity that transcends our own bodies and even our own reality. The Cosmics aspire to be among the sentient who can access this Conscious Plane, to exist at a level beyond ourselves. Are you all right, Amira? You look pale."

Amira nodded, exhaling slowly to steady herself. After her years on the New Covenant and subsequent life as a neuroscience student, the theories regarding consciousness were not alien to her, but the way Dr. Mercer described the Conscious Plane – she knew it must be real. She'd experienced it at the Gathering, the day she ran up the hill with that young boy, and more recently, the moment she found Singh near death. The faith she had rejected, the core tenets of the compounds, carried a kernel of potential truth.

"So back to the Trinity," Amira said. "Aside from both believing in the Conscious Plane, any idea why the Cosmics would partner with the Trinity? Have you heard of a drug called Tiresia?"

Through the grainy video, Dr. Mercer's pixelated face underwent several transformations – surprise, concern and realization in rapid succession.

"I wonder," he said. "I haven't heard the name, but my colleague mentioned a Cosmic experiment, after the Drought Wars, to test a new drug. A group of Cosmic scientists who wanted to take what the compounds had done with Chimyra to another level. Instead of just hallucinating and glimpsing a shared consciousness, they wanted to actually allow individuals to merge into a single consciousness, even if temporarily."

"Shared thoughts?" Amira asked, transfixed. The Elders had always preached the importance of the group over the individual and exalted the idea of losing oneself to the Conscious Plane, which bound all living things. It made sense that such as experiment would interest the compounds.

"More than shared thoughts, Amira," Dr. Mercer said, glancing nervously over his shoulder. "Shared action. Ten people, twenty, a hundred – all acting in unison. Of course, this is just a story. But the rumor is that Victor Zhang hosted experiments in his own vacation home, along with other Cosmics who supported the idea, and that he had some communications with compound Elders along the way."

Amira dropped her cup of tea. The Eye connection flickered as she collected herself. Her heart sank in her stomach, like the cup landing on the floor with a dull thud. Henry appeared in the lens and leaned into Dr. Mercer's ear.

"Amira, I must go," he said. "There are lights moving up the pathway, so we need to get out. We spoke before about my new home. I won't say where, in case we are being listened to, but you and your friends will find a way to reach me if needed. Be safe!"

The screen went static. Amira stared at it, massaging her temples.

An experiment that removed free will. An army of adherents, acting as one. A terrifying weapon in the wrong hands – and both the Cosmics and the Elders had demonstrated how they might use such a weapon.

Could Tiresia be that weapon? An invention of Victor Zhang's, one the Cosmics and the Trinity had decided to steal together, an alliance with a shared purpose? If so, Rozene may have been more expendable than they realized. A public ploy to mask the true goal of the Soma attack – finding Tiresia.

The boat swayed gently, rocking her exhausted body. Amira thought about Valerie Singh and whether she was at peace. She thought of Rozene – whether she was alive still, frightened, suffering, and bereft of hope. Amira closed her eyes and recited a message to Rozene in her mind, a vain attempt to reach out to her through the Conscious Plane.

Stay strong. I will find you.

CHAPTER THIRTEEN

Parallel to Orbit

The harbor at Sullivan's Wharf was achingly cold in the early morning hours before the sun peered over the eastern mountains. Chilling winds followed the Pacific currents to shore, leaving the taste of salt in the air. Amira blew into her numb fists for warmth as she paced along the wharf's northern fence, through which row after row of cargo containers sat, loaded with supplies and equipment destined for space.

An elderly stevedore with a green hat emerged from behind a container, hands in his pockets. He glanced casually around him before nodding curtly in Amira's direction, her cue to scale the surrounding fence. She gripped the mesh wall, cold air biting at her fingers. She pulled herself up as quickly as possible, aware that another stevedore in the surveillance room had, only briefly, disabled the camera along the north side. He would later blame a technical glitch.

Mr. Pham, D'Arcy's father, had a team that trusted him. For that reason, they helped Amira without asking questions.

Because she was a fugitive, Amira's options to enter the Carthage were limited. When passing security checkpoints, the new Eye marked her as an elderly man with a tall frame and pale eyes. The Parallel's security would immediately catch that discrepancy, and a simple facial recognition scan would unmask her as a wanted woman. Since Amira could not enter the mid-ocean facility as a civilian, D'Arcy concluded, she would have to enter as cargo. Something that Mr. Pham could facilitate. From there, her fate lay in Hadrian's hands.

Moving quickly, Amira followed the stevedore to a brown container the size of a school bus, a windowless structure shaped like a rectangle with each corner severed. D'Arcy and Mr. Pham waited with an older, stocky man who she marked as the head wharfman. He carried himself with an unmistakable air of authority. She shook his hand.

"We'll load you in this one," he said. "It'll be pressurized on the way up, so you won't need any oxygen and your head won't explode. It's carrying some bacteria for research, so it's more regulated inside. Also got some boxes of food for the food court up there – curry and fries and whatnot."

"So I won't starve, at least," she replied jokingly, but the man did not return the smile.

"It'll still be rough on the way up," he said. "It's not meant for moving people and you isn't trained for space travel is what I'm guessing, so I can't guarantee you won't pass out."

"I know the risks," Amira said. That seemed to satisfy him. He tipped his hat and walked back toward the wharf's office buildings.

D'Arcy helped her climb into the container's opening. They faced each other. The first traces of sunlight illuminated D'Arcy's tired face.

"I'm sorry to bring your family into this," Amira said. "To have your dad take this risk."

D'Arcy shook her head.

"You're our family too, Amira," she said. "My dad didn't hesitate when I told him we were in trouble and needed to get you up there. Just be careful."

A whistle blew in the distance. Loading had begun.

They clasped hands briefly. Amira's pulse hammered in her ears. As D'Arcy retreated to the detached stevedore's office, Amira cast a final glance at the looming Westport skyline. Her city.

Amira sank back into the container as the door closed and her surroundings vanished into darkness. Through the thick walls came distant sounds of machinery at work, cranes and pulleys moving cargo into the Bullet train that left for the Parallel. *Illuminate*, she thought, and a faint light shone out of her Eye, revealing the tight quarters of her temporary home. There was little room for her to maneuver. She pressed her back against high rows of boxes and assorted cartons surrounding her, with labels such as 'fragile' and 'handle with care: contains food products'. She imagined the boxes cascading on top of her during the ascent and quickly pushed the thought aside. She traced the scars on her palms, feeling the ridges rise and fall along her fingers, breathing deeply.

The box reminded her of the routine punishments she endured in the New Covenant. At first, Amira would scream in panic when she heard the turn of a lock or bolt. After a time, however, she learned to embrace the calm and let her mind wander and guide her where she pleased – through the walls of her prison and up over the domed houses, past the compound walls into the mountains and beyond. The Elders undoubtedly intended it as punishment, but Amira came to think of it as a kind of freedom. In the stillness, her mind could roam and its boundaries were limitless.

A sudden jolt shook Amira from her sedated state, followed by the sensation of the container's floor leaving the ground. Amira's heart skipped at the first tilt of the floor, and she extended shaking arms for balance. The stevedores had loaded her onto the shuttle.

The Pacific Parallel sat on a string of islands in the Pacific Ocean, near the equator. It served as the base for the Western Hemisphere's space elevator, which took both passengers and cargo to the North American Space Harbor. Elite passengers traveled in private shuttles up to NASH in technology-centered cities such as Zurich, Singapore and Westport, but most tourists and casual visitors went through pods in the space elevator. Satellites traveled into low Earth orbit in a similar fashion, propelled upward by the elevator's powerful cables.

The container docked in position on the Bullet train with a generous thud, followed by the clicking of its sides being locked into place. Amira had watched the Bullet depart Westport in violent bursts of speed more times than she could count. As the engine growled in anticipation, she braced for acceleration. The train gained momentum and then shot forward in a heart-lurching burst of power, thrusting Amira against the cargo boxes behind her. Outside of her dark confines, she knew the Bullet now glided several feet above water, traversing the Pacific Ocean through a vacuum tunnel.

Amira crossed her arms tightly over her chest. Years ago, when she first arrived in Westport and wandered through Union Station with bare, bloody feet, she had stared up curiously at the clear, expansive tube that ran across the station, high above the other train tracks and directly underneath its arched, ornate ceilings. A sharp scream had announced the Bullet train's arrival, and she shrieked as a dark shape sped through the long tube, there and gone in a matter of seconds. A middle-aged man with dark skin and cropped gray hair explained to her that the train was only passing through, and her fear of the train gave way to fascination when he patiently explained the science behind the Bullet (a combination of vacuum-based maglev design and jet propulsion). The man who stopped to talk to the dirty, disheveled girl with a small backpack over her shoulder was Dr. Mercer, her first friend in Westport. Impressed by her questions that day, he had secured a placement for her as a conditional student at the Academy.

At this memory, her thoughts turned once again toward Rozene and what her first days in this dizzying, chaotic city entailed, how she ended up on Hadrian's ship and later in Aldwych, signing her freedom away with the stroke of a pen. She ached to see Rozene again. Which Rozene would her captors be dealing with? The meek, broken woman Amira first met? Or the girl who revealed herself in her memories and in the final stages of pregnancy, sharp and defiant? Amira hoped for the latter. It might keep her alive longer, give her hope.

The Bullet slowed. Amira sensed the inertia in the train's deceleration and felt queasy. The reclined passenger seats typically rotated on the trains to help travelers adjust to the reduction in speed, but Amira, on her knees and entombed by boxes on all sides, did not have the luxury of turning herself around, not without losing her balance and crashing sideways into packages of frozen chicken korma. Her head spun and stomach lurched as the Bullet's brakes screeched to a halt. They were at the Parallel at last.

Aside from brief snippets of footage on the Stream, Amira had never seen the island station. Curiosity defeated caution, and she pushed the container's inner latch to peer out. To her surprise, the door relented and a thin sliver of sunlight seeped inside.

The Pacific Ocean surrounded her, a mass of rich blue interlaced with the simmering white foam of waves breaking along the coast. On shore, teeming crowds filled the concrete pathways. Families stood excitedly in a queue for tickets or rested in sparse patches of grass. Palm trees lined the walkways, rustling agitatedly in the breeze. Eyes flashed from every direction, taking final pictures before entering the space harbor's dead zone. Crowds gaped at something to Amira's right, and she twisted her head to follow their gaze. She nudged the door a little further and saw it at last – the Parallel's space elevator, a gigantic base structure from which three carbon nanotubes emerged, extending skyward until they vanished into the clouds.

Amira inched the door further open, taking in the yawning, bunker-like entrance and surrounding gardens, laced with lines of tourists. Tourists from as far as Japan, China and Russia flocked to the Pacific Parallel to travel spaceside and experience Earth from staggering heights. They wore bright clothes and applied sunscreen, as though preparing for a theme park ride, in grim contrast to the stevedores steering containers on the other side of the entrance.

Amira's view was suddenly blocked by a large pair of bulging eyes and she shrieked, falling backward into a stack of boxes.

"Amira Valdez, right?" the voice behind the eyes said. "Pham said you needed a *discreet* ride up to NASH."

Gasping for air, she managed a nod.

"I'm Terry, one of the crew," he said, opening the door slightly wider to reveal a middle-aged man with a round, open face. "Don't know what you're up to, miss, and don't care. You're a friend of the Phams, and that's all I need to know. Now, we don't have a lot of time here, so here's the deal – I'm going to seal you in, since it's pretty cold up there. You've got oxygen in here, so you should be ok to breathe and all. When you get into NASH, I'll knock on the door twice before unlocking the hatch and I won't do that until the coast is clear. If you don't hear the knock and it opens, try to hide."

Amira nodded, although her options for hiding places in a loaded rectangular box were limited.

"Gotta go," the man said, looking anxiously around him. "I'm locking you in now." And with that, the hatch closed with a loud thud, followed by the hiss of a compressed seal.

Amira settled back, sun spots still waltzing across her closed eyes. *Brace for ascent. Focus. Breathe.* The silent mantras lasted until her eyes adjusted to the dark, impending panic replaced by a newer threat

– the slow, gnawing anxiety of waiting for something, anything, to happen.

The din of the crowds died down and the cranes resumed work, presumably loading cargo containers into position along the space elevator. After what felt like an hour passed, the walls of her own container vibrated as the crane's claws gripped its sides. The stevedores shouted commands and directions at one another outside, and Amira felt the container lift off the ground. It swayed back and forth slightly as it was carried away. This was it.

Amira sat back on her heels and pressed her hands against the boxes on each side of her, steadying herself for the climb. The knot in her stomach tightened further with each second of stillness.

Amira knew this much – the container box had been fixed to one of the elevator's climbers, each fastened to one of the three nanotubes connecting the Parallel to NASH. The harbor moved in complete synchronization with the Earth's rotation so that it was stationary relative to the Parallel. The nanotubes were attached to a counterweight at the base of the station, where claw-like machines maneuvered cargo and passenger pods inside their respective holding areas.

Amira drummed her fingers against the side of the boxes, letting the steady rhythm fill her ears.

And then it started. A whistle sounded and Amira's knees burrowed painfully into the container floor as it rose skyward. It accelerated with each passing second, rattling and shaking while the climber grated against the nanotube. Amira gritted her teeth at the wail of metal against metal. The screeching filled her ears until they suddenly and painfully popped, leaving a dull hum behind.

When the ascending container reached maximum speed, Amira's stomach flipped and she pressed her forehead to the floor to salvage the breakfast her body fought to expel. Every bone in her body weighed her down, heavy as lead. She shivered, fighting back waves of dizziness. She tried to push her forehead back off the floor, but it was too heavy to move. Paralyzed under the weight of the acceleration, she curled helplessly on the floor, fighting for each breath.

Then, in a single moment, the container's driving acceleration stopped as it entered low Earth orbit and Amira became weightless, floating among the cargo. Small beads of sweat drifted away from her clammy forehead, forming tiny crystal globes in front of her. Slowly, her heart rate came down. She exhaled, her head light and airy as she adjusted to the abrupt change in speed and gravity. For the first time, she was in space.

The crushing weight of gravity and anxiety gone, Amira laughed. She laughed again, louder this time, her voice echoing along the container. Stretching her arms wide, she arched her back and turned in slow, backward flips amid the floating boxes. Her hair spread in every direction. Space, at last. A compound girl's dream in the desert, now realized. Her mission, the dangers lurking in every shadow, the violent men she was terrified to face and the threat of mobilizing compounds...all of it faded in the face of her elation. In that moment, nothing else mattered.

The container continued to glide along the elevator, albeit in a more benign fashion, as it passed through the lower and medium Earth orbits toward NASH.

Amira sensed movement in a different direction. Careful to avoid the suspended boxes, she slowly turned upright again, adjusting to the sensation of zero gravity.

Just as she righted herself, they hit something solid and gravity returned. Amira and the neighboring cargo collided with the floor. She activated her Eye, shining a light into the now disheveled container. Rubbing her elbows delicately, she stood up and climbed on a nearby box to listen through the hatch door. Muffled conversations and laughter suggested that she had reached the holding bay, where workers unloaded cargo onto NASH or redirected it to the research stations. She folded her arms anxiously, feeling the first sense of claustrophobia now that the end was near, and waited for the knock.

Minutes later, she jumped at a sharp rapping on the lid. The latch turned. The coast was clear.

Amira pushed the top open. Mr. Pham gave her a quick salute before rounding the corner. The crew traveled up the elevator in their own passenger pod, D'Arcy had informed her, but still took turns ascending in the elevator to avoid health issues. NASH proposed using robots to man the elevators in their stead, a proposal repeatedly vetoed by the union.

She stood in the middle of an expansive room with high ceilings, inundated with row after row of cargo boxes and containers. It had the greenish, sterile lighting and chalky floors of a typical warehouse, albeit one with windows displaying the void of space outside. Warning signs plastered the double doors on the far end of the room. Probably the airlock.

A hand gripped her arm. She spun around to face Hadrian.

"Keep your voice down, love," he said. "You're supposed to be contraband, remember?"

"You scared me." She rubbed her arm and once again marveled at his chameleon-like ability to change his face, literally and figuratively. The NASH badge gleamed against his blue jacket. Several small cuts decorated his freshly shaved face, and his eyes shone with alertness.

"Listen carefully, love, because I don't have loads of time," he said, peering around the corner of the container before he continued. "They've shut down the shipments and prisoner transports to the Carthage."

"What?"

"Nothing goes in, nothing goes out. The station ignored our requests to board, so NASH countered with a lockdown of their own. You won't be able to hitch a ride with me, I'm afraid."

"But how do I get there?" Amira asked anxiously.

"You'll have to figure that out, you and Lee. This should help."

He pulled out a white coat and wrapped it around her shoulders. Amira fingered the badge fastened to the lapel, bearing her face.

"For access inside the Carthage," Hadrian said. "It only works in the Carthage, though, so you'll have to be a little stealthy until you can get yourself there."

A device in Hadrian's shirt pocket flashed and he scowled as he read a message on its screen.

"I've got to run," he said in a low voice. "This could go many ways. It's been on the news for a while that the Carthage hasn't been playing nice with NASH. Refusing inspections, ignoring directives. Your instincts were right – something is happening there. The suits in NASH command will try to do nothing, as usual. I'll fight to board and see what Parrish is hiding. I don't know which side will win out, but you know as well as I do that helping our Rozene is not NASH's priority. If you want to get there first, you're on your own for now."

With that, he dipped in a shallow bow and walked away.

Amira cursed under her breath, alone in a room full of stagnant cargo. It was time to test the most crucial part of her plan.

She blinked sharply and activated her Eye. As she focused her thoughts on her targeted contact, a message appeared in small blue text across the corner of her right eye.

Lee. Are you there?

After a brief pause, a reply appeared below her text.

Affirmative. Swtch 2 speaking mode if u can, itz easier.

She smiled but changed the chat mode on the conversation to 'speak and listen'.

"Lee?" she whispered.

"Good, I can hear you," Lee's voice replied.

It was unlike anything she had experienced – his voice was loud and clear, though he was over a thousand miles away, and seemed to be coming from inside, rather than outside, her ear.

"This is amazing!" she said, struggling to keep her voice soft. "Better than a Two-Way communicator. Does the Eye send the spoken text directly to the other person's auditory cortex? It must have to hit the primary at least."

"No idea," Lee replied, impatience edging into his typically neutral monotone. "Where are you now?"

"Is she ok?" D'Arcy's voice joined in the background.

"Completed the hike on time." They had agreed to keep their communication as cryptic and vague as could be managed, in case their Eyes were intercepted.

"Ok," he said. "Have you found passage to the old city yet?"

"Change of plans," she said, walking briskly down a row of red containers. "The trail is blocked and – oh, hell, I don't know how to say it – all cargo transport to the Carthage has been shut down. I can't get in that way."

"Let's see." Lee's voice remained calm. "I'm pulling up a floor plan of NASH to see where you need to go next, then."

"You got through their servers?" Amira asked eagerly. The coded speech had failed within the span of a few sentences, but at least one part of the plan succeeded.

"Hadrian may have given me a password or two. Got past the initial firewall, but there's an extra encrypted set of files I don't have. It's ok, though, because what I got is pretty good – floor plans, a map of personnel locations, station docking traffic, the important stuff. The bad news is, since you can't go on the cargo ships, we'll have to get to the restricted area's docking bay. Looks like you'll have to cross the entire station."

"Terrific," Amira said, her heart pounding. "Lead the way."

CHAPTER FOURTEEN

The Ghost Harbor

The main hall of NASH's public zone teemed with bodies moving in every direction, leaving Amira lost and disoriented. The entrance to the Space Travel Museum and Planetarium glinted across the hall, next to the gift shop. Neon signs circled the station's upper level. A long food court offered everything from synthetic hamburgers to Caribbean-fusion sushi. Despite her rush to cross the walkway, she couldn't resist pausing at the enormous model of the first planned Titan colony (*Coming in 2275!*) in the center of the floor. A statue of Tenzing Norgay, the Sherpa who led Edmund Hillary up Everest, towered over the main hall, a tribute erected by the powerful Tibetan Sherpa's Guild, who managed all space tourism on the facility.

An enormous window spanned nearly an entire wall of the main hall, revealing the 'spacewalking zone', where tourists could don sleek silver space suits and, after a minimal orientation under the direction of a Space Sherpa, venture out into nearby space. Within the giant netting that surrounded the harbor, hundreds of suited figures floated and glided through space, some taking pictures with older handheld cameras in place of their disabled Eyes.

In the throes of the crowd, Amira did her best to appear inconspicuous as she navigated the lower floor with Lee's commands in her ear.

"It's hard to pinpoint you with all these people," Lee said tensely. "Get up to the walkway along the window."

Amira walked briskly up the stairs. The happy tourists in their space suits reminded her of children in a cordoned beach, except the ocean was airless and unimaginably cold and punctuated with glimmering light that separated stars and worlds. She paused to lean over the walkway rail.

And there it was – Earth, glowing and suspended below them. The home planet appeared deceptively peaceful from a distance, a luminescent swirl of cloud and sea and dirt. It was surreal and beautiful in every sense. No outsider passing by would ever imagine the chaos raging below the veil of clouds; the machinery and burning factories, the plagues and natural disasters, the wars and terrible carnage that raged for thousands of years and the lives that played out across its vast surface. Amira understood now why so many paid small fortunes to visit NASH. From a great distance, one could see the world without its borders and blemishes, a small, floating rock teeming with life, death and the infinite potential between.

"Amira, are you still there? You need to get across the room to the second level."

Amira tore herself from the window.

"Lee, how am I going to get to the Carthage if everything is blocked off?"

"It's going to be tricky but I have an idea," he said over the clicking sound of furious typing. "First thing is to get out of crazy town here and get to the restricted area for scientists and NASH personnel. Since you have full station access, M. William Young, you should be able to get past without too much trouble."

Amira admired his confidence but refused to share it. The knot in her stomach tightened further as she reached the end of the walkway and ascended the stairs. The side pathway ahead of her was marked with the ominous yellow sign – *Authorized personnel only. Trespassers will be prosecuted according to the International Code of Space-Orbital Regulations.*

"Lee, we have a problem," she whispered when she reached the top of the stairs.

"What is it?"

"Is everything ok?" D'Arcy asked, her voice quieter than Lee's but thick with tension.

Amira switched to text. *Armed guards at entryway. Looking closely at everyone who passes. They'll notice the mismatch when my Eye is scanned.* At the Academy and the tolerant enclaves of Westport, no one would question the masculine name attached to a young woman, but she sensed the stern-faced guards ahead would treat her with a higher degree of scrutiny, and a single facial recognition scan in a back office would end the charade swiftly.

"Can you sneak past?"

No. Need distraction.

"I got it," he said. "Keep walking."

Amira drew closer to the security checkpoint. She glimpsed the small, inconspicuous camera near the ceiling and pulled her hoodie around the sides of her face. The security guards stood directly ahead, peering closely at badges and faces as they waved people through.

Suddenly, the music blaring from the hall's main speakers cut off abruptly, replaced by loud, ecstatic moans that drowned out the hum of the crowd. Bewildered, hundreds of eyes turned to the screens that flanked the curved walls of the room. The generic footage of smiling Sherpas and Tibetan cuisine had been replaced with the source of the moaning – a naked woman engaged in enthusiastic sex with an indiscernible number of equally willing partners, both human and mechanical.

A moment of stunned silence was followed by shrieks and gasps. Parents rushed to shield innocent eyes, while others remained transfixed by the screens, pulling out handheld cameras to record the moment. The two guards floundered for several seconds, equally distracted by the scene, until both ran forward to help a beleaguered woman with the main monitor, where the actress was now performing a handstand with her legs spread wide, and Amira walked swiftly and silently past the now-abandoned checkpoint. *Welcome back, M. Young*, the checkpoint screen read as she crossed into the restricted area and rounded the corner.

"Nice work," she said softly as the chaotic sounds of the main hall faded behind her.

"I'd already hacked into the communication channels, so the switch was easy, but they'll override it soon," Lee said.

Amira pictured the sullen teenager with the smile that was evident in his voice.

"I should never have taken you to the Satyr Road with me," Amira replied, though she was grinning.

"The other kids here think it was a great idea," Lee said over roaring laughter in the background. "Now take a left and go down two levels to the docking zone."

Past the security checkpoint, Amira walked swiftly, keen to evade scrutiny. With Lee's help, she navigated through the dimly lit hallways of NASH's restricted zone. She lowered her head, avoiding eye contact when the occasional NASH employee crossed her path.

The NASH docking bay resembled its maritime equivalent. It comprised of a long line of shuttles at its center, each with its own air-locked exit. Beyond the parked transports was a landing area through an arched door, where worker robots signed in departures and arrivals.

"How am I getting out of here?" Amira asked softly.

"You're not going in a shuttle," Lee said. "I've checked the security log and it looks like they aren't letting anyone or anything into the Carthage, like you said. Even in the private docking bay."

Amira sighed. Two women in lab coats walked past her and she stood upright, pacing as though waiting for someone to arrive.

"There has to be a way out," Amira continued in a low voice. "Is the Carthage too far to get to in a space suit?"

"Let me check," Lee said over a flurry of typing. "Yes. You won't have enough oxygen and power to get there from its current location in orbit."

"Then there's no way to get there, if there's no traffic allowed."

"Wait," Lee said. "You just gave me an idea! There are no shuttles going to the Carthage from *NASH*."

"Right."

"Doesn't mean no shuttles are going there at all." Lee went silent for several minutes while Amira continued to pace.

"Found it!" Lee said with triumphant satisfaction. "This is going to be tough, but I have a plan."

Minutes later, Amira stood in a narrow, isolated corridor below the restricted area's private docking bay, quickly fitting into a slim, silver-toned space suit, the flag of New Tibet fastened to the lapel. She slid on the helmet, wondering how something so sleek and simple could keep her safe from the cruel vacuum that awaited her beyond the airlock. Only decades ago, space suits were twice the size, but demand had fueled a new necessity for something light, minimalist and even stylish.

"Hurry up," Lee said tensely.

"Is someone coming?"

"More like someone's going," he said. "I've been watching NASH's radars on everything in orbit in the area. There's a shuttle heading toward the Carthage. It came from the Atlantic Harbor, looks like."

And Amira understood how Lee intended to get her to the Carthage.

"Amira? You ok?"

"I think so. Lee, you should be in the Academy, you know that?"

Lee met her compliment with silence. Amira longed to see his reaction – excitement, dismissal, apprehension. Given his stoic demeanor, the likeliest reaction was none at all.

"If I make it back in one piece, let's talk about it again," Amira said seriously.

"Ready?" Lee asked.

"Ready. Let's do this."

In her years at the Academy, Amira completed her share of space simulation training, an unspoken requirement for ambitious students who planned futures in orbit. Despite this, she lingered for several minutes in the airlock, gripping its handles to steady herself. After several deep breaths, she opened the outer door and passed through.

Overwhelmed by the black canvas before her, she stared at her feet as she rotated around the airlock's entrance. The door closed behind her and Amira fought the urge to retreat back into the harbor. Space was not welcoming – Amira felt consciously alien in her infinite surroundings.

"Amira?"

She drew in a sharp breath at the closeness of Lee's voice, surreal in her surroundings.

"Still here," she croaked.

"How is it?" D'Arcy shouted in the background.

"It's...." Amira's voice trailed away. She faced Earth, tracing the familiar borders between land and sea. Night fell over the western

Americas, the horizon spreading along the deep blue of the Pacific. Along the coast, the bright lights of Westport shone back at her like a flare amid the web of roads and habitation, marking the spot where Lee and D'Arcy sat on a ship, guiding her. The American southwest, a patch of darkness amid intricate webs of city light, peered through a curtain of swirling clouds, where Amira once gazed into the sky every night in search of passing stations. Now, she looked back.

"Incredible, indescribable, amazing," Lee finished for her. "Amira, you need to move diagonally away from the station, to your northeast. I'm sending you the path on your Eye."

Guided by the coordinates, Amira propelled herself forward with her suit's jetpack. Despite her many hours of anti-gravity training and space simulations, she sensed the beginnings of motion sickness. Her stomach flipped with each movement of her legs and feet, which searched in vain for solid ground. She closed her eyes, but it only worsened the feeling of being upside down. Instead, she focused on the navigator displayed on her Eye.

Earth was to her left and she kept it in her vision, a reassuring anchor in the void. On the other side, the Osiris station shone brightly despite its considerable distance, the only station besides NASH that operated in geostationary orbit. The remote station's purpose was the subject of much speculation, and though curious, Amira had no desire to deviate off course.

"Turn your lights off," Lee said. "The shuttle's getting closer."

Amira switched off the reflection on her suit and the small light in her helmet, rendering her invisible for the crucial part of Lee's plan. The suit she wore was identical to the ones at the Academy, a small comfort as she steered ahead.

Then she saw it. A single compact shuttle, speeding forward with a thin sliver of fuel exhaust trailing silently behind. Gently, she propelled herself toward the vehicle, timing her forward momentum carefully. As it approached, she pressed firmly on her jet accelerator and sped alongside its center. Her stomach lurched violently but she continued to accelerate. She reached forward. Her fingers barely wrapped around the handle of the side door when it veered slightly. Her arm jerked violently as her body swung against the side of the craft, but she maintained her grip as the shuttle neared medium Earth orbit. Amira clung tightly to the handle, hoping no one inside heard the impact of the collision.

She would not have long to find out. The Carthage station grew larger and larger by the second as the ship slowed in approach. It was modest in size compared to many other research stations but still made for an imposing sight. The station's body was disc-shaped, three levels high with oval, blue-tinted windows encircling its perimeter. Several prong-like shapes stretched out from its base in every direction like the spokes of a spinning wheel, where shuttles could dock and depart.

"Approaching the dock, Lee," she said. "Can you see anything on your radar?"

Silence on the other end. The map in the corner of the Eye flashed in and out, accompanied by faint static.

"Lee, can you hear me?"

No response.

"Lee?" she asked again in a smaller voice. Lee and D'Arcy were gone, out of her reach. A low rumble signaled the shuttle's connection to the Carthage, and Amira felt a loneliness she had never experienced before. An isolation that surpassed even her escape from the New Covenant.

She remained alongside the shuttle while it docked on one of the station's spokes. Her breath rattled back at her in her helmet, loud and sharp. After waiting for a period, hoping the shuttle's passengers had all boarded the Carthage, she opened the hatch. Though at first she'd been terrified to step into space, Amira felt her heart now racing as she prepared to leave it, unsure of what or who would await her inside the shuttle. Counting to three, she pulled herself into the airlock.

After confirming she was alone, Amira unfastened her helmet with a sigh of relief. The air felt cool and electrifying. The shuttle was thankfully empty, though it yielded no clues as to who took it to the Carthage and why.

The entrance into the Carthage from the shuttle's airlock was closed. Every station in low Earth orbit had a quote or proverb inscribed on each of its entrances chosen by its founder to signify the purpose of the station. The Carthage was built to research the effects of long-term space travel on the human body and mind, and its motto read:

The seeds of life – fiery is their force, divine their birth, but they are weighed down by the body's ills or dulled by limbs and flesh that's born for death. That is the source of all men's fears and longings, joys and sorrows. They cannot see the heaven's light, shut up in the body's tomb, a prison dark and deep – Virgil.

Amira tentatively pulled down on the door latch of the Carthage station. She floated in zero gravity along the stretching, narrow pathway into the station's main body, also known as the harbor.

Something was wrong. Amira felt it the moment she passed the airlock. The air was thick with apprehension and her head throbbed as a high-pitched ringing pierced her ears. It grew louder with each pull forward along the corridor.

Amira clutched the railings on the sides of the wall, her hands sliding with sweat. Eventually she paused, reeling from the pain in her head, and reached with careful fingers to pull out the Eye. To her surprise, the ringing lessened, leaving behind a faint, nagging echo.

The lights in the narrow corridor flickered on and off. Another wave of dizziness struck Amira and a new sound rose above the faint ringing, clouded as though coming from a whispering voice. The voice was human, the words unintelligible. She could not tell if the voice was male or female, fearful or calm, nor what was being said or where it came from, but the whispering continued relentlessly until it rose in volume, reigniting the dull pain in her skull. She looked back at the entrance.

At the end of the corridor, framed under convulsions of light, a body floated lifelessly.

The body belonged to an old man with long, wavy gray hair that fanned out in every direction under zero gravity. He was clearly dead with bloodless, waxy skin and open but unseeing eyes. Before Amira had time to open her mouth to scream, the lights flickered again and the figure of Victor Zhang vanished, along with the whispering, ringing chorus in her ear.

Trembling, Amira longed to turn back, away from this place of corpses and ghostly, distant whispers. But she heard new voices now, the sound of footsteps and muffled shouts from the harbor. She pressed forward.

At the end of the corridor, she pulled out her badge.

Don't let me down, Hadrian, she thought, pressing the badge against the lock.

The red light changed to green. With a sigh of relief, she pushed the door open.

Inside the spinning harbor, gravity returned. She landed clumsily on her knees. Wincing, she pulled herself upright, every bone heavy and lethargic as her body adjusted to the renewed sensation of weight.

A corridor ran along the perimeter of the Carthage's central harbor area, a high-ceilinged circular pathway around the station that cut through several floors. Along its inner ring, doors led to interior rooms and stairways climbed the walls, up to walkways for two rows of visible prison cells. Stepping as softly as possible, given the return to gravity, Amira circled the perimeter. She noted the empty floors, the lack of guards and staff patrolling the station.

Jeers greeted her from above. On the highest level of the station, arms dangled through bars and eyes peered from the back of dark cells. The prisoners called out to her, suggesting clothes to remove, body parts to suck. Others took no interest in her arrival, staring numbly ahead or rocking back and forth in their cells.

Their words did not faze her but the attention they attracted did. She walked with brisk purpose, readying her hands to flash her badge at any passing guards. None revealed themselves, only a long row of convicts, subjects of science's farthest boundaries. She scanned their feral faces, hoping to find either Parrish's prisoner or a lone female face, framed in red hair, in the long row of men.

Halfway around the station, the row of convicts ended. Amira entered the inner portion of the harbor through an open door. Her body tensed at the sound of new voices, angry, but different from the wild jeers of the prisoners. An argument underway.

She followed the trail of the voices around the walkway and up to the second level. The muffled voices took shape near the door.

"This is ridiculous, Tony, just tell us where it is!"

"And what does M. Morgan want with Tiresia?"

"It's none of your damn concern!"

"It is very much my concern, since it is my intellectual property. In either case, I couldn't tell you where the last of it is now."

"If you don't surrender it, we'll have no choice but to create more of it. Go back to the Osiris and resume the process. I know neither of us wants that."

While Amira's eyes remained fixed on the door, something in the air shifted behind her. She spun around to face a man in a red uniform and black ski mask.

He grabbed her by the throat before she could react. In a swift motion, he pulled her roughly through the door.

She struggled to her feet, disoriented. The guard grabbed the backs of her arms and pushed her into a chair. She kicked furiously in every direction but he was strong and quickly forced her arms behind the chair's back.

"Amira Valdez? How did she get here?"

As the man bound her hands roughly, Amira turned to the source of the question – Alistair Parrish stood anxiously before her, clearly thrown by her unexpected presence. To Amira's right, Tony Barlow was similarly bound to a chair. He sat in dispassionate silence and turned to Amira with an odd, knowing smile.

She scanned the room in earnest. Through the dim lighting, the walls were the dull, grimy color one would expect to find along a sewer. In addition to Parrish, the man who bound her joined a second man in a ski mask. Guards for Parrish and the Cosmics, wearing the same uniforms she saw at the police station. Another man sat strapped to a chair across the room, surrounded by trays of equipment. Though his face was bruised and bloody, Amira recognized him as the man who chased her and Lee through the Satyr Road alongside Reznik. He stared stonily ahead, ignoring the array of tools and monitors around him.

As though the scene was not surreal enough, an even more disturbing sight awaited across the room – behind a glass partition lay a young woman, strapped to a complex apparatus of wires and feeding tubes. Her chest rose and fell softly. For a moment, Amira's heart stopped. Had she been too late?

Upon closer inspection, the woman was not Rozene. Her skin was the color of dark, thick honey, her jaw and angular cheeks unmistakably Valerie Singh's, while her deep red hair, cropped around her neck, was the same copper shade as Alistair Parrish's.

Barlow muttered under his breath beside her. "Time deceives us. We are all things and nothing at once."

"Is that Maya?" Amira asked Parrish, ignoring Barlow's strange prayer.

"What's that?" He blinked confusedly as he spoke, as though shaken awake from a dream. "Yes, that is my Maya. We brought her to the Carthage last year to try some experimental treatments that aren't approved yet in Westport, but with no progress. She is as good as dead. Amira, you shouldn't have come here."

Bound to a chair, far from home and her friends, Amira felt as if Parrish had given voice to her own feelings. But as the Cosmic guards glared at her with pure hatred, she refused to give in.

"I was following him," she said, jerking her head toward the bound Trinity man. "Trying to find Rozene. Is she here?"

"No," Parrish said, glowering at his compound captive. "But this gentleman here should be able to answer that question for us. Once he understands that he has no choice but to cooperate."

"We need to be quick," one of the masked guards interjected, addressing Parrish. "The Morgans will hold back NASH a little longer, but we don't have forever. We need all three of these agitators to start squealing, any way we can make them."

The Trinity man closed his eyes and muttered rapidly under his breath, a prayer.

"Alistair, think about what you're doing," Barlow said as Parrish grabbed a pair of sensory pads from one of the trays and placed them on the man's temples. "This is barbaric and unnecessary."

And at that, Amira realized what was about to happen and slumped back into her chair weakly. While she had no affection for the man who tried to kill her, she had no desire to see him suffer.

"What happened to Rozene?" Amira asked in a quavering voice, hoping to delay Parrish, if only for a few seconds. "You were with the Trinity when they took her. I heard it all. You were working *for* them. Why don't you know where she is?"

Parrish faced her, his bewildered expression shifting to anger.

"We were lied to," he replied venomously. "She was supposed

to be brought to us first, so we could finish our testing for our own purposes. But Elder Young had a different idea and dropped contact after the initial seizure. He separated from me and failed to take her to the meeting point. Our people found him in the Satyr Road and tried to bring him in. Caused too much commotion and he got away. But not this one."

"You were going to do tests on her and then hand her to *them*?" Amira asked furiously.

"Trust me, M. Valdez, you don't want the details," Parrish said impatiently.

"The Trinity didn't want the clone to be born," Barlow said simply. "And they didn't trust you, with good reason. This unholy alliance was doomed to fail from the start, Alistair."

Ignoring Barlow, Parrish continued his setup on his other, less talkative captive.

"But why would the Cosmics want to help the Trinity Compound destroy Pandora?" Amira whispered to Barlow. "Aren't they scientists? Shouldn't they support the project?"

"Yes and no," Barlow said smoothly. "There is division among the Cosmics, many of whom have ties or at least sympathies with the holy communities. They entered an alliance, with the intent of both sabotaging the cloning effort on Pandora, as well as procuring something of mine. They have succeeded on the former but not the latter, which is why I have been invited here, to give up my property."

"The property of the Sentient Cosmology movement," the first guard said angrily at Barlow. Clearly, he was more than a hired gun. "You didn't invent it alone."

The Tiresia. What did that vial of clear liquid contain that inspired an assault on a facility, a kidnapping, and factional infighting among the Cosmics?

But Barlow stared intently at Alistair Parrish, his eyes fixed and unblinking, as if to shorten the space between them. He used silence like a blunt weapon, Amira realized in that moment.

"Have you really given up, Alistair?" Barlow asked. "You had the same vision as I not that long ago."

"It was a dangerous and foolish idea," Parrish said roughly, though with sadness in his eyes as he turned to the figure behind the glass. "The time for your fringe science has passed, Tony. I carried false hope, because of Maya, but I have faith in the Conscious Plane. Something better awaits her and us at the end, a better world."

The Trinity man spat on the ground in disgust. In other circumstances, Amira would have been amused by his revulsion. Life beyond life, reward after death. But the compound man would deem Maya Parrish as unworthy of the Nearhaven.

"Faith," Barlow said, so that the word twisted out of the corner of his mouth. "So you at least are wise enough to distinguish faith from fact. But tell me, Alistair, if you have such faith that a parallel universe awaits, one where Maya can walk and feel the air on her face, why do you keep her alive, hanging on to hope? Do you fear death?"

"We don't," the guard interjected. "And we will release her to the Conscious Plane before we leave."

"No!" Amira cried.

"Enough!" Parrish shouted. He paced back and forth with his fists pressed to his temples, as if to prevent the contents of his mind from bursting through his skull. "We must get Rozene Hull back, for her own sake as much as ours. The clone cannot be born. Once it is, more will follow, and it will be a Rubicon we cannot turn back from."

"The Rubicon has been crossed already, Alistair," Barlow said, and an unsettling smile spread across his face. "My 'fringe science' that these occultists told you was impossible? It is done."

Silence filled the room. Even the engine seemed quieter.

"You—?" Parrish whispered. "How? To the subject, to... Rozene?"

Barlow nodded.

"What the hell is he raving about?" the guard barked, eyes glaring through the slits in the ski mask.

"Did Valerie know?" Parrish asked Barlow.

"No," Barlow said. "I made my own *unilateral* decision and I will live with the consequences. We need to see what happens, Alistair, when it is born, to both mother and subject. If it works... if we succeed...."

Though baffled, Amira sifted through Barlow's cryptic words. *It is done. To Rozene. Live with the consequences.*

"It was you," she said loudly, rounding on Tony Barlow. "You were the man Rozene saw that night! I saw her memory! You snuck in and injected her with something, did something to her. It was the Ti—"

Barlow shot her a meaningful glance and she stopped speaking. Though his face was its usual mask, it was evident that he did not want her to say *Tiresia*. Amira did not name it, but could not contain her anger. All of these scientists, with their great minds and sweeping ideas, saw Rozene as disposable, her body and mind as a sandbox to be played in.

"You did something to her!" Amira's voice rose in anger. "You tampered with her memory to try and kill her!"

"I did not, actually," Barlow said softly. "Although I can see how it would appear that way. I have no desire to harm M. Hull, quite the opposite." He nodded at Parrish.

"If not you, then who?" she asked, realizing the answer as she spoke.

"It was Victor Zhang's mistake," Parrish said with disgust. "He foolishly visited the Soma before he disappeared, to search for something, and passed by M. Hull's ward. She recognized him, despite his efforts to disguise himself in the Trinity. Her face gave it away. And so we had the memory of his visit removed. M. Hull was already experiencing the same problems as the others by this time and no one expected such a detail to be noticed." He nodded at Amira with somber respect.

"How did you get those memories removed?" Amira asked in disbelief.

"We had it arranged quickly," Parrish said. "One of our own. Gifted as you are, you are not the only skilled holomentic reader in Westport, Amira."

"A real reader," the guard sneered at Amira. "Not a nobody, Academy brat like you."

"I still don't understand," Amira said, scowling at the vicious guard before turning back to Barlow. "The memory tampering wasn't the only thing wrong with Rozene – you did something before that even happened. What did you do?"

Barlow inclined his head toward Parrish and the guards, then looked intently back at Amira. The message was clear – not in front of the Cosmics.

Amira remained silent, her anger toward Barlow now compounded by a new rush of apprehension. She always found the quiet, observant man suspicious, but now she saw him in an entirely new light. Though bound to a chair, he was revealing himself to be the smartest, perhaps most dangerous man in this room.

Parrish was also processing Barlow's revelation.

"We have to get the girl back," he said softly.

"Alistair," Barlow warned.

Parrish ignored him, positioning himself in front of the machine from which the sensors connected to the man's head.

"Where did Elder William Young take Rozene Hull?" Parrish asked.

The man spat on the ground.

Parrish turned the dial on the machine and the sensors lit up in crystalline blue around the man's temples. At first, nothing happened, but after several seconds, the man began twisting and contorting in his seat, his jaw clenching, his teeth grinding. His hands tightened, gripping something invisible, as he thrashed in unmistakable pain.

"Where is Rozene Hull?"

When the man remained silent, Parrish turned the dial up further. The man, who had previously allowed only a faint whistling sound to escape from between his teeth, now opened his mouth in a full howling scream, thrashing and struggling against the chair binds.

Amira responded in kind, her breathing shallow as she doubled over in her chair, fighting and failing to block out his rising screams.

"Stop!" she yelled, tears threatening. "Stop, make it stop!"

Blood pounded in her face, her vision blurring and tunneling, while the man continued to writhe in agony at the end of the tunnel. The ringing in her ears returned.

Amira struggled fruitlessly against her binds. The screams continued and she lowered her head, sobbing, and in that unbearable moment, the world shifted out from under her.

She rose to the high ceiling. She tried to call out, but she had no mouth, no voice – they remained in the chair below with the rest of her body, now motionless. After an abrupt shift, the familiar sensations returned. The newfound calm, the taste of rust. Beneath her unnatural perch, Parrish continued his grim interrogation, the man continued to scream and thrash and Barlow remained bound, watching Amira with keen interest. She observed the scene dispassionately, calm for the first time since her ascent from the Parallel that morning.

From the ceiling, she pulled even further away. The room grew smaller and smaller, until she passed through the Carthage's intricate walls, past wires and insulation, moving backward further and further until she was out of the station itself, floating above the spinning structure in space.

She was in space. Without a body, without air or protection, and yet the station spun before her, the stars surrounded her.

Amira drifted further away until the Carthage became a distant object in the panorama of her mind, moving in orbit alongside the blue atmospheric ring of Earth. In space, the sensation differed from her past disassociations, a detail she accepted with some concern for what it meant. She tasted rust, heard the buzzing in her ears, but did not sense the usual eyes upon her. Did the invisible observer's reach not extend into space? She vaguely wondered if she would return, or remain a floating, conscious entity in space forever. Some distance away, a small shuttle approached the Carthage. Everything was quiet, free of engines and screams, and Amira focused on the Carthage, willing herself back inside its walls.

Then Amira returned to the room at once, gasping as she lurched forward in her seat. Her hair hung over her shoulders and a bead of sweat fell from her forehead to her knees. Panic and fear returned when she regained her body.

The captive continued wailing under Parrish's turning dial. Amira felt Barlow's eyes still on her.

"You disassociated, didn't you?" he asked quietly.

"I don't know what you mean," she said.

"You left us," Barlow said. "An 'out-of-body experience'. But you're a psychology student, Amira Valdez, you know exactly what I mean when I say disassociation."

"Yes," she said after a pause. Her face flushed with anger. "I've done it all my life, but it's gotten worse."

Barlow nodded.

"Someone's coming," she mouthed to Barlow. "A shuttle." He nodded again, shooting a careful glance at Parrish. Alerting Barlow might have been a mistake, but between his ties to Hadrian and his cryptic conversation with Parrish, Amira had concluded that his agenda included keeping Rozene alive, and that she would need his help.

"What have you done?" Alistair Parrish shouted at the screaming man. "You've killed her, haven't you? Does life mean nothing to you?"

"Alistair, enough," Barlow said firmly. "This is madness. Even if you get an answer, you can't know it's the truth. This man will simply lie to end the torture. Perhaps we could use another resource at hand?"

"You mean M. Valdez?"

Every eye in the room turned to her.

"You have a holomentic device," Barlow continued. "And Amira Valdez has unquestionably proven her abilities in that arena."

* * *

The Trinity man scowled at Amira as she activated the holomentic sensor. It was outdated, but the basics of the machine were no different from the ones she used in Westport. The disc began spinning and she wordlessly attached the sensory pads to the man's head. She loosened his bindings to improve his circulation for the reading. His swollen, bloodshot eyes caught hers.

"You'll die screaming, apostate filth," he said.

"Access visual cortex," she said into the sensor. She kept her voice steady and calm, willing the rest of her to follow.

To read the prisoner while he was fully awake, free of Oniria or other medications that would ease the navigation of his subconscious layers, would be extremely difficult. She turned a dial on the reader and as she feared, the first visuals it generated were haphazard and fragmented. The man's primal, conscious mind was an orgy of violence and rage, every flash of thought tinted in deep red as he struggled to shake the sensors off his head. On the holographic display, Barlow's severed head turned on a spit, Parrish ran down a dark alleyway before being cut in two, and as the man glared at Amira, she materialized in the hologram, lying bloody and dismembered on train tracks. Parrish gasped and turned away in disgust, but she continued to pull deeper into the man's mind. When he realized what she was doing, the man made a concerted effort to visualize the most gruesome, shocking scenes his undeniably active imagination could conceive.

Amira let him. He could imagine what he liked but could not control his subconscious. Once it was breached, she would unlock its contents until all his secrets lay bare. She held on to that thought as the man began laughing shrilly. The hologram displayed a naked Amira spinning in circles like a macabre top as layers of her skin and flesh unraveled onto the floor, peeled away like an apple.

An alarm sounded. The second guard ran to the radar screen.

"A shuttle's on its way," he said to Parrish. "NASH police craft. They'll be here in ten minutes."

Parrish cursed. The power of the Cosmics had its limits – Hadrian, in pursuit. Adrenaline flooded Amira's senses, along with a strange cocktail of relief and dread. Would Hadrian's team get the upper hand? And would she be able to find Rozene's location before the imminent showdown between Parrish's guards and Hadrian's?

"Quickly, find where she is," Parrish yelled at Amira. "And you two" – he addressed the Cosmic guards – "destroy all of the data. I want every file wiped out! Disable everything except Maya's chamber, and get the shuttle ready! Take him!" He pointed to Barlow.

The men sprang to action. One grabbed Barlow under his arms and roughly dragged him away while the second swung a chair against the wall of monitors behind them. Amira continued to navigate the holomentic sensor amid the chaos. In the disjointed reel of the man's active mind, Elder William Young flickered before them for only a second. The man cried out angrily, pushing the thought away.

Amira darted across the room and grabbed a lab coat from its hanger. She ignored the chaos around her. All that mattered was finding Rozene in the tempest of her new subject's brain. And she would.

"What are you doing?" Parrish shouted.

"Cutting through the clutter," she retorted, and tore at the coat's sleeve. She tied the cloth around the man's eyes before stuffing pieces of fabric into both ears. His external senses muted, the frenetic reel of imagery began to slow, the mind's eye coming into focus.

Amid the sounds of shattering glass and equipment crashing to the ground, Amira turned the sensor toward the brain's phonological loop.

Parrish had pressed his hostage with questions about Rozene, a mistake. The Trinity man had probably seen her only once or twice, if he had encountered her at all, so her name did not inspire strong memory triggers. As his mind calmed, Amira pulled the cloth from one ear and spoke a different set of words.

"Elder Young. Andrew Reznik. Where are they hiding?"

And there it was – Elder Young standing in the desert, a glowing ring of blue around his head and a team of young women behind him, in front of a large house overlooking a cliff. With gaping glass windows and bold geometric shapes that stretched over the cliff's edge, supported under angular beams, it looked nothing like the simple round homes that defined the compounds.

"They're about to dock!" one of the guards cried.

Then the image dissolved into another one, of a group of men in black standing in an enormous room with wide glass windows. An old man with long, wavy white hair was on his knees in front of them, head hanging in resignation. She recognized him immediately, as anyone in Westport would.

"Victor Zhang," Parrish said, realization dawning on his face. "That's his home. They're hiding in his house in Utah. Let's go!"

In the hologram, Victor Zhang recited from a piece of paper.

"*—to my ultimate corruption, which led me to believe that I could play God. I hope for atonement with my death and with my renunciation of my role in the terrible crimes of—*"

Suddenly, the Trinity man twisted out of his loosened bindings and lunged out of his chair at Amira, knocking her to the floor. Startled, she struggled to push him away, panicking as he gripped her arms with surprising strength. His teeth found the side of her face and sank into her ear, releasing a hot spurt of blood as the flesh tore. Pain, white-hot and staggering. She screamed and struggled to get out from underneath him. The man fell sideways off her to the sound of a hideous crack, taking a piece of her ear with him. She looked for the source of the blow and found Parrish, wielding a small monitor. He raised it again and brought it down on the Trinity man's head.

During the scuffle, the holomentic machine fell over. Its many parts scattered across the floor. The small disc on which the imagery was stored had dislodged from the reader. Trembling with shock, fighting the urge to vomit as the man's blood swelled in a black puddle across the floor, she felt a moment of clarity fight its way through an enveloping fog of terror.

Grab the disc. Find Rozene.

Amira crawled forward on her knees and elbows, swiftly grabbed the disc and jammed it into her pocket.

"They're here, inside!" Parrish shouted.

Shouts rang out from the prisoners' quarters, accompanied by thundering footsteps. Someone grabbed Amira by the arm and dragged her onto her feet. Shouts, gunfire, glass breaking. Forcing back her fear, she ran, dodging loose wires and blown fuses as they sprinted down the stairs toward the shuttles. The prisoners above them rattled the bars, yelling incoherently. When she slowed for a moment, a pair of rough hands shoved her forward in the direction of the outreaching hallways.

Zero gravity returned when they left the rotating harbor. Amira grabbed a rail along the wall, momentarily disoriented, as frantic shouts echoed behind her. Something pressed against her ribs on her left side. The barrel of a handgun.

"No rescue for you," the masked Cosmic growled. "Move!"

She pulled herself along the narrow corridor as fast as she was able, recalling a space orientation class in which the teacher asserted that guns do, in fact, work in zero gravity. Her arms burned from the effort but fear kept her grappling across the pathway's horizontal ladder, fear and the realization that she had to leave this station and find Elder Young, even under the barrel of a gun.

When she reached the end of the corridor, Amira ducked through the airlock into the shuttle to find Barlow already secure in his seat. The armed guards and Parrish followed behind her. It was incredibly compact, with five passenger seats in a circle and two pilot seats in front. One of the guards pushed Amira into the seat next to Barlow, who, judging from the cut on his forehead, had also attempted escape.

Parrish and the second guard sat in the pilots' seats, hastily flipping switches and turning dials as a chorus of shouts echoed down the corridor. Amira's heart quickened at a familiar voice.

"Hurry!" Parrish yelled as the airlock door began to close.

The engine started, heating the ground below their feet.

As the door closed, something powerful slammed against it. It flew open. Hadrian barreled in through the airlock.

"Save me a seat, kids!" Hadrian shouted, surveying the scene with triumph.

The guard who was not co-piloting sprang into action, leaping out of his seat with his pistol drawn. Relief, temporary and powerful, gave way to fury. Amira stuck out her foot for a sharp kick, sending him hurtling sideways. Hadrian grabbed the guard's arm, the pistol's muzzle pointing and waving toward the ceiling as the two men wrestled in midair.

"Don't fire it, you'll kill us all!" Parrish cried in alarm as the two men battled for control of the gun.

The door locked and the shuttle separated from the Carthage.

The Carthage was shrinking steadily through the narrow rear window, but a second shuttle on the end of a docking bay was also departing – Hadrian's team in pursuit.

Hadrian gripped the guard's throat with one hand and used the other to slam the man's arm against the wall. The gun slid from his fingers, drifting out of reach. Amira leapt for the gun when a loud bang shook the spacecraft. A second bang followed, and the lights went out. Amira let out a small cry, startled by the sudden darkness.

"Call them off!" Parrish yelled at Hadrian.

"They're only shock propellers," Barlow said from his seat. His voice retained its mild, calm tone. The dark outline of his head remained motionless. "A warning to scare us. An ISP agent is on board and there are far too many valuable people in here for them to shoot us down."

"Don't get too confi—" Hadrian began before the craft shuddered.

Light returned and the shuttle shook even harder, making Amira's teeth and eyes rattle in her skull like the engine of a dying car.

Suddenly, the shuttle tilted. It swayed and veered sharply to one side, sending everyone who was unfastened crashing against the walls.

"It's not them," Parrish said, running his fingers down the control screen hurriedly. "Something was damaged when the shock waves hit. This is not good – secure yourselves!"

Another jolt shook the craft again and they all fastened into their seats, the pistol abandoned in the air. Amira gripped the sides of her seat. Her insides sloped and churned in time with the swaying shuttle. She forced her eyes shut and clamped her jaw too tight to scream.

"Entering atmosphere," a mechanical voice intoned from the cockpit. Amira watched thin flames leap up hungrily around the shuttle window upon re-entry into the Earth's atmosphere. The vehicle accelerated, continuing to shake as it dove through the sea of clouds below them.

Everyone gripped the sides of their seats, uttering soft prayers or curses. Hadrian's eyes darted wildly around the shuttle before he slammed his fist aggressively against the wall. Only Barlow seemed calm, or as close to it as possible under the circumstances, his hands folded on his lap and eyes closed as though in deep meditation.

"This moment has already happened and this moment has yet to happen," he said. "All things are possible, every outcome probable. I am dead and alive at the same time." A Cosmic prayer, a last rite.

Amira's face contorted in terror. Tears leaked out of her eyes and rose as salty orbs into the air.

"Hang tight, love!" Hadrian yelled.

The shuttle tilted again. As it fell sideways, the outline of a lake glinted through the window above Hadrian's head. The craft maintained its speed, approaching the ground fast – too fast.

Panic consumed the shuttle. Hadrian yelled something unintelligible at the pilots. The guard fumbled for something under his seat and Hadrian unfastened his safety belt, careening sideways.

"Brace yourselves!" Parrish shouted from the pilot's seat.

Amira moaned weakly as the craft stalled and descended in a sudden, sickening drop. They were falling and spinning at the same time, glued into their seats by the powerful centrifugal force, careening toward the Earth. Then, as quickly as it happened, the craft stabilized and descended at a steadier pace. They were too close, far too close to the ground. A package was thrust into Amira's hand. She looked up to see Hadrian strapping a parachute around his shoulders, managing a wink. She followed suit, fumbling desperately at the clasps with shaking fingers. She struggled to recall the steps from a basic shuttle emergency seminar at the Academy, so long ago. Her ear throbbed, and she realized it was still bleeding. She felt a hot trail of sticky blood down her neck.

Shouts and screams accompanied the roar of the dying shuttle. Amira could not see where they came from or what the other passengers were doing. All she saw was the rocky surface through the crack of the window, drawing closer and closer. Someone pushed at the ceiling to open the top door and screamed. She reached for the door next, pressed her fingers against the metal and drew them back quickly when melting heat ran down her fingers. Terrible shrieks followed, which she then realized were her own. She crouched on the floor, cradling her burnt fingers. Hadrian swung at the latch with a large red object, and Amira stood upright in preparation, but her knees buckled under the force of the descent. The ground was close now, close enough to make out the individual trees on the hills. She gripped the deployment cord on her parachute. Though she never prayed, she silently hoped it wouldn't fail her.

This is it. She couldn't die yet. Not here and now, under rushing heat with screams in her ears. Before she had a chance to truly live. Before she could save Rozene and start again.

The top of the shuttle tore open and a dizzying gust of air rushed through the narrow space, sending equipment and objects flying in every direction. Amira was suddenly airborne as she twisted past sky and earth in a terrifying spin, her feet struggling to find solid ground to land on. She was falling.

The dusty terrain stretched before her and her fingers found the latch on her parachute. A gust of air whipped her face; her body jerked back. Her world went black.

CHAPTER FIFTEEN

The Holy Country

Amira crawled out from underneath the parachute into harsh sunlight, coughing up dirt. The left side of her face was caked with blood from her wounded ear. Every part of her body hurt to varying degrees, but she shakily rose to her feet to prove to herself that she could indeed stand, alive and relatively intact.

Taking several deep breaths, she surveyed the immediate scene. Parrish's coordinates hadn't betrayed them too far; she stood in the American southwest. She recognized it in the color of the soil, the gentle coating of sagebrush over gravelly rock and sand, and the dryness in the air. The terrain was hilly, with treeless mountains the color of rust in the distance.

A trail of black smoke, rising in spirals into the sky, revealed the location of the shuttle several hundred feet away in the shadow of the hills. She jogged toward the wreck.

Amira saw the first casualty as she neared the wreckage – one of Parrish's armed guards, his face mask partially torn off, lying with his legs in grisly contortion across the sand. A small pool of blood leaked from the center of his body, his pale mouth agape in dull surprise. The heat from the wreckage warmed Amira's face; the hot air burned her nostrils.

Amira heard a loud, retching cough and spun around to see the other guard lying on the ground, spitting up thin strands of blood. Most of his red uniform had been charred away. Hideous burns covered his arms and hands and black skin slid down his fingers. She grimaced but knelt beside him to check his pulse. His eyes met hers and widened with fear. His pulse was fast but faint.

"I'm going to look for a first aid kit," she said, getting up. Rummaging through the torn gap in the shuttle, careful to avoid the still-hot metal and the body hanging outside, she grabbed a small case with the red symbol across its cover, miraculously intact.

By the time she returned, he was dead. She pulled back the remains of his mask gingerly, revealing a young face. This had been the one who grabbed her and taunted her in the Carthage. She knew it, somehow, but could not find any satisfaction from his burned, broken body, lost to this plane of existence.

She searched the wreckage for Hadrian, pushing and kicking smoldering debris aside, but found no trace of him. Her stomach lurched at the thought that there may only be traces left to find. Hadrian had his parachute on before the shuttle tore apart – perhaps he had landed elsewhere, as she had.

Parrish and Barlow were also nowhere to be found. Given the violence of the crash, they were equally likely to be dead or alive. In any case, she would need to locate Victor Zhang's house and find a way inside, preferably not alone.

The sun began to slip behind the high ridges in the distance, turning the sky a glowing pink, when Amira reached the base of the nearest mountain for shelter. Early dusk brought with it a cool breeze, and Amira pulled her hoodie tightly around her head. Her ear ached but had stopped bleeding. Under the shelter of a singular juniper tree, she cleaned up her ear with the first aid kit, calmed the burns on her hands and planned her next steps.

Amira reached in her coat pocket and found her Eye, which she had not worn since removing it in the Carthage. She carefully placed it back in her right eye, blinking several times as the cold silicone slid along her lens.

For about a minute, the Eye did not respond, and Amira wondered if it received too much damage on the descent back to Earth before the unsettling greeting, "*Welcome, William Young,*" appeared in the corner of her vision. She immediately called Lee.

Lee? Are you still there?

Lee's exasperated voice boomed into her ears.

"Amira, where have you been? We lost you on the way to the Carthage. D'Arcy's been freaking out."

"I lost the signal," Amira said. "Something on the station switched the Eye off, but never mind. I'm back on Earth now."

A silence spanned several seconds, while the teenager presumably processed the information.

"Do you know where?" Lee asked.

"I may need your help." Amira pulled up a satellite map on her Eye, which placed her location in southern Utah, close to the Arizona border. Lee let out a low whistle.

"You're in compound territory, Amira," Lee said. "The heart of the Holy Country."

He was more accurate than he realized. In the aftermath of the chaotic escape from the Carthage, Amira realized that she knew the strange, geometric house in the Trinity man's memory – she saw it years ago, the day she evaded tear gas and rubber bullets to encounter a strange house across the valley, and disassociated for the first time. The house turned out to be Victor Zhang's.

"Lee, I need you to look and see if there's a house nearby," Amira said. "They're keeping Rozene in Victor Zhang's house in the desert, which is—" She screamed when a cold hand gripped her arm.

Hadrian. He stumbled forward, haggard but elated. Scratches lined his face and his ISP jacket was coated in a solid layer of dust.

Terror turned to joy. Amira threw her arms around his neck and let out a muffled sob of relief.

"I see the strong survived," he said, clapping a hand on her shoulder before grimacing. "That was quite a ride, eh? Is that Lee you're talking to? Lee, can you hear me? You better be running those updates to my servers! And take the trash out."

"Sounds like Hadrian's ok," Lee said drily. "I'll review your current location and let you know if I find any houses in the area."

Amira and Hadrian faced one another, Hadrian bouncing on the balls of his feet.

"Have you seen any of the others?" Hadrian asked.

"The two security men are dead. I found them by the crash site. Haven't seen Alistair Parrish or Barlow anywhere."

Hadrian sat down under the juniper and winced slightly as he stretched his legs out in front of him. He had no obvious injuries, but despite his manic posturing, he was clearly exhausted and shaken by the crash. He lunged forward, retching.

"What's happening?" Amira asked, startled.

Hadrian looked weaker than she had ever seen him. His eyes carried the same hollowness as on the night they listened to Victor Zhang die. He tried to speak but only managed a thin rasp. She searched the first aid kit and pulled out a small bottle of water. Hadrian took a deep drink and leaned in toward her ear.

"Got any stims in there?"

"Stimulants? Really? Is that why you're the way you are most of the time?" Exasperated, Amira rummaged through the first aid kit again before finding one, the same medication she had injected herself and Rozene with in the Soma.

Hadrian's face came back to life as she pulled the syringe needle out of his arm. He stood up again, his eyes alert to their surroundings.

"Any sign of the others?" Amira asked.

"I saw Parrish on his parachute landing east of here," he said. "Haven't seen Barlow."

"Yes, about Barlow," Amira said. "Tell me more about him."

Hadrian looked up at her with a cryptic smile, but Amira had reached the end of her patience.

"He did something to Rozene in the Soma," Amira snapped. "Then he had you use me to get this Tiresia. The two of you are buddies for some reason and I don't care why, but I want to know who he is and what he's up to."

"You're making some mighty big assumptions, love, by saying I'm mates with Tony Barlow," Hadrian replied. "But we go back a-ways, that much is true. As to your questions, I've been trying to learn the same thing, ever since Victor Zhang disappeared. Here's what I know – Barlow is gifted, a true talent, but also rogue. Bit like me, in a way. A Cosmic, but doesn't follow the party line, it seems. He's one of the most senior scientists up there, as you can tell by the company he keeps, but he doesn't wear the Aldwych Council badge or the black coat – on purpose, I reckon. Barlow prefers to be behind the scenes. Oh, and one more thing – he's one of the few names with full access spaceside. Meaning the Osiris, where he always goes when he comes to NASH."

Osiris, the shadow station. The notoriously secretive research done there was information that few in space, even NASH security figures like Hadrian, knew much about. It made sense, Amira thought, with Barlow's unexplained presence on the Pandora project that he was in a position of influence. He was also clearly in opposition to other Cosmics, refusing to give Parrish the mysterious Tiresia, although he had somehow persuaded Parrish to change direction on the Carthage. What was Barlow's goal and who would stand to gain if he reached it?

They strategized further under the last gasps of sunlight. Hadrian's men had followed Parrish's shuttle closely when entering the atmosphere, but appeared to have lost the trail. His team should be searching for them, Hadrian informed Amira, but could not be counted on for backup. The sky cloudless and empty above them, an old unease settled in Amira's stomach. Back in the Holy Country, even the dry air felt hostile, draining strength and confidence from her. Amira tried to shake off the suffocating apprehension. She left this place a child. A lot had changed since then.

Amira described the Trinity man's memory of Zhang's execution, and explained that his desert home was the likely hideaway for Elder Young and Rozene. Hadrian listened intently, his face flickering darkly at the mention of the famous scientist's death.

"No surprise that it was the Trinity," Hadrian said. "I figured it was just because he was part of the cloning club in Aldwych, but seems there was more to it than that."

"These Cosmics," Amira said in agreement. "They were in some kind of alliance with the Trinity and it's gone sour. They both wanted Rozene, but also the Tiresia, though I still don't know why. But Parrish may have changed his loyalties, based on something that Barlow told him. He's trying to find Rozene as well, but hard to say what his end game is right now."

"If Parrish hadn't killed him," Hadrian grumbled, "I could have gotten a confession out of that Trinity bastard."

Amira pulled out the slim disc from her pocket.

"It's in here," Amira said. "The memories loaded from the holomentic display. I was thinking that if I could get it to Detective Pierson and get the police down here, it might help clear my name. But I don't have a way to send them or upload them. It won't work with my Eye."

"First things first, love. We have a damsel in distress to find."

"Should I contact the police?" Lee asked, and Amira jumped. She relayed the question to Hadrian and he shook his head.

"My team up in the sky can be trusted, but Westport PD, the rest of NASH, anyone with a badge could be compromised. There's a dead man in the Carthage and you're a fugitive. What kind of help do you think we'll get? And if they help us rescue Rozene, where does she go? Those Cosmic folk wanted her badly enough to aid a terrorist attack and try to snatch you from police custody. I'd expect they'll jump at the first clue of her whereabouts. No, love, we're on our own for now. Unless my damn crew finds us."

They unpacked the remainder of the first aid kit. To Amira's relief, they had two days' supply of hydration tablets and sustenance packages, a set of thin powders designed for space travel. The lack of solid food and water would be unpleasant, but they would survive. There was also gauze, antiseptic and a healing gel for deep wounds. She reapplied it generously to her maimed ear when Lee's voice came back on.

"I've been going through the NASH satellites and I think I found the house you're looking for. It's east of where you are now, about seven miles away, over a gap in the hills. It's pretty big and looks like it's on some high clifftop."

"That sounds like it," Amira said, recalling the Trinity captive's flashing memories of the house, as well as her own. "And that's not too far – that would probably take us a few hours, with all of the switchbacks."

"Right," Lee said. There was hesitation in his voice. "So Amira, what do you know about Victor Zhang?"

"Famous scientist, headed the Volta station. He's been reported absent for months on the Stream, Lee, but he's actually dead. The Trinity killed him in his own home."

"Ok, I've been reading about him on the Stream, and he's called an 'eccentric' a lot," Lee said, ignoring the detail of his violent homicide. "Looks like there were stories about him building weird things in his houses, experiments of his. And...."

"Yes?"

"The satellite images of the house are kind of funny as well. There's this really bright light in the center of the house, but it's not a reflection from the sun. There's all these forums where people post theories on what it might be, and...."

"Lee, there are all kinds of crazy things that get shared on the Stream," Amira said, smiling as Hadrian shot her a puzzled look. "And it wouldn't change anything if any of it were true. If Rozene is there, then we need to go and find her."

But Amira recalled Dr. Mercer's last words to her about the Cosmics. A team running strange experiments in Victor Zhang's home, attempting to form a single consciousness. What would they find in the house, aside from a retinue of heavily armed Trinity fighters?

After Lee sent the coordinates of the house to her Eye, Amira and Hadrian discussed their options. Both agreed that breaking into the house at night was the best chance of getting in and out quietly, although they would have to anticipate some security if Elder Young was indeed there. As a result, they would sleep for about three hours and start walking at 10:00 p.m. toward the house to ensure an arrival when it was still dark.

Before the sun disappeared behind the distant peaks, Amira walked along the base of the hill to explore. A rare opening between worlds had been discovered not far from here, the wives told her during the Gathering, a temporary tear in the universe's fabric that revealed the Otherworlds to Elder Cartwright. Of course, the Feds had done their best to hide the evidence, so terrified were they that the word would spread. Creatures from the Nearhaven, ten times our height, walked through these canyons during the Cataclysm, the wives added. Their bones were excavated but hidden from the faithful. Even as a child, Amira had to stifle laughter at the compounds' artless mixture of Otherworld lore and government conspiracy.

In the clearing on the other side of the hill were remnants of the Gathering. Amira felt like a spirit passing over familiar ground, echoes of an old life hanging in the still air.

A rotting piece of wood was partially buried in the sand. Amira knelt and brushed the sand away from the exposed beam, revealing the skeleton of the podium built to lead prayers and deliver sermons – on sin, passage, and the upcoming battle between good and evil that the compounds' children would inherit.

Amira's chest burned and her eyes quickly followed. She shed hot tears of grief and rage for the past she still carried and would always carry, and for others at the Gathering who remained, forgotten and waiting. Westport had become her home, its residents her new family, but she would always be bound to the compounds, molded by the scars they left her. They would always shape her future.

Amira rejoined Hadrian and they returned to the hill near the crash site to rest for the night. The smoke no longer rose from the wreckage, though a dark cloud hovered over them as the sun began its descent over the ridge.

They dined on energy bars from the first aid kit. Amira tended to her ear, which no longer bled but would never fully heal, chunks of bloody skin lost to the Carthage. Hadrian wrapped his jacket around her shivering shoulders as they lay down.

CHAPTER SIXTEEN

House of Apparition

It was pitch black when Hadrian shook Amira awake. She massaged a sore neck, body protesting as she stood. Her limbs ached for another hour of rest, but delaying their trek was not an option. They began the long walk in the darkness, Amira's Eye shining the faintest of lights in front of them. Even that small beam of light made Hadrian nervous; he feared it would draw the Trinity to their location, but Amira pointed out that they were more liable to plunge down a ravine without something to guide them.

As they hiked the trail up the mountains, Amira silently thanked the Academy for their grueling physical exams. Though it was challenging, she knew she would complete the trek and arrive at their destination with energy to spare. Energy she would need in spades.

Following the mapped directions on Amira's Eye, they turned the final corner along the trail and there it was – a single house on the edge of a high cliff, dim lights shining from several windows.

Hadrian let out a low whistle.

"It's impressive, I'll give it that."

"And full of Trinity men, no doubt." The Eye zoomed in. A low wall encased the house and a garden on three sides – the fourth side reached out over the plunging chasm below the cliff. There was no visible sentry outside or through the windows.

It was not unheard of for Westport's wealthy elite to own homes in the American southwest near compound territory. To escape polluted skies in the densely populated cities, those who could afford it built their retirement homes in the few remaining remote areas in North America. For some, the mountainous regions in the western Rockies and the Pacific Northwest; for others, the Baja peninsula, which remained pristine but heavily dry, the cost of water considerable even decades after the Drought Wars. For many, though, particularly the scientists of Aldwych, it was worthwhile to be able to see the night sky, free of smog and city lights, so Amira understood the desert's appeal to Victor Zhang and others like him.

They descended the hill toward the house to get a closer look. Large boulders and scraggly pine trees punctuated the long downhill, providing cover as they advanced.

Hadrian suddenly threw out his arm in front of her to stop.

"Over there," he whispered.

It took a moment of scanning in the dark before she saw what Hadrian was pointing at – Alistair Parrish propped against a tree, wrapping a torn piece of cloth around his midsection, where a large bloodstain spread like watercolor paint across the right side of his shirt. He tightened the makeshift bandage, oblivious to their presence.

Hadrian and Amira stayed back, silently exchanging the same look. *What now*? Amira distrusted Parrish, but for now at least, he shared their goal of rescuing Rozene from Elder Young. He had knowledge and resources at his disposal that they did not. And though he helped the Trinity Compound abduct her, the alliance between Cosmic and compound appeared to be over, along with Parrish's own allegiance to the Cosmics. He wanted Rozene alive for whatever purpose Barlow had alluded to.

Amira stepped forward slowly.

Parrish sprang upright at the sight of Amira. No sooner had he stood up than he sank back down again, the color drained from his tired face.

"I have a first aid kit," Amira said, taking another step forward. "Do you need help?" Hadrian approached him slowly, hands in his jacket pockets.

Parrish took the hint and raised his hands in the air before nodding at Amira.

As Amira helped dress and bandage his wound, a deep gash directly below his ribs, Parrish began a delirious, rambling speech, directed at himself as much as Amira.

"I have made some terrible mistakes, M. Valdez. You know, I changed once I learned that Maya would never wake up. I couldn't accept it – that with all my power and influence, I could not change that one fact. The only thing that really matters – the awards, the research, all should be secondary to the ones we love. When cloning became closer to reality, which Valerie had been fighting forever to legalize, I saw the chance to bring Maya back somehow, born again as a genetic copy. This was before Pandora, Amira. Valerie was different. She never believed in looking back, however much she wished it. Everything always had to move forward, forward, forward."

"Raise your arm a little higher, Dr. Parrish," Amira said.

"But as we struggled and fought," Parrish continued, "I found comfort in the teachings of Sentient Cosmology. You must understand, I was in deep depression – they say that to bury one's child is the worst, most unnatural thing, but I didn't even get the finality of a burial. No, my child resided in limbo, as the Catholics used to believe, between consciousness and death, not here but not gone, and the pain of it was unbearable. Truly unbearable. They told me what I wanted to hear, that there was more to us than these short, meaningless lives. Other realities, other planes of existence, that we are not what we fear ourselves to be – something brief and temporary and small."

"You became an official Cosmic?" Amira asked. She recalled seeing him on that hazy day at Infinity Park, tears streaming down his face at the Cosmic lecture. It made sense to her. Some, like Dr. Mercer, patched their losses with a robot, reliving old memories through a crude imitation of the past. Parrish needed something more powerful.

"It took time, but they pulled me into the fold," Parrish said, his pale head nodding in confirmation. "They convinced me that Pandora was a mistake, a potentially catastrophic one. They promised treatment for Maya, based on new insight into consciousness. I'm ashamed of myself. And now Valerie is gone, I saw to that! For all her faults, and she had many, she did not deserve the fate I delivered her – the desolation I wreak on everyone I touch. Maya, Valerie, Victor…I am running out of people to hurt, Amira. Only I am left."

Parrish laughed bitterly and winced as the bandages tightened.

Hadrian paced impatiently, gun held loosely at his side, crushing pine needles under his heavy boots. Amira finished wrapping Parrish's bandages, nodding to him as he spoke. Despite everything, she pitied him. Her own father, she always sensed, was a skeptic at heart. He had only truly surrendered to the doctrine of the compound after enduring losses of his own – Amira's brother of three days, the son he always wanted. There is no reason in grief, no logical deductions that can heal its deep wounds, but faith could slow the bleeding.

With his wound treated and contained, Parrish led them further down the hill. The sky remained dark as they approached Zhang's house. The Trinity's presence was finally confirmed by the two men standing sentry in the front yard, cradling large, archaic machine guns. Neither looked to be on high alert, but they were sufficiently armed for any surprises. Hadrian jumped from the sturdy juniper tree he used to survey the scene.

"Any luck with your Eye?" he asked Amira.

Amira cradled the fragile lens in the palm of her hand, silently pleading with it, willing it to activate. Shortly after treating Parrish, she realized that it was dead. Like most modern Eyes, it operated on solar energy and after her lengthy trek in space and walk through the dark, it had no power left.

She shook her head angrily. They were on their own.

Hadrian nodded and gestured Amira and Parrish forward.

"I can take them out," he said. "I'll move quickly and knock them cold while you two climb in through those windows. Only problem is that we don't know what's inside and how many are in there."

"That sounds terribly risky," Parrish said.

"Any tactical assault ideas you'd like to share, scientist?"

"Listen, I knew Victor Zhang well," Parrish said in a low voice as they crouched down in a close circle. "I've been in that house many times before and know the layout. Something to know about Zhang is that he took his most important work home with him, and we might be able to use that in our favor."

"What do you mean?" Amira asked, intrigued.

"There was a project conceived decades ago, during the Drought Wars. The North American Alliance decommissioned it by the time Zhang took the Volta station, but he never stopped working on it. It was an experiment in using single-conscious commands for mechanized warfare, specifically robotic warfare."

Hadrian shook his head in confusion, but Amira understood the concept. Dr. Mercer had devoted entire classes to it at the Academy.

"Using singular conscious navigation to control something with artificial cognition, like an advanced computer or a robot," she said.

"Exactly. A team of people, a single person even, can direct an army, making them move and act through mental focus. Victor Zhang spent years on it after the war ended. It's in there. Not an entire army, but robots that can attack and fight with someone directing them."

"You've seen it work?" Hadrian asked eagerly.

Parrish paused.

"It wasn't perfected when I saw a demonstration of it," he conceded. "But the basic science is correct. The devil was in the details of execution. I know the logistics of his technology and I'm confident that I can activate it if it comes to that."

"You're suggesting that one of us sics these mind-sharing robots on the Trinity?" Hadrian's eyes betrayed his doubt and the faintest trace of fear.

"You go look for the girl," Parrish said firmly. "As quietly as possible, and hopefully, we can slip out undetected. But if someone sees us, and I suspect they will, I'll make my way to the equipment Victor set up for his project and give us a weapon in return. We're outnumbered and outgunned. This is our best chance to do this with only the three of us."

"And what if the Trinity have already figured out how to use whatever's in there?" Hadrian asked with a shrewd smile.

"A frightening prospect, but I doubt it. The world of inter-conscious navigation is very much out of their realm."

Hadrian frowned as he searched for a counter-argument, but said nothing.

Amira nodded at Parrish in agreement. They had no Eye, no contact with Hadrian's unit, and no allies available to help them. But she had an idea.

"If I find a computer in there, I can upload the disc from the holomentic machine and send it back to Lee in Westport," Amira said. "Hadrian, I know we planned for you to do it, but I think you'll need to back up Dr. Parrish if things...go badly. After it's uploaded, my friends can route it to the police."

Though Parrish shuffled uncomfortably, no one objected.

Hadrian moved first. Amira and Parrish obediently waited behind the wall of trees near the complex. Exhausted and restless, Amira bounced on the balls of her feet, craning her neck for a view into the entrance.

With adept swiftness, Hadrian pulled up over the wall, landed on the other side softly, and sprinted with his head low toward the first of the two guards. He swung his arm around and pressed a small round device against the man's head, sending him crumpling silently to the floor. When the second guard turned and raised his weapon, Hadrian brought the instrument around again, rendering him unconscious.

Hadrian dragged the men around the building. The swift brutality of Hadrian's attack jolted Amira out of her tired state. The hairs on her arms raised to attention, her entire body tense with the realization that their plan had become action, and events were outside of her control.

Parrish made his move over the wall. He gestured at Hadrian toward the window along the nearest corner. The two men pried the window open and quickly pulled themselves inside.

Amira waited, ears straining to hear any indications of activity in the house.

Suddenly, there was a faint shout, followed by the muffled sounds of a scuffle. They had been discovered already, as Parrish predicted.

Her heart pounded. It was just past 5:00 a.m. – the sun would soon rise and the rest of the house with it, if the intrusion had not awoken them already. Fighting back panic, Amira considered her options. To follow them now would be reckless and most likely ineffective, as they tackled an unknown number of assailants, but she could not sit idly by either.

Another idea struck her. Instead of clearing the wall, Amira raced to the back of the complex. She followed the low cement wall until she stood before a narrow door of heavily tinted glass, an entrance to the house's backyard. Taking a deep breath, she knocked.

The compounds had their differences in doctrine and lifestyle, but also shared common customs. One was that women always used the rear entrances to houses wherever possible, while men freely passed through front doors. If there were any women in the house, this would be the way to reach them. It was early morning, when younger compound women began chores and cooking. She knocked again, louder.

After a moment, the cloudy silhouette of a slight figure appeared through the other side of the door. A lump formed in Amira's throat. If this didn't work....

"Who's there?" A soft, frightened, and unmistakably feminine voice.

"Please open the door, Sister in Faith," Amira said, adopting the compound term for a woman of unknown marital status. She struggled to keep her voice calm, as though she were just a passing neighbor. "I need your help."

A bolt turned and the door cracked open, revealing a sliver of a young face with dark eyes.

"Who are you?"

"Sister, I was born in the Children of the New Covenant Holy Community and I'm looking for my friend, Rozene Hull. I am worried for her safety and want to see her. Is she here?"

"There is no one here with that name, Child in Faith," the young woman replied. She addressed Amira as an unmarried woman. A fair assumption to make, given her modern dress and uncovered hair.

A distant crash came from the house and the young woman's eyes fearfully darted sideways. Amira's chest spasmed under another rush of adrenaline. Time for Rozene, for all of them, was running out. Desperately, Amira searched for the words that might reach her on a common plane of understanding.

"Please," she whispered. "Woman to woman, all I want is for one of our own to be treated fairly. Please let me in and I'll make my own way. If I'm caught, I'll say I broke in without help."

The door opened wider to reveal the young woman in full. Like Rozene, her face was heart shaped, partially concealed under a periwinkle lace veil, through which several ringlets of dark, curly hair escaped around her forehead. The light purple color of her veil signified a woman past her first year of marriage.

Amira gasped.

"Marlee?"

"How do you know my name?" Marlee asked, eyes widening in fear. Her eyes had lost the sparkle she saw in Rozene's memories, their dark centers now dull and weary.

"Rozene told me about you," Amira said. "How close you once were."

Marlee flushed slightly but continued to stare back at Amira through the narrow crack. Her hand remained pressed against the door, blocking Amira.

It was surreal, looking back at a person she had never met before, who regarded her as a stranger, though Amira knew her most private and intimate moments, at least through Rozene's eyes. Knowing Marlee on some level, Amira used it to her advantage.

"You know what they're going to do to our friend," Amira continued, lowering her voice further. "If you stop me, I know you'll regret it. You must still care about her in some way. Maybe not as you once did, but you don't want her to suffer, I'm sure of that. Please. Do this for her now."

Marlee finally relented, casting a final anxious glance behind her before she opened the door. Amira exhaled, flooded with relief. Marlee would not turn her over to the Trinity. Whispering her gratitude, Amira stepped into the backyard, which looked unsettlingly commonplace; patio furniture covered in white cushions, checkered with a pattern of palm trees and camels. A grill sat on the edge of the brick patio next to a large, beautiful cactus plant with spiky, outstretched arms adorned with purple flowers. The backyard's intimate, personalized touches gave Amira a pang of grief for its former resident, a man she had never met.

Marlee gestured to the door by the patio.

"Down those stairs," Marlee said in a high whisper as Amira pulled the sliding door into the house. "She's being kept down there."

The floors creaked under the echoes of distant footsteps. The sounds of the earlier scuffle were gone – either Hadrian and Parrish had won and were making their way through the house or, Amira thought with a cold shudder, they were no longer in a position to escape. In either case, she was on her own. Amira found a veil on the coat rack and hastily tied it around her head. Light blue, the color for a newly married woman. A woman's coat rested on a hanger, smelling faintly of dirt and cooked onion, and she pulled it on, her body enveloped in its woolly protection.

The marble-tiled staircase beckoned behind the coat rack. Lowering her head so that the veil shielded most of her face, she descended with soft, swift steps. When she reached the first landing, she paused, reeling and light-headed as a strange sensation overtook her, the same disorientation she experienced in the Carthage station. Her ears rang. She leaned against the rail for support as she heard pounding footsteps from the level above her, followed closely by men's shouts and several loud crashes. Amira silently hoped that Parrish had been able to reach Victor Zhang's invention, or it was likely to be a short fight.

"What are you doing here?"

A stern woman of about fifty emerged around the staircase from below. She peered suspiciously into Amira's face.

"I – I'm a—"

"Speak, girl, I don't have all day!"

"I'm...Marshal Sarka's new bride. My father brought me in late last night," Amira said, keeping her head lowered. Her pulse drummed along her neck. "I – I came down because I heard some strange noises from the entrance of the house."

The older woman's face flickered with pity, probably at the thought of being married to Sarka, before resuming her scowl.

"We can all hear the commotion, girl, that's where I'm going. Move on and pack your things. The Elder will send us away in a hurry if the Feds are here."

Amira continued down the stairs. The next level contained an office and a den, with large screens and a bar that had been spray-painted with religious slogans. A hallway beyond the den led to several additional rooms, where Amira guessed the other Trinity members slept. The stairs continued to another level below, its pathway dark and unlit. A fitting place for a prisoner.

A shout came from the hallway and Amira darted behind the door. She pressed against the wall. Her hands trembled. Two men ran into the room. Through the sliver in the door jamb, she could see both men toted large guns with ammunition chains around their necks. One of them shouted down the stairs.

"All hands upstairs!" the man yelled. "We're under attack!"

"Is it Feds?"

"Reznik told us to stand guard no matter what," chimed in a second voice from below.

Guard. Amira was in the right place.

One of the men spat and cursed softly. Less than a foot away, Amira held her breath, willing every muscle in her body to remain still.

"Did you hear me? We're under attack, grab your weapons and come fight, you sodomist clowns!"

'Sodomist' was a common insult at the Trinity, according to Rozene. It gained popularity following a brutal purge of gay men in the compound, becoming a general term for any man one disliked. Between the persecuted gay men and the young straight men who were expelled to eliminate competition for young wives, Amira wondered at there being any men left other than the greedy, lecherous Elders.

She forced her back further against the wall as the guards from the lower level ran upstairs to join the action. Resisting the urge to follow them, to scream a warning to Hadrian and Parrish, she continued the descent to the next level.

She stood in Victor Zhang's wine cellar, or whatever was left of it. Most of the bottles had been smashed, though some were intact but empty. The fumes from the broken bottles had saturated the wood-paneled walls and hardwood floor, strong enough to make Amira feel light-headed. The room was closed off entirely with no sign of Rozene.

Several tall refrigerators lined the wall at the end of the room. As Amira drew closer, she gasped and clapped a hand over her mouth.

Crammed in the center fridge was an old man with long white hair, mouth slightly open. His head pressed against the clear glass door, revealing an opening in the side of his head from which blood streaked down his white hair. The wine refrigerator had not been cold enough to preserve the body entirely – the visible skin was waxy and green, bones protruding where the skin had broken apart on his hands. It was the same decayed face she saw a flicker of in the Carthage, the apparition at the end of the tunnel. Victor Zhang.

Amira knelt on the floor and retched. After a moment, she breathed in deeply and tried to steady herself, but as the pungent decay filled her nostrils, she doubled over and retched again.

A high cry rang out from beyond the wall. She stood up, searching for the source of the sound when she heard it again.

Help!

And as she looked back at the horrific sight of Victor Zhang, she understood. He was not only a hidden trophy, but a distraction from what was behind his tomb.

She moved to one side of the fridge containing Zhang and pushed it with her fullest strength, using her shoulder to nudge it sideways. It gave, scraping along the floor. As she suspected, the fridge concealed a door. At the third cry for help, she went through.

The next room contained a large, drained indoor pool, though about five feet of brownish water remained at its deeper end. Next to the pool, Tony Barlow sat on a chair with his arms bound behind his back. In the deep end of the pool, a metal cage similar to a rabbit hutch had been placed in the water, partially submerged. Inside, Rozene clung to the top of the cage with her head above water, her small face pale and petrified.

Relief momentarily flared in Amira. Rozene, alive! But fury quickly burned the relief away, and Amira gritted her teeth.

"Ah, M. Valdez," Tony Barlow said mildly, as though they had just run into each other on the street. "We could use your help. As you can see, M. Hull was placed in the water overnight to induce labor. You may want to reach her first."

Rozene looked up at Amira with wide eyes. She took in several short, sharp breaths as she wrapped her thin fingers tightly around the thin metal wire.

"Get me out of here!" she screamed.

Amira ran to the edge of the pool and jumped into the water. She came up alongside the cage as Rozene hit her palms furiously against the top of the enclosure. Amira felt the wiring. Though it resembled the chicken wire used back at the compound for smaller animals, the material was something stronger, not easily torn or broken through. A lock sealed the narrow hatch underneath the water.

"No, don't leave," Rozene screamed in panic when Amira climbed out of the pool.

"I need to find something to open it with," she called back.

"There are keys somewhere," Barlow said. "Keys for my handcuffs and for the cage."

Amira ran frantically around the pool area, searching under furniture and on the tables. A standing camera loomed near the diving board, pointed directly at Rozene's cage. It was turned off but Amira did not want to think about its purpose. The key chain rested on top of the camera.

"Quickly," Rozene cried as Amira ran toward the pool again. All three looked up to the ceiling at the burst of rapid gunfire, followed by the bellow of a shotgun.

"The police?" Barlow asked with interest.

Amira shook her head.

She dropped back into the water, drew a deep breath and submerged. She fumbled with several keys in the lock before the right one slid in place, then she blew out a steady stream of bubbles as she wrestled with the hatch door. Rozene plunged under the water to squeeze through, barely fitting past the mesh wire with her swollen belly.

Gasping for air, Amira and Rozene stood in the water and faced each other.

"How did you find me here?" Rozene asked between coughs.

"It...well, it wasn't easy."

Another round of machine gun fire rattled above them and Amira pulled Rozene out of the pool. It took Rozene a moment to find her footing after her extended suspension in water. As she teetered on her swollen, waterlogged feet, Amira unlocked Barlow's cuffs with no effort to be gentle. She had not forgotten his mysterious experiment on Rozene, but she needed allies for whatever was transpiring above them. After seeing Victor Zhang, she would not leave Barlow to the Trinity.

"How did you end up here?" she asked in a low voice as Barlow stood up, rubbing his wrists.

"I landed a little too close to the target," Barlow replied. "Two men on patrol found me under my parachute and had guns trained on me as soon as I landed. It has not been a fortunate week for me, M. Valdez. Or maybe it has, since you've found me for the second time now."

"Let's get going," she said in way of reply.

As the three began to climb the stairs back to the main level, Barlow held up his arm in warning.

Amira peered around the corner. A man stood sentry outside, near the back entrance through which Amira had entered. A small group of women gathered in a circle behind him on the patio, all billowing dresses and bonnets, arms folded while they anxiously awaited orders, to escape or return. The guard stood with his back to the house, although he frequently turned to listen to the increasingly loud sounds of fighting inside.

Marlee stood in the crowd of women and caught Amira's eye. Shifting casually away from the group, she began talking animatedly to the guard. Marlee cocked her head, twirling a loose strand of hair underneath her veil, and the guard relaxed his grip on his weapon, entranced by the rare attention the young woman bestowed. A dangerous move for a married woman and a young, unmarried marshal. Amira raised her hand in thankful acknowledgment Marlee's way for the risk she had taken, but if Marlee saw it, she didn't react, focused on the guard.

"Now's our chance," Amira whispered. "Go!"

They moved swiftly past the exit door.

Amira breathed a sigh of relief, but Marlee's intervention also meant that they could not escape through the back entrance, forcing them toward the ominous cries of a battle in motion.

The sounds of gunfire grew louder as they advanced through the hallways. Rozene clutched at her stomach with gritted teeth.

"Rozene," Amira said. "Is that a contraction?"

Anxiety tightened Rozene's face. "It feels like a cramp, times a hundred," she managed, squeezing her eyes shut. "And my back hurts like nothing else."

Amira exchanged a concerned look with Barlow. Her labor was beginning. Amira linked her arm with Rozene's for support.

A long hallway ended at an enormous room with a domed glass ceiling and tall pillars along its edges in the style of a Roman atrium. The beginnings of sunrise turned the visible sky the color of dark coral. At the center of the room was an enormous glass structure in the shape of an inverted pyramid, comprised of thousands of smaller triangular shapes inside. A machine of some kind sat atop the structure with a laser beaming into it from the ceiling. Upon closer inspection, something bright flashed in its center and then disappeared just as quickly.

"What is that?" Amira murmured, her fingers stretching in the direction of the mysterious device. The object's shape suggested a prism, but it was far too complex to be a simple light refractor, and the machine propped above the glass resembled an old holographic simulator on display at the Academy, but was not the same. She turned to the senior scientist in the room.

"That is *very* interesting," Barlow said with a slight smile. His face came alive as he examined it while Rozene pulled impatiently at Amira's arm.

"We need to go," she said.

Rozene clutched her lower back as she hobbled forward, squeezing Amira's arm through another contraction.

The windows were too high to exit from. They continued past the strange structure into the next room in search of a way out. The rising sound of gunfire warned them away, but perhaps they could make their escape without drawing attention. Peering through the open door, they found themselves on a landing overlooking the main living room of the house, where an incredible scene was underway.

At least a dozen robots about eight feet high fired electromagnetic weapons at several armed Trinity men across the room. The Trinity men returned fire, blocking the front door leading out of the house. The robots moved in near unison, occasionally advancing only to pull back under the vigorous storm of bullets.

Alistair Parrish and Hadrian took shelter behind the line of robots. An intricate metal cap encased Parrish's head, with bright blue wires reaching out to his temples and above his eyelids. He kept close to the ground, immobile aside from the occasional jerk of an arm or leg, while the machines moved in perfect synchronization, firing and defending in tandem. Hadrian shielded Parrish from the gunmen, sporadically lobbing a round from his own weapon with an accompanying taunt or insult.

Victor Zhang's robots resembled nothing Amira had seen before. In Westport, robots tended to adopt either a conventional human-like aesthetic or something more harmless and endearing, but these robots looked anything but human. Their appearance was more likely inspired by nightmares. Their limbs were unnaturally long, their faces bloodlessly white and emaciated like skulls, teeth bare in wide, ghoulish grins with hollow black slits for eyes, like masks belonging to ancient, terrible gods. They moved with a spider's swift, predatory crawl.

The Trinity men, however, did not retreat. Sarka stood at the front of the group, spraying bullets in every direction while other fighters used the wall partitions and overturned furniture for cover. Like Parrish, Elder Young crouched on the ground, hands raised in the air while he recited prayers over the gunfire. Through smoke and falling dust, his temples glowed faintly in the same blue light from Rozene's memory. Three Trinity men stood in unison, firing their weapons at the nearest robot.

Amira clutched the railing, color draining from her face. Rozene had not imagined the Elder's strange power. The Trinity Compound had their own tricks to bring into battle. The memory of Rozene, flailing like a marionette at her Sisters in Faith, flashed into Amira's thoughts, and her heart sprinted in response.

A stray bullet ricocheted off the high ceiling's chandelier and hit the staircase where Rozene, Amira and Barlow stood.

The three new arrivals, who had been observing the scene mutely from above, took their cue to retreat. Their movement, however, drew several eyes upward, including those of the grinning robots, who turned in time with Parrish.

Elder Young pointed at Rozene and yelled something incoherent.

At that moment, two of the robots lunged forward at the Trinity men.

A young, lanky man charged to meet them, ripping apart his black coat to reveal the wires strapped around his chest. He unleashed a battle cry.

"Get down," Hadrian yelled.

The sound and force of the explosion shook the landing as debris flew and scattered across the room. Amira fell on her knees, feeling the floor tremble beneath her. Barlow also lost his balance, yelling something she could not hear over the powerful ringing in her ears.

Shaking, Amira looked up. The explosion was not as large as it felt, leaving most of the men dazed but mobile, but there was little left of the two robots and nothing of the young man remaining in the small, smoking crater in the center of the living room floor. The chandelier fell to the ground, sending shattered gold-colored glass in every direction. The ringing in Amira's ears subsided, replaced with low curses and coughs as everyone collected themselves following the blast, feeling for missing limbs or open wounds.

Elder Young leapt up and pointed to the landing. "Kill the apostates, kill them all!" he screamed.

"Let's move back," Barlow said in a low voice while Rozene moaned in pain.

Below them, Hadrian had the same idea, lifting a weak Parrish over his shoulders and sprinting up the staircase as the Trinity men resumed fire. The robots followed in a reverse retreat, stepping backward but continuing to fire along the way. Electromagnetic fire struck two Trinity men in near unison. Both let out a strangled scream and gaping holes appeared where their chests and abdomens existed seconds earlier.

Rozene hurtled toward Hadrian when he reached the top of the stairs, gripping him in a fast, friendly embrace before resuming her retreat. She hobbled through the door and Hadrian clapped Amira on the back of the head, still balancing Parrish around his shoulders.

"Family's back together again!" Hadrian crowed, extending his arm around the door for a final volley of bullets.

They tore at breakneck speed down the corridor, but when they entered the room with the prism-like structure, the Trinity guards from the back entrance waited under the door's archway, blocking their escape.

"Quick, behind the pillars," Hadrian shouted to Barlow as the rest of the Trinity men poured out from behind them.

They were trapped.

Suddenly, a Trinity man toppled forward, blood spurting from his chest. The other men spun around.

Several voices rose in a battle cry. Through the falling dust, D'Arcy, Lee, Maxine and a small group of teenagers charged into the room, brandishing rifles and stunners. Speechless, Amira dropped to her knees.

The Trinity men took positions behind the pillars on the other side of the prism. The new arrivals crouched in positions on the far side of the room, firing at the Trinity men. Hadrian bolted to join them, dodging fire in the open space. All from Hadrian's ship, several looked no older than sixteen. The oldest was a girl Amira recognized, aiming her rifle with visible skill. Lee immediately adopted the role of leader, barking commands.

D'Arcy fought her way toward Amira, her dead eyes and frozen face betraying battle shock. Amira embraced her and could feel D'Arcy tremble. With one shoulder still bandaged, D'Arcy wrapped her other arm around Amira. A bullet struck the pillar above them, raining dust over their heads. Either the dust or the sight of Amira roused D'Arcy from her terrified state and she smiled.

"I couldn't stay on the ship," she yelled over the gunfire.

In front of them, the Trinity men advanced on Parrish.

Though ashen-faced and limp, Parrish rallied and the robots resumed their attack while Amira and D'Arcy helped Rozene. Several robots moved to protect them but struggled under the hail of bullets and Parrish's weakening state – they reacted slower, their movements stilted and sporadic, which emboldened the Trinity men. The sides of the pillars that sheltered Amira and Rozene came under heavy fire, cracking and sending additional trails of dust into Amira's face.

Behind a nearby pillar, Maxine spat, reloading her weapon. Her eyes met Amira's and she winked, before unleashing a fierce torrent of electromagnetic fire. The Trinity men continued their assault, seemingly targeting their part of the room. Targeting Parrish. Targeting Rozene.

Rozene slumped against the pillar, her arms folded over her stomach as she mouthed a prayer of her own. She remained a believer, Amira realized, in her own way. While Amira readily left everything behind her except for the small bag she carried on the train to Westport, Rozene always carried a heavier burden on her shoulders.

Amira leaned forward to say something encouraging, but before she could speak, Rozene looked up at her and shook her head. Her eyes were heavy with resignation. She was preparing to die. Amira clutched Rozene's hand in response and the two women shrank down together behind the pillar, surrendering to fate.

Bright light filled the room, the earlier coral sky now blue and crisp with the sun's emergence over the mountain's high ridges. At this new influx of light, the glass pyramid also illuminated and the machine above it came to life with a whirring growl.

The machine's awakening brought a lull to the fight, as both sides behind the pillars paused to process the strange phenomenon unfolding in front of them.

Light gathered at the pointed base of the pyramid, growing in brilliance until beams shone from all four corners of the prism in a blinding burst of energy. The glare of light subsided, and Amira gasped when she suddenly saw herself, D'Arcy and Rozene huddled together on the far-right side of the square room, then again to her left and right on the other side of the glass. She stood up and her three copies stood up with her. There were other figures as well – Barlow, Maxine, Parrish, Elder Young, Trinity men, all apparently in several places at once.

And then Amira understood. The machine was both hologram and prism, using the sun to reflect everything the light touched and refracted through the glass, so the holographic copies materialized from all sides of the room. Victor Zhang had built a hologram unlike any other. The images were vivid and real. From a distance, there was no telling reality and illusion apart.

Mass confusion enveloped the room as its occupants appeared to quadruple in number in an instant. Zhang's robots spanned every corner, along with Trinity men firing in all directions. Figures darted and ran across floors and past pillars, bullets flying ineffectually through bodies that turned out to be air and illusion. Other bullets found their target, each strike causing four identical bodies to fall to the ground in perfect unison. Hadrian darted around the pillars, capitalizing on the confusion as he fired, though he often shot at the wrong targets since they adopted the same tactic of continuous motion. Parrish's robots were no wiser, unable to distinguish between flesh and phantom, striking at anything with two legs and a weapon.

The chaos provided a fleeting opportunity to escape. Amira grabbed Rozene by the arm and they made their way toward the door leading to the house's entrance, dodging men and machines from pillar to pillar. Rozene sank to her knees before reaching the exit, moaning at the onset of another contraction. Amira called for D'Arcy, but she had joined the other compound children to help them reload.

Lee collapsed onto the ground and clutched his leg. Rozene let out a low, guttural sound before doubling over again. Hadrian yelled in fury, rushing around his pillar and spraying a hail of bullets at the Trinity fighters.

The battle grew fiercer near its end. Half of the Trinity men were dead, wounded or retreating. A sizable force, however, remained scattered across the room, including Elder Young and Sarka, who lobbed a grenade at one of the robots. The machine sank into the ground, a dense plume of smoke rising where its head once sat.

Amid the confusion, one man in the room walked with calm purpose. Andrew Reznik kept his eyes trained on Parrish, one of four, as he moved intently through the melee. A small pistol rested at his side. Amira's ears began to ring again, loud static through the already deafening sounds of battle.

"Stay here," Amira shouted to Rozene over the blasts of gunfire.

A shot struck the ground close to a copy of Parrish, kicking up dust residue from the floor. Across all four sides of the room, Parrish remained still. Reznik fired near another pillar opposite the room, and this time, all four images of the man coughed and shielded their eyes.

Reznik had the real man in his crosshairs. The corners of his mouth curved in a malicious smile. Barlow suddenly ran from behind a nearby pillar toward the real Parrish, further confirming his target. Reznik strode deliberately forward and fired a single shot into the center of Parrish's abdomen.

Parrish slumped to the floor, fumbling at the metal cap on his head. Amira watched in horror as the remaining robots froze, kneeling on the ground with their twisted grins in place. The room went quiet when the remaining Trinity men realized what was happening.

Hadrian ran forward to shield Parrish, firing at Reznik.

Reznik smoothly stepped sideways and returned Hadrian's fire, hitting him in the left shoulder. Hadrian fell to the ground. The Trinity men advanced.

Amira sprinted toward Parrish as well, then dove to her knees to examine him. Shaking, he moved his hand to reveal a black pool of blood bubbling below his ribs, which soaked the still-bloody bandage on his right side.

Quickly, Amira removed the cap from Parrish's head and placed it on her own. It felt warm against her scalp and tightened when she slid the sensors on her forehead as Parrish had done.

Immediately, a sensation unlike anything she had experienced seized her. Her body was heavy and her head light as kinetic warmth spread from her forehead to her eyes, traveling through her blood until it reached her brain. Her surroundings dissolved in a single moment. It was as though her skull had been opened and the contents of her mind spread across the room thinly like butter on toast. Every footstep was sharp and clear, but she heard each sound from ten different places at once. The room unfolded in a panorama above her, but every detail was known to her – a bead of sweat running down Elder Young's forehead, Rozene's eyes glassy as she looked skyward from behind her pillar, offering a soft, final prayer. Opening her eyes was too overwhelming, Amira realized, so she closed them and tried to focus her thoughts, as she had done many times as a child confined to dark, punishing places. And all at once, everything was clear. She felt the presence of others in her mind's eye, other bodies and minds, and they would move where she wanted them to. She had many arms at her disposal, metallic arms that could crush and stun anything in their path. She could jump and climb the walls around her, free of all obstacles in her way.

Swiftly, she summoned these visitors, and the robots rose together in perfect unison. Elder Young, who was advancing toward her and Parrish, stopped in his tracks.

Amira flung one robot at Sarka, firing its weapon, while two others leapt to the left in Reznik's direction. He slid behind a pillar to avoid their crushing feet. Two Trinity men charged toward D'Arcy and Amira spun the nearest robot around, pulverizing them in a hail of bullets. Amira never felt so powerful or free, to climb and leap and destroy. She was the solitary conductor of a deadly orchestra, each instrument playing its own harmony to a song that only she could hear. Her enemies were falling around her, bones crunching like dry leaves under her metallic feet, but she could not stop or relent, so great was the rush of anger that rose before each strike and the triumph as they fell, one by one.

Then something changed. A tremendous force hit one of her bodies and ripped it in two, wiry innards erupting with the split, and her control was shattered. From her other eyes, she watched the robot collapse to the ground. She tried to focus but became acutely aware of how weak her own body, her real body, had become. Her arms were too heavy to lift and she was slumped sideways against Alistair Parrish, whose ragged breathing was painfully audible.

The prism flickered weakly. Dark clouds stretched over the house and the domed ceiling was streaked with tears of heavy rainfall. With no sunlight, the holograms around the room vanished, leaving the remaining survivors visible, a small group surrounded by ruin and death. The robots were immobile. Though Victor Zhang's cap remained fastened to her head, Amira could sense them but not revive them. Everything was too blurry, too unclear.

Hadrian yelled something, but she could not untangle the words in her cluttered mind.

Through this fog, a figure approached her. Elder Young had his arms outstretched in front of him like a monster in an old horror movie, his sallow features twisted in a furious snarl. His halo of blue light snaked across his forehead, like bulging, radioactive veins. In seconds, his hands were on her throat.

"Apostate bitch," he snarled as he delivered a sharp blow across her face. Somewhere in the room, D'Arcy yelled.

She reeled, her focus shifting back and forth from the robots and her own aching body. His hands moved up to the cap on her head, trying to pull it off.

He could shoot but he wants me alive first, she realized.

Finding her last reserve of strength, she grabbed his face and pushed him back, adrenaline pulsing through her every muscle as she fought in those last seconds for her life, for Rozene's life, and the unborn life within Rozene struggling at that very moment to enter the world. She dug her nails into Young's face. The cap on her head heated against her skull and together, they screamed in pain. New images flashed before her, faces she had never seen before of bloody men kneeling on the ground, one after the other, followed by a young girl lying on red-stained sheets and crowds moving together in prayer. She tried to pull away but when she opened her eyes, her own horrified face stared back at her. It was surreal, watching the fury in her own black eyes while a pair of weathered hands tightened around her throat. The world grew smaller as she watched herself being strangled, the vision of her face blurring as the hands tightened. She tried to move her own arms and found that she could, tightening her grip around Elder Young's face. She pressed her fingers deep into his eyes.

Pain shifted to rage, rage into fear as she spun on an invisible axis, so that she was in her own body, then Young's, then her own again. She heard a voice cry out, *shoot her now*, and she screamed with all the force she had left, so that the scream rang through her ears and filled every corner of her sentient mind, leaving nothing but a raw, red fury that coursed through her entire body.

The prism exploded, the force of the blast knocking Amira off her feet. Her head throbbed and she clutched at her ears, desperate to stop the piercing ringing sensation that blocked out everything around her. She raised her head to find herself suddenly high in the air, on a level with the glass dome, looking down at the chaos below, where friend and foe alike crawled or lay unconscious on the ground.

Now accustomed to the sensation of leaving her body behind, Amira reacted without alarm until she noticed something strange on the atrium floor. While her own body writhed on the ground, hands clasping her ears, Andrew Reznik contorted on the floor in similar fashion across the room. Déjà vu passed through her. She sensed a presence she had only felt once before, and looked up to find another figure hovering nearby – Reznik, surveying the scene with passive disinterest.

Amira understood why Reznik seemed familiar when she saw him in Rozene's memory, beyond their brief encounter at Westport. She had seen him before, as the young boy who pushed her and ran up the hill during the Gathering, only to find a strange house. This house.

Their eyes met and Amira was back on the ground, gasping as though she had been submerged underwater. She looked up to find Reznik staring back at her through the clouds of dust and chaos. His face, normally unreadable, shifted like an old silent movie reel, delivering revelations in staggered motion – first shock, followed by fear, then a sinister interest that shone in his eyes, the realization of a shared mystery.

The floor tilted and Amira fell to her hands and knees, struggling against the blackness that passed over her eyes. She fainted, the chaos of the room fading to a distant echo.

CHAPTER SEVENTEEN

Mothers of Evolution

Amira regained consciousness in a remote, distant world. Everything was far away, from the faint, echoing shouts of the blurred figures around her, dodging shards of glass and falling debris, to the sensation of her own body.

As the room came back into focus, she realized she had been unconscious for mere seconds. Everyone around her was reacting to the blast. Hadrian lay flat on his stomach, staring at her incredulously, while Barlow, forehead bleeding, watched her with a knowing, almost appraising smile. Lee was struggling to his feet but buckled, and several of the other children rushed forward to carry him.

The Trinity men, or what was left of them, retreated to the back of the house. Reznik and another man grabbed Elder Young by the arms. The Elder babbled incoherently, his face stretched in terror. Reznik was wounded as well, hobbling awkwardly as he attempted to drag the Elder away, shooting a final glance in Amira's direction not unlike Barlow's.

We will meet again, it promised.

Sarka lay dead on the floor with a large shard of glass planted in the middle of his forehead. At least fifteen other compound men were dead, either from the earlier battle with Zhang's fighters or from the impact of the blast. Tiny pieces of glass scattered across the floor like winter's first snow.

Lee let out a triumphant war cry, joined by the other compound children. Though several appeared badly injured, the lifeless bodies belonged to the Trinity and the robots, who absorbed most of the assault.

Hands gripped Amira's arms from behind. D'Arcy, her face pale, lifted her off the ground with help from Maxine.

A cold, clammy sensation overcame Amira as she scrambled to her feet. The battle was over but her sense of danger, if anything, heightened.

Barlow knelt over Parrish, trying to slow the bleeding from his abdomen, but he shook his head grimly at Hadrian. Hadrian winced when he touched his injured shoulder. The wound was considerably less severe than Parrish's.

"Help me move him," Barlow said softly. "We need to keep him lying down. Try to relax, Alistair."

Harsh fumes of smoke filled Amira's nostrils as the men supported Parrish.

"We need to go," Amira said.

"Let's be careful to keep him immobile," Barlow said. He tore the side of his shirt to create a new bandage. Amira approached the door the Trinity men had just retreated through, only to be greeted with a gust of heat. At the far end of the house near the backyard entrance, the first traces of orange flames licked at the carpet.

This had all happened many times before, night after night – the same clammy fear that awoke her, the dream of the burning house she could not escape.

"Fire!" she screamed. "Run!"

The fire was already spreading at alarming speed, forcing them back to the main entrance, or what remained of it. Amira found Rozene behind the same pillar where she'd left her. She pulled her up roughly. Hadrian and Barlow carried Parrish, whose tall body swayed as they sprinted out of the atrium. D'Arcy joined Amira to help her support Rozene.

The fire moved quickly. It brought with it a fierce heat and even harsher smoke, a shadow that hovered in the air above them and blackened the walls as it chased them into the main entrance.

At first, Amira kept pace with Rozene and D'Arcy but soon, her legs grew heavier and weaker with each step. Panic choked her, her chest spasming as the heat drew nearer. She couldn't run. She couldn't breathe. Something about Victor Zhang's weapon had drained her, like it had weakened Parrish. Her energy left her, mentally and physically, whereas the smoke appeared to have lit another fire in Rozene, who hobbled ahead of D'Arcy toward the door, her face set with determination.

"What's happening?" D'Arcy yelled as Amira slowed down further. She shook her head, struggling to speak. D'Arcy wrapped her arm across her shoulder and continued to run.

They reached the landing stairs that led down to the front entrance. Rozene stumbled at the first step but gripped the rails. Righting herself, she descended the stairs alone, eyes trained ahead. Still on the landing, Hadrian looked darkly at the ailing Parrish before raising his eyebrows at Amira and Barlow.

Barlow, reading his expression as Amira did, shouted above the roaring fire.

"We can't leave him here to die!"

And so they continued down the stairway, stepping over broken glass and the charred remains of Zhang's soldiers. Before they reached the front door, a loud crack followed by a rushing sound stopped them. A wooden beam from the upper level fell directly in front of the exit, bringing with it a new rush of heat and flame.

The fog within Amira returned; her legs gave way and she collapsed to her knees. D'Arcy was shouting something and Hadrian was smashing a nearby window, but she could not move another inch in any direction. She curled up on the warm floor and waited, inhaling deeply as the crackling flames reverberated from the hardwood floor into her eardrum.

Maybe I'll suffocate before I burn, she thought. In either case, it would be over soon.

A pair of hands gripped her roughly under her arms and lifted her. Another set of hands grabbed her ankles and then she was flying, weightless, until a burst of fresh, clean air filled her lungs and she landed roughly in the grass, its earthy scent filling her nostrils.

Behind her, Hadrian, D'Arcy and Barlow were retching. Hadrian's fits were interlaced with a string of curses. He and D'Arcy must have thrown her through the window along with Parrish, who coughed violently nearby. Relieved, Amira tried to move her legs again. Her left knee bent slowly at her command, followed by her right, and she crawled toward the front gate, distancing herself further from the roaring heat. As she reached the gate, a loud *boom!* sounded behind her. The second level had caved in, engulfing the entire house in flames. The rain continued to fall but the fire was beyond control and would end of its own accord.

An engine sounded and Amira whipped around to see an all-terrain vehicle speed away from the house and across the desert. Reznik sat at the front, leaning forward in exhaustion, but thankfully the vehicle's occupants didn't spot Amira and the others as they retreated. Two surviving Trinity fighters in the back of the vehicle tended to Elder Young, now screaming incoherently. Another all-terrain followed closely behind, carrying the Trinity women. Amira caught Marlee's curls flying in the wind and her heart fluttered with relief at the girl's survival.

Barlow and Hadrian were carrying Parrish in her direction, moving him further away from the fire, but the urgency had passed. They were out of danger.

"First aid kit?" Hadrian asked Amira.

She wordlessly pulled it from the interior of her jacket, and Hadrian set about patching his shoulder while Barlow and D'Arcy administered a shot of painkillers to Parrish. Maxine lay on her back, coughing.

"I'll never smoke again," she gasped.

The children had apparently escaped before them and taken shelter under a nearby tree. Lee was still alive but alarmingly pale. Maxine grabbed some gauze and wound sealant from Amira's first aid kit, which she threw at the kids between fits of coughing.

Amira lay on the ground for another minute, feeling her strength return. Her head cleared slowly, the fog lifting as she watched the fire begin to devour the house's frame. She noticed Lee looking around, his face tight with fear. After a pause, she rose to her feet, knees buckling slightly.

"Where's Rozene?" she asked.

The men looked around the garden.

"Where is she?" Amira shouted, panic rising. No one answered.

Amira ran through the front gate into the desert and found Rozene sitting under a single parched juniper tree. Her legs were spread wide, her long red hair trailing down her spine as she leaned back and breathed deeply.

Rozene was never in a more vulnerable position than now. The moment had arrived.

Amira knelt by Rozene as she began pushing in earnest, her small features contorted in silent pain. When Amira took her place next to her, she felt a sudden calm, now that they were here, in this long-awaited moment. Rozene kept pushing and breathing, Amira patiently by her side.

Neither woman was a stranger to childbirth; in the compounds, new life was welcome, the arrival of a new soul from the Conscious Plane, destined to travel in death across worlds. Amira had witnessed and sometimes assisted as brothers, cousins and neighbors entered the world to screams and tears, an ancient feminine rite as normal as preparing dinner at the end of a long day.

For a birth unlike any other in human history, it was remarkably ordinary.

A small creaking noise escaped between Rozene's clenched teeth during each push, her fingers digging into the sand. Amira grabbed one of her hands and inched closer to her feet.

"You can do this, Rozene," she said. "Don't give up!"

Hadrian ran toward them, Lee hopping and stumbling behind with gauze tight around his calf. They slowed down to a nervous hover as they took in the scene transpiring under the tree.

"Get over here and help," Amira barked.

Rozene let out an audible groan, her loudest so far, and she rested back onto her elbows. Her face was wet, rain and tears rolling together down her pale cheeks.

Hadrian crouched behind Rozene, holding on to her shoulders while Amira remained in front of her, squeezing her hand and uttering the occasional word of encouragement. In pain but unable to stay back, Lee knelt beside Amira and they exchanged a nervous, excited glance.

"Good to see you again, little Rozene," Hadrian said quietly.

Then Rozene cried in a single, piercing wail and Amira leaned forward to grab the head that appeared at last, and another scream, smaller but sharp and announcing, joined hers as the first human clone emerged into the world.

The infant girl screamed in Amira's arms, raising her tiny red fists as the rain fell. Wordlessly, Lee whipped off his jacket and handed it to Amira, who wiped the newborn clean. Hadrian handed Amira a small pocket knife and she cut the umbilical cord. The children watched the scene from a distance, silent and respectful.

"How is she?" Rozene asked in a daze. "Is she normal?"

"Of course." Amira handed her to Rozene, whose face reflected the gamut of emotions that greet every new mother – joy and awe, a look of powerful, frightening love accompanied by the realization that the frail life in her arms depended on her completely for survival.

Hadrian breathed a sigh of relief behind Rozene's shoulder and Amira smiled. For that fleeting moment, they were safe.

The sound of heavy footsteps announced Barlow's approach; he and D'Arcy half carried Parrish, now alarmingly pale. He stumbled and they laid him down on his back, his hair and beard blending in with the soil, in contrast to the thick red blood on his abdomen.

"He shouldn't be moved out here," Hadrian began warningly, but Amira understood. Parrish wanted to see the clone, Valerie Singh's final and greatest endeavor.

Rozene understood this as well. Smiling, she lowered the baby down to Parrish's eye level. The infant was no longer crying but looking around her intently, as though searching for clues to decipher the strange shapes and sounds that made up her narrow world. She found her mother's face and rested her gaze there.

Parrish turned to face the baby and touched her cheek lightly with a shaking hand.

"Perfect," he said in a faint voice. "Just perfect. Valerie was right about this. And about you." He looked up at Amira.

"They wanted to get rid of you," Parrish continued weakly. "The Cosmics, when Pandora turned around, thanks to you. But by then it was too late – Valerie was going to get her clone. And so we let the Trinity Compound take care of things, and I told them that would be the end of you. But I was tired of killing or letting others be killed. Victor, then Valerie...lost forever, each in their own way. Great minds. Valerie, following Maya into the world between life and death. You remind me of Valerie when she was younger, Amira Valdez, and I didn't want another great mind thrown away in the cause of faith.

"And to you, I'm so sorry," he said, turning back to Rozene. "I'm sorry for what was done to you and what you must face now. Take care of her. She is precious to us all."

Rozene nodded, her wide eyes welling with tears. Amira glared coldly at Barlow, who smiled calmly back.

Parrish died shortly thereafter. They injected him with aggressive doses of morphine from Amira's first aid kit to keep his final moments as painless as possible. As the chemicals took effect, he watched the baby with smiling eyes then turned his gaze to the sky. Amira knew that he was searching for the Carthage, where Maya remained. He did this for his final moments, turning from his old child to the new and back again, until both slipped out of his reach forever.

⋆ ⋆ ⋆

The rain died down in the afternoon, but the house continued to smolder. One corner of the structure remained standing, albeit heavily damaged. While Rozene rested in the shade with her newborn tightly wrapped to her, Amira combed through the remnants of Zhang's den, populated by computers in varying states of damage.

Barlow's shadow emerged behind her while she examined the charred insides of the largest quantum processor. She moved on to the next one, ignoring him.

"Our friend Agent Wolfe found an all-terrain vehicle in the hills out back," he said. "The Trinity men must have left it behind when they escaped. There were fewer of them going out than came in, it's safe to say."

Amira didn't answer. She opened the second processor and inspected the hard drive, singed around the edges but relatively intact. There was no power, however, and the wires were destroyed. She lifted it up toward the window to test for solar capability.

"Is there any urgency in getting a connection to the outside world?" Barlow asked.

"Parrish is dead, Victor Zhang is in a freezer, and the house is littered with bodies," Amira answered. "And I have the holomentic readings from the Carthage. If I can get them to my friends in Westport, they can send them to the Westport PD. I was their number one suspect after the Soma attack, and I'd like to get my name cleared."

"Ah." Barlow leaned forward and peered at the hard drive Amira was trying to recharge. "Before we invite the police and the rest of Westport over, perhaps we should discuss the plan for M. Hull and her...copy."

Amira at last turned to face Barlow, her expression hard with anger.

"Good idea. What did you do to her the night you snuck into her ward?"

"Before we get to that," Barlow began placidly, "and believe me, M. Valdez, we will get to that before long, we need a plan for the girl. When Dr. Singh still headed Pandora, which is now my project to continue, by the way, the plan was to keep M. Hull at the Soma under close monitoring while she and the clone underwent medical tests and observation. She would then be moved to a house in Aldwych, probably in the Rails, to continue our observations."

"Too risky," Amira said immediately. "She and the baby are still targets for a lot of people. The Cosmics want them both. And neither one of them will have a normal life the way you described it."

"I don't disagree," Barlow replied. "And I welcome your suggestions for where to house her. But she must be observed closely. It is not just ensuring that the clone develops the way a...naturally produced infant would, without defects or mutations, but to see the impact certain developments have on M. Hull herself."

"The Tiresia you injected her with," Amira said. "The drug Hadrian had me steal on your orders. What does it do?"

Barlow laughed.

"On my *advice*, M. Valdez. I don't think anyone gives Hadrian Wolfe orders. Yes, what you removed from the Soma was the last of my Tiresia supply. I knew the Cosmics wanted to get their hands on it and I needed it in a safer place."

"They were afraid you'd do what you ended up doing," Amira said.

"I'm not sure they knew I was using it secretly in Pandora, but they know what Tiresia does. To answer your question, it was developed years ago by myself and Victor Zhang, among others – and perfected in this very house, in fact. The process for creating Tiresia was...horrific, in many ways. Difficult, and something the

Cosmics swore to avoid repeating. But we succeeded. Its original goal was to discover a means of achieving a singular consciousness. You witnessed that with Victor's robots, but machines are less complex, easier to manipulate. The Cosmics, with endorsement from some ambitious compound Elders, wanted to meld the minds of many into one. Feed the individuals into a hive mind, a higher level of cognition and awareness."

The ground spun.

"They could control people," Amira said slowly. "Make them do things they didn't want to, lose their free will."

"Concerns I shared as well," Barlow said. "But my view ended up in the minority. Victor and others were eager to see it in action, and the mellow, Chimyra-addled sheep of the compounds made ideal test subjects. The partnership with the compounds began then."

"So the Cosmics want this as well?" Amira asked.

"A faction of them do," Barlow said, his forehead wrinkling in disgust. "I had other ideas and made sure the last of the supplies of my drug remained out of their hands. In the meantime, I ran my own experiments and learned of other side effects. Some opportune, some less than desirable."

"Such as?"

"In small doses, they are minimal. But the medication can cause severe confusion and a fractured sense of self due to the impact it has on conscious perception, traumatizing an already traumatized individual further."

"Which is what nearly turned Rozene crazy, along with some random Cosmic tampering with her memory," Amira said before she remembered another detail. "Nina Leakey and Jessica Alvarado! They were both administered the drug. It was on their records. You did the same thing to them."

Barlow said nothing. Amira sat down in shock.

"I still don't understand," she said. "Why give it to them? They were supposed to carry a clone to term, so why give them something that harms them, makes them lose themselves?"

"That brings me to the other effect of Tiresia," Barlow said, and he knelt to face her directly with an intensity that was unnerving, even by Barlow's standards. "Before I explain it, let me ask you a question, Academy student – are you familiar with the concept of 'roaming consciousness'?"

Amira frowned.

"We touched on it at the Academy," she said. "But it wasn't anything proven and so complicated.... It's the idea of being in a universal consciousness outside of the body, right?" She gasped, and understood Barlow's leading question. "It's the Conscious Plane that the Cosmics believe in."

"Exactly. Consciousness is tied and connected to the body but still a separate entity, this much we know. What we have failed to prove either way is whether consciousness can exist permanently outside of the body. However, we have compelling evidence that consciousness can shift in and out of the body from time to time. In layman's terms, they are sometimes called 'out-of-body experiences'. There are signs that a visceral, traumatic experience makes these disassociations from one's own physical body more likely. Scientifically, what may be happening is a temporary merging of our personal consciousness – stored in our brain structure – with a wider conscious plane separate from ourselves, a plane that interacts with the material world around us in ways we can observe through quantum study."

Though she did not understand the direction Barlow was going, Amira sat transfixed. She had experienced this phenomenon more frequently than she would have liked. It happened when she stood over Valerie Singh on the night the Trinity attacked. It happened in the Carthage, and again in Victor Zhang's house. And it happened for the first time, with unmatched and visceral power, at the Gathering. The charred floor beneath her swayed with this sudden realization, that her ability was not accidental – it was born in this house. The house where Barlow and his team ran the first Tiresia experiments – with the tacit approval of compound Elders.

"I'm this way because you did something here," Amira said in a shaking voice. "During the Gathering, when you knew there would be people nearby who could be exposed. I was near this house over ten years ago when something happened to me. I floated above the ground. I thought I was possessed."

Barlow nodded with interest.

"Do not grieve for yourself, M. Valdez," he said with uncharacteristic softness. "You had the ability for out-of-body experiences long before you crossed paths with this house, but the Tiresia undoubtedly enhanced its effects in you. You are correct. We released Tiresia in a unique way – not through swallowing a liquid or inhaling a gas, but through the remarkable light apparatus that runs through this house. The details will astonish you, if you ever let me explain them to you. It changed you. You can exist at a level of consciousness that many spend years trying to attain. It is a gift, to be one of the sentient."

"How?"

"We discovered that Tiresia can also cause this separation of consciousness," Barlow continued. "But rather than the conscious waves just flitting in and out of the body, part of it can remain detached from the body for a longer period of time, until it merges with something else it is directed to."

"I don't understand," Amira said, but her heart quickened slightly.

"You don't, but you're starting to see what this means," Barlow said with growing excitement. "It means that if administered properly, your consciousness can exist where it is now, inside your own body, but also *somewhere else* outside of the body. A pathway to immortality, where the end of the body is not the end of your existence. Amira Valdez, no concept, no theory being toyed with in Aldwych or the spaceships spinning above us is more important than this one – the extinction of death."

"What you're talking about isn't new," Amira said as calmly as she could manage. "It's been talked about for years, figuring out how to permanently move our consciousness into robots or computers, so we can keep existing outside of our bodies. No one is close to figuring that one out, though, which is why the science now is all about prolonging life as much as possible, not changing what life *is*."

Barlow laughed.

"An answer right out of a textbook. Forgive me, M. Valdez, I don't mean to trivialize your argument, which is correct in the essentials. Robots and computers are a pipe dream; no one knows how to steer something as intangible as conscious existence into a machine, beyond the crude warfare you demonstrated earlier. But a body that is genetically identical to its host…that is a more feasible matter to be tried."

And finally, Amira understood. She stood up and looked out the window at Rozene, who was nestled on a patio lounger with the baby asleep against her chest.

"You – you transferred Rozene's consciousness into the clone while she was pregnant," Amira said. "That's why you gave her and the other subjects the Tiresia. So the baby will have Rozene's consciousness in addition to its own. The baby will have part of Rozene in her."

"That's one possibility," Barlow said patiently. "It was done early in the pregnancy. It's possible that Rozene's consciousness will dominate the infant in development, so that she becomes practically Rozene reborn. Or the child may have an identity of her own but absorb some of Rozene's memories and perceptions as she develops. I will admit I was very curious to see what would happen immediately after the birth. It's too early to tell. Will the infant retain Rozene's thought patterns, personality, even memories? Will she be linked mentally to her mother beyond the usual bond? The possibilities are endless."

"But you figured you'd just try it and see?" Amira exploded. She was shaking with anger; of everything she could have imagined, she did not expect this. It was no wonder that Barlow had enemies in Aldwych, but he had also grossly betrayed Valerie Singh's trust, turning her final accomplishment into something dangerous and unethical in the extreme. She paced for a moment, her anger swelling as Barlow waited calmly.

"Why are you telling me all of this?" Amira asked.

"Because we need each other, Amira Valdez," Barlow replied. "You're invested now in this girl's safety and have your own welfare to consider as well. In the course of your brief career at Aldwych, you have already attracted the attention of some very powerful, very dangerous people. I can protect you from them. Unlike Dr. Singh, brilliant as she was, I know how to use the Cosmics and their endless infighting to my advantage and continue my work."

"And what do you get by me helping you?"

"I think you have an idea of that already, but you're afraid to articulate it. You are an impressive holomentic reader and therapist, which will undoubtedly come in very handy as we observe mother and child. But you have other things to offer. I've observed it firsthand, when you completed your test on the Academy's Placement Day. I watched you through an observation room, and understood what had happened, even if the Academy didn't. And your remarkable show of power with Victor Zhang's creations a few hours ago confirmed what I have suspected – you are special in your ability to manage your conscious mind and to escape its trappings within yourself. Your mind can wander where it needs to, and even sense things before they occur. Preconjecture. I saw you in the prism room – you knew the fire was coming before it happened. It is that ability that I am particularly interested in. We will need it, to prevent our shared enemies from using Tiresia for their own purposes."

Through Amira's swirling thoughts, Elder Young's face emerged, snarling under phosphorescent blue light. He aimed to do what Amira had done with the robots, but on a larger, deadlier scale. Using Tiresia gifted by the Cosmics, Elder Young planned to control the compounds, mobilizing their congregants into a single, conscious entity under his control. An army. Men, women, children – all marching in unison, puppets to one man's will. Amira shuddered, imagining such an army marching on Westport. Did the Cosmics realize the plague they could unleash on the world, giving such power to the Trinity Compound?

Amira turned away and walked along the remaining wall in Zhang's den. Pictures, certificates, newspaper clippings all detailed a long life rich with accomplishments and a mind to legacy, but Zhang ended it in a compact freezer while most of his trophies and prizes melted in the heat. Was this all that was left in the end – a fading collection of souvenirs, or in Zhang's case, the passing of knowledge to the living, who may use it for any purpose, however noble or cruel?

Barlow spoke again.

"I know you think I'm a monster for what I chose to do. Perhaps I am. History will judge. I have done unconscionable things in the past that I regret deeply, and though you may not understand it now, this is part of that atonement. But there are other monsters out there, Amira, bigger and more dangerous. To defeat them, I must persuade the Cosmics that my vision for Tiresia is the correct one. If I succeed – if *we* succeed in this, and let Rozene and others live countless lifetimes from body to body, there will be no price too high for what humanity will reap. It is evolution in its final, most perfect conclusion, and we shall be its engineers."

Amira faced Barlow and thought back to their first unsettling encounter at the Academy. It took him little time to understand her, but he remained an evasive and suspicious presence for Amira from the moment they first shook hands and he gave her that cryptic, appraising look, as though he could mentally strip her bare and see the facets of herself she did not care to reveal. She had that ability too, to find the dark corners in people's minds, and he valued her for that. Though she could not trust him, she would have to grow to understand him. Perhaps Perkins had summarized him best – *Aldwych demands the dedicated.* None seemed more dedicated than Tony Barlow, but Amira could perhaps influence the means he used to gain his ends.

"You're in charge of Pandora now?" she asked.

"I am."

"Then if you want me to help in your consciousness transfers, or use me as a guinea pig, you'll need to keep me on Pandora as well. I want Rozene away from Aldwych, and I don't want the birth announced until she's ready."

"I cannot guarantee such a thing," Barlow said with a dryness that was reminiscent of Valerie Singh. "The cloning method works, and believe it or not, there is a huge demand to put this technology to market. But I'll see what arrangements we can make for her well-being."

"No deal," Amira said firmly. "If you want my cooperation, that's my price."

They negotiated further and after Amira explained her plan, one that had been brewing since Rozene gave birth, they came to an agreement, or at least a détente for the near future.

Hadrian arrived with the abandoned all-terrain from the valley. He was covered in grease, ostensibly from fixing the engine, and in high spirits.

"Excellent," Barlow said. "M. Valdez has identified our next destination. We need to take a detour before returning to Westport."

Westport. The city would no longer be the same refuge she knew before, when it represented endless possibility. Its glamor and sheen had been stripped away by harsh truths and secrets. But amid the charred remains of a great scientist's refuge and the sounds of a new life letting out its first cries, she understood now that Westport was not just a place she called home but an idea, a vision for a better world, and though imperfect, it was one worth fighting for. And they would have to fight, from both outside and within.

They prepared to leave. D'Arcy helped the children into the all-terrain vehicle. Maxine and Lee climbed to the top, both struggling to find signals for their Eyes. Hadrian woke Rozene up as Amira returned to the ashes for a final attempt to activate one of the computers. Failing, she was ready to leave the decimated den when she noticed a map on the wall. It was burnt on one half but still readable. As she looked closer, Amira noticed pins and marks on the map, which spanned greater North America. Three large pins had writing in red marker next to them, naming three compounds.

The Remnant Faithful. The Trinity. The Children of the New Covenant. Three communities, about to be united as a single force against everything Amira stood for. And in the space in between all three, a red circle with another word.

The Gathering.

EPILOGUE

Baja

The long stretch of beach in the heart of the Baja peninsula remained secluded and untamed, the lap of the dark Pacific waters and rustling palm trees in harmony after sunset. The drought along the American West Coast scared away most residents generations ago, as small towns and even larger cities witnessed an exodus motivated by thirst and a desire to escape the cruel summer months, leaving long stretches of Baja primarily for the wealthy and reclusive.

Dr. Mercer's house was on such a stretch of land, quiet and relatively undeveloped on either side, though there was a small fishing village several miles away where groceries and other essentials could be obtained. The Gradient line also ran to San Diego, providing a convenient route to Westport and other transportation hubs.

Rozene loved the ocean. She greeted Dr. Mercer warmly and the robot Henry with bemused cordiality, but took the earliest opportunity to rush out onto the sand and watch the sun slowly dissolve over the Pacific, the baby resting on her arm.

The baby had a name by the time they reached the Baja peninsula – Nova. Rozene stumbled across it during her research. She was drawn immediately to the sound and the meaning, since the child signified new beginnings. The concept of a nova in deep space, a star bursting with sudden brightness, also had a romantic appeal. Amira liked the name and Barlow ceded it was 'fitting', adding that Lucy Dunning, the founder of the Academy in Westport, had a partner who was a renowned sculptor, Nova Kidane.

While Rozene lingered along the shore, gently dipping Nova's tiny feet into the water, Amira and Barlow talked with Dr. Mercer. The professor had reacted with delight when Amira called him from a gas station in northern Mexico, finally able to recharge her

Eye. Before they parted, he had mentioned his newly-constructed home in Baja, a haven even more isolated than his refuge in the mountains, and that is where he'd fled after the attack on the Soma. After reassuring him that she was alive and safe, Amira explained the basics of her plan.

The arrangement was logical from a purely transactional perspective. Rozene would provide Dr. Mercer with purpose and much-needed company in his retirement years, while he would give Rozene and her child support, safety, privacy and non-invasive observation. Barlow talked in more detail with Dr. Mercer about the type of observation to document and report back to him in Aldwych, carefully avoiding the exact nature of what was done to Rozene during the pregnancy. Better, Barlow explained earlier to Amira, for Dr. Mercer to be a non-biased observer until something significant occurs, if it even does occur. It was possible, he conceded, that his attempt to shift Rozene's consciousness had failed completely, and that would be evident before long. Amira doubted that.

Amira looked outside at Rozene, laughing with her feet in the water as she gently swung the baby from side to side over the moon-lit waves, feeling a fierce pang of guilt that Rozene, too, was in the dark about Barlow's experiment. Despite this, Amira agreed to remain silent, at least for the immediate future. Rozene needed, above all things, a period of peace and normalcy.

At the house, Amira was at last able to use Dr. Mercer's computer to transmit the evidence from the holomentic disc. With Rozene safe, Dr. Mercer said with a smile, Amira's name would be cleared, although she would still need to address her escape from the police station.

With his leg bandaged but healing, Lee stretched across the couch in Dr. Mercer's living room, watching Rozene through the screen door. He reacted similarly to Hadrian when he held Nova, relieved at her apparent normalcy while also scanning her carefully for some tell-tale sign of artificiality. There was none to be found. Nova looked and acted like any other newborn. She was, all in all, a remarkably unremarkable baby, with wide eyes and an unsmiling, inquisitive face in those sparse moments when she was not sleeping or wailing.

After Rozene came back inside, Dr. Mercer and Henry showed her around the house, leading her upstairs to the room that she and Nova would occupy. They made an odd group; an elderly professor, a robot, and a young woman carrying a baby who would soon become the most famous and discussed infant on Earth – for some, an abomination to be feared and for others, a tentative, exciting step into a bold and uncertain future. The news could not be hidden, Barlow warned Amira. They had to announce the success of Pandora, which would inspire attempted replications, and soon enough the initiation of the cloning industry as the Soma made its services (though not its patented technology) available to the public. Rozene would avoid the brunt of the public scrutiny, her location a closely guarded secret among the small group in the house, but at some point, mother and child would have to show their faces to the world.

Amira walked out onto the patio, took in the cool breeze and the salty smells of the deep ocean it carried, and tried to push the future out of mind.

Hadrian sat outside on a lounge chair, tightening the bandage around his shoulder. He nodded with a tired smile as she approached.

"Taking off already?" she asked. "Getting back to the ship?"

"The remaining kids'll be fine without me for another day, love, even without Lee keeping them in line," he said. "No, I need to get back up to NASH. Need to report officially that I'm alive and kicking and find out what happened to my crew."

Amira nodded. She had forgotten after the chaos of their crash in the desert that the NASH security crew was in pursuit of them as well, though the point where they lost the chase was unclear.

D'Arcy joined Amira on the patio.

"You ladies try to stay out of trouble for the next couple of days," Hadrian said pointedly. And with that, he stood up unceremoniously and walked toward the dark street. His footsteps faded as they crunched along the gravel driveway, and Amira fought the urge to call out a final goodbye. She would miss him. The air had already shifted, less charged somehow, in his absence.

D'Arcy stood behind Amira.

"Ready to go home?" D'Arcy asked.

The wide leaves on the palm trees trembled with each powerful gust, a hypnotic dance that calmed her as she scanned the sky. No stations were visible through the clouds. Smog rolled in from San Diego along with the Pacific tide, muting the moonlight as it bounced off the gentle water. Hundreds of miles up the coast, she imagined the lights of Westport spreading into the sky, drowning out the stars.

Forces pulled at her from different directions like the churning currents of an undertow. Westport to the north, her friends all around her, and the skies above them, from which the universe spread – all drew her closer, reaching to that part of her in search of home.

Home. Though there was much Amira did not yet understand – about her own abilities, the challenges and dangers that awaited her – she knew that she was a scientist of Aldwych, and Westport was her home. Her feet felt steady on its concrete streets, rooted in purpose. The pursuit of knowledge, in aid of those she loved, was her life's purpose, and that purpose gave her the power to overcome anything that the compounds or Cosmics threw at her.

Someone called to them from the living room. Dr. Mercer was in deep conversation with Barlow in the kitchen. Amira folded her arms against the strengthening winds. With a final glance in the direction of Westport, Amira followed D'Arcy inside.

ACKNOWLEDGMENTS

It takes hard work, focus and a pinch of masochism to finish a novel, but it takes a village to bring it to life. Firstly, a huge thank you to my brilliant, tireless agent, Naomi Davis from Bookends Literary Agency, for working with me to address the elements in earlier drafts that weren't working and strengthen the parts that were. I couldn't ask for a better advocate and supporter, always ready to talk through a plot hole or a new idea. I'm also grateful to my editor, Don D'Auria, and the Flame Tree Press team for believing in this novel and working with me to sharpen the prose and work through those small but critical details.

I'm also indebted to those who gave me feedback on the first drafts of this novel, as well as family and friends who supported me through the ups and downs of the writing process. Thank you to the Lighthouse Writers Workshop in Denver, for giving me the opportunity to get some crucial early feedback on my first pages. Heather Webb, who I met at the Rocky Mountain Fiction Writers' Conference, for her excellent insights that greatly improved my later drafts. Thanks to Laila Arand and Kathy Breining for their kind but constructive input, and to Adrianne Kolano and David Bender for their willingness to be early beta readers. To my English teachers in high school, Neil Horner and Alistair Pugh, for that report card in which they said I could be a published writer one day. And last but not least, to my grandparents on both sides of the family, gone but present in so many ways, thank you for being great storytellers and instilling that same instinct in me.

FLAME TREE PRESS
FICTION WITHOUT FRONTIERS
Award-Winning Authors & Original Voices

Flame Tree Press is the trade fiction imprint of Flame Tree Publishing, focusing on excellent writing in horror and the supernatural, crime and mystery, science fiction and fantasy. Our aim is to explore beyond the boundaries of the everyday, with tales from both award-winning authors and original voices.

•

You may also enjoy:
American Dreams by Kenneth Bromberg
Second Lives by P.D. Cacek
The City Among the Stars by Francis Carsac
Vulcan's Forge by Robert Mitchell Evans
The Widening Gyre by Michael R. Johnston
The Blood-Dimmed Tide by Michael R. Johnston
The Sky Woman by J.D. Moyer
The Guardian by J.D. Moyer
The Goblets Immortal by Beth Overmyer
The Apocalypse Strain by Jason Parent
A Killing Fire by Faye Snowden
The Bad Neighbor by David Tallerman
A Savage Generation by David Tallerman
Ten Thousand Thunders by Brian Trent
Two Lives: Tales of Life, Love & Crime by A. Yi

Horror and suspense titles available include:
Snowball by Gregory Bastianelli
Thirteen Days by Sunset Beach by Ramsey Campbell
The Influence by Ramsey Campbell
The Wise Friend by Ramsey Campbell
The Haunting of Henderson Close by Catherine Cavendish
The Garden of Bewitchment by Catherine Cavendish
Boy in the Box by Marc E. Fitch
Black Wings by Megan Hart
Will Haunt You by Brian Kirk
We Are Monsters by Brian Kirk
Those Who Came Before by J.H. Moncrieff
Stoker's Wilde by Steven Hopstaken & Melissa Prusi
Until Summer Comes Around by Glenn Rolfe
They Kill by Tim Waggoner
The Forever House by Tim Waggoner

•

Join our mailing list for free short stories, new release details, news about our authors and special promotions:

flametreepress.com